Other Crooked Lake mysteries by Robert W. Gregg

A Death on Crooked Lake

The Man Who Wasn't Beckham

Setting the Stage for Murder

The Scarecrow in the Vineyard

The Cottage with Too Many Keys

A Crooked Lake Mystery

Robert W. Gregg

ISBN 978-0-7414-6015-8 Paperback
ISBN 978-0-7414-6946-5 eBook

Printed in the United States of America

Published December 2012

INFINITY PUBLISHING
1094 New DeHaven Street, Suite 100
West Conshohocken, PA 19428-2713
Toll-free (877) BUY BOOK
Local Phone (610) 941-9999
Fax (610) 941-9959
Info@buybooksontheweb.com
www.buybooksontheweb.com

Many people have contributed in one way or another to my Crooked Lake mysteries. In this case, I am especially grateful to my wife Barbara for her thoughtful and creative suggestions regarding the plot and the dialogue, and to my good friend Lois Gregg for editing which far exceeded the usual search for grammatical faux pas. For the fourth time since I began my contemplation of murder on and around Crooked Lake, I wish to thank Dr. Melissa Brassell for her guidance on matters relating to forensic pathology. She has been a patient counselor from whom I have learned much. All of my Crooked Lake books have benefitted immeasurably from Steve Knapp's beautiful photography, and once again Brett Steeves has worked his computer magic to enhance my covers.

This book is dedicated to Barbara, Patty, Bobby, Kevin,
Brian, Amy, Stephen, Laura, and McKinley,
all of whom continue to bring sunshine into my life.

CHAPTER 1

It had been a long and tiring day. Four hundred and some odd miles, the last thirty of which seemed to have taken forever. Between the two of them, they had given voice to their impatience half a dozen times before they finally pulled in behind their cottage on Crooked Lake.

"Now we can start complaining about what a pain unpacking is," Bill Claymore said. His tone of voice made it clear that he didn't much care for the task of lugging suitcases and boxes of staples and what they thought of as summer stuff into the cottage. It was always like this, he thought. They enjoyed the lake once they got there and settled in, but getting there and settling in was always another matter.

It was the 5th of May, and it was still chilly. In fact it was downright cold. They had debated postponing opening the cottage until Memorial Day weekend, but Bill was anxious to get in some fishing before the summer crowd arrived, and Helen's term as president of her book club had come to an end in April. So here they were, nearly an eight hour drive from their home in New Jersey, contemplating a cottage which had been closed up since the previous September. A cottage which would be every bit as cold inside as it was outside. A cottage whose refrigerator and cupboards would be bare, except for odds and ends of spices and sacks of flour and sugar, tightly sealed to frustrate the mice which seemed to find their way into the place during the long months which separated one summer from the next.

Tomorrow they would stock the larder. Today they faced the task of unloading the car, turning on the water and electricity, and checking to see what if any damage winter snows and winds had done to The Summer House. The Summer House. A weathered wooden sign with those words on it hung above the back door, telling them that they were back at the lake. Bill hated the name. It was so unimaginative, so unclever. Why hadn't the family accepted his suggestion that the cottage be called Wanderlust, or Jersey on the Lake, or maybe Serendipity? But he

1

had been outvoted, not that any of the others had a better idea. The Summer House had become the default choice.

Bill popped the trunk while Helen gathered up an armful of books from the back seat. He set the two suitcases down on the back porch and fished in his pocket for the key. It was 6:20 in the evening. The sky was blanketed by clouds, the early evening light already dim.

"Why don't you just take it easy," Bill said. "I'll flip the circuit breakers and then I'll finish unloading the car. We can put things away tomorrow."

She gave him no argument. The lights came on, and in fifteen minutes he had moved everything from the car to the living room and turned his attention to the task of heating some water for tea. But of course there was no water. Like many of the residents along the lake, the Claymores drew their water from the lake, which meant shutting down the pipes in the fall and opening them up in the spring. It was a familiar ritual, necessitated by the fact that the pipes would otherwise freeze and burst during the cold winters typical of upstate New York.

"I've got to go down and open the pipes," he announced. "Just give me a few minutes, and we'll have some tea."

And toilets that flush, he thought.

The task required a trip to the pump room, a semifinished basement with a dirt floor, a maze of pipes, and a number of valves whose function he had mastered over the course of several frustrating summers. Bill smiled to himself, recalling that their youngest son, Barry, had been afraid of it as a little boy. Heaven knew what creatures he thought lurked down there, but it was not until he was into his early teens that Barry had cautiously ventured down the steps and into the dreaded pump room.

Bill flicked on the hall light and opened the door to the basement. He thought he detected a strange odor. It was not strong, but it seemed different from the usual musty damp smell he had come to associate with the pump room. He turned on the flashlight as he made his way down the stairs, shining the beam around the floor, expecting to see a dead mouse or some other small animal that had somehow made its way into the room and expired there over the long winter.

There may have been a dead mouse in the pump room, but Bill Claymore was quickly aware that what he was looking at was much larger and more shocking than a mere mouse. There on the dirt floor, folded into an awkward sitting position against the far wall, was a human being. A woman, by the look of things. And it was doubtful that she was sleeping, not in this cold room, not in a cottage which had been locked up since the previous September. He had had no experience with such things, but he was as certain as he had been about anything in his life that there was a dead woman in The Summer House.

CHAPTER 2

It was over eight months earlier that Amanda Kershaw and her daughter Jennifer had watched the small commercial airliner land at the regional airport, taxi to the terminal, and disgorge a dozen passengers. One of those passengers was a young woman, actually a girl not yet out of her teens. She was tall, blonde, and attractive, and she walked purposefully across the tarmac towards the Kershaws.

Amanda had seen photos of the girl, of course, but they hadn't begun to convey the full picture of Annika Lindstrom, the foreign exchange student from Sweden who was coming to live with the Kershaws. For one thing she was even taller than Amanda had imagined, towering nearly half a foot over her own daughter. She walked with comfortable assurance, giving off no hint that she was in an unfamiliar land, about to meet unfamiliar people. Nor had the photographs done her justice. She was not only attractive; she was beautiful, the healthy beauty of someone born with good genes who was no stranger to exercise. Her clothes were the uniform of high school age girls in much of the western world, but she wore them well and it seemed impossible that she had actually lived in them on the whole of the long trip from her native Sweden to Crooked Lake. The only thing to catch Mrs. Kershaw's eye that was not pleasing was the jewelry on the girl's face – a small silver ring on each eyebrow and a silver stud piercing her nose. Jennifer will now want to similarly adorn her own face, Amanda thought. She didn't look forward to that argument.

"Mrs. Kershaw?" the girl said, but it was less a question than a greeting. She wrapped her arms around her host in a tight embrace, and then turned to hug Jennifer, who seemed overwhelmed by this show of affection.

"How was your trip, my dear?" Mrs. Kershaw asked.

"Fine. Just fine. The layover in New York wasn't bad at all."

Such perfect English, Amanda thought. You'd never know she wasn't a native speaker.

4

"Your luggage should be off the plane in a few minutes," Amanda said, taking the girl's arm to steer her in the direction of the terminal entrance.

"This is all I brought with me," Annika said, shifting a large shoulder bag from one arm to the other.

"Really? You can't be serious." Amanda was momentarily taken aback, imagining that she might be looking forward to a lot of shopping and not sure any of the area stores would have outfits that would fit this young woman, much less suit her.

"No, I'm only kidding," Annika said, laughing. "I'm afraid I've got two other bags. Lots of stuff in them, including bathing suits. You said the swimming here is great."

Mrs. Kershaw hoped her daughter would end her silence, jumping at the chance to say something about how good swimming was in Crooked Lake. But Jennifer had nothing to say.

It took only fifteen minutes to collect the bags, stow them in the trunk of the Ford, and head for the Kershaw residence, Annika riding up front with Mrs. Kershaw and Jennifer in the back seat. The conversation in the front seat was animated, but Jennifer did not join in. Her mother kept glancing in the rear view mirror, and what she saw was a face that could only be described as bored, even unhappy. Something was wrong. Her daughter had been looking forward to the arrival of a new friend from Sweden, or so she had said. But Amanda had seen that look on Jennifer's face before. Indeed, she had seen it all too often of late. Jennifer was sulking.

Anxious to make their visitor feel at home and attract attention away from Jennifer's unpleasantness, Amanda became even more voluble, peppering Annika with questions and calling attention to a variety of sights along the way, most of which she knew would be of little interest. It was only a forty minute drive from the airport to the Kershaw home in Southport, but Amanda was exhausted from the effort to sustain a conversation. And annoyed that her daughter had contributed nothing to it.

"Let me see if Brian is home," she said as they climbed out of the car. "He can help take the bags up to your room. I know you'll like it. Nice southern exposure, and that's a good thing during the long winters up here."

"Don't worry. Remember, where I come from the winters are even longer than yours. It can get dark by early afternoon."

Annika laughed as she described Sweden's winters. "They say Swedes get depressed by all that cold and darkness, that it turns us into alcoholics and makes us suicidal. I don't believe it. Besides, I love it. Summers are okay, but you can't ice skate in the summer."

Jennifer rolled her eyes and disappeared into the house.

Brian hadn't come home yet, and Annika declined Mrs. Kershaw's offer to help with the luggage and carried it up to what was to be her bedroom herself. The room had been a spare guest room, decorated with fussy landscape prints and artificial flowers, but Amanda had put them away in the attic in order to give their guest a chance to fix it up according to her own taste.

"There's not much here right now," she said, "but we'd like you to feel free to do what you want with the room. It's going to be your home away from home until next June, and you ought to make yourself comfortable in it. Do you have any favorite colors?"

"Blue. Definitely blue. Anyway, it's just fine as it is. Where's Jennifer's room?"

"Just down the hall, across from Brian's. I'm sorry we don't have more bathrooms. There's just the one. Other than my husband's and mine, that is. But I'm sure you'll work it out. Brian and Jennifer have."

That was not true, and Amanda anticipated that there would be trouble as the three teenagers vied for time in the bathroom, especially in the morning before school. She fervently hoped that Jennifer would be cooperative, something she most assuredly had not been where her brother was concerned.

After a few more assurances that Annika was to consider herself part of the family, Amanda urged her to have a shower, change clothes, do whatever she wanted to do.

"Come on down any time. Brian should be along any minute, and Mr. Kershaw is usually home by six. That's Bob. He'll probably prefer you call him by his first name."

She had no idea what Bob would wish to be called by their house guest, but she'd heard that the Swedes were an informal people.

Mrs. Kershaw retreated to the kitchen to prepare Annika Lindstrom's first meal in her new home. She had wanted to make a stop in Jennifer's room to see what was the matter, but she knew she would be told either that it was nothing or that it was none of her business, depending on her daughter's mood at the moment. She hoped that her son would be more welcoming. Why did teenagers have to be so difficult?

It was 6:15 when the four Kershaws and Annika Lindstrom settled into chairs in the living room for the pre-dinner drink that had been Bob and Amanda's custom for many years. Only in the last year had Brian been allowed the occasional beer, and while they were sure that Jennifer was not unfamiliar with alcohol, they didn't allow it at home. As a result, Brian and Jennifer typically spent their parents' 'happy hour' in their rooms. On this particular night, however, it seemed appropriate for the whole family to be present.

"A ginger ale, Annika?" Amanda asked. "Or maybe a coke?"

"I'll have a beer, thank you."

"Me, too." These were Jennifer's first words to her parents since meeting Annika at the airport.

It was an awkward moment, but Mr. Kershaw got up and went to the refrigerator for beers for the three members of the younger generation.

"So tell me," he said, resuming his seat and eager to move the conversation to safer ground, "what's it like this time of year back in Stockholm?"

"Okay I think," Annika said, "but I haven't been in Stockholm in a year. I'm from Malmo. It's down in the south, just over the bridge from Copenhagen. That's in Denmark. I spend a lot more time in Copenhagen than I do in Stockholm."

Amanda was embarrassed by her husband's gaffe. He had been little involved in the decision to host an exchange student, as was now becoming apparent.

"And what is it that your parents do in Malmo?" Bob asked. This, too, was something which Amanda knew and which her husband ought to have known.

"Daddy's in publishing. Mum's an invalid. She doesn't do much. It's been eight years since the accident. Daddy's much better, but he does a lot of his work from home."

"I'm so sorry," Bob said, belatedly aware that the more questions he asked the more he would demonstrate how little thought he had given to the fact that the Kershaws would be hosting an exchange student for a whole school year.

Amanda was about to take over the faltering conversation when Brian spoke up.

"You have a boy friend back home?"

Annika didn't seem to mind the question.

"Sure. I haven't done the math recently, but I think I've got three of them." A big smile spread across her face as she said it. It was obvious that she found Brian's question amusing.

"How do you manage that?" he asked.

"I guess we all work at what gives us pleasure."

"I'd have thought you'd have a hard time giving up all that pleasure and coming over here where you don't know anybody." Mr. and Mrs. Kershaw thought their son was being rude. But Brian, like Annika, was having fun.

"I'm always up for new experiences," Annika said, enjoying the banter. "I've heard good things about America. About American schools, American guys. I'm very happy to be here, living with you nice people. How about you? Do you have a girl friend?"

Jennifer, quiet since she had asked for a beer, snorted.

"What's that supposed to mean?" Brian flashed a nasty look at his sister.

"You know, and she'll find out soon enough. He can't hang on to a girl, can you, Brian? First Jackie, now Paula. Jackie, she went off to college – out of sight, out of mind, right? And Paula, she just dumped him. You'll meet her, you'll see what I mean."

Annika Lindstrom may have been enjoying the cocktail hour, but Amanda Kershaw wasn't. She managed to steer the conversation to other subjects and then decided that it would be a good idea to have dinner a bit sooner than she had originally planned. The food was good according to Bob and Annika. The table talk left more to be desired. Brian spent most of the meal staring at Annika. Jennifer spent most of it staring at her plate.

Annika offered to help with the dishes, and Amanda gratefully accepted the offer. She didn't really want help in the kitchen, but it would have the effect of separating their guest from Brian and Jennifer, who for reasons of their own, and without apparent provocation, had decided to be obnoxious.

To say that the months Annika Lindstrom was to have spent in Southport as a guest of the Kershaws had gotten off on the wrong foot would have been an understatement. Or so Amanda

Kershaw believed.

The fall semester at Southport High School was scheduled to begin in less than a week. Perhaps when the young people became immersed in their classes and the activities which engaged them after class, the prickliness which had been so much in evidence that afternoon would vanish. Surely a bond would develop between two lively and attractive girls of the same age. It was even possible that Brian would develop a crush on Annika. The thought caused Amanda, who was a romantic at heart, to smile. But later, while she was trying to fall asleep, she found herself thinking that such a relationship might not be such a good idea. And what if the fact that Jennifer and Amanda were both lively and attractive girls of the same age fostered not friendship but an unhealthy competition?

Before she finally fell asleep, Amanda had begun to worry that her decision to host an exchange student might have been a mistake. And it was only late August. There are still ten months to go, she thought. Of course she had no way of knowing that Annika would only be with them for five months, or that what lay ahead was far worse than anything she had imagined.

CHAPTER 3

"It's her. It's got to be her," Carol Kelleher, sheriff of Cumberland County, thought as she digested the news of William Claymore's shocking discovery. The 'her' was Annika Lindstrom, a foreign exchange student at Southport High School, who had, to the puzzlement and consternation of the lake community, gone missing back in January. Carol wasn't sure why she was sure the dead woman would be Lindstrom. She couldn't imagine why her body would be in the cottage of summer residents, a cottage which had been closed for the winter for eight months, antedating the girl's disappearance by nearly four of those months. Moreover, Lindstrom had sent a post card to the Southport family she had been staying with, telling them that she was in Ohio and not to worry about her. But Carol trusted her intuition. The body in The Summer House would turn out to be that of Annika Lindstrom.

She remembered all too well the crisis that had erupted in January when the Lindstrom girl disappeared. She had been staying with a family named Kershaw in Southport. The *Gazette* had run a feature story on this attractive young visitor from Sweden back in the fall, and word had circulated that she was both a very good student and an immensely popular one. Then one wintry day Mrs. Kershaw had called in a state of near panic to report that Annika had not come home the night before. Carol had suggested that the girl could have stayed with a friend, or even that she might have become homesick and decided to go back to Sweden.

But Mrs. Kershaw had already inquired of Annika's friends' mothers, and she had been doubtful that this polite and seemingly well adjusted girl had set off for home without saying anything to her host. Carol had placed a few calls on behalf of the Kershaws, but had assumed that there would be some simple explanation for what had happened and that Annika would show up as suddenly as she had disappeared.

By the end of that week, the girl had neither been seen nor heard from, and her disappearance had become the biggest story in

Southport and all around Crooked Lake. Carol had spoken several times with Mrs. Kershaw and had even placed a call to Mrs. Lindstrom in the Swedish city of Malmo, but had learned nothing except that they were both worried. And then one day a post card arrived from Ohio. It was signed AL, and read simply "Don't worry, I'm all right."

Receipt of the post card had not assuaged the Kershaws' guilt or anxiety, but it had alleviated their worst fears. It also had had the effect of relegating the story of the missing girl to yesterday's news. Carol had not been entirely satisfied that the case of the missing exchange student was at an end, but she had been preoccupied with law enforcement problems in the county and Annika Lindstrom had gradually dropped off her radar.

Bill Claymore's 911 call on the evening of May 5th changed all that. Carol was cleaning up after dinner when she got a call from the emergency response team that she should get over to the Claymore residence. Right away. She grabbed some tissues to cope with her hay fever and headed for Crooked Lake. It was 7:27 pm when Carol made her way down the stairs into the pump room in The Summer House, followed by the paramedics and the owner. Her flashlight was an improvement over Claymore's, but an overhead light would have been better.

"Is there no light down here?" she asked.

"Sorry, sheriff. There's something wrong with the connection, and I just haven't gotten around to fixing it."

"This'll do," she said, turning the flashlight beam on the silent figure against the back wall. It took but five steps to reach the body, and it was immediately apparent that the face which was illuminated by Carol's flashlight was that of Annika Lindstrom. She was dressed in jeans, a hooded winter coat, and a pair of boots. The position in which she was lying didn't look comfortable, not that she would have cared. Her head looked as if it might have taken a hard blow from some kind of blunt instrument or from a fall. There was the faintest hint of something disagreeable in the air. Early stage decomposition? With her hay fever, Carol couldn't be sure.

It had been a particularly cold winter. Early spring had not been much better. Carol guessed that the temperature in the pump room was no more than a degree or two above freezing. She did not know how long Lindstrom had been dead, but it was likely that she had met her death in January at the time of her disappearance. If that were the case, and she had spent the intervening four months in the Claymore's pump room, she would almost certainly have frozen solid, with thawing and decomposition not beginning until very recently as the temperature in the cottage had slowly begun to rise.

Fifteen minutes later, Carol had sent the paramedics on their way, called the coroner's office, and retreated with the Claymores to the living room where it was still unpleasantly cold.

"Now, Mr. Claymore, let's see if we can make some sense of this. You tell me that you had never seen the woman in your cellar before this evening. That you don't know who she is, or didn't until I told you her name is Annika Lindstrom. Had you heard that Miss Lindstrom had gone missing from Southport last winter? It was big news on the lake."

"No." It was an emphatic 'no.' "Like I said, sheriff, she's a complete stranger. I can't imagine what she's doing in my cottage or how she got here. When we leave the lake in the fall, I get right back to my job at the state university and neither Helen nor I pay much attention to what's going on up here. I suppose we'd have heard about the woman from neighbors once we'd gotten settled in, but we haven't seen anybody yet. Except you, that is – and that dead woman in my pump room."

"And you, Mrs. Claymore? Ever hear of Annika Lindstrom?"

"Never. Who is she?"

Carol didn't try to correct her use of the present tense.

"She came over here from Sweden in late August as an exchange student. She was attending Southport High when she disappeared. That was in January. She'd been staying with a Southport family named Kershaw. Do you know them, by any chance?"

"No, we don't know any people down in Southport. None, that is, except a few of the merchants, like Fran Wilkie who runs that gift shop or Betty Merrill from the little restaurant on the corner."

"So how do you suppose that a young woman you'd never heard of ends up dead in your cellar?" Carol had expected – no, she had hoped – that there would be some connection, however slight, between Lindstrom and the couple in whose cottage she had been found. There had to be a reason why the woman's frozen body was slowly beginning to thaw in the Claymores' pump room.

"I wish I knew," Mr. Claymore said. "And with the place locked up and all."

"It's possible that the cottage was broken into. We won't be sure until it's light tomorrow and we can check all the doors and windows. But let's talk about it being locked. How can you be sure?"

"It's what we do every fall. You can see what kind of a place this is," he said, waving his hand at the walls around him. "There's no insulation, no furnace – just those baseboard heaters. We're just a fishing cottage, really. You'd freeze to death if you tried to stay here over the winter. So we shut the water off and lock up when we leave – do it around Labor Day every year."

The irony of his reference to freezing to death struck him and elicited a brief apology for what sounded like a thoughtless remark.

"I'm sure you would," Carol said. "Freeze to death, that is. What you're saying is that after you close up and lock up at the end of the summer you don't come back until around now. But how can you be sure you locked up? Maybe you forgot. Maybe one of you thought the other had done it."

"Usually I do it myself. Last September, I asked Bud Harbaugh to do it. He's a contractor who was redoing the upstairs bathroom for us. The job wasn't done when we packed up and left, so he closed the place after he'd finished. That was towards the end of September. There was a note with the bill he sent me, said he'd shut off the water and locked the cottage just like I asked him to. So I'm sure it was locked. Everything just like it always is – refrigerator empty, water turned off, power off. And locked up, tight as a drum."

Carol didn't choose to argue with him, but she knew that in spite of what the contractor had said, he might have failed to make sure the cottage was locked. But she doubted it. In all likelihood the cottage had been locked when the remodeling job was finished, well before Annika Lindstrom's disappearance in January.

"I gather that neither of you had occasion to come back to the lake at any time between September and today."

"No, we didn't. Bill has his job to tend to. I've got my

13

clubs, my friends. Long as we've owned this place, I can only think of one time when we had to come back, and that was because I'd forgotten some things I really needed. That happened two years ago."

Carol thought it would have been easier for Mrs. Claymore to ask a neighbor to package them up and mail them to her. But would a neighbor have had a key?

"Is there anyone other than the two of you and this contractor who has a key to the cottage?"

"Well, of course," Claymore answered. "But no one who would have had anything to do with putting that woman in the pump room."

"Be that as it may, why don't you tell me who the other people are who have keys to the cottage."

"Our son has a key, but I don't think he ever uses it. He's in college, but he occasionally joins us for a few days during the summer. Joe Cabot's got one. He and his wife. They're neighbors, just a couple of cottages away. They live here year around, and it helps to let them have access in case there's some problem. Sort of look after the place over the winter, that's what they do."

"They called us once, I think it was in late January or February." It was Helen Claymore. "Joe said they'd had to shovel snow off our back roof after a bad storm."

"But that Lindstrom girl in the pump room, that's not Joe's doing," Claymore said. "No way."

"Is that it? Your son, your neighbor, and your contractor. No one else?"

"None I can think of. And Harbaugh and Cabot are trustworthy. I've known them for years. They both know to lock up after themselves."

"Did this man Harbaugh finish the upstairs job?" Carol asked.

"I'm sure he did. Like I said, he billed me, said he had taken care of the water. But we haven't been upstairs to see what the new bathroom looks like. It's been crazy ever since I found that woman."

"Why don't you go take a look now," Carol said.

Bill Claymore went upstairs, returning in a minute to report that Harbaugh had indeed finished the bathroom as he had promised.

"Nice job," he added. "He's done other things for me when we're away, and he always leaves things in good order. I'm sure he locked up."

"Excuse me for repeating myself, but you're sure that no one else has a key?" For some reason Carol doubted that she now had a complete inventory of keys to The Summer House.

"That's all. What's that make, five?"

"Wait a minute, Bill." Something had just occurred to Helen Claymore. "Didn't Roger have a key? Seems to me I remember he said he needed one when he visited us last."

Bill Claymore made a face.

"That was three years ago, Helen. Your brother hasn't been back here since then, and you know I'd rather he stay away for another three years. Or permanently."

Mrs. Claymore started to defend her brother Roger, thought better of it, and suggested that they needn't wash dirty family linen in front of the sheriff.

Carol was interested in what the problem with Roger was, but chose not to pursue the matter.

"So what does that make it? One key for each of you, one for your son, one for Cabot, the neighbor, and one for Harbaugh, the contractor. Five keys, plus the possibility a relative name Roger may have one. You don't know anything about Annika Lindstrom, so I'm to assume that you had nothing to do with her being dead in your cellar. You have vouched for your son, for Cabot, and for Harbaugh. And I assume that whatever differences of opinion you may have about Mrs. Claymore's brother, you can't imagine him having anything to do with Miss Lindstrom's death. Right?"

"That's right," Claymore answered. "Roger's got problems, but he wouldn't have killed the girl or stuck her down in our pump room. He wouldn't even know who she is, anymore than we do."

Maybe, maybe not, Carol thought. Same with the other holders of keys. She didn't know any of them. It was conceivable that the Claymores had given keys to yet other people and either forgotten about doing so or chosen not to mention it. And there was no guarantee that one or more of those five or six keys hadn't been copied. Or that they hadn't been mislaid and come into someone else's possession. She was quite sure that she didn't begin to know all there was to know about keys to The Summer House.

15

It was after nine o'clock, and Carol had another more immediate problem to contend with.

"I don't like to say this, but unfortunately I'm going to have to ask you to spend the night in a motel. My men will be over here first thing in the morning to check for signs of breaking and entering and to give the cottage a thorough going over. We have to see if we can find anything that will tell us who it is that's responsible for what happened here. And when. I can't imagine you'd be very happy bedding down in the cottage tonight anyway."

"Aren't you going to remove the body tonight?" Claymore asked.

"Yes, of course. Just as soon as the coroner gets here and does his thing. But it doesn't matter. I guess you could say that your cottage is now a crime scene, which means we need to close it up until we've done what we have to do. It won't take long, but I'm still going to have to ask you to bear with us. I'll call and get you a place for the night. And my department will pay your bill."

Bill Claymore started to protest, but his wife shushed him and said she didn't think she could possibly sleep in the cottage, knowing there had been a dead woman in their pump room just hours before she went to bed.

By 10:20 the Claymores had plucked a few necessities from their suitcases and departed for a motel in Yates Center. The coroner had arrived, rendered his preliminary verdict, and gone back to his poker game in Cumberland. Lindstrom's body had been removed from the pump room and transferred to the county morgue to await Doc Crawford's autopsy. The sheriff had contacted two of her officers and filled them in on what they would be doing the following morning. And she had relieved the Claymores of one of their two keys to the cottage.

As for herself, tomorrow would be a very busy and very difficult day. Among other things, there would be a painful overseas call to Sweden, plus another to the Kershaws. No, she thought, I shall pay Annika Lindstrom's host family a visit and break the news in person. And then would begin the task of searching for whoever had killed Miss Lindstrom. Killed her and left her body in a cold cellar in a vacant and locked cottage on Crooked Lake. A cottage whose owners claimed never to have heard of Annika Lindstrom.

CHAPTER 4

The sheriff rolled over and fumbled for the alarm clock. The dial told her it was 6:45. She desperately wished she could stay in bed for another hour, perhaps all morning. Her head was throbbing, and it felt like a migraine. To make matters worse, Carol had not had such a bad case of hay fever in years, and she knew that if she got up and went about her business her eyes would water constantly and her nose would run like a faucet. She was exhausted. Nonetheless, she crawled out of bed and made her way groggily to the bathroom. Two things motivated her to do what her body told her not to do. One was that she had not missed a day's work since she had become sheriff of Cumberland County, and somehow it didn't seem right to allow a headache and a bout of hay fever to end that streak. More importantly, she owed both Annika Lindstrom's parents and the Kershaws a report of the sad news that the young woman was dead. She had told the Claymores not to talk with the Kershaws, but what if they mentioned it to someone who in turn could pass the information on to the couple who had played host to the Swedish exchange student? Carol knew that she had to be the one who broke the news.

Better to take care of it right away. It was 7:35 when she finished breakfast, which meant that it was early afternoon in Sweden. She found the number which she had used to call the Lindstroms back in January and placed the call. It took a couple of minutes, and the woman who answered said something in Swedish which Carol did not understand.

"Is Mrs. Lindstrom available?" she asked. For all Carol knew, the woman who had answered the phone was Helga Lindstrom. In view of the fact that she was known to be bed ridden, it was probable that she was at least in the house and hence available.

"No, Mrs. Lindstrom cannot come to the phone," the woman said. Her English was passable. "May I take a message for her?"

This was not what Carol wanted to hear. You don't ask a

housekeeper or a nurse to pass along the news of a daughter's death to her mother.

"I really need to speak with Mrs. Lindstrom myself," she said. "I'm calling from the United States."

She hoped the fact that the call was long distance and presumably of some importance would be sufficient to make Mrs. Lindstrom available. Apparently it did.

"Let me see," she was told.

It was after another three minutes that a much weaker voice came on the line.

"This is Helga Lindstrom. Who's calling?"

"Mrs. Lindstrom, I'm Carol Kelleher. We last spoke back in January. I am the sheriff in a county in New York State, the place where your daughter Annika was visiting as an exchange student. I'm calling to share some bad news with you. Your daughter is dead."

She wasn't happy with the way it had come out, but there really wasn't any point in beating around the bush. Mrs. Lindstrom would have guessed the reason for the call as soon as Carol had identified herself as the sheriff.

"I have been expecting this call for four months, sheriff."

Was it her imagination, or was the woman's voice actually stronger than it had been when first she spoke?

"I am so very sorry to have to be the bearer of such sad news," Carol said. "We only found her yesterday, and I wanted to let you know just as soon as I could."

"Of course. I appreciate that. But Lars and I have been prepared for this for a long time, so I probably don't sound as devastated as you might expect. You don't know us, but if you did I think you could understand me when I say that in a sense we lost Annika many years ago when we had our accident. It might be better to say that Annika lost us back then. She was a lovely girl, but given the circumstances of our lives and hers we haven't been close since she was eight years old."

Carol was uncomfortable. What she was hearing was something very close to a confession, a brief and unhappy epitaph to a failed relationship.

"I suppose I should ask how she died," Mrs. Lindstrom went on, "although I'm not sure that I want to know. I only hope that it was mercifully quick."

"We don't know," Carol said. "As I said, we only found her body late yesterday, and it wasn't clear how or when she died. It may take a few days before we have the answer to those questions. If it helps, she didn't look as if she had been abused."

That was only a half truth. There was trauma to the head, but she did not know whether it had come from a fall or from a blow administered by an attacker. And saying that Annika did not appear to have been abused was Carol's way of saying that there was no superficial evidence of sexual abuse. Not yet at any rate.

"I'm sure you'll let us know the cause of death when it has been determined. Lars isn't here at the moment, but he will be in touch with you to make the necessary arrangements for shipping her body back to Malmo. There is no way we can come over there to take care of things. I'm sorry about that, but we have trouble getting around, as I'm sure you have heard."

After Carol hung up the phone, she sat quietly in her chair for another minute, reflecting on the strange conversation she had just had with Annika's mother. It had been almost as if they were talking about some stranger.

That unpleasant task behind her, Carol was on the road by 8:15. Skies were clear, temperatures still cold. Not typical hay fever weather, Carol thought as she blew her nose.

Traffic was light, but twice she had to stop and wait while yellow school buses picked up students. The mood on those buses making their way to the schools in Southport would be noticeably different than it had been a week or two earlier. The semester was winding down, and students were beginning to count the days until they could put the books away and start living the good life that came with summer on the lake.

Two of the students who got off the bus at the Southport High School and went up the steps and into the long, low red brick building at the south end of the lake were named Kershaw. The brother, Brian, was a senior for whom graduation was now just a month away, the sister, Jennifer, a junior who had recently fallen just six votes short of having been elected the school's May Queen. They had shared their home with Annika Lindstrom from just before Labor Day until January, from her arrival in Southport until her mysterious disappearance shortly after the beginning of the spring semester. Over the course of those months they had formed very different impressions of their house guest and had had very different relationships with her. Whereas most of their classmates had largely stopped talking and thinking about Annika as winter turned to spring and her disappearance became old news, Brian and Jennifer had found it much harder to forget her and get on with their lives.

Sheriff Kelleher would later regret that she had not been the one to tell these two young people what had happened to Annika Lindstrom. To tell them she was dead and where she had been found, and to observe the way in which they reacted to the news. It was their mother who would break the news to them, having heard it herself from the sheriff that morning while her son and daughter were seeking to master the intricacies of calculus and European history.

Carol circled the town square in Southport and followed Mountain View Road past a number of old homes until she came to the Kershaw residence. It was just after 8:55. She had not wanted to call and make an appointment, so she could not be sure that anyone would be at home. But there was a grey Ford van in the driveway, so she parked across the street and went over to the house. It was on the third ring that a woman in a bathrobe came to the door. She looked to be in her forties, and was probably regretting the fact that she had not dressed and put on makeup.

"Yes?" she said, puzzled to see a uniformed officer of the law at her doorstep.

"Hello, Mrs. Kershaw. I'm Sheriff Kelleher. You may remember me."

"On, yes, of course. I'm Amanda. But what –"

"May I come in? I need to talk to you."

"Of course, but has something happened? To my Bob? Not the kids, I hope."

"No, Mrs. Kershaw. I'm sure your family is okay. Let's find a place where we can sit down." The woman seemed unable to move away from the doorway, so Carol stepped into the foyer and taking her by the elbow guided her into what looked less like the living room than it did an old fashioned parlor.

"This is about Annika Lindstrom," Carol said, getting right to the point of her visit. "I'm afraid I have bad news. Miss Lindstrom is dead."

Amanda Kershaw sighed deeply and sank down into an overstuffed chair that didn't look as if it would provide much comfort.

"She is?" Her voice was small and weak.

"I'm afraid so. I know you must have been worried about her all of these months since she disappeared. Now at least we know. She has very likely been dead since the day she didn't come home back in January."

"But she was in Ohio." Mrs. Kershaw was trying to process this information, searching for something that would prove that it wasn't true.

"We don't know about that post card from Ohio. What we do know is that she was found last night in a cottage on the lake, just a few miles north of here."

"I don't understand," Mrs. Kershaw began. "How could she have –"

"I know that this must be very hard for you. But I have to ask you a few questions. We have no idea why she was killed or by whom. Or precisely when. And we don't know why or how she got into that cottage. You may be able to help us."

"But sheriff, I told you everything I could when she went missing. I don't know – I can't imagine why she turned up dead right here, I mean right on the lake. I've always hoped that she'd just run away, heaven knows why. Maybe a boy. Maybe there was trouble with her parents that she didn't want to talk about. I tried to tell myself it wasn't my fault."

"It wasn't your fault," Carol said, interrupting. Or had the Kershaws had something to do with it? But this was no time to add to Mrs. Kershaw's feelings of guilt. Better simply to encourage her to talk, to talk about what kind of a person Annika had been, what kind of relationships she had had with members of the family, with students at the school. What had made her happy, what had made her sad. They had been over some of this ground in the days after she had disappeared, but that had been months ago and perhaps there would now be other things that she would be willing to share.

"I'd be interested to hear what Annika talked about. Did she seem willing to talk with you about what was on her mind? Did she have much to say about her life back in Sweden? Her relationship with her parents?"

Mrs. Kershaw considered this.

"Do they know that she is dead?" she asked.

21

"Yes. I called this morning just before I came down here to tell you. Do you have any impression of them, based of course on what Annika said?"

"It's interesting," Mrs. Kershaw said. "She talked very little about them. She was so young – I guess you could say vibrant – whereas they were old and somehow more like grandparents than parents to her. You know they had been in a terrible accident when she was a little girl, and it left her mother bed ridden and in chronic pain. Her father couldn't get around very well. He worked from their home. I don't think she didn't love them, but I got the impression that they weren't a very important part of her life as she grew up. She didn't have the responsibility for caring for them, and I think they recognized that she was a smart, self-sufficient girl who didn't need constant attention like most kids do – like mine do. Annika didn't write them often, and I don't suppose she received more than two letters from them all fall."

"You once told me that Annika's mother was worried sick about her disappearance."

"Well, I suppose I did. What mother wouldn't be worried? But I had the feeling she figured her daughter would turn up, that she was self-reliant, able to look after herself."

"Did she think it strange that Annika had just walked away without saying anything to you?"

"I've thought about it a lot," she said. "She didn't say it, but I suspect she figured it was a boy. She thought Annika was mature – you know, old beyond her years. And I don't think it would have surprised her, or even bothered her, if she developed a serious relationship with some boy over here."

"And did you see any evidence that Annika was developing a serious interest in a boy?"

It was immediately apparent that this was something Amanda was reluctant to talk about.

"I'm not sure. Teenagers can be awfully private. They don't want adults poking into their lives."

"But how about Annika? You must have some idea whether she was doing more than just going to school dances and coming home at a decent hour."

Mrs. Kershaw looked as if she had suddenly remembered that she was still in her bathrobe. Her hands went to her hair, then returned to her lap.

"This is really a family matter, sheriff. I'm just not comfortable talking about it."

"I'm sorry, but I don't know what it is that you're not comfortable talking about."

"It's my son, Brian. And it's nothing. Really, it's nothing."

This conversation had gone too far to stop now.

"I understand that it's personal. But I'm sure you can appreciate how important it is that we get to the bottom of Miss Lindstrom's death. We need to know everything we can about her. I'm not investigating your son, Mrs. Kershaw. I'm investigating what happened to Annika Lindstrom, and if there is something about her relationship with Brian that I need to know, I think you should tell me."

Carol knew that Brian's mother was smart enough to know that if there had been a relationship between the two, there could also have been a conflict. And now Annika Lindstrom was dead. Could a conflict have turned violent? Could Brian Kershaw have been responsible for Annika's death?

"I want you to know that Brian never had a relationship with Annika. He found her fascinating, but so did we all. She was so different from most of her peers. You know all about the statistics, I'm sure. A lot of high school kids are sexually active. Even in Southport. Bob and I don't kid ourselves about it. And I'm as sure as I am of anything that Annika was sexually active. Things she said, things she didn't have to say – she'd had several partners back in Sweden, and it would have been naive to think she wouldn't be looking to have several more here in the States. My guess is that she'd have been only too happy to go to bed with Brian. It isn't that she was a bad girl. It was just her nature. Can't you imagine someone who is promiscuous but somehow still innocent?"

Carol didn't think she'd ever considered that particular paradox.

"But you know that they never had a relationship?"

"If you mean did they ever have sex, I'm sure the answer is no. It would have been difficult under this roof, and besides, Brian got wind of the fact that she had been seeing Eric Mackinson. If it had been a high school acquaintance, that's something else. But Mackinson is out of school and he must be at least eight years older than Annika. It was a wake up call for Brian. He never told me how he felt about Annika, but he did make it a point to tell me that he knew she was sleeping with Mackinson. I'm not sure why he told me. Maybe he thought I'd talk to her about it, but I wouldn't have known how to do that."

"What about your daughter? She's about Annika's age, as I remember. They must have talked a lot. Did she ever say anything about what Annika was like? Who she palled around with at school? Anything that might have hinted at trouble?"

Once again Mrs. Kershaw looked uncomfortable. Carol was patient.

"Actually, Jennifer didn't get along very well with Annika." She hadn't wanted to say it, but now that she had the words came more easily. "Jennifer doesn't share much with Bob and me. She never said what it was about Annika that bothered her. But I had the feeling that Jennifer was jealous of her. No, let me take that back. Jealousy isn't the right word, and it isn't fair to Jennifer. But Annika was so perfect – well, not to me, but for another teenage girl. I mean she had it all – looks, smarts, poise, maturity. She was only 16, but she could have passed for 23 or 24. And it had obviously come so easily for her. I'll bet if you asked around the high school you'd find that a lot of the girls resented her. It was like everyone else was diminished by her presence."

Carol had never met Annika Lindstrom, but from what she had heard she could imagine that Mrs. Kershaw was right. And that her daughter had indeed felt diminished.

"As far as you know, did Annika date someone who had been dating your daughter?"

"Jennifer wasn't dating anyone. Of course I don't know whether she would have liked to date someone that Annika hung out with. Who knows what she might have been thinking. But I know she didn't have a boyfriend back then."

I'm going to have to talk with Jennifer, Carol thought. Jennifer and Brian, too. In all likelihood they would know much more about what Annika Lindstrom was doing and with whom during her semester at Southport High School than their mother did. If, that is, they would condescend to talk to her.

"How about you and your husband?" Carol asked, aware that this might be an even more sensitive question. "You had opened your home to an exchange student, a very kind thing to have done. I'm sure you looked forward to a pleasant experience.

Forget if you can that it ended tragically. How did you feel about Miss Lindstrom?"

"I wish I could forget that it ended tragically, sheriff. That's impossible. But like I told you, she was an impressive young woman. I didn't like it that she was so casual about sex. Otherwise, she was easy to get along with. Never complained about anything. If she didn't like my cooking, she never said so. I asked her to honor the hours I'd set for my kids – home by midnight unless it was some special occasion – and she went along without a fuss."

"Did your husband share your feelings?"

"Yes, he did. Bob doesn't involve himself much in these things. I doubt that he spent much time talking with Annika, so he probably knew less about her than the rest of us."

Carol had never met Mr. Kershaw, and she had no idea how he may have felt about this girl-woman who had moved into his home. She hoped that Amanda Kershaw was right in her assessment of her husband's lack of interest in Annika Lindstrom.

They talked for another quarter of an hour. Most of those minutes were devoted to trying to convince Amanda Kershaw that she need not feel guilty about what had happened to Annika. But Carol knew that if she had been in the woman's shoes, she herself would be feeling guilty. And that it would be a long time, regardless of who turned out to have been Annika's killer, for that feeling of guilt to go away.

CHAPTER 5

Carol decided to make a brief stop at the Claymore cottage on her way back to the office. It wasn't that she had no confidence that Sam Bridges, her deputy sheriff, and Bill Parsons, her most experienced officer, would do a thorough job. It had everything to do with a burning curiosity about how Annika Lindstrom's body had gotten into the cottage. She needed to know whether someone had used a key or had broken in. She wasn't sure which means of access would make her investigation easier. Either way, she had her work cut out for her; but she had to know and she had to know before she did anything else that day.

Bridges and Parsons were still there when she drove up behind the cottage. Three police cars on the point. The neighbors would already be calling each other to see who knew what was going on at the Claymores. For all she knew, Bill or Helen Claymore had already spoken with the Cabots or another of their neighbors. At least they had followed her instructions and not called the Kershaws.

Although clouds had begun to gather, it was still a beautiful if cold morning. A moderate breeze from the northwest was keeping the blue lake waters in motion. There were even two sail boats on the lake, helping to create a picture of tranquility which was at odds with the harsh fact that a murder had almost certainly been committed there. She had tried unsuccessfully to imagine another cause of Miss Lindstrom's death, although she knew that she wouldn't know for sure until Doc Crawford had done the autopsy.

She grabbed another bunch of tissues from the box on the seat beside her and walked around the cottage, where she found Bridges at one of the windows. Parsons was presumably inside.

"Find anything interesting?" she asked.

"Depends on how you define interesting," Sam replied. "This place isn't what you'd call secure. It's old. The seal on the windows isn't very tight. The locks are pretty simple. Somebody who knew what he was doing and wasn't pressed for time could probably break in. Here, let me show you."

They went over to the front door where he pointed out what was indeed a simple lock, probably one that had been installed several decades ago. Carol knew that someone with the skills of Lawrence Block's fictional burglar, Bernie Rhodenbarr, could have picked it easily. She had no idea whether the person who had stashed Annika Lindstrom in the cellar had the skills of a Rhodenbarr.

"What's your opinion?"

"I thought it would be easy," Sam said. "We'd find obvious signs of a break-in, or we wouldn't, in which case someone used a key. But now I'm damned if I know. There are places that look like somebody might have been monkeying with a couple of the windows, but I don't think the marks on the frame and sill are new. Could have been done when they were scraped for painting. Bill found something inside. Want to take a look?"

Of course she did, and they went in to where Parsons was helping himself to a glass of water.

"There are two possible problems as I see it," he said. "One of them is upstairs, where the sash locks are missing on two of the windows. Opening them would be a piece of cake, although I have trouble seeing someone putting up a ladder and carrying a body up to the second floor and pushing it through the window. Of course your killer could be a strong guy who happens to drive a truck conveniently equipped with an extension ladder."

Parsons' smile suggested that he didn't believe in that scenario. He took another drink of water and led them into the living room.

"Now here's a real puzzle. See those marks?"

He was pointing at a window which looked as if someone had taken a chisel to it, gouging out small pieces of wood over an eight inch wide stretch of the sill.

"That's fairly recent, and it sure looks suspicious. But I can't figure why somebody who was already inside would tear up the window sill when he could simply walk out the door. Besides, the sash lock is still fastened."

"I agree," Carol said. "The killer's problem would be getting in, not getting out. I don't know what it means, but I doubt that it has anything to do with Miss Lindstrom being in the pump room."

Frustrated by the fact that they couldn't rule out the possibility that the killer had gained entry without use of a key, they turned their attention to other things.

"There doesn't seem to be anything out of order elsewhere in the house," Sam said. "They look like they left it pretty neat when they moved out, and the workmen who did the remodeling upstairs did a good job of cleaning up after themselves."

Officer Parsons interrupted.

"It's probably nothing, but there's one thing. I noticed it when I was going through the bedrooms. All the beds were made up nice and proper, blankets tucked in, pillows fluffed up. With one exception. At least I think it might be an exception. One of the beds isn't quite as neatly made up as the others. Not a huge difference, but considering how fussy whoever made up the rest of the beds was, you couldn't help but notice that one of them was different. Either she got tired of being a perfectionist before she got to that bed or someone lay down on it after it'd been made up and didn't bother to straighten it up again."

The minor discrepancy her colleague had noticed in the condition of the beds might be important. Perhaps someone had used that bed since the Claymores vacated the cottage in September. Perhaps. It was equally possible, of course, that Mr. Claymore had taken a short rest on the bed in question after it had been made up and before they had headed back to New Jersey.

"I want to look at the beds," Carol said, and headed for the stairs.

What she found was that there wasn't as great a difference between the one bed and all the others as she had imagined. If someone had used it, he had tried to neaten it up afterwards but had not been quite as meticulous as he might have been. What could be more important was that the bed in question was not in the master bedroom, the one where Mr. and Mrs. Claymore presumably slept. It was a single bed in a sparely furnished bedroom down the hall, a bedroom which was decorated in a way that made it look very much as if it belonged to a young man or a boy. Why would Mr. Claymore have flopped down on that bed in that room rather than on his own bed in his own room?

Carol filed that question away in the back of her mind and suggested that she'd like to take another look at the pump room.

"We didn't find anything down there," Sam said. "Just

some scuffing in the dirt where the body had been. If there were any shoe or boot marks on the dirt floor, they would have been wiped out last night."

"I know," Carol said, acknowledging the implied criticism. She was only too well aware that she and Claymore and the paramedics would have obliterated such prints as they poked around in the pump room. "Was the floor damp back by the wall where the body had been?"

Decomposition had barely begun, slowed by the fact that the room had still been very cold, but with decomposition comes purge fluid and the odor which she thought she had detected. Perhaps some fluid had begun to seep out of the body.

"I don't think so, but let's go see."

The pump room had no window to the outside, and without a functioning light it was still pitch black. Their flashlights produced circles of light on the floor, but behind the stairs it remained nearly black and dark shadows formed and reformed elsewhere as the lights shifted their focus from one part of the room to another. Carol went to the corner where Annika Lindstrom's body had been and knelt down to examine the floor. If there had been a seepage of fluid, it had been so slight as to be unnoticeable to the naked eye in bad light. She studied the area more carefully than she had the night before, and decided that Sam had been right. The pump room seemed to be devoid of clues to the mystery of why Miss Lindstrom had been left there and by whom.

"I'm going to leave you two to continue your search of the cottage," she said as they went back to the first floor. "I want to hear about anything – anything! – that's the least bit unusual. Like that bed upstairs. It may turn out to be nothing, but I'd rather we be wrong than miss something."

She paused at the back door.

"By the way, if any curious neighbor comes by, not a word about what we found here. Let's not mention Lindstrom's name. It'll get out soon enough, if it hasn't already. Just tell them someone thought he'd seen a light in the place, and we were checking it out."

"Would it have taken three police cars and more than an hour to do that?" Sam asked, sounding doubtful.

"No, but I'm sure you can make it sound plausible. I'm

going to call their motel and talk to the Claymores before they come home and start unpacking."

With that, Carol set off for her office, still unsure how Lindstrom's body had gotten into the Claymore cottage. And with no idea why that particular cottage, out of the hundreds on Crooked Lake, had been chosen as its hiding place.

CHAPTER 6

Carol never made it to the office after leaving the Claymore cottage. She stopped en route to pick up some more antihistamine tablets, examined her puffy face in the car's rear view mirror, and decided to spend the rest of the day at her house in Cumberland. She could just as easily call the Claymores in Yates Center from there as from the office. She could also call Doc Crawford. There was no way he could have completed an autopsy. He might not even have gotten started. But she could tell him what she knew about the girl's disappearance back in January, and she could make it clear that she needed his report at the earliest possible date. If the throbbing in her head would only ease up she might even be able to put her mind to thinking hard about how she should go about trying to solve the mystery of Annika Lindstrom's death.

Back home, she first called the office to tell them where she was and what she was doing. And that she would take calls if something important came up. Then she swallowed two aspirin and an antihistamine tablet and lay down on the bed. She had planned to rest for a few minutes, but it was nearly five o'clock when she woke up. Aware that she had slept away the afternoon, Carol practically leaped out of bed and immediately regretted it. Her head was still throbbing painfully. But she had to call the Claymores. She could picture them, cooped up in the motel room, eager to know when they could return to their own cottage.

A call to her office revealed that Bill Claymore had dutifully phoned, only to be told to sit tight until he heard from the sheriff. Only a minute later he heard from her.

"Sorry to be so late getting back to you," she said apologetically. "But if you and your wife feel like moving back into the cottage, you can go ahead and do so. I would appreciate it, however, if you would stay out of the pump room for a couple more days. The water's on, so it really shouldn't be necessary to go down there right now."

"Is there still some problem in the pump room?" He

sounded worried. Was the sheriff going to stage a recreation of Annika being stowed away there? No, of course he wouldn't think that, but he might well have worried that she had found something that necessitated further police presence.

"Not that I can see, Mr. Claymore, but I'd like to wait until we have the autopsy report. There's always a chance that it will tell us we should take another look." Carol herself could think of no good reason to continue treating the pump room as off limits to the owners of the cottage, but she couldn't quite dismiss a nagging doubt that they had learned everything they could from the crime scene.

That bit of business completed, she dialed Doc Crawford's number. He wasn't available, so she left a message stressing the urgency of an autopsy and then went out to see if the mail had arrived – it had, but no letter from Kevin. Headache or no headache, she finally settled down in her study to brainstorm what was looking suspiciously like yet another of Crooked Lake's annual murder mysteries.

At the moment, she knew almost nothing. What she did know for sure was that the Claymores, summer residents on the lake, had returned to find the body of a young woman in their cellar. And that the young woman was Annika Lindstrom, an exchange student from Sweden who had come to Southport the previous August, enrolled in the local high school, disappeared mysteriously in January, and just as mysteriously turned up dead four months later. Beyond that, nothing was certain.

The owners of the cottage had insisted that their cottage had been locked since the previous Labor Day, but there was no proof that that was so. They had also insisted that there were five, possibly six keys to the cottage, keys which might have been used to gain access and put Miss Lindstrom in the cellar. But it was possible that those in possession of some of the keys were not the ones who had been identified by the owners of the cottage. It was also possible that there were even more keys floating about.

It was not clear how Miss Lindstrom had died. That she had been murdered was most likely, given the fact that her body had been found – been hidden? – in what was a most unlikely place, but even that would remain uncertain until the autopsy had been completed. Why was her body in the cottage of Bill and Helen Claymore, who claimed not to know who she was? And who had put her there?

Amanda Kershaw, in whose home Annika Lindstrom had been living before her disappearance, had provided information about the girl and her life style. But was that information reliable? She would need to talk with many more people, and even if they were honest in their assessment of the late Miss Lindstrom, an accurate image of her might not emerge. Moreover, some of those people might have their own reasons for lying or shading the truth.

Carol needed to know who had been Annika's friends, as well as who had disliked her and why. She needed to know who the boys – and perhaps the men – were that she had dated. And which of them, if any, she had slept with. She needed to know a lot more about the Kershaws. And about the Claymores, for that matter.

She counted at least eight people she wanted to talk with right away. Three of them were the other members of the Kershaw family with whom Annika had lived for nearly five months. Jennifer, the daughter who had 'felt diminished' by the beautiful young woman from Sweden. Brian, the son whose budding interest in her had soured when she started dating an older man. And Bob, the husband who had allegedly paid her little attention. Then there was that older man, actually a twenty-something named Eric Mackinson, who had reputedly been having an affair with Annika. The other four people on her must see list were there because the Claymores had identified them as possessing keys to their cottage. One was a neighbor, Joe Cabot, who kept an eye on the place over the winter months. A second was Bud Harbaugh, a contractor who had been doing some work on the second floor of the cottage. A third was the Claymore's son, Barry, who was in college somewhere, but was known to visit his parents' summer home on occasion. Finally, there was a Roger somebody, Helen Claymore's brother, who might or might not have a key.

Carol put down the note pad on which she had been jotting down these thoughts about a case not yet 24 hours old. She started to get up to take another antihistamine, but just as quickly sat down as another thought occurred to her. There had been a post card from Lindstrom to the Kershaws back in January, just shortly after her disappearance, a post card from Ohio that assured them that she was all right, that they should not worry. As soon as she had recognized the body in the pump room as Annika

Lindstrom's, Carol had assumed that she had disappeared because she was dead. If that were true, how could she have posted a card to the Kershaws from Ohio? Had someone else written and mailed the card? Someone who wanted people to believe that she was alive when in fact she was dead?

As she thought about it, Carol remembered that she had never actually seen the post card. Amanda Kershaw had told her about it, told her what it said and how relieved she had been to hear from Annika. And – yes, now she remembered. According to Amanda, the card had been signed AL. Those were indeed the girl's initials, but why had she signed herself in that way instead of 'Annika'? Was it that AL would be easier to forge than Annika?

Suddenly, in addition to all of those people she needed to talk with and soon, she needed to see that post card. If, that is, it had not been tossed out. She hoped that Amanda would have held onto it, reassuring proof that Annika Lindstrom was okay and that she need not feel quite so guilty about her disappearance. Even as she reached for the phone to call the Kershaw residence, however, she started to have second thoughts. It was, after all, possible for Annika to have gone to Ohio when she disappeared from Southport and posted a card from there. She might then have decided to come back to Crooked Lake, only to face death and four months as a frozen corpse in the Claymore's cellar. Possible, but not, she thought, likely. She placed the call.

It was Amanda who answered the phone.

"Mrs. Kershaw, this is Sheriff Kelleher again. How has your family taken the news about Miss Lindstrom?"

"Bob isn't home yet, but I did talk with Brian and Jennifer. It's always hard to know just how the kids are feeling about things. They both said something about how terrible it was, but they didn't seem to want to discuss it. Anyway, Brian acted as if he wasn't surprised. Jennifer actually seemed more upset than her brother, which sort of surprised me. They both thought it weird that she'd been found in somebody's cottage. They've been texting their friends ever since I told them. By now just about everybody in the high school must know that Annika's dead and where you found her."

Interesting, Carol thought. Interesting but probably not surprising. Jennifer and Brian didn't want to discuss Annika's death with their mother, but they were immediately sharing the news with their peers.

"Look, I'm calling about that post card that you received from Annika back in January. The one that said she was okay and that you shouldn't worry. Do you by chance still have it?"

"I think so," Mrs. Kershaw said. "But then I don't really know. I'm not all that well organized, and I never made a file up on Annika. Would you like me to look for it?"

"Yes, I'd very much appreciate it if you would. We now know that Annika was wrong when she wrote that she was well and that you shouldn't worry about her. What we don't know is whether she was in Ohio. There is a possibility that she didn't write that post card. I'm not sure we could prove it, one way or another, but I'd like to have a good look at it."

"That would be terrible, wouldn't it? I mean if someone tried to make us believe she was all right when she wasn't."

Yes, indeed, it would be terrible, Carol thought, and said as much to Mrs. Kershaw. Not as terrible, however, as killing her. If that is what happened. In spite of all the unknowns she had written down on her note pad, Carol was still very much of the opinion that Annika Lindstrom had indeed been murdered. Murdered and left in the Claymore's pump room, murdered and left there before a forged and false message had been posted from Ohio.

It was shortly after six o'clock, and Carol was debating with herself whether to uncap a beer. Her head still ached, but not quite as badly. Her nose was still running, but the antihistamine had made a difference. The question was whether the beer would exacerbate her problems or help her relax. She opted for the beer, deferring for the time being the matter of fixing supper.

As she nursed the beer, she went through the day's mail that she had set aside without opening after finding no letter from Kevin. There was nothing that engaged her attention, and she focussed instead on the letter that wasn't there. Not that Kevin owed her a letter. They had spoken on the phone just three days earlier, and she knew he was busy with end of semester duties at Madison College. In fact he would probably be returning to the lake within a matter of days. That prospect was even more of a pick-me-up than the beer.

It had, all things considered, been a good year. Or as good a year as was possible in view of the fact that his job kept him down in the city while hers kept her upstate, in and around Crooked

Lake. Things had been better in the fall, when his teaching schedule had allowed him to spend every other weekend at the lake. But he had been unable to avoid Friday and Monday classes in the spring, with the result that they had seen each other only once since the first of the year, and that way back during his spring break in March. It wasn't only that two months without sharing his company seemed like an eternity. She missed the daily reminders that they were not only the best of lovers but also the best of friends. But she also missed the opportunity to share with him the ups and downs of the law enforcement business. He had thrown himself into the investigation of Father Brendan Rafferty's murder in the fall with all of his accustomed vigor. She would have nailed the killer without his help, of course, but she had to admit that she had loved the enthusiasm with which he played amateur detective. She would even have to give him credit for the occasional brilliant idea.

Carol knew that Kevin would find the problem of Annika Lindstrom's death intriguing. She had no idea how her investigation would play out. There was much she didn't know. Actually, there was almost everything she didn't know. But it was always possible that what looked daunting today would look simple tomorrow. Someone would say something or do something which would let all the pieces of the puzzle fall into place. She and Kevin could then concentrate on enjoying each other's company.

It was possible, but if past was prologue, it wasn't probable. It was more likely that solving the Lindstrom case would be difficult and time consuming. And one of these days the citizens of Cumberland County would begin to ask themselves why Carol Kelleher's tenure as sheriff had resulted, not in a drop in the crime rate, but in an unprecedented string of murders. Carol felt her headache worsening.

CHAPTER 7

Carol awoke without benefit of the alarm clock on Saturday morning, and for nearly fifteen seconds luxuriated in the knowledge that for the first time in almost a week she felt like a human being. Unfortunately, the recollection that Annika Lindstrom was dead kicked in almost immediately, bringing the sheriff quickly back down to earth.

Nor was it just that she was now face to face with a puzzling case that dampened her mood. It was also the realization that there were things she ought to have done that had gone undone, questions she ought to have asked that had gone unasked. It appeared that she could no longer use a bad headache and an equally bad case of hay fever as an excuse for the oversight. There would be no R & R over the weekend.

The coffee started, Carol put her mind to those things she had failed to address on Friday. The most important, she decided, was a search of Miss Lindstrom's room at the Kershaws. She hadn't even asked if the room had been restored to its condition before Annika's disappearance. She hoped it hadn't been. The girl had vanished with only a shoulder bag in her possession, leaving behind two suitcases and heaven knows how many personal items. Carol remembered that when she first heard about it, she had been worried by the fact that Annika had not taken these things with her. Her failure to do so had suggested that she might not have left Southport of her own free will. But the post card from Ohio had the effect of moving the matter to a back burner. Now it was a priority matter.

She also knew that it was of critical importance to talk again with all of the students whose names had surfaced when she and Mrs. Kershaw had made inquiries about where Annika had been the night she disappeared. Those names, all presumably friends from Southport High, were in a skimpy file at the office. Back in January, none of these students had been helpful. A few of them had seen Annika that night at a party, but it had been one of those roving parties, with kids drifting from one house to another. No one was able to say when or where she had dropped out of sight. Now that she had been found dead right on Crooked Lake, perhaps one or more of her friends would be able to recall something that had not seemed important at the time. She could only hope so, and the possibility made it necessary to begin making contact with all of them. Carol was suddenly aware that the prospect of interviewing a flock of teenagers face to face was unsettling. What if they were all as opaque as Amanda Kershaw had said her own daughter was?

Saturday or no Saturday, this was going to be a busy work day. First a brief stop at the office to pick up the old Lindstrom file and then a trip to Southport to examine Annika's room. The rest of the day would be spent calling on Southport High students. With any luck, one or two of them would be at home.

To her surprise, all of the Kershaws were at home. For a brief moment she entertained the idea of talking with Mr. Kershaw and both Brian and Jennifer before she tackled Annika's room. But on second thought, that seemed to be a poor idea. She should talk with each of them separately, not in the presence of the others. Better yet, she should talk with them separately without having to emphasize that that was what she wanted to do. No reason to make them suspicious that she might be checking on whether their stories matched. With luck, she would catch one of them alone later that day. If not, there would be other days.

For the second time in two days Amanda Kershaw greeted Carol at the front door of the house on Mountain View Road. This time she had gotten herself dressed, although she didn't look any more eager to talk with the sheriff than she had the day before.

"Have you learned something about what happened to Annika?" she asked. Her tone of voice suggested that she was sure the answer would be 'no.'

"I wish I could say that we have, but I can't," Carol replied. "As it happens, I'm here to do something I didn't get around to yesterday."

Amanda Kershaw stepped aside to let the sheriff past. They went into the living room, where Bob Kershaw was reading a newspaper. It looked like the *Wall Street Journal*. Introductions over, Carol got right to her reason for being there.

"What have you done with Annika's things?"

The Kershaws looked at each other, as if unsure how to

respond to a simple question. I'll bet they disagreed about what to do with them, Carol thought. Bob had obviously prevailed.

"I could see no reason to leave the guest room like she had left it," he said. "She wasn't the neatest person, you know. Anyhow, once we knew she'd gone off and settled somewhere else, it seemed to make sense to pack her things away. I stuffed them in the suitcases and put them up in the attic. In case she came back or sent for them. The room is pretty much as it was before she got here."

"But of course you didn't know that she hadn't gone off and settled somewhere else," Carol said, as if to assure Mr. Kershaw that what he had done was perfectly reasonable, even if she wished he had left everything just as it was. "Tell me, did you put everything in the suitcases? I mean, did you throw anything out, or did you save it all?"

Once again the Kershaws exchanged glances.

"I don't think we tossed anything that's important," Mrs. Kershaw said. "We dumped the wastebasket, as well as used toiletries and things like that. As far as I know, it's just her clothes that went into the suitcases."

"Did you find a diary? Anything that looked like she kept track of dates, put down the names of people she knew?"

It was Mr. Kershaw who answered this question.

"The only thing she had written except for some school papers was in a small booklet, about the size of an envelope. I don't know what you'd call it. But it was in Swedish, which we couldn't understand, so I got rid of it along with the other stuff Amanda mentioned."

Carol was not in the habit of swearing, but at that very moment she wanted to. The little booklet might have contained nothing of interest. On the other hand, it might have had something important to say. The fact that it was in Swedish might only reflect the fact that it was Annika's first language. But she might have resorted to Swedish because she didn't want the Kershaws to know what she was writing, just in case they should snoop around in her room.

"You didn't tell me about that," Mrs. Kershaw said to her husband.

"It didn't seem important," he said dismissively.

"If it wasn't important, why did you steal it from my

room?" It was Jennifer, who had suddenly appeared on the stairs. It wasn't clear how long she had been there.

"This isn't any of your business, Jennifer," her father said, obviously irritated that she had injected herself into their discussion with the sheriff.

"You know I don't want you in my room. Why can't you respect my privacy?" Jennifer was angry and made no effort to conceal it. It was Carol's first introduction to the generational tensions in the Kershaw family.

"Hello, Jennifer. I'm Sheriff Kelleher and I'm investigating Annika Lindstrom's death, as you might have guessed." Carol was trying very hard to be matter of fact. And friendly. "The reason I'm here today is so I can look over Annika's belongings. Maybe they will help us figure out what happened to her. Apparently you had this notebook of hers in your possession. How did you happen to have it in your room?"

Jennifer came down the last several stair steps and took a seat. She addressed the sheriff, but her eyes remained focussed on her father.

"When she disappeared last winter, I wondered why, just like everyone else. I'd hardly ever been in her room, but I was curious, so I went in. That diary or whatever it was was there, and I borrowed it. Of course it wasn't in English, so I couldn't read it. But I had an idea that maybe I could find a Swedish-English dictionary or something like that and figure out what she'd written."

Mr. Kershaw interrupted her.

"You're accusing me of not respecting your privacy, Jennifer, but it looks like you didn't respect Annika's privacy."

"Oh, come on," the young girl said. "She's dead and I'm not. Or hadn't you noticed?"

This unpleasantness is interesting, Carol thought. But irrelevant.

"Let's forget the privacy issue for a moment," she said. "Did either of you find anything in the diary – the notebook, whatever it was – that you could understand?"

Carol assumed that Jennifer had skimmed through it and she thought it likely that her father had, too. Hopefully they had seen something that wasn't in Swedish, like names and phone numbers.

"I don't remember," Jennifer said. "There may have been

some names, but I can't recall any right now."

Carol was frankly puzzled. It was, after all, a small high school, and it was hard to imagine that Jennifer would not have been interested in and remembered whom Annika might have written about. Was she being deliberately evasive?

"How about you, Mr. Kershaw? Do you remember any names from the notebook?"

"I wasn't interested in it. I was just getting rid of Annika's stuff."

Jennifer couldn't let that pass.

"So why did you go in my room and hunt for it? I didn't leave it out in plain sight, you know." It was a direct challenge, and her father was not pleased.

"That'll be enough, Jennifer. The sheriff doesn't need to be a witness to your rude behavior."

"Don't worry, I'm leaving." And with a flourish, she got up and headed for the door.

Carol's question caught her just before she marched out.

"You said you were going to see if you could translate some of what Annika had written. Did you succeed?"

"No, I didn't. Swedish isn't like French or Spanish. It's weird. The library didn't have anything, and I don't know anybody who speaks Swedish. Can I go now?"

Jennifer Kershaw didn't wait for permission to leave.

The atmosphere in the room could charitably be described as chilly. Amanda Kershaw had clearly been upset by the confrontation between her husband and her daughter. Carol decided to stop talking and spend some time going through Annika's things. At her request, Mr. Kershaw brought the suitcases down from the attic and the sheriff was left alone with them in Annika's old room.

Carol could see nothing in the room to suggest that it had been occupied by a young woman not that many months earlier. The furnishings were fussy, the pictures on the walls old fashioned. She opened the dresser drawers and those of the bedside stand. As she expected, they were empty. The closet was equally empty except for a dozen or so hangers. Just to be sure, she searched under the mattress and on the floor under the bed. Nothing.

She put the first of the two suitcases onto the bed and

opened it. Bob Kershaw had said he had stuffed Annika's things into the suitcases, and indeed he had. Nothing had been folded, no effort had been taken to separate clean clothes from those that needed to be washed. Carol emptied the suitcase and examined each item before putting it back. The end result was a neater job of packing than that which had been done by Mr. Kershaw, but she found nothing of interest. A few of the items were of a style with which Carol was unfamiliar, but then Annika had assembled her wardrobe in Sweden, not the United States. Otherwise, it appeared that she had dressed like many another teenager.

The second suitcase contained more clothes, but it was also the repository of what might be described as small hardware. There was a small cotton bag with assorted jewelry and a number of personal appliances which would be among most women's bathroom accessories. There were also two vibrators. Carol allowed herself a wry smile. In a side pocket of the suitcase were four small pill bottles. Two of them were instantly recognizable, and a third appeared to contain birth control pills. If it became necessary, she would inquire of the local pharmacist what the other pills were for.

It was what wasn't in the suitcases which was most troubling, and that was the booklet that both Bob and Jennifer Kershaw had mentioned. The booklet which Jennifer had 'borrowed' from Annika's room, the booklet which her father had then removed from his daughter's room. The booklet which had stirred an unpleasant debate about privacy. The booklet which was now long gone via a routine trash pickup along Mountain View Road.

It was doubtful that the suitcases contained anything which would be of further use in the investigation of Annika Lindstrom's death. It was equally doubtful that Annika's parents would wish to have them sent to Malmo. But until she was sure that they would be of no further use, they would have to be placed under lock and key. Which meant that she would be taking them back to Cumberland with her.

Brian Kershaw made his first appearance of the morning as she was coming down the stairs, a suitcase in each hand. He offered to help her with the bags, and she gladly let him do so.

"These look like Annika's," he said.

"They are, and I'm taking them back to our office." Carol took advantage of the fact that none of the rest of the family was present to pose a question. "I'm the sheriff, and I've been going through Annika's things. There don't seem to be that many. But I just need to make sure that we have in our possession everything that she left here when she didn't come back that night in January. So I need to ask if by any chance you may have taken anything – anything at all, no matter how small – from her room."

"No, why would I have done that?"

"I'm not accusing you of anything. It's Brian, isn't it? But it would have been perfectly natural for members of the family to have been in and out of her room over these months. So I'm asking all of you if you have anything of Miss Lindstrom's."

"What would I want with any of her stuff? Souvenirs from Sweden? No, not me. You might get a different answer from Jennifer."

"Thanks for the advice. I'll ask her. Now I need to say good-bye to your mother and father, then you can help me put those suitcases in my car."

CHAPTER 8

Carol had no children. Now in her late thirties, her biological clock ticking inexorably away, it was increasingly likely that she might never have any. Barring some as yet unforeseen development in her relationship with Kevin Whitman, she could not even be sure that marriage was in her future. But if having children meant having to look forward to what she had just witnessed in the Kershaw house, she wasn't sure she wanted any part of it. Imagine, she thought as she drove, slogging your way though your fifties with your teenage offspring alternately ignoring you and being rude and disrespectful. Carol knew, of course, that all teenagers weren't like Jennifer Kershaw or all households as tension-ridden as the one on Mountain View Road. She had gotten along well with both her own mother and father, and her brother's brood had been a veritable Norman Rockwell poster family.

By the time she reached the town square in Southport, she had brushed this unproductive line of thinking from her mind. Or tried to. After all, it only had the effect of stirring up her worries about where her relationship with Kevin was going, and she didn't want to think about that. It was while she was trying to refocus her attention on the Lindstrom case that she spotted the rude, disrespectful daughter. She was standing by herself on the corner near Cameron's Ice Cream Parlor, looking glum. At least that's how she appeared to Carol.

Let's see if I can get her to talk to me, Carol thought, and pulled over to the curb.

"Jennifer?" she said, trying to convey pleasure at this chance meeting. "I didn't expect to see you so soon. I was going to stop for an ice cream cone. Will you join me?"

The girl's face was a blank. She looked around, perhaps hoping to see a friend who could spare her the necessity of saying yes to the sheriff. But suddenly her face brightened. I'll bet she's decided that there might be a certain cachet in being seen talking with the sheriff, Carol thought. Her friends might be impressed.

"Sure. Debbie must have had something she had to do, so why not kill some time while I wait for her?"

Carol finished parking. There had been no time for a handshake at the Kershaw house, so Carol made amends as she came around the car.

"Want to sit outside?" She was sure that would be Jennifer's preference, the better to be seen. She was right. They placed their orders and took seats at an empty sidewalk table.

"I've been wanting to talk with you," Carol said. "After all, you lived with Annika for several months. I imagine you knew her better than anybody else. I never met her. I only know her from pictures. When we're up against a case like this, we need to learn all we can about people, especially the victim. So you're in a great position to help me."

Jennifer didn't look ready to start volunteering information, so Carol was more specific.

"Was Annika popular?"

"I suppose it would depend on who you asked," Jennifer said, obviously weighing her words. "Everybody was curious about her, that's for sure. I think kids thought she was exotic."

"You mean being from a foreign country, being a stranger at school?"

"Well, yes, that's true. But there was something about her. I heard a couple of the guys say she seemed sort of dangerous. Know what I mean?"

"I'm not sure I do," Carol said. "What about her might have made her seem dangerous?"

"It was like she had lived a different kind of life than kids did around here. Like she grew up faster."

"Maybe she did. You know her parents had been badly hurt in a car accident. They probably didn't supervise her as much as most parents do."

"Yeah, I know," Jennifer said.

"When you say faster, are you suggesting that she was into drugs? That she was maybe more casual about sex than they are here in Southport?"

"Everybody knows all about drugs and sex. We're not naive," Jennifer said, not wanting the sheriff to think that she and her crowd weren't with it. For some reason, this intimation that she might be into drugs and might have had sex lacked conviction.

"So Annika was exotic. What kind of a relationship did you and she have?"

"It was okay. There weren't any problems. Except maybe over the bathroom, but that was more my brother's fault than hers. But I already had a lot of friends, so she wasn't a problem."

This was a rather indirect way of answering the question. And it didn't square with what Mrs. Kershaw had said.

"Would you say the two of you were friends?"

"Sure, in a way. She did her thing, I did mine. We didn't mess with each other."

It was a strange way of defining friends, and Carol was about to try again when a couple took seats at the neighboring table. Unless she wished the conversation to be overheard by these people, she would have to bring it to an end.

"I have to be going," Carol said. "It's been nice talking with you. In fact, I'll probably want to do it again soon."

They walked to the sheriff's car where, out of hearing range of the couple at the other table, Carol asked Jennifer one more question.

"By the way, did Annika have a boyfriend? Someone she seemed most interested in?"

Jennifer considered the question.

"Yeah, she did. His name's Bruce Bachman. She told me so herself. Said he was definitely the sexiest guy she'd met here."

"Bachman," Carol said, making a mental note of it.

"Right. He's a brainy jock, not your usual Neanderthal."

As she drove off, Carol could see Jennifer Kershaw, still standing on the sidewalk, waiting for her friend Debbie to show up.

There had been something disingenuous in what Jennifer had told her. In fact, she couldn't be sure that anything she had heard was true. Or if true, that it was the whole truth. It had been only a brief conversation, and there hadn't been an opportunity to press for more answers or for clarification of just what the girl had meant by some of the things she had said. Was the fact that Jennifer had been vague simply a manifestation of her difficult teenage persona? Or was she deliberately trying to mislead her? And if so, why?

Carol drove around the square and down a side street, where she parked and took out the file she had picked up at the office. It contained the names, addresses, and phone numbers of the students she had contacted back in January. Mrs. Kershaw had identified three of them as Annika's friends – Debbie Selfridge, Karen Leeds, and Sue Marinelli. Bruce Bachman's name had not been on the list. In fact, none of the students she had spoken with in January were boys. Carol reread the notes she had taken after talking with them. The Leeds girl had claimed that Annika was at her house early in the evening she had disappeared, but had left mid-evening without saying where she was going. Marinelli had also remembered seeing her at the Leeds house, and thought she might have been with a group of her fellow students heading down Water Street sometime later.

Okay. Debbie Selfridge was supposedly meeting Jennifer, so she would leave her for later. She would first pay a visit to Karen Leeds, assuming she was at home. If not, she would try Sue Marinelli, or perhaps Bruce Bachman.

To get to the Leeds' address, she had to pass through the town square again. Jennifer Kershaw was no longer there patrolling the sidewalk in front of Cameron's.

It took less than two minutes to reach the Leeds' residence, an old stucco house with green shutters not far from the lake. Carol took a deep breath as she climbed the front steps and rang the bell. She knew that this would be only the first of many homes she would be visiting in the next few days in her quest for information about the Swedish exchange student.

To her surprise, the girl who answered the door introduced herself as Karen Leeds. Carol's surprise wasn't due to the fact that Karen was home, although she had doubted that she would be. It was that she stood barely five feet tall – and she was wearing shoes. Annika Lindstrom was reported to have been close to six feet tall and much taller than Jennifer Kershaw. But Jennifer, whom she had just left in Southport's town square, was in turn much taller than Karen. A picture of the three of them, standing side by side and arranged in order of height, flashed through her mind. In fact, Carol realized that for the first time she was focusing on what Jennifer looked like. She had been paying more attention to what the Kershaws' daughter was saying than she had been to her appearance. Five foot five, just slightly overweight, dark brown hair worn with a pony tail, attractive face (when she wasn't looking surly). Miss Leeds, by contrast, was the epitome of cute. It wasn't just her height. She was small all over, including her facial features. Everything in proportion.

Carol forced herself to concentrate on the reason for her visit.

"Hi. I'm Sheriff Kelleher. You may remember, we talked on the phone back in the winter after Annika Lindstrom disappeared. I assume you've heard that Annika is dead."

"I know. That's so terrible. We can't believe it. I mean, she was such an awesome person."

Awesome? Not an adjective Jennifer had used.

"How so? No, let's wait a minute. May I come in? I'd like to talk to you a bit about Miss Lindstrom."

"Sure. Come on in."

Karen led the sheriff to a living room which did indeed looked lived in. Not cluttered, just much used.

"I'm grateful for the opportunity to talk with you, Karen. I've been hoping that some of you who knew Annika might be able to help me form a better picture of her. You see, I never met her. All I know is what the family she lived with have told me."

"Oh, the Kershaws. Well, there are several sides to every story."

So. This should be interesting, Carol thought.

"Yes, I'm sure there are. But first, you called Annika awesome. Why don't you tell me what you mean."

"Just awesome. You know, kinda unbelievable. Did you ever see one of our soccer games?

"No, I'm afraid not."

"Well, if you had you'd know. A year ago we were lousy, won only three games. But last fall, with Annika, we really turned it around. Eleven wins! I mean she was fantastic. Her size made a difference, but that's not all. She was quick, she could see the whole field, she moved the ball around like a pro. Like I said, she was awesome."

"I take it you're not referring only to soccer."

"No way. She was leading the basketball team in scoring when she went away. She aced all the tests, got along with everyone. I'll bet she'd have made May Queen if she were still here."

"She does sound impressive. And popular. Did everyone like her?"

"Mostly." Karen Leeds suddenly lapsed into silence.

"Can you explain what you mean by mostly? It sounds as if not everyone found her awesome."

"I shouldn't criticize my friends. But a couple of the girls didn't like her. You mentioned the Kershaws. They're really nice people, but Jennifer – she's their daughter – she wasn't so keen on Annika. I always figured that it was like it is with sisters. You know, both living in the same house, day after day. It can get on your nerves. Jennifer's a good friend, but she and Annika weren't real tight."

"How about the guys? Did Annika seem to have somebody she hung out with? I know she wasn't here all that long, but she must have had time to do some dating."

Karen broke into a little laugh.

"She could have had just about any guy she wanted. You should have seen them, everybody watching her in the cafeteria, in the halls between classes. Everywhere. I've never seen so many guys on the sidelines when the girl's soccer team was practicing."

"How about Bruce Bachman? I've heard she was really interested in him."

Karen frowned.

"Bruce? Where'd you hear that?"

"I don't remember," Carol lied. "I must have picked it up somewhere. Probably just gossip around town."

"Well, that's crazy. I mean Bruce is a nice guy. Too nice for Annika, if you know what I mean. She had a fast reputation. Don't get me wrong, but she was always looking for somebody who could keep up with her. But Bruce? If he wasn't such a great football player, people would probably call him a nerd. Straight A, church choir. I don't think he ever said a cuss word in his life. No, he definitely wasn't Annika's type, and I'm sure they never dated."

Well, well, Carol thought, there seems to be a real difference of opinion here. If not Bachman, who is – or who was – Annika's type?

"Do you remember who she was going with when she disappeared?"

"There wasn't just one guy," Karen said. "She hung out a lot with a senior named Rickie Lalor. And there's another guy, Michael Stebbins. She sure wasn't going steady."

Maybe it was part of what made her awesome.

"I'd like to go back to the night Annika disappeared," Carol said, changing the subject. "What do you remember about the party you and she went to that night?"

"I told you everything I know when you called," Karen said.

"I'm sure you answered my questions as best you could. But now that she's dead, it's even more important that we figure out just what happened that night. I'm hoping that you might be able to remember something else, something that would help us. So I wish you'd think hard about that night, that party. You told me it was here, at your house. Why don't you begin by telling me who was at the party?"

"I know you'll think this is funny, but it's hard to say." Karen probably figured that parties were different back in the day when the sheriff had been a teenager. "Nobody sends out invitations. Word gets around, and if you're in the group, you just drop by. It started here, but like always it continued at other places, like Debbie's and Sue's. I'm not sure all the same kids were at each house."

"But can you remember who showed up at your house?"

"There were maybe ten or twelve of us, including Jennifer, Debbie, Sue – oh, and Annika, plus Michael and Rickie and – sorry, I'm forgetting."

"Why don't we slow down. Can you give me those names again, first and last names?"

It took a minute or two, but eventually Carol had jotted down the names of all the people Karen was sure had been at the party that night. She hadn't followed them right away to Sue Marinelli's, apparently the next stop in the evening's peregrinations, but she was able to attest to the presence of some of the original dozen as well as a latecomer or two by the time they made their final stop of the night at Debbie Selfridge's. Unfortunately, she had lost track of Annika somewhere along the way.

"Do you remember when you last saw Annika?"

"I'm sorry, but no, I don't. We didn't do roll call." Karen seemed to think this was funny, then immediately sobered up when she realized that the sheriff wasn't smiling.

"So you didn't see her wander off with someone?"

"I wish I had, but the last time I saw her was when she left here. And she was with the whole gang."

Hopefully Sue Marinelli and Debbie Selfridge would remember where Annika was and with whom later that January night.

There didn't seem much point in prolonging her conversation with Karen. It had been interesting, but ultimately frustrating. She was left with the question of just who Annika Lindstrom really was. The awesome young woman Karen Leeds had described so admiringly, or the one whom Jennifer Kershaw appeared to dislike. Was the nerdy Bruce Bachman the lucky guy on whom she smiled, or was it one of the 'faster' ones, like Lalor or Stebbins? Had Annika had anything to say about these young men in the diary which Bob Kershaw had lifted from his daughter's room and then summarily tossed into the trash? Had she said anything in it about her plans for the night she had disappeared?

The fact that she would be holding conversations over the coming week with any number of Southport High School students was depressing. Based on what she had heard today, what lay ahead promised to be a variation on the Rashomon effect – memories and perceptions different, the truth about both Annika Lindstrom and the January party frustratingly elusive. She would persevere, of course, and one or more of these young people might reveal something, intentionally or inadvertently, that would actually put her on the track of Annika's killer. But as she climbed back into her car, Carol made a snap decision to leave Annika's student acquaintances for tomorrow and the week ahead and focus instead on keys. And because she was already in Southport, she would start with Bud Harbaugh, the contractor who had put in a new bathroom for the Claymores and a man who was known to have one of the keys to their cottage.

CHAPTER 9

Carol had never met Harbaugh, but she had heard of him. There weren't that many contractors in the Crooked Lake area who specialized in kitchens and bathrooms. The year before, when she had briefly considered modernizing her own kitchen, she had checked out the names of people who could do the job. Nothing came of that plan, the result of a conversation with Kevin that hinted that they might be edging cautiously toward marriage. Nothing had come of that, either. But at least she knew that Harbaugh worked out of a shop south of town. She circled the town square again and turned onto the Old Trout Run Road.

The stately old homes with well mowed lawns and rocking chairs on their porches gave way after a mile to a rural landscape. The houses were smaller and fewer, some with chickens in the yard. One had a roadside sign announcing that honey was for sale. Another called attention to an adjacent shed, overflowing with antiques. Finally, she came to a place that obviously doubled as a residence and a business establishment. The latter section had been given a face lift and sported a sign proclaiming that it was Harbaugh's Kitchens and Baths.

Carol pulled off into a gravel parking area and made her way into a small but attractive show room. The room was empty, but the sign on a desk near the entry way said that Mr. Harbaugh or whoever was on duty would be back in five minutes. It wasn't clear when the clock had begun running on those five minutes, but before Carol had a chance to think about it a handsome, rugged looking man came in through a back door.

"Good afternoon, I'm Bud Harbaugh," he said. "To what do I owe the pleasure of a visit from law enforcement?"

The smile suggested that he didn't find the presence of a uniformed officer worrisome.

"Hi," Carol said, extending her hand. "I'm Sheriff Kelleher."

"Planning on doing some remodeling?"

"I probably need to, but that's not my agenda today. This

may take a few minutes. Okay if I sit down?"

"Of course," Harbaugh said as he removed the 'back in five minutes' sign on his desk and took a seat opposite the sheriff.

"I understand that you did some work for Bill Claymore last year. Remodeled the bathroom in his cottage on the West Lake Road."

"Right. Does he have a complaint?"

"No, no, not that I know of." The Claymores actually did have a complaint, but it had to do with their pump room, not the bathroom. "It's clear that you aren't aware of what happened at the Claymores. It's not a pleasant story."

Harbaugh waited for an explanation.

"When the Claymores returned from New Jersey on Thursday, he went down to their basement to open the water pipes. What he found was a dead body. It was Annika Lindstrom, that student who disappeared last winter. Do you remember hearing about her?"

"Oh, yes. It was quite a big story at the time. But my God, how awful to find her dead – and in your own house."

It apparently hadn't dawned on Mr. Harbaugh why the sheriff was sitting in his office, telling him this.

"No question it was awful," Carol continued. "But what is particularly strange is that the Claymores tell me the cottage was all locked up and had been since last September. We know that Miss Lindstrom was alive until at least mid-January, so somebody had to have gotten into the cottage at that time or shortly thereafter and left her body there."

"Why did you come here to tell me this?" Harbaugh asked. He still didn't get it. Or was he doing a good job of acting innocent?

"I'm here, Mr. Harbaugh, because I'm going around checking with all the people who, according to the Claymores, had keys to their cottage."

Bertram Harbaugh, owner of Harbaugh's Kitchens and Baths, suddenly sat up in his chair, mouth open, eyes wide.

"My God," he said for the second time in less than two minutes. "You can't possibly think I had anything to do with it."

"We only learned about this two days ago, Mr. Harbaugh. In fact, it wasn't even 48 hours ago. There seem to be several keys to the Claymore cottage, and you have one of them. I am not suggesting that you are responsible for Miss Lindstrom's body being in the cottage. And I'm not suggesting that you had anything to do with her death. But somebody did, and that somebody almost certainly had a key. We know that you were in the cottage after the Claymores left last fall. You were doing that work on the upstairs bathroom. And Mr. Claymore had left you with a key so you could get in and finish the job."

Carol paused to let this sink in.

"But I shut the water off and locked up when I finished the job. You can't leave the water on in a place like that. The pipes would freeze. And Claymore made it very clear that I was to make sure the place was locked up. Besides, I never saw that girl in my life."

"Somebody got into the cottage, Mr. Harbaugh, and there's no sign of forced entry. We're pretty sure somebody with a key opened it and put Miss Lindstrom's body down in the cellar. I'm going to talk with everyone who had a key, and I thought I'd start with you because Mr. Claymore tells me you were the last person he knows of who was in the cottage. I'd like you to –"

"Wait!" Harbaugh interrupted, almost shouting the word. "Eric Mackinson! It could have been Eric Mackinson."

But almost as quickly as he had spoken Mackinson's name, he shook his head as if to take back what he had just said.

"No, that can't be right. Eric would never have done something like that."

Carol had heard Mackinson's name just the day before. Amanda Kershaw had mentioned him in the course of explaining why her son had lost interest in dating Annika.

"Why did you bring up Mr. Mackinson?" she asked.

"It's because he had a key. But I know he isn't responsible for what happened to that girl."

"And how do you know he had a key?"

"Because he was subbing for me. I'd finished my work at the Claymores, but the bathroom still needed wall papering and painting. Eric does that sort of thing, and I've used him before. He's pretty good, so I hired him to finish up the job. I suppose I could have given him my key to the cottage, but instead I had a copy made for him."

"Did he give you back his key when he finished?"

"No. I went back to the cottage when he was done, just to

make sure the job was done right before I shut the water off and sent my bill to Claymore. But I plain forgot to ask him for the key."

"So, hypothetically, Eric Mackinson could have used that key to get back into the cottage at a later date."

"But he wouldn't have." Harbaugh was feeling guilty he had identified Mackinson as someone who could have been responsible for what had happened to Lindstrom. "Do you know him?"

"No, I've never met him."

"Well, take my word for it, he's a sweet boy. Well, not exactly a boy any more. But he's hard working, honest as the day is long. Hell, he's still living in his parents' home, and they're real nice, God-fearing people."

"Nonetheless, Mr. Harbaugh, I shall have to talk with him, just as I have with you. You needn't worry that I'll be accusing him of anything."

At least not yet, Carol thought as she drove back toward Cumberland. Was this the first breakthrough in the Lindstrom case? She had known that there were too many keys to the Claymore cottage, and that it was almost certain that one of them had been used to gain access to the cottage and put Annika's body in the pump room. And she had begun to learn a few things about the Swedish girl's relationships with people in her new home away from home and her dating habits. But now, for the first time, she had learned about a connection between these two lines of inquiry in her fledgling investigation. One of the people Annika knew and had allegedly dated also had a key to the Claymore cottage.

Carol knew better than to allow herself to become prematurely excited. Other people had keys and might have used them. She had no proof that Annika knew Eric Mackinson, much less that she was sleeping with him. Brian Kershaw had told his mother as much, but was he sure of it or was he simply sharing school gossip? She had spoken with Brian only briefly when he carried Annika's suitcases out to the car. For all she knew, he was as unreliable as his sister. She would have to question him. More importantly, she would have to question Eric Mackinson. Why not do it now?

She pulled off the road and consulted the file which contained a growing list of the names and addresses of people she would need to talk to. Most of them were students at Southport High. Eric Mackinson was quite a few years past high school, although Harbaugh had said that he was still living with his parents. The file told her that the address was on Edgeware Lane. Five minutes later she rolled to a stop in front of a modest house only a block away from where she had met with Karen Leeds not much more than an hour earlier.

A lazy spaniel saw her coming and came down the front steps to meet her. She patted it on the head and rang the bell. The woman who came to the door was wearing an apron and, to Carol's surprise, a big smile.

"I saw the police car drive up," she said. "I hope you've arrived to add some spice to my day."

If she knew why I'm here, Carol thought, she wouldn't be quite so happy to see me.

"I wouldn't know about that," she said, returning the smile. "It's Mrs. Mackinson, right?"

"Yes. I'm Joyce."

"Nice to meet you. I'm Sheriff Kelleher, and I'm here because I was hoping I might talk with Eric."

The smile on Joyce Mackinson's face quickly faded.

"Has he gotten into some kind of trouble?"

"No, I just need to talk with him. It will only take a few minutes."

"I'm sorry, but Eric isn't here. He and some of his friends left several hours ago. I don't have any idea where they went or when they'll be back. He's all grown up, you know, and he doesn't like it when I ask him what he's up to. I still forget sometimes that he's a big boy, got a job and all."

"Well, then, I don't need to bother you further," Carol said. There would be other days, other opportunities to speak with the young man who had one of the keys to the Claymore cottage.

"Can I give him a message? Tell him what you wanted of him?"

"No, that won't be necessary. If I need to, I can get in touch. By the way, whatever's cooking smells awfully good."

"Saturday's my baking day," Mrs. Mackinson said, the smile returning. "I promised Eric I'd have some cookies for him to take over to his girl friend's tonight."

"I bet he'll be pleased," Carol said.

Later, on the way back to Cumberland, she wondered just how pleased Eric Mackinson would be that his mother was baking cookies for his girl friend. She was willing to bet that Eric's mother was too much involved in her son's life. What had she thought about his interest in Annika Lindstrom? Assuming, that is, that Eric had been interested in the Swedish exchange student. And that gave rise to another question. If they had been in a relationship, where did they spend their time together? Almost certainly not at the Kershaw house. The Mackinson residence? That struck her as equally doubtful. Where would a twenty-something high school graduate and his allegedly fast, sexually active girl friend go to get away from her host's worried supervision and his mother's smothering presence?

Carol hated to tip her hand by calling ahead to make appointments to see the many people on her list. But she might have to do so if she were to see Eric Mackinson any time soon. And that was something she needed very much to do.

CHAPTER 10

While Carol was worrying about Eric Mackinson and the many other people she would have to talk to in the days ahead, Kevin Whitman, associate professor of music at Madison College, was worrying a decision that could not be postponed much longer. He was sitting in his office on the third floor of Sherman Hall, staring at a crowded desk. The spring semester had just ended, and most of the papers that cluttered the desk could be disposed of without further thought. A few would need to be filed, of course, but deciding which ones to file and which ones to toss wasn't what was worrying him. The problem was that he faced a conflict.

He wanted to pack up and head back to the lake for the summer. That's where Carol was, not to mention the change of scene and the change of pace which always buoyed his spirits after a hard year in the trenches of academe. But he also had to finish the paper he had promised to deliver at a conference in Copenhagen. The conference was only a week away, and he was having difficulty bringing the paper to closure. It wouldn't have to be in publishable form, but he feared that the current draft would not impress the audience he would be addressing. And that would only lead to professional embarrassment.

Kevin was realist enough to know that if he were at the lake, even for a few days, with Carol sharing the cottage, he wouldn't be able to concentrate on the paper. He would make a stab at sharpening his argument, but the result would be disappointing. So he would have to stay in the city until the paper was acceptably coherent and persuasive. But if he did –

Annoyed with himself and his indecision, Kevin impulsively swept a batch of the papers off the desk and onto the floor. He'd have to pick them up, of course, but it made him feel momentarily better. It was nearly 5:30, and there was a good chance that Carol would be at home. In their last conversation, she had said nothing about a crisis which was likely to have tied her up on a Saturday. He'd call her.

But the sheriff was not at home. He had trouble picturing

her at the office so late in the day on a weekend; in any event, she and Kevin had long ago agreed that they wouldn't call each other at their offices unless it was an emergency. Probably shopping or visiting a friend. He'd call again mid-evening.

He caught Carol in a bad mood. Her hay fever had returned. She hadn't been shopping, which meant that there hadn't been anything worthy of the name in the house for dinner. And she was still feeling frustrated that Eric Mackinson had not been at home.

"Sheriff Kelleher." It was not a warm and welcoming voice.

"Hi, it's Kevin. You okay?"

Carol's reply was much friendlier.

"Oh, sure. Sorry if I sounded formal. What's up?"

"What's up is that I'm missing you, but then what else is new? I've been trying to clean up the usual end of semester mess with only limited success. Do you ever have days when you think you're regressing?"

"I've just had one."

"Really? What's the problem?"

Carol had chosen not to tell Kevin about the Lindstrom case. It was the reason she hadn't called him since the young woman's body had been discovered in the Claymore's pump room. She knew that the minute he heard about it he'd want to drop everything and hurry back to Crooked Lake.

"Nothing,"

"Since when is a bad day nothing?"

"Why don't you tell me about your day?"

"You're changing the subject," he said. "Okay, I'll tell you about my day. I've been wrestling with a dilemma – we've talked about it, but now I've got to do something about it. You know that paper I'm supposed to give? The one about the King Lear opera Verdi never wrote? Well, semester's over, and the Copenhagen conference is no longer later, it starts next Friday."

"And the paper isn't done, right?"

"I'm afraid so. Oh, I could wrap it up in a few hours, but it would be a pretty poor excuse for a scholarly piece of work. Trouble is, I want to be up there with you."

"What you're telling me," Carol said, "is that you know that once you're at the lake the paper won't get written. I don't think you've ever gotten much writing done up here. And I'm the thief of your time, right? Do me a favor. Stay where you are, write the paper, go to the conference, and then you're welcome to come back to the lake. You'll chew yourself out all summer if you blow this gig in Copenhagen."

"I know, and you shouldn't have to remind me about my priorities. But it's really your fault. If you weren't so special, we wouldn't be having this conversation."

"Yes, and if I told you to forget the paper and get yourself back to the lake, you should have nothing more to do with me. I love you, but I'm not going to sabotage your career."

"She who must be obeyed," Kevin said with a laugh. "Good. Now that's settled, what's new up there?"

"I wasn't going to tell you, because I knew you'd want to drop everything and come back up here yesterday. But now that I know you'll be professionally responsible, I'll let you in on our latest murder."

"Murder?"

"You heard me. Thursday night one of you summer people had just gotten back from wherever he spends the rest of the year, and guess what?"

"He was killed by one of Crooked Lake's many lunatics?"

"No, this is serious business. He found a dead woman in his cellar. And we don't know how she got into the cottage. The place was locked up, had been since last September, and there's no sign of a break-in."

"If I didn't know you so well, I'd wonder what you've been smoking. You're sure it's murder? Again? How many does this make since we met?"

"It makes five, six counting the one that brought us together in the first place. This one's a young woman – a girl, actually. She was a high school exchange student from Sweden who was living with a family in Southport. She'd been missing since January, which means she'd probably been a frozen corpse in that cellar for almost four months."

"Sweden, you say?"

"Right. Some place called Malmo. But she seemed to fit right in. Excellent English, very popular, lots of friends. At least that's the preliminary verdict."

Kevin, who had been peppering Carol with questions, had no comment.

"Are you still there?" Carol asked.

"Yes, very much so. And I'm thinking."

Oh, no, she thought, he's going to finesse the paper and come rushing back to the lake.

"Kevin, let's take a breath."

"No, no. I'm not about to change my plans. But I've got an idea."

"You don't know anything about it. How can you have an idea?"

"This woman, girl, whatever, she was from Malmo, you said. That means she has a family over there, people who knew her, people who could give you a picture of just who she was, maybe help you make sense of why this happened."

"I've already talked with her mother."

"Good, but that's just a beginning. Now here's my idea. That town where she's from, Malmo, it's just across a new bridge from Denmark. From Copenhagen. I'm going there for my conference in less than a week. You can come with me, meet the family, talk with this girl's friends. We'd both be doing our jobs – and stay at the same hotel, maybe have a nice dinner or two at Tivoli. What do you think?"

"Very creative, Kevin, but the answer is no. If I have questions, there are police in Malmo who can do my footwork for me. Besides, how do you think it will look if I go running off to Europe with you? People do know about us. They'd say their sheriff was off on a lark with her lover boy. Talk about really bad public relations! No, I'm not going to Copenhagen with you. And you're not going to go snooping around Malmo, looking for heaven knows what dirt on Annika Lindstrom."

"Lindstrom, that's her name?"

"Why? Did you know her?"

"Of course not. But I still think it's a good idea."

"It's a very bad idea. Would I like to go to Copenhagen with you? Of course. Maybe we can do it someday. But not now. And I mean it when I say I won't have you pretending to be a private detective between panels at a convention on opera. You can discuss Verdi and Wagner and the rest of the operatic greats to your heart's content, but Lindstroms are out of bounds. Is that understood?"

"Aye, aye, sir. Now that we've agreed that I won't be seeing you for another week, maybe ten days, do you want to tell me more about this latest chapter in the Crooked Lake crime wave?"

"There's not much to tell, unfortunately. We don't have the autopsy report yet, and I've just begun to question people who knew the girl."

"I'll bet they all say she was a sweet, wonderful girl, loved by everybody," Kevin said. "But sweet, wonderful girls don't get themselves killed and stashed in the cellar of some vacant cottage, do they? So you've got a problem."

"Actually, not everyone I've spoken with would agree that she was sweet and wonderful. Beautiful, yes, but that's something else. Anyway, you're right; I've got myself a problem. It looks like I'll be talking to half the kids in Southport High School plus heaven knows how many people who have keys to that cottage where she spent the winter. I'd be very surprised if we get to the bottom of this one before you get back from your conference."

"Which means I may still have a chance to demonstrate my powers of deduction."

"I'd much rather give you a chance to demonstrate some of your other skills," Carol replied.

They promised to stay in touch, with Kevin providing updates on the progress of his paper and Carol keeping him informed on the status of her investigation of Annika Lindstrom's murder. They both knew they were doing the right thing, but neither was happy that their summer together had just been postponed, even if for only a week.

CHAPTER 11

While Kevin closeted himself and struggled with the task of completing his contribution to the debate over the opera that Giuseppe Verdi never composed, Carol again turned her attention to Eric Mackinson. Or tried to. But her plans were briefly sidetracked by an unexpected development on Sunday morning.

As she drove past the Claymore cottage on her way to Southport, she noticed that there were now two cars, both with New Jersey license plates, parked there. It was not until she had gone another quarter of a mile down West Lake Road that it occurred to her that the second car might belong to the Claymores' son, Barry. Or to Helen Claymore's brother Roger. There were many other possibilities, of course, all of them more likely. After all, Barry was off in college somewhere and Roger was apparently unwelcome at The Summer House. But what if one or the other of these men, both possessors of a key to the cottage, had chosen to pay Bill and Helen Claymore a visit? What is more, Carol had not seen the Claymores since the night Annika Lindstrom's body had been discovered in their pump room. She should be paying them a visit herself.

She found a place to turn around and a minute later pulled up behind the cottage. Her arrival had been noticed, and the door opened just as she was about to ring the bell.

"Sheriff Kelleher, so good to see you again." It was Helen Claymore. "You know who did this thing?"

"No, Mrs. Claymore, I'm afraid not. It's only been a little over two days since we found the body. How are you and your husband doing?"

"We're okay." She did not sound as if they were okay.

"I'm sure it can't have been easy. I mean getting used to the idea that someone had gotten into your cottage and put that girl's body in your cellar."

"You're right. We can't stop talking about it. Whoever would have believed something like this."

"Mrs. Claymore, would you mind if I came in?" Carol

asked.

"Oh, my, what's happened to my manners," the woman said, stepping aside and making room for the sheriff. "Let me get you some coffee. And you can meet Barry."

So, it was the son. Had his parents called to share the news of their macabre discovery? Had he found the news so unbelievable, so bizarre, that he had cut classes and made the trip to the lake out of natural curiosity? Or had he expected the call and wanted to be on the scene to get a first hand impression of how people were reacting to what had happened? Carol realized that she had not given any thought to Barry Claymore. She knew he was of college age, but she had no idea where he went to college or anything else about him. Would he have known Annika Lindstrom? How could he have known her? She would have been in Southport while he was elsewhere.

Carol set these thoughts aside, accepted the cup of coffee, and went on into the living room where she had heard two male voices in conversation.

"Ah, it's our sheriff." Mr. Claymore extended his hand in greeting and turned to introduce his son. "I want you to meet Barry. His semester has just ended and he decided to come back here when he heard about our little mystery."

The young man stood just under six feet in height, carried his weight better than his father, and didn't seem to be embarrassed to still be dressed in pajamas and bathrobe, hair uncombed, face unshaven.

"Pleased to meet you," he said, his grip strong on Carol's hand. "I got in late last night. Had to see what all the excitement's about."

"I was going to stop by to see how your parents are doing, but it's a bonus to be meeting you as well."

Bill Claymore took charge.

"I see Helen's gotten you some coffee. Why don't you sit over here on the couch?" He picked the Sunday paper off the cushions and adjusted a pillow. "We're just now getting back to normal, as you might have guessed. Unpacked finally. Haven't been down to the pump room, though."

He flashed a nervous smile as he said it.

"Any more information about that girl?"

"No. Like I told your wife, we're still feeling our way. I'm talking to people, but it's going to take time. I'm sure you're getting a lot of calls from friends, neighbors. It must get tiresome, being the center of attention in a matter like this."

"Well, it hasn't been all that bad. Mostly just understandable curiosity. Haven't heard from anybody who seems to have known that Lindstrom girl. I'll bet there's been a lot of talk among the students down in Southport, though."

"I'm sure you're right about that." Carol turned her attention to Barry Claymore, who was sitting in a big armchair across from the couch, his bare feet tucked under him. "How about you, Barry? Did you know Miss Lindstrom?"

"No I didn't. I understand she came here as an exchange student last fall, but I was off in Ohio by then."

Ohio. That's where the post card had come from, the card telling the Kershaws that Annika Lindstrom was all right. The card that had almost certainly not been written by Annika.

"You're in college out there?"

"Right. McLean. It's a small liberal arts school south of Akron. You've probably never heard of it."

"I'm afraid not. Do you like it there?"

"It's okay. A little isolated, like a lot of those other small Ohio colleges. We get over to Columbus quite a bit."

"What's your major?"

This was surely an irrelevant question, but Carol wanted to hear Barry Claymore talk.

"I just finished my first year. You don't have to declare a major until second year. I'll probably do econ."

"McLean coed?"

"Of course," he replied. "It used to be all guys, but they started admitting girls a long time ago. Not many single sex colleges left."

Carol recalled the movement away from all men, all women schools. It had taken off well before she went to college. Her father had been worried that his daughter might be living in a dorm where guys shared bathrooms with girls.

"Do you spend much time here at your parents' cottage?" Carol asked, changing the subject.

"Not anymore. Back in the day, before college, I used to be here a lot. But then there were summer jobs back home, and now – well, I doubt I'll find time to be here more than a couple of long weekends."

"How about when you were still in high school down in New Jersey. Did you come up here much, get to know any of the local crowd?"

"Some. I mean I was here some, knew some of the kids from around the lake."

"How was that? Were they neighbors on the point? Did you hang out with any of the crowd down in Southport?"

For the first time, Barry hesitated. Was he trying to remember specific people he had known? Was he trying to figure out where the sheriff was headed with her questions?

"There wasn't what you'd call a crowd. I knew a few guys in the high school, a couple of them from the Yacht Club. Dad has a membership."

Mr. Claymore nodded, confirming what his son had said.

"It's sort of the equivalent of a country club," he said. "Good people. We often race on the weekend."

"I understand from your parents that you have a key to the cottage," Carol said, stating a fact.

"He does, but he doesn't use it." It was Bill, not Barry, Claymore who spoke up. "Barry knows the story."

There was a moment of silence.

"Look, Dad told me about the business with the keys," Barry said. "But I'm not here when my parents are away."

The Claymore's living room again became silent.

"I'm sorry, sheriff, but this is a bit awkward," Mr. Claymore explained. "We had a little problem awhile back. It must have been almost two years ago. Barry had some friends over one time when Helen and I were away. We got back and found the place in a mess. The stereo was busted and the toilet was backed up. Helen, she said this can't go on. So we laid down some rules. One of them was that Barry wasn't to use the place when we weren't around."

"It was your rule, Bill," Mrs. Claymore interjected.

"Okay, but you didn't object. I remember it was the condition of the kitchen that bothered you the most."

"All right, Dad, can't we let it go? That was way back when I was in high school. Have I ever broken your rule?"

It was obvious that Barry Claymore was embarrassed to have the sheriff hearing this. A young adult, a year of college under his belt, he didn't like it known that he was denied use of his family's cottage unless his parents were present.

"All I was getting at," Carol explained, "is the matter of keys. Someone seems to have used a key to get into the cottage and leave Miss Lindstrom's body in the pump room. I'm trying to account for keys to the cottage.

"I don't understand," Barry said, suddenly more animated. "Why would you even think I might have had something to do with that girl being in the cottage? I didn't even know her."

"I didn't mean to suggest that you had anything to do with what happened here," Carol said, her voice calm. "But keys can be lost. Misplaced. Do you still have your key to the cottage?"

"Of course I do." Barry got up from the chair and disappeared upstairs. He was back in half a minute with a ring containing quite a few keys.

"Here." He handed the key ring to the sheriff, identifying the one that opened the cottage.

Carol looked at it, then at Mr. Claymore.

"It looks right," he said, then fumbled in his pocket and extracted another key ring. He picked out the cottage key and held it up for the sheriff to compare with the one on Barry's key ring. They matched.

"Have these keys always been in your possession?" Carol had no reason to believe otherwise, but the question had to be asked.

"Of course," Barry answered, his voice suggesting that he found the sheriff's question offensive. Just as quickly he adopted a more polite tone.

"I'm sorry, sheriff. I know you have a problem about the keys, but I've never given my key to the cottage to anyone. I even doubt that it's been used since that party Dad told you about."

Mr. Claymore nodded his agreement, as if to assure the sheriff that his son had conscientiously lived up to their bargain on use of The Summer House.

"Okay, so you've never given your key to the cottage to anyone. Right now, however, I'm afraid I'm going to have to ask you to give it to me."

Later, as she continued her drive to Southport and the conversation she hoped to have with Eric Mackinson, Carol reviewed her reaction to what she had learned from and about

Barry Claymore. He seemed like a normal young man of college age. But could she – should she – take at face value everything he had said? There was the fact that he was in college in Ohio. There was the impression that he had agonized over how to answer her question about friends on the lake. There was the episode concerning the abuse of his parents' cottage. Surely none of this would prove to have any bearing on the murder of Annika Lindstrom. But she couldn't put aside a small, nagging sense of unease about what she had heard in the Claymore's living room.

I wonder if any of the young people in Southport will tell me that they know Barry Claymore, she asked herself. She would certainly be asking them. And she would find an occasion to have another conversation with Barry himself, this time without his parents present.

CHAPTER 12

As Carol turned onto the town square in Southport, her mind was occupied with the worrisome possibility that Eric Mackinson would once again not be at home. Which reminded her that she faced the same problem with all of the other people she knew she would have to question, many of them students at Southport High School. What is more, the list of people she would be interviewing was certain to grow as new names popped up in the course of her investigation. Her task would be simpler if she could simply place calls and make appointments. But that was not the way she liked to proceed. It eliminated the element of surprise and gave people time to plan their answers to her questions, to decide what to say and how to say it. Carol had always preferred to try to catch people off guard.

Unfortunately, she was unlikely to catch many of the students who had known Annika Lindstrom off guard. By the end of the school day on Monday, if not before, almost everyone in the high school would be aware that the sheriff was questioning Annika's acquaintances. Jennifer Kershaw would have spread the word. As would Karen Leeds. Which meant that all of those students who were only names to her – people like Debbie Selfridge and Rickie Lalor and Bruce Bachman – they would all have had a chance to think about how they would wish to describe their relationship with Annika and what they would choose to remember about that fateful night in January.

Carol considered going directly to the high school and arranging with the principal to call these students out of class for a series of interviews in some quiet corner of the building. But that might only send the alarming message that the investigation of Annika's death was focussed on her fellow students, which was simply not true. It would, of course, be helpful to talk with the principal and perhaps with some of her teachers about their impressions of the beautiful exchange student. But that was another matter, and would be unlikely to expedite her round of interviews.

No, she thought, this is simply going to take time. And there is no way that I can prevent the rumor mill from preparing Annika's friends – and enemies? – for a visit from the sheriff. Carol turned her attention back to Eric Mackinson. She was now only a block from the house he shared with his parents. Hopefully, he would be at home.

But for the second time over the weekend, Eric had chosen to be elsewhere.

"I'm sorry," Mrs. Mackinson told her. "He said something about going up that ravine at the south end of town. You know, the one down where the old Iroquois Road branches off from Meadowbrook. He likes to shoot at cans up there."

"Do you remember when he left?"

"Not exactly, but it must have been around 9:30. What's that, an hour ago?"

"Something like that," Carol said. "I'm not sure whether I'm up to hiking up the ravine this morning. If I don't catch up to him, I'll be around another time."

"Is there something Eric has done that he shouldn't have done?" Joyce Mackinson sounded concerned that the county sheriff had come looking for her son twice in two days.

"Not that I know of," Carol said. "I'm just talking to people who might have information about a case we're working on."

It was not an answer that would put Mrs. Mackinson's mind at rest, but she saw no point in mentioning Annika Lindstrom without having talked to Eric. If he wanted to explain the sheriff's interest in him to his mother, he was welcome to do so. But first she would have to find him. The entrance to the Iroquois Road ravine was barely a mile away, and hopefully he would be there. Preferably alone.

A white panel truck was parked off the road near the entrance to the ravine. It bore a hand lettered sign, Mackinson's Paint Jobs.

The ravine was considerably wider than most of those which surrounded Crooked Lake. From the road it looked more like a gravel pit than a channel though which water coursed down off the hill into the lake. But Carol knew that around a bend and out of sight from the road, this ravine narrowed and climbed rather precipitously. She had no idea where Eric Mackinson was in the ravine. She might have a strenuous hike ahead of her, and she had not worn shoes suitable for such a hike.

While it had been a chillier than normal spring, it had not rained a lot, with the result that there was relatively little water in the ravine. This made walking easier than Carol had feared, and she negotiated the first several hundred yards fairly quickly. But still no sign of Mackinson. Why would he have gone so far up the ravine just to shoot at tin cans, something he could have done more easily near the road?

A shot rang out from somewhere up ahead of her.

Carol decided that she had better call out, letting him know that she was in the ravine. No need to take a chance that an errant shot might hit her.

"Mr. Mackinson? Is that you? I need to talk with you. I'm not far below where you are – please hold your fire and wait for me."

"You the sheriff?" came a voice from somewhere close.

Why had he assumed that it was the sheriff? Obviously his mother had told him of her visit the previous day. But what made him think that she would have come looking for him less than twenty-four hours later in the Iroquois Road ravine?

He was sitting on a ledge just beyond a shallow pool of water where the ravine widened and leveled off temporarily. Fairly tall, dark blond hair, jeans, navy blue polo shirt, athletic shoes that looked far more comfortable than what she was wearing. He held an air pistol in his right hand. It looked to her like a Crosman, but she couldn't be sure. Some distance away across the ravine a row of three small cans stood on a shelf of shale. Several others lay on the floor of the ravine, testimony to Eric Mackinson' skill with his air pistol.

"Good morning," Carol said as she approached. "I hoped I'd find you here."

"You are the sheriff, right?" Had she been in uniform, the question need not have been asked. This Sunday morning Carol had chosen to wear a pair of jeans and a windbreaker which she had zipped all the way up. She thought Eric looked cold in his polo shirt.

"Yes, I'm Sheriff Kelleher. And you're Eric Mackinson. We need to talk."

Carol sat down beside Eric on the ledge.

"What do we need to talk about?" he asked. You know what

we need to talk about, Carol thought, but she didn't say it.

"I'm looking into what happened to Annika Lindstrom. Have you heard about it?"

"Sure. Everyone's been talking about it. It's crazy, her being found in someone's cottage. Really unbelievable."

Not just someone's cottage, Carol said to herself. Bill and Helen Claymore's cottage, a place you know well.

"Tell me, Mr. Mackinson, did you know Miss Lindstrom?"

"Not very well. We'd met."

This made two conflicting stories. Jennifer Kershaw and Karen Leeds disagreeing about Annika's interest in Bruce Bachman. Now Brian Kershaw and Eric Mackinson at odds over whether Eric had been dating Annika. Eric should know whether he had been in some kind of relationship with Annika. But if he had, he might not want to admit it. Carol could not leave it at that.

"You say you'd met," she said. "How did you meet?"

"I'm not sure, but I think it was at a game last fall."

"I presume you're talking about a Southport High soccer game. Do you still go to their games?"

"When I can," was the laconic answer.

"So you were introduced, talked to each other. What was your impression of Miss Lindstrom?"

Mackinson apparently had to think about this before answering the sheriff's question.

"She seemed okay," he finally said. "Pretty girl. I remember being surprised she spoke such good English. She wasn't from America, you know."

"Yes, I do know. You say you didn't know Miss Lindstrom well. Maybe then you can explain why I've heard that you used to date her?"

Another moment of silence.

"Well, I suppose I did. Sort of." No attempt to deny it, or even to ask where the sheriff had gotten this information.

"I'm sorry, but I don't understand. Dating sounds like more than just meeting someone."

"It wasn't serious," he said, trying to minimize whatever relationship he had had with Annika.

"What did you do when you and she were together?" Carol asked. "Where did you go? Did you go out with other people?"

It was obvious that Eric was uncomfortable. He must have

realized that the source of Carol's information would be one or more of the high school crowd and that there was no point in denying that he had been in some kind of relationship with Annika. But providing a more detailed account of the nature of that relationship was another matter.

"We just hung out around town," he said.

"I'm sorry to bother you with these questions, Mr. Mackinson, but I never met Miss Lindstrom. All I know about her is what people tell me. If you were actually spending time with her, you must know more about her than most people in Southport. Besides, it's been quite awhile since I was going out on dates. I have no idea what dating is like now days here in Southport."

It was, to say the least, a most indirect way of broaching the subject of whether Annika and Eric had been intimate. Her subtlety was not lost on Eric.

"You want to know if we were sleeping together, don't you?"

"Were you?"

"No. It's like I said, I didn't know her very well. Besides, where could we have ever been alone? Not in my house, that's for sure. And the Kershaws – that's where she was staying. I mean, can you imagine me seeing her over there? Mr. Kershaw, he would've kicked me out of the house."

Carol had to acknowledge that neither the Mackinson house nor the Kershaw house sounded like a promising place for intimacy. Unless, of course, no one was at home. Moreover, there might be other places where Annika and Eric could have gone. Eric had been adamant that his and Annika's relationship had not involved sex. But he had sounded as if the possibility of sex had entered his mind.

"Mr. Mackinson, it is my understanding that back in January, the night that Miss Lindstrom disappeared, there was a party. Annika was there, so were a lot of her school mates. Were you there, too?"

"No. I heard about it, but I wasn't invited. It was just the Southport High kids. You know, teenagers. I graduated seven years earlier, don't have much to do with the high school crowd."

"Except Annika," Carol said. "I was just wondering if that might have been one of the nights when you and she got together."

"Well, it wasn't. In fact, by that time I don't think I'd seen her for a month or more. I'd heard that she was seeing a guy named Lalor. Like I told you before, I didn't really know her very well. It didn't matter what she was doing. By January I'd moved on."

Carol got up and walked the twenty or so yards to where the cans were sitting, all in a row, beyond a shallow pool of water.

"Do you come up here often to shoot at these things?" she asked. There was so little water running down the ravine, making so little noise, that she didn't have to raise her voice to be heard.

"Sometimes, when the mood strikes me," Eric said. "The mood to be alone. I do it more to get away from the house than because I enjoy potting tin cans."

"I used to have an air rifle, can you believe that?" Carol said. "It was a Daisy, one of those Red Ryders that used to be popular with kids. My Dad believed I should be a good shot. He never knew I'd grow up to be a sheriff, that I'd wear a gun to work."

"I didn't know girls – I'm sorry, I mean women. I didn't know they went in for shooting."

"Some do, some don't. It's like guys. I don't think the man I'm going with has ever owned a gun, much less fired one."

Why had she said that? Carol wasn't in the habit of calling Kevin the man she was going with. It was hardly a good description of their relationship. She wondered what Eric would think of this comment about her private life. In all likelihood he thought of dating as something that high schoolers did. He probably didn't like it that the sheriff kept referring to what he and Annika had been doing as dating.

It was time to bring up the subject of keys.

Carol came back to where Eric was sitting, but she didn't take a seat on the ledge.

"Do you know where Miss Lindstrom's body was found?" She was pretty sure he did, but he had spoken of 'someone's' cottage, and it was possible that he hadn't heard that it was the Claymores'.

"The word around town is that it was a cottage belonging to people named Claymore."

"And you don't know them?"

"No I don't."

That was probably true, inasmuch as Harbaugh had hired

Mackinson sometime in September after the Claymores had moved back to New Jersey. But she found it hard to believe that he wasn't aware of whose bathroom he had been painting. And that he hadn't wondered about the fact that his former 'date' had been found in the same cottage where he had been working.

"Mr. Mackinson, you may not know the Claymores. You may never have met them. But you have been in their cottage. It was last September, and you were helping Bud Harbaugh finish up a job on their upstairs bathroom. Do you remember that?"

"Yeah. I guess I did do some work there. The bathroom, and one of the bedrooms needed some painting, too."

"That's better," Carol said. "So you realize that you've been in the cottage where Miss Lindstrom's body was found."

"But I was just there on a job," Mackinson said, now aware that this was not just a conversation about whether and when he had dated Annika Lindstrom. "I had nothing to do with Annika being in the cottage."

"I'm not saying that you did. But I find it interesting that her body was found in a cottage that was all locked up, and that you had a key to that cottage."

The young man had sounded uncomfortable. Now he sounded as if he might be scared. He looked it, too.

"You can't possibly think I'm responsible for what happened to Annika. I wasn't going with her or anything. I didn't even know she'd disappeared until somebody mentioned it one day when I was gassing up at Smitty's BP Station."

"Let's talk about the key," Carol said. "Mr. Harbaugh says he gave you one so you could finish up the Claymore job. And that he never got it back from you. He wasn't accusing you of anything, only answering my questions about his work on the Claymore cottage. Do you still have that key?"

Whatever Mackinson thought about what Harbaugh had told the sheriff, he didn't deny that he had indeed had his own key to the cottage.

"I honestly don't know where the key is. I haven't thought about it since I finished that job, and that was back in September."

"Wouldn't it be on your key ring?"

"I really don't know," he said. "Probably."

"You wouldn't have given it to somebody else, would you?"

Mackinson thought about that for a moment. He's probably wondering if it's in his interest to say 'yes,' Carol thought, whether it's true or not. But he didn't.

"No, I wouldn't have done that. I should have returned it to Bud, that's what I should have done."

"Right now I'm in the business of accounting for keys to the Claymore cottage. Why don't you take a good look at what's on your key ring, see if it's there."

He unclipped his key ring from his belt and examined what appeared to be a dozen or more keys.

"I don't think I could recognize it," he said. "You know how it is with keys – it's hard to be sure what they're all for. Except for the ones you use all the time."

"Maybe I can help," Carol said. She took Eric's key ring from him, extracted from her pocket the key she had taken from Barry Claymore that morning, and, one by one, compared it with Eric's keys.

"You still have it," she announced, holding up a pair of matching keys. "You won't be needing it any more, but I will."

Carol added it to her growing collection of keys to the Claymore cottage, and within a few minutes was on her way back down the ravine, leaving a worried Eric Mackinson to resume target practice.

CHAPTER 13

While Carol was considering which of the Southport residents on her must-see list should be her next stop, Bob and Amanda Kershaw were engaged in a conversation which had turned from slightly testy to downright unpleasant.

There was no one else in the Kershaw household. Jennifer and Brian had left to be with friends, and the silence that descended on the house after their departure gradually acquired an almost oppressive quality. It was only a matter of time before either Mr. or Mrs. Kershaw would puncture that silence with a remark that was guaranteed to offend. It was Amanda who put down her knitting and gave voice to something that had been bothering her.

"Why did you have to be so unpleasant to your daughter yesterday when the sheriff was here?"

"My daughter? She's your daughter, too. And she's the one who's being unpleasant."

"I know, but she'd just going through a stage. It's what teenagers do. But we're adults. We don't have to be like that. You really embarrassed me – you embarrassed all of us, right in front of the sheriff."

"I'm tired of making excuses for our children," Bob said. He tossed aside the newspaper, signaling his intention to focus on what he disliked about their offspring rather than what he disliked about the state of the nation.

"I'm not making excuses for them. But hollering at them doesn't get us anywhere."

"I didn't holler. When have you ever heard me holler at Jennifer?"

"Oh, stop nitpicking, Bob. Call it whatever you want, but it wasn't nice. What will the sheriff think of us?"

"She'll think we've got a selfish, disrespectful daughter, which we have."

"Yes, and that we're part of the problem," Amanda said.

Bob Kershaw made no attempt to hide the fact that he was

annoyed. He had put on an angry face.

"Damn it, Amanda, she was telling me where to get off. Are we going to let her get away with that?"

"She was only objecting to you going through her things and taking Annika's diary," Amanda said, trying to sound reasonable.

"Annika was our house guest, not hers. It's our business to take care of her things, not Jennifer's. What's she want with the diary anyway?"

"Well, what did you want with it?"

Bob looked at his wife as if he could not believe what he had heard. It was at that point that the exchange between the Kershaws began to turn nasty.

"What kind of an accusation is that?"

"It's not an accusation," Amanda said, "I was only wondering why you had to go through Jennifer's things looking for the diary."

"We were getting rid of her stuff, weren't we? The diary was part of her stuff."

"How did you know that Annika even had a diary?"

The storm that had been slowly brewing in the Kershaw living room came to a head. Bob got up off the couch and stormed out to the kitchen. Amanda sat quietly, her knitting in her lap, staring straight ahead and waiting for him to return. She was certain that he would.

"I'm tired of your insinuations," he said when he returned, beer in hand. He may not have been hollering, but he had raised the decibel level to a point not far from it. "What's the matter with you anyway?"

"There's nothing the matter with me," she said, her voice under control. "What I don't understand is what's the matter with you. What was it between you and Annika?"

"Between me and Annika? Are you out of your mind? I can't tell you how many times you told me I should pay more attention to her, try to make her feel more at home. Now you're implying I was too interested in her. Is that what you're trying to say?"

"All I'm saying is that you were interested in her diary – interested enough to sneak into Jennifer's room to get it. Why? What did you think was in the diary?"

"Nothing. Nothing at all. And I resent that remark about sneaking into Jennifer's room."

"I wasn't born yesterday, Bob. You didn't care much where Annika was from or what her interests were. What you did care about was that she was a beautiful young woman. You couldn't keep your eyes off her."

"That's ridiculous. Absolutely ridiculous. She was just a kid who was living in our house, thanks to you and your silly notion that we'd be doing something for the cause of world peace if only we took in an exchange student."

Amanda Kershaw was having none of it.

"You don't even know how obvious you are," she said, her tone of voice now matching her husband's vitriol. "I saw you watching her going up the stairs. Watching her swish her tail, watching her stretch so she could show off her boobs. I'm sure she had a starring role in your fantasy life."

Bob stared at his wife as if he had never seen her before.

"That's nonsense, all of it." He was still angry, but something in the way he said it seemed to lack conviction.

"No, it's not nonsense, it's what I saw, day after day, for months. If she hadn't been killed, I'd still be seeing it. I'm not naive, Bob. I'm aware that men aren't immune to the charms of young sexy things. But you weren't just charmed. You were fixated, and it wasn't pretty to watch. That's why you wanted the diary, isn't it?"

"This is ridiculous," he said, repeating himself. "I don't read Swedish, you know that."

"You didn't know when you stole the diary from Jennifer's room that it was in Swedish. Or if it was, maybe she talked about you. You'd have recognized references to Bob or Mr. Kershaw. What did you expect to find? Some flattering comment about how good looking you are? How virile? How smart? Or were you afraid that she might have said something about some indiscretion, like you'd kissed her or pinched her bottom, or something like that?"

"I can't believe we're having this conversation. Or that you have such a sick imagination. There was never anything between that girl and me. Nothing. We lived in the same house, that's all. My God, Amanda, we've been married for twenty two years, and we've never had a problem. Now, out of the blue, you're accusing me of going all gaga over some high school student. What's next? That I snuck into her bedroom at night? That I was making out with her? Where in hell was that supposed to have happened?"

"No," Amanda said, "I'm not saying you ever had sex with Annika. Maybe you wanted to, but I don't think you're that dumb. But why were you so anxious to see the diary? What did you expect to find? And why did you get rid of the diary?"

"I already told you. The diary was just part of Annika's stuff that we didn't need to keep in case she came back."

"Maybe so. But why should that have been your decision, not Jennifer's? What would have been the harm if the diary had stayed in Jennifer's possession?"

Bob Kershaw, who had been so vocal in his own defense, declined to answer this question.

"This has gone on long enough. I'm tired of defending myself against your baseless accusations. And I'd suggest that you put your mind to something else, like what we're going to do about our unpleasant daughter. I'm going out to take a walk. Maybe I'll have calmed down by dinner time."

Just before he left the house, Jennifer popped in, Debbie Selfridge with her.

"Hi. We'll be down in the game room. New movie." She waved the DVD in the direction of her parents, and she and Debbie disappeared down the stairs to the basement.

Thank God, Amanda thought, they hadn't made their appearance earlier. And then another thought struck her. What if it were true that Bob had done something foolish with Annika, and what if Annika had told Jennifer about it? The two girls had not been close, but she had no idea what they did talk about when they talked. Now she had two things to worry about. The hurtful conversation with her husband, and the possibility that their own daughter might have been privy to her father's infidelity.

CHAPTER 14

It was almost six weeks since the vernal equinox had come and gone, yet nothing like what most Crooked Lake residents thought of as spring had materialized. A brisk and cold wind was blowing in off the lake and chasing odds and ends of paper across the playing fields of Southport High School. Carol was standing at the edge of a crowd of students, her uniform jacket collar turned up, watching the activities on the sideline of the soccer field.

This was not where she had expected to be at ten o'clock on Monday morning, but her plans had changed when she got a call from Betty Engelman the previous evening. Betty was a friend who taught English and coached the drama club at the high school, and she had thought Carol should know about a memorial service which had been planned for Annika Lindstrom.

"I have no idea whether you'll want to attend," Betty had said, "but I know you're going to be working on the Lindstrom case. So I thought I should alert you to what the school's got planned."

Nobody had said anything about a memorial service. And Carol was not really interested in spending her morning back in Southport. But the more she thought about it, the more she felt that it would be a good idea to be there. She would see Betty and talk with her a bit about Annika. Betty might be able to point out some of the students who were alleged to be friends of Annika's. It would only take an hour or two.

The main event of the service seemed to be the planting of several small trees in Annika's memory along the path that led from the school building to the soccer field. There had been a couple of speeches, both mercifully brief, one by the principal, the other by a boy Betty identified as the president of the student body. The wind and the fact that she was standing quite some distance from the podium made it impossible for her to hear all of what was said. There were the predictable remarks about what a lovely person Annika had been, how privileged they all were to have known her, how sad that one so young had had her promising life cut short. She listened in vain for an anecdote or two which would have shed light on the real Annika Lindstrom. The tributes to her were little more than boilerplate. Was that because she had been a student at Southport for such a short time? Or was it because she had generated controversy, and that respect for the deceased dictated avoidance of personal reminiscences?

The students, who appeared to number close to a hundred, looked properly thoughtful and reverent. All except for a small group off to her right who seemed to be trying to suppress laughter at something one of them had said. Carol's eyes searched the crowd, looking for a familiar face. In due course, she would probably be talking with quite a few of these young men and women who were now nameless. But this morning she spotted no one she knew. Not Jennifer Kershaw or her brother. Not Karen Leeds. No, that wasn't true. Several girls closest to the school building began to drift away from the tree planting exercise, and she recognized one of them as Jennifer. Was she planning to duck out of this event in honor of a girl she hadn't much cared for? Whether that had been Jennifer's intention or not, neither she nor her friends actually left the scene. But they had clearly ceased to pay attention to what was going on, preferring to talk among themselves.

Carol asked Betty about several students whose names had been brought to her attention. It was a small school, and Betty recognized all of the names. She was able to point out Debbie Selfridge, a friend of Jennifer's and one of the 'hosts' of the roving party back in January. She also spotted Michael Stebbins and Rickie Lalor, both of whom Annika was reported to have dated. Carol would not be speaking with them today, but she tried to fix in her mind what they looked like. It was impossible, not to mention irresponsible, to try to form an impression based on such a casual sighting.

"Do you think it would look bad if we went back to your classroom?" Carol asked Betty. "I'd like to ask you a few questions about Annika Lindstrom."

"No problem," was the answer. "I've done my duty. The teachers weren't required to be here."

They walked back to the main entrance to the building, where the American flag, now at half mast, was flapping vigorously in the wind. Had the school tried to find a Swedish flag for the occasion? Probably not. She doubted that anyone in Southport would have been familiar with protocol for such a situation.

"This would have been my free period anyway," Betty said as they made their way to her classroom. "I think we've got another ten minutes."

Carol took someone's seat in the front row, selecting it instead of others because it was the neatest.

"Let me ask the big question. I can get back to you on specifics later. How would you say Annika was regarded by her fellow students?"

"How about how she was regarded by the teachers?" Betty asked.

"Okay. Do you think there was a consensus?"

"More or less." Betty smiled as she said it. "I don't know whether any of the men were mesmerized by her looks. But among my colleagues I talk with most, the book on Annika was that she was very bright, obviously a product of a challenging school system in Sweden. She was almost certainly better informed than almost any of our local kids. Unfortunately, she knew it. She had a good opinion of herself, and she tended to have a condescending opinion of most of her peers here. If she'd put herself to it, she would have broken the curve in just about any class she was in. But she could see that she would do well without all that much effort, so she coasted. Needless to say, most people in my business don't think much of an attitude like that."

"Do you think the students reacted much as you have?"

"It depends. Some of them practically worshipped her. There were a few who resented her. A bit of jealousy in that, of course, but the most observant ones saw through her."

"Was she part of a clique?"

"Thank God, cliques aren't that bad here. Oh, I suppose there will always be in-groups, but I don't see much in the way of kids being ostracized by their peers. Annika was close to several of the girls, and there were a few boys you'd see her with frequently."

"How about the Kershaws? Did she seem close to Jennifer and Brian?"

"I've never had Jennifer in class. Probably next fall. But considering that Annika lived in the Kershaw home, they didn't seem that close. Brian was another story. He was the proverbial puppy dog for awhile. He went to a lot of trouble to sit next to her in my class. But it didn't last. I don't know what happened, but I'd bet she told him to get lost. He's got a good head on his shoulders, however, and he seemed to take it in stride."

"Who were the boys she hung out with?"

"I'm not a very reliable witness, Carol," she said. "I didn't follow her around school, and I tend to disregard gossip. My best guess is that the guy she was closest to was Rickie Lalor. He's a senior, has a scholarship to Syracuse in the fall. Good looking kid, does drama as well as football. He'd be lost in a big high school, but he's a big man on campus here in Southport."

"How about Michael Stebbins?"

"I'm not sure. He's a friend of Rickie's, but what his relationship was with Annika I wouldn't know."

"Bruce Bachman?"

"Where did you get these names?"

"They come up in conversations."

"Well, Bruce is one of our best students. He could probably have held his own with Annika in a conversation about Mark Twain or Fitzgerald. Even Melville. But I don't believe I ever saw them together."

"There's one other thing," Carol said, but the bell was ringing and a bunch of students came bursting into the classroom.

"I'm sorry," Betty said as she turned to answer a question from a member of her class. "We'll have to continue this another time. Give me a call."

Carol thanked her, smiled at the the students who were conspicuously interested in the presence of an officer of the law in their classroom, and set off for the visitors' parking lot.

It had been a wasted morning. Nothing she had heard or seen at the tree planting in honor of Annika Lindstrom had made any impression. Betty Engelman's observations about Annika reinforced what she had been told by others, but added little or nothing to what she already knew. If anything, her visit to Southport High School had simply ratcheted up the dread which she felt about the prospect of interrogating a small army of teenagers. How many would there be before she was through? Five? Ten? A dozen?

By the time she had driven half way back to Cumberland

she had made a decision. What was for her a big decision. She was going to have to delegate the task of interrogating these students to her staff. She hated to do it. She had never been a good delegator. She always harbored doubts that Bridges or Barrett or any of the others would be as thorough as she was. Or as she liked to think she was. But if she were honest with herself, she knew that all of her men were competent. Each had his own strengths, but none of them had ever let her down.

She'd prefer to find a way to let Kevin be the one to talk to the students, but Kevin was down in the city writing a paper for a conference. And then he'd be off to Copenhagen to give that paper. She couldn't afford to wait for his return to the lake. When she got back to the office, she would give the assignments to her officers. Maybe she'd give Bridges the task of sizing up someone named Rickie Lalor. Parsons, Barrett, Byrnes, Grieves, the others, they'd all be tasked with interviewing the students on her list.

Then, Carol said to herself, I'll be free to pursue the question of who has a key to The Summer House.

CHAPTER 15

Keys to The Summer House were also on Bill Claymore's mind, and he wasn't waiting for the sheriff to take the initiative in tracking them all down. He thought he knew where they all were, but he couldn't believe that any of the people he had entrusted with them would have had anything to do with breaking into his cottage and putting Annika Lindstrom in his pump room. On the other hand, someone had done it, which meant either that his trust had been misplaced or that one of the men to whom he had given a key had allowed that key to fall into someone else's hands.

Bill had considered the possibilities. He had no problem with Barry. His key had been accounted for, just as he had expected it to be. Barry would not have dreamed of disregarding his father's wishes, especially after the unpleasant episode of the trashed cottage. Nor could he imagine that either Joe Cabot or Bud Harbaugh would have lost their key or shared it with anyone else. He would talk with them both, of course, but he would only be confirming what he already knew. Finally, there was his brother-in-law, who probably still had a key. Bill didn't like Roger Chase. He was a sponge, not to mention a man who had never outgrown his frat house youth. His string of failed marriages was testimony both to his poor judgment and to a wandering eye that led to seemingly endless infidelities. Yet he knew that it was highly unlikely that Roger was responsible for the break-in, either directly or indirectly. He lived too far away, and his sins were of a decidedly different kind.

Which left him with Bud Harbaugh and Joe Cabot. Joe was a neighbor, so he'd talk with him first. Actually it would be more likely that he'd be talking with Ellie Cabot. Joe was a custodian at Southport High School and did some part time work elsewhere. He would either be at the school or on one of his other jobs. It didn't matter. Ellie was better organized than Joe was, so she'd be quite able to vouch for the key.

Bill set his breakfast dishes in the sink and called the Cabots. As he expected, it was Ellie who answered the phone. She'd be happy to see him. It was but a short walk. The Cabots only lived two cottages above his, but their old and much weathered Cape Cod was hidden from sight due to a tall, thick hedge which a former resident on the point had planted many years ago.

"Well, well, if it isn't our resident celebrity," Ellie Cabot greeted him at the door. "Word is that you've been playing host to a murder victim."

"I'm afraid so. It's publicity we could do without. I'm sorry I haven't been in touch with you and Joe sooner, but first there was that awful discovery, then the sheriff, then Barry's arrival – this has been one helluva weekend. Oh, and I forgot that we had to spend our first night back here at a motel. The sheriff wanted us out of the cottage while her people poked around. Wonderful homecoming."

"We figured you were busy as sin, thought we should leave you alone until things settled down."

"Have you got a little time?" Bill asked.

"Sure. But I promise not to pump you for information. You've probably had enough of that to last all summer."

"It hasn't been too bad. Anyway, we don't really know anything. The sheriff either doesn't have it figured out or she's being cagey. But I didn't come over to talk about our little surprise."

"No? Is Helen okay. No bad news on the health front, is there?"

"We're both in pretty good shape, all things considered. But we've got a puzzle. We can't figure out how that girl got into our cellar. I mean the place was locked up and the sheriff says it doesn't look like somebody broke in. But somebody must have. Right off the bat the sheriff wanted to know who had keys to the place. We told her, gave her a list of people we'd given keys to. So she knows that you and Joe have one. Has she been in touch with you?"

"She's never talked to me. Or to Joe, unless she called him this morning down at the school."

"Well, she'll be talking with you, I'm sure of that. Anyhow, Helen and I are worried. We know everyone who has a key, and we know that none of you had anything to do with this. But whoever lugged that Lindstrom girl into the cottage had to have had a key. You see my problem?"

"I do, and I appreciate it that you aren't accusing Joe and me of anything."

"Of course not," Claymore said. "You're the best neighbors anybody could have, and it never occurred to us that you even knew the girl. I guess what I'm asking is whether there's any chance that your key was ever out of your possession. You know, it got lost or something."

Bill Claymore looked uncomfortable. He knew that he had suggested that the Cabots might have been responsible, however indirectly, for what had happened.

"The keys never left this house, Bill. Except, of course, when Joe went over there to check on things. Or the time when I had to borrow Helen's juicer. We'd ordered some oranges from down in Florida – something to bring a little sunshine into our dreary winter. So, no, the keys are –"

"Keys?" Bill interrupted. He looked puzzled. "You've got more than one key?"

"Two. It seemed like a good idea to make a copy."

"I don't understand," Bill said, his anxiety rising. If the Cabots had more than the one key he'd given them, then the number of keys to The Summer House that were floating about was larger than he knew. Larger than the number he'd reported to the sheriff.

"It's okay," Ellie assured him. "When I went over to your place for the juicer, I accidentally dropped the key in a snow bank. It took me a good five minutes to find it. We decided it would be a good idea to have a spare, so Joe had one cut. They're both here."

Bill trusted his neighbor, but he knew that he had to be sure.

"Sorry to be a worrier, but given the circumstances it's hard not to be. Would you mind checking to see if both keys are here?"

"No problem," she said, but the look on her face said that she thought him a bit paranoid.

He waited patiently while Ellie went in search of the two keys to his cottage. She was gone longer than he expected.

"Well, here's one of them," she said. "It was in the drawer of that little work desk in the kitchen. The one that's always on a hook inside the back door doesn't seem to be there. Maybe Joe has it with him. Do you want me to call him?"

Bill had expected his visit to the Cabots to be uneventful. An exchange of some beginning-of-the-season pleasantries, a confirmation that their key to The Summer House was right where it always was. But now he was faced with the information that his neighbors had two keys and that one of them could not be accounted for. He was unable to hide the agitation he felt.

"Yes, please," he said. "I wouldn't think Joe would carry our key around with him, but give him a call. Can you do it now?"

"I'll try. He should answer his cell." Ellie wanted to offer words of reassurance to Bill, but could sense that he would be satisfied with nothing less than concrete evidence that the key was safely in their possession.

She rang her husband down at Southport High, waiting patiently for him to answer. The owner of The Summer House stood by, waiting less patiently.

"Joe, it's me," she said when he answered his phone. "I'm talking with Bill Claymore. He's concerned about the keys to his cottage. It's about that girl and how she could have gotten into the place last winter. I can't put my hands on both of our keys. Do you have one of them with you?"

Bill watched her face, and knew immediately that the Cabots' second key was not on Joe's key ring.

"You're sure?" Further silence.

"Where do you suggest I look?" Another pause.

"I already looked there." Ellie looked at Bill and shrugged.

"Okay, but we've got to give the house a thorough search when you get back. Do me favor and pick up a quart of milk on your way home."

Bill Claymore would have liked to tear the place apart himself, but that was, of course impossible. He did his best to sound pleasant, even if he didn't feel that way, and cut his visit short. He was now more anxious than ever to place a call to Bud Harbaugh, custodian of yet another key to their cottage.

The second Monday in May was not destined to be a happy one for the Claymores. Harbaugh was at his place of business, and was obviously pleased to hear from one of his clients.

"Yes, it's a great job, Bud. Helen is particularly pleased. I should have been in touch sooner to thank you, but things have been a little hectic since we got back to the lake. Do you know about what happened at our place? The dead girl in our cellar?"

It was clear that Harbaugh had heard about it, but Bill wasn't interested in hearing the contractor commiserate with him.

"It was a shock, all right. That's the reason I'm calling. I'm trying to account for all of my keys, trying to figure out how that girl could have gotten into the cottage. You had one, of course, and I was wondering if you're sure where it is. I mean, can you be sure someone else couldn't have –" Bill let his thought trail off. "You see what I'm driving at?"

Then he listened while the man who had remodeled his bathroom explained that the sheriff had already asked him the same question. And informed him that a sub, a man named Eric Mackinson, also had a key.

"He still has it?" Bill Claymore was having trouble believing what he was hearing. Keys to The Summer House were proliferating at an alarming rate. He was reminded of Mickey Mouse's turn as the sorcerer's apprentice in the movie *Fantasia*. Except that that was a fondly remembered delight. This was not.

"I like your work, Bud, but I'm not happy that you gave a key to somebody I don't even know. For all I know, this man Mackinson was involved in that business with the Lindstrom woman. Someone smuggled her into the cottage, and I can't imagine it was you or any of the other people I know."

He held the phone away from his ear. Bud Harbaugh was protesting, and doing so loudly.

"Say what you will about this guy Mackinson," Bill continued, "somebody killed her, somebody who had a key, somebody who knew where I live. This is a terrible thing we've been through. I've never seen Helen so upset. And here I am, chasing down keys I didn't know even existed. I know, we can't undo what's been done, but I wish you'd handled it differently."

When he hung up the phone, Bill knew that his relationship with Bud Harbaugh had been badly strained. Harbaugh would probably not wish to do further work on the Claymore cottage, and Bill was not sure he would offer him another job. He knew that he would now have to meet this man Mackinson, although it would probably be best to talk with the sheriff first. Hopefully, she had already been in touch with him.

He was about to share this discouraging news with Helen when another thought occurred to him. What about Roger? His irresponsible brother-in-law Roger. It was Roger, he thought, not Joe Cabot or Bud Harbaugh, who was most likely to have lost a key or for some dumb reason had another one made. Yet in the space of half an hour he had learned that both Joe and Bud had in fact been responsible for making extra keys. And one of those keys could not be accounted for and the other was presumably in the possession of someone Bill had never heard of. If Cabot and Harbaugh could not be trusted with his keys, heaven knows what Roger might have done.

Bill knew full well that Roger was aware that he was persona non grata at the cottage. As far as he knew, Roger had not been inside The Summer House in three years, and then only during a brief summer visit. But he still had a key. Or did he?

"Helen, can you come down for a minute?" he called up the stairs.

"Is something the matter?" It sounded that way to her.

"Come on down. We've got to talk."

And so they did, for nearly half an hour.

"I can't get it out of mind that Roger has a key to the cottage," Bill said when they had taken seats in the living room.

"But of course he has," Helen said. "He's had one for years. You know that."

"But what if he doesn't. Or what if he has more than one?"

"What are you talking about?" Helen sounded as if her husband had taken leave if his senses.

"This has been a bad morning," he continued, trying to put his anxiety into context. "I've learned that both the Cabots and Bud Harbaugh didn't just have a key to the cottage. They both had two keys, and neither of them can account for one of them. No, that's not quite right. Ellie can't find their second key, and Harbaugh gave his to a subcontractor and never got it back. Don't you see? That means that there could be even more people who could have gotten into the cottage. No wonder that girl got left in the pump room. It could have been anyone."

"What does this have to do with Roger?"

"It's about keys, don't you see? All of sudden there are more keys to our cottage out there than we thought there were. Which brings me to Roger. How do we know whether he still has a key? Or two keys?"

"You're not making sense," Helen said. "Why worry about Roger? He doesn't look after the place like Joe, or redo our bathroom like Mr. Harbaugh. He hasn't been in the cottage in ages. He probably doesn't even know where his key is."

"That's exactly my point. Maybe his key got into the hands of whoever broke into the cottage."

"You know what? You're sounding paranoid. Roger lives in Watertown. You certainly can't believe that somebody from Watertown came all the way down here, killed the Lindstrom girl, and used Roger's key to put her in our cellar."

"Maybe, maybe not," Bill said, not willing to let it go. "Maybe it was someone from around here. That's more likely."

Helen stood up and headed for the kitchen.

"I'm pouring myself some coffee. Want some?"

"This is serious, Helen. Come on, sit down, let me explain."

"Explain what? How my brother gave someone who knew Lindstrom a key so he could stow her in the pump room after he'd killed her?"

"No, nothing like that. But we've got to account for all the keys to this place – all of them. I'm sorry if I sound like I'm obsessed with keys, but I can't help it. I've got to find out where Roger's key is and where it's been."

"Why don't you leave that to the sheriff? She'll know how to go about this better than you or me."

"It's our cottage, Helen. I'm going to talk to Roger."

Helen decided to have that cup of coffee after all.

"I'll get you a cup, too. It'll calm your nerves."

"When has coffee ever calmed anyone's nerves? But, yes, while you're up you can get me some."

"Let's do this my way," she said after settling back down with her cup of coffee. "If you've got to talk with Roger, let's do it here. Let's invite him down for a couple of days. If you call him and ask him to account for his key, you'll only make it more obvious that you don't like him, that you're suspicious of him."

"Well, I am," Bill said. But there was a certain amount of logic in his wife's proposal.

"I know, but he deserves the benefit of the doubt. Chances his key had anything to do with what happened here are pretty slim. As far as I'm concerned, they're nonexistent. Anyway, there's no point making this a family feud."

"Okay, have it your way. But you call him. I can't trust myself to be pleasant. Just make sure he gets down here right away."

"I know you think he just lies around, wasting his life away, but he might have something he has to do. Can't you relax for a few days?"

"I'll try, but see if you can't hurry him up. And tell him to bring his keys."

"His key, Bill, and I don't know if that's a good idea. Won't it sound like we suspect something?"

"Okay, tell him we're going to change the locks – which, by the way, is a good idea. I just want to see that key. And get it back."

By noon on this Monday in May, it had been arranged that Helen Claymore's wayward brother would spend the following weekend on Crooked Lake and the sheriff had been notified in case she also wanted to question him. What Roger thought about the request that he bring his key to the cottage, Helen and Bill didn't know, but he promised to do as he was asked.

CHAPTER 16

"Hey, Sue, over here!"

It was Karen Leeds, the Southport student Carol had thought of as the epitome of cute, who called across the cafeteria to her friend.

12:20. The sheriff would not yet have gotten back to her office in Cumberland. Deputy Sheriff Bridges did not yet know that he would be tasked with interrogating a young man named Rickie Lalor. Nor did the rest of her officers know that they would soon be talking to the late Annika Lindstrom's other friends at Southport High School. The other friends who were now sitting around a table in the school cafeteria, discussing not the memorial service most of them had just attended but the death of the girl for whom the memorial service had been held.

They all knew that she was dead and that her body had been found in the cellar of a cottage on the West Lake Road. They all knew that she had gone missing after a party on a cold night back in January, a party that had taken place over a period of several hours at several different places. And most of them had been at that party, at least some of the time.

"Where've you been?" someone asked Sue.

"The bathroom, if it's any of your business," Sue said.

Everyone laughed, including Sue.

"How can you eat that stuff?" A sharp featured blond guy asked as he took his own fork and prodded at what looked like a salad of apples and raisins on Karen's plate.

She brushed his hand away from her tray.

"Unlike you, Michael, I watch my bod. That's why."

Her companions oohed in appreciation of the witticism. One of the guys said something to the effect that they'd been watching her bod, too.

"That's the kind of stuff Annika ate, and look where it got her," Sue said.

"That's cruel, Sue. I don't think it was her diet that did her in." It was Brian Kershaw.

"Well, you should know."

"What's that supposed to mean?" Brian shot back.

"Just kidding. If it wasn't her diet, though, what did happen to her?" Sue Marinelli was suddenly serious.

"I thought we'd already decided that," a big, muscular guy in a Green Day T-shirt said.

"You decided, Rickie. I don't remember taking a vote."

"Oh, c'mon, Debbie. Nobody's got a better idea." Karen Leeds was siding with Rickie's theory.

Sue Marinelli, the latecomer to the cafeteria table, wanted to know just what Rickie Lalor's theory was.

"He thinks she got roaring drunk, passed out, then froze to death," said Karen.

"That's bullshit," Brian Kershaw spoke up. "Why wouldn't somebody have noticed? Can any of you remember a time when Annika didn't have a bunch of people hanging around her?"

"You were just pissed because you never could get her alone." Brian's sister had said something for the first time.

"Oh, for Christ's sake, Jennifer. Don't be an idiot."

Rickie came to the defense of his theory.

"Well, I was there. And what I remember – what all of you remember if you think about it – is that the group was never all together. I don't know where everyone was all the time – Sue's maybe, heading over to Debbie's, who knows. Everybody doing his own thing. So, were any of you with Annika all that evening? Come on, anyone? I thought not."

"Don't you think someone would have missed her?" It was Sue.

"They'd have figured she was at one of the other houses. Or maybe hooking up in some upstairs bedroom. Live and let live."

Brian snickered.

"You thought she was hooking up with someone, and you just said 'oh, what the hell?' I thought she was your girl."

"You're way off base, Brian," Rickie said. "I never said I thought she was doing it with some guy. Fact is, what did occur to me was that she might have gone home – to your house. She'd had one too many, felt sick, decided to call it a night."

"It could have happened that way," Karen said. "I've done that once or twice."

"Well, I'll tell you one thing," Brian said, "Annika never

came home that night, drunk or sober."

"You have an opinion, Michael?" Sue turned to Michael Stebbins, who'd watched the give and take much as one might watch a tennis match, but had not contributed to the discussion.

"Not really. Rickie's probably got it right. Hard to figure it any other way."

"Anyone for dessert?" Debbie Selfridge stood up and waited for company. "No takers? Too bad."

Everyone knew that the bell would ring shortly, their lunch hour over.

"You guys amaze me," Sue said as she organized things on her tray. "Suppose she collapsed in the snow on the way back to the Kershaws, like Rickie says. Suppose she did freeze. How in hell did she get into that cottage? She couldn't have walked all the way up there, could she? It must be a good six miles. Besides, she's supposed to be frozen stiff. Anybody got a theory about that?"

No one spoke up. It was Jennifer Kershaw who broke the silence.

"I'm betting on Barry Claymore."

Had she said Justin Timberlake, the response could not have been greater. The small group erupted as one.

"Barry?"

"Yes, Barry. I'm guessing, but why not? Word is the cottage was locked, so it took someone with a key. Barry would have had a key. And he knew Annika from last fall, remember? Suppose he came back to see her, they had a quarrel, he killed her, then took her back to his parents' cottage."

"Excuse me." It was Sue Marinelli. "Who is this Barry Claymore?"

Jennifer started to answer, but Karen Leeds interrupted.

"Let me do it. I'm the local expert on Barry, as Debbie will be happy to tell you. He's spent summers here on the lake since he was just a kid. His parents own the cottage where Annika was found, and he's in college now somewhere out in Ohio. But you know how it is with those guys who arrive on the Fourth of July and leave on Labor Day. They go looking for local girls, and us local girls are easy prey. Well, Barry started paying attention to me. That was this past July. It lasted for about two weeks, then he disappeared. When I saw him next, he'd found somebody else, newly arrived just like you, Sue. Guess who? It was Annika Lindstrom. He barely said 'hi' to me."

"So you agree with me," Jennifer said.

"No, I don't. Why would Barry want to kill Annika? And why would he leave her body in his parents' cottage where they'd be sure to find her? He's not dumb, you know."

"If I were you." Jennifer said, and she was talking to everyone at the table, "whether you agree with me or not, I'd think about what you're going to say when the sheriff comes round to talk to you about Annika."

"The sheriff?"

"Yes, the sheriff. She'll get all of us aside, and she'll pump us about what we think of Annika. And what was going on that night when she went missing. I don't think she'll buy a lot of crap. Better decide what you want to tell her before she starts asking questions."

"Why shouldn't we tell her the truth?" Debbie Selfridge asked.

"Ah, but who knows for sure what the truth is," Brian Kershaw said. "Excuse me, I'm just quoting from that fountain of wisdom who teaches my next class, Mr. Weldon."

Jennifer glared at her brother.

The bell rang at that moment, and the group began to split, gathering up their belongings and heading for the next class. It was Rickie Lalor who had the final word as they left the cafeteria.

"While we're thinking about what to say to the sheriff, it might be a good idea to consider an old Southport alum. Know what I mean? His name's Eric Mackinson."

CHAPTER 17

Had it been possible, Carol would have spent the Monday noon hour as a fly on the wall in the Southport High School cafeteria. Instead, she planned to hold a meeting with a few of her officers, brief them on the progress of the Lindstrom case, and send them off to question members of Annika's circle of friends. Unfortunately, that plan was derailed – or, more properly, deferred – when she came upon a car on the roadside, its hood up.

It was a familiar sight, one Carol had encountered numerous times since assuming the job as sheriff of Cumberland County. She did not, of course, spend most of her time cruising county roads. That was a task that occupied most of her fellow officers during many, even most, of their hours on duty. But she was the officer who had come upon this motorist in distress, and it was her responsibility to stop and see what she could do to help.

Having parked on the gravel shoulder, she was in the process of climbing out of her car when she realized that she had seen the car ahead of her somewhere. And very recently. The New Jersey license plate told her where, and whose car it was. Barry Claymore's.

As Carol approached Barry's car, it was apparent that no one was in it. She tried the door. It opened. Where had he gone, leaving the vehicle untended along the road? It was while she was trying to decide what to do that she spotted him, a distant figure, walking toward her, almost a quarter of a mile away. She waited, watching him watching her, probably trying to decide what he would tell her.

"Having some trouble, I see?" she said as he reached the car.

"A little. How'd you know about it?"

Carol smiled.

"I didn't. I was just on my way over to Cumberland when I saw a motorist in distress. It's our job to stop, offer help. Where've you been?"

"It isn't far down to the Yacht Club. I thought I'd see if

anybody there could help me."

"You might have called your Dad and Mom. I'm sure they'd have come along."

"I know, but I didn't want to bother Dad. He'd just be annoyed."

Carol thought that Barry looked younger than she'd remembered from their first meeting on Sunday morning. At least he was dressed and wearing shoes this time.

"What's the problem with the car?" she asked. "Out of gas? Overheating?"

"No idea. To tell you the truth, I don't know anything about cars. Some red light on the dash. I pulled over and checked the manual. It said not to drive if it was on."

"Sounds like good advice. I take it you didn't find anybody at the Yacht Club who could give you a hand."

"Yeah. It was deserted. This early in the season, I suppose they don't open up except on weekends."

"Let me take a look," Carol said as she slid behind the wheel. "Let me have the key."

It was not a tough call.

"It's your oil pressure warning light. Have you had the car serviced recently?"

"I don't think so."

"You don't think so?"

"Okay, I've never had it serviced. That's why I didn't call Dad. He thinks I don't take care of things."

And it looks as if he's right, Carol thought. She got out of the car and looked under the hood. Barry's car had what looked like a very bad oil leak.

"Tell you what I'm going to do," she said. "I'm going to drive over to Jardine's in Yates Center, have them take it in and check it out. You come with me."

She locked Barry's car, set out a couple of her reflecting triangles behind it, and waited until he'd climbed into the passenger seat of her car. I wonder if he's ever been inside a police vehicle, she asked herself. That thought led to another. Why not use the occasion to have a good talk with Barry? To pursue some of the questions that had come to mind on Sunday when they had been discussing his key to the cottage and his knowledge of Annika Lindstrom.

"How about joining me for a cup of coffee?" she said when they pulled away from Jardine's twenty-five minutes later. It would apparently be the better part of an hour before they could dispatch a tow truck for Barry's car.

"It's okay with me if you have the time." He didn't sound enthusiastic, but until the car was ready he was the one who had time on his hands.

The coffee came and Barry waited for the sheriff to say what was on her mind. Carol stirred some sugar into her cup and showed no sign of initiating the conversation. She out waited him.

"Is there something you need to ask me?" he finally said.

"Is there something you'd like to tell me?"

Barry Claymore was nervous, and it showed. He took up his spoon and proceeded to stir his coffee. He had used neither sugar nor cream.

"No, I don't think so. Why, should there be?"

"I don't really know," Carol said. "But I'm interested in the fact that your father doesn't want you using the cottage when he's not around. And that you didn't want to call home to report that you were having a car problem. Do the two of you get along okay?"

"Pretty much of the time," Barry replied, but the color had risen in his face. "It's like I always have to prove myself. I guess I'm not as responsible as he thinks I should be."

"I suppose that's something a lot of parents worry about. You might say it goes with the territory. What do you think your father would say or do if he found out you'd used the cottage when he'd told you not to?"

This was a question Barry had not expected. The color drained from his face.

"Who told you about that?"

"About what, Barry?"

"You know, about –" The young man stopped, apparently having decided he should be more careful about what he said to the sheriff.

"You asked who had told me that you used the cottage when you weren't supposed to. Actually, no one told me any such thing. It was a rhetorical question, Barry. A what if question. But I think you answered it anyway. You did use the cottage against your father's wishes at some time, didn't you?"

Barry was obviously trying to frame an answer which would undo what he believed to be a damaging admission.

"Well, there was one time," he said, adopting a casual tone.

"And when was that one time?"

"Last summer, I believe. I don't remember just when."

"You needed your key, right?"

"Sure. They always lock up when they're not home."

Carol sipped some coffee, thought about where this conversation might be going. Where she hoped it would go.

"You're sure it was in the summer?"

"It had to be. I left for college in late August."

"And never came back to the lake until this past weekend?"

"That's right." He said it emphatically. "What are you trying to get me to say, that I was here when Annika was killed?"

"No, all I'm trying to do is find out what happened to Miss Lindstrom. By the way, when we spoke yesterday you said you'd never met the girl. But you just called her Annika. May I infer that you really do know her? Most people don't refer to people they've never met by their given names."

Barry Claymore was regretting that he'd agreed to have a cup of coffee with the sheriff.

"I think my parents called her Annika," he said.

"I'm sure they did," Carol said. "Let's go back to August when you were moving to Ohio to start college. I'd be interested in when the fall semester started out there."

"Let me think," Barry said, trying to figure what the implications of his answer might be. He thought about it and decided that it was the Wednesday before Labor Day. Carol knew that she could easily verify when classes had begun at McLean College, but her mental picture of the calendar told her that they had probably begun when Barry said they did.

"And you were there for the first week of classes?"

"I was."

If that were true, Barry could not have met Annika Lindstrom before Labor Day. Which would mean either that, as he had claimed, he had never met her, or that he had returned to the lake sometime after his parents had closed up the cottage for the season. What if he had disobeyed his father's rule about use of the cottage, not during the summer, but sometime in the fall? Or in January? What if he had been at the lake the night of the fateful party? What if he had not only been present when Annika Lindstrom disappeared, but had been responsible for her disappearance? For her death and for the fact that she had spent a long, cold winter in the Claymore's cellar?

She knew she had no proof, but Carol was almost certain that Barry had met Annika Lindstrom. And she was almost equally certain that he had met her after his parents had closed and locked the cottage and moved back to New Jersey. Even if she were correct, however, it did not follow that Barry had killed Annika. She did not begin to know enough about his relationship – or non-relationship – with the Swedish exchange student to jump to that conclusion. Moreover, even if it turned out that he had killed her, Carol could not imagine why he would have left her body in the pump room of his parents' cottage. Which left Carol with two questions. One concerned the key. The other concerned Barry's Crooked Lake friends.

"I know you must wonder why I'm throwing all of these questions at you," Carol said, her voice matter of fact. "It's just the way we work when we're confronted with a crime. I'm in the process of asking questions of everyone who knew Miss Lindstrom, everyone who had a key to your parents' cottage. So I appreciate you bearing with me. You realize that there's a problem with keys. You had one. Was there ever a time when that key wasn't in your possession? When you couldn't find it?"

"No, never. But wait," he said, as if something had suddenly occurred to him. "I think there was a time. I lost my key, just temporarily. I don't remember the circumstances. I looked all over for it. It turned up in a pair of my jeans."

"And when was this?"

"Sometime last year, I'm not sure just when."

"How did you happen to know it was missing? I mean, you weren't in the habit of using it. It looked to me as if your key ring has a whole bunch of keys on it, so many you wouldn't be likely to know if one you never used was missing."

Once again, Barry was conspicuously nervous. Carol had seen that look on other faces. He was trying to decide how he should answer her question.

"I know this sounds lame, but I don't know how or when I knew it was gone. It doesn't matter, does it? I mean it's not as if it really got lost."

There's something he's not telling me, Carol thought. Something he doesn't want me to know. I wonder why he even mentioned losing the key? She changed the subject.

"When we talked yesterday, you said you had a few friends up here that you'd see in the summer. But I never heard any names. Why don't you fill me in? Who, specifically, are your Crooked Lake friends?"

"Nobody close," he said. "I wasn't around enough to make close friends. Like I said, there were some guys at the Yacht Club that I sailed with once in awhile."

"You were going to tell me their names."

"There were really only two. They're both seniors in high school now. One's Rickie Lalor. He's the one who's got the boat. Then there's his friend, Michael Stebbins. They sail together a lot, and when I'm here I go along sometimes."

Lalor and Stebbins. Both alleged to have been among Annika's dates.

"Would you say you know them quite well?" Carol asked.

"We're hardly real close. I've probably been out with them four, five times."

"Did they ever take girls with them when they went sailing?"

"Not that I remember."

"How about dates?"

"Did they ever go out with girls?" Barry asked, puzzled by the question.

"I'm sure they did," Carol said. "What I mean is did you ever double date with either of them?"

Maybe the expression 'double date' was no longer in vogue, but he'd know what she meant.

"Maybe once or twice."

The coffee was long gone, and Barry had said 'no' to a refill. No doubt he was hoping for the promised call from Jardine's that his car was ready so that he could bring an end to this interrogation. Unfortunately, it was more likely that they hadn't yet sent the tow truck out to pick it up.

"Whom were you dating back then?" she asked.

"Different girls. You won't know them."

You might be surprised, Carol thought.

"Tell me anyway," she said.

"They weren't serious, you understand. Just casual dates. One was Brenda Miles. And there was Karen Leeds. Somebody called Jackie, but I can't remember her last name."

"Do you recall whom Lalor and Stebbins dated?"

"They mostly played the field. I think Stebbins was interested in a girl named Jennifer Kershaw."

"Do you know Kershaw?"

"Sort of. Not well."

This conversation was nearing its end. Carol consulted her watch.

"I'm afraid I have to get back to my job," she said. "If you like, I'll give you a ride back to your parents' place. Your Mom or Dad can take you over to Jardine's when the car's ready. Or maybe they'll drop it off at the cottage."

"No, that won't be necessary. I'll just hang around town until it's ready."

She couldn't imagine what he'd do for the next couple of hours, but he seemed to prefer killing time in Yates Center than facing his father's criticism for failing to take his car in for routine checkups.

"Okay, whatever you say. By the way, how long do you expect to be around? You going back to New Jersey? Or is it out to Ohio?"

"I'll probably stick around for the rest of this week. Then I've got to look for a summer job."

"Good luck."

"Oh, thanks for the lift," Barry Claymore called out to the sheriff as she made her way down the aisle and out into the early afternoon sun.

CHAPTER 18

Nothing had gone as Carol had planned. First there was the memorial service for Annika Lindstrom. Then the unexpected encounter with Barry Claymore. Not that the day had been wasted. The conversation with Betty Engelman had been informative, and she was grateful for the serendipitous breakdown of Barry's car. But now it was close to mid-afternoon and her plan to convene a brief staff meeting and make assignments to interview Southport High School students had not gotten off the ground.

That meeting was destined not to take place. Carol had gone only a little more than a mile beyond West Branch when she was confronted with an accident which had closed the road to Cumberland. A large black Cadillac sat crosswise of the road, its radiator still steaming. The car had obviously been struck on the passenger side by a small Honda which rested half on and half off the road to the right. Both vehicles had sustained considerable damage. The road was strewn with pieces of metal which had been sheared off the two cars when they collided. From their positions, it looked as if the Honda had backed out of a driveway and into the path of the northbound Cadillac. A Cadillac which must have been going much too fast. A third car was on the scene. It belonged to the Cumberland County Sheriff's Department, and Jim Barrett, one of Carol's younger officers, could be seen, leaning into the Cadillac, presumably talking to the driver.

She pulled in behind Barrett's car and made her way through the debris.

"Jim, it's me, Carol. Is everyone okay?"

"It looks that way. Scared, but not hurt. Just my luck I was only a few hundred yards behind the Caddie when it happened. What are you doing here?"

"On my way back to the office. Have you checked the Honda?"

"It's an old lady. I don't think she looked before she backed out into the road. Do you want to talk to her? I've got to get some information from this guy and then call for a tow or we're going to have a nasty backup here."

"I'll make the call," Carol said, and hurried over to the Honda to see about the old lady.

It turned out that she wasn't that old, and the words with which she greeted the sheriff suggested that she might not be a lady either. Carol guessed that her age was somewhere between fifty and fifty-five. If she had been hurt, there was no evidence of it. But she was angry.

"I hope you've arrested that bastard."

Carol ignored the demand that the other party be arrested.

"I'm Sheriff Kelleher. My colleague says he was only a short distance behind when your accident occurred. What's most important is how you and the other man are doing. Do you think you've suffered any injuries?"

"No, I'm fine, no thanks to him. Stupid fool, he barreled right into me. Had to have been going close to a hundred."

Speeding, perhaps, but surely not 100 miles per hour, Carol thought.

"Does it hurt when you move?" she asked.

"No. Like I told you, I'm all right. But the car's a wreck. Brand new car, haven't had it three months. That idiot better have insurance."

Carol had no idea who had been at fault in the accident. It wouldn't surprise her if both drivers shared responsibility. Barrett would make sure that the relevant insurance information had been exchanged. At the moment, however, she was more anxious to make sure that the drivers had not suffered injuries.

"If you're sure you're okay, it might be a good idea to step out and walk around a bit." Carol held the door open, ready to offer an assist as the woman got out of her car.

"How am I supposed to get to Southport?"

Carol had no ready answer for this question, but she knew that she would be unable to offer ad hoc taxi service. The woman, who said her name was Sarah Ballester, had no more trouble walking than she did talking, so the sheriff excused herself and made the call for a tow-truck.

It was almost another fifteen minutes before she was able to get away, leaving Officer Barrett to route traffic around the accident and otherwise wrap things up.

The clock on the wall above her desk read 3:36 when she

finally sat down and turned her attention to the day's mail and messages. None of her officers was in the building, which meant that it would be impossible for her to assign them Southport High School students to interrogate. At least not that afternoon. Perhaps it was just as well. She had begun to have second thoughts about doing so. The accident she had just encountered made the point quite effectively. She realized that she couldn't simply pull her officers off the highways of Cumberland County. Even murder could not be allowed to preempt the routines of law enforcement on and around Crooked Lake. More importantly, she knew that she was the one who should talk with Jennifer and Brian Kershaw. They had lived with Annika for more than four months and ought to have known her better than any of the others. Yet what she had heard about their relationship with Annika was disturbingly vague and unpersuasive. Why had Jennifer disliked her? Why had Brian not been more interested in her?

No, she thought, I'll handle Jennifer and Brian myself. As for the others – the girls who had reportedly been Annika's friends, the guys who were said to have dated her, the ones who had been at the January party – I can brief Bridges on what I know and what I've heard and let him tackle a few of them. Just the two of us. Simpler that way, even if it means we move forward more slowly.

Carol spent what was left of the afternoon winnowing the pile in her in basket and making routine phone calls. Her hay fever had pretty much gone away, but she still didn't feel like herself. She was normally the last one out of the office. Today she would be the first.

Dinner for one was disappointing, and had done nothing to improve her mood. She spent several minutes scanning the titles of the assorted books which had been her father's collection, hoping to find something she might enjoy reading before bed. Not surprisingly, she found nothing which suited her mood. They had always had different tastes in both fiction and nonfiction. Big Bill Kelleher had been a voracious reader, but Carol had never shared his affection for tales of travel and adventure. As she passed over one title after another, she found herself wondering what Kevin read for relaxation. She pictured him listening to his operas rather than immersed in a book. And opera wasn't her thing either. Perhaps she should begin to broaden her horizons.

It was while she was considering that possibility that the phone rang.

"Hello, this is Sheriff Kelleher." She hoped that she wasn't being called in her professional capacity, but she had made it a practice to identify herself as the sheriff, taking a leaf from her late father's book.

"Hi, Carol. It's me, Doc Crawford. What are you doing tonight?"

The sound of his voice gave an immediate lift to her spirits. It wasn't just that he handled autopsies for her, although that had become a very important part of their relationship in recent years. He also happened to be a charming man with a good sense of humor and an inexhaustible stock of yarns about medical practice and malpractice.

"Hello, Doc. What I'm doing tonight is trying not to feel sorry for myself. Dare I hope that you have news that might cheer me up?"

"Missing that man of yours, are you?"

"You know about him?"

"Carol, I've been doing what your Daddy would do if he were with us – waiting impatiently for you to find a man. So, naturally, I've had my eyes and ears open. But I didn't call to talk about the professor. I thought you'd like to know that the autopsy on that Lindstrom girl is done."

"That's great," Carol said, and it was clear that she meant it. "I was afraid it would take a few more days."

"Well, we don't have a very big backlog up here. And I work fast, rumors to the contrary."

"What can you tell me?"

"What I'd like to do is drop by your place. We could talk over a glass of cognac, assuming, that is, that you've kept that bottle of your Daddy's VSOP. It improves with age, you know."

Carol had no idea whether there was any cognac in the house. She remembered that her father had liked his cognac, but she didn't. No matter, Doc Crawford would settle for whiskey, even a beer.

"You're always welcome, Doc, so, yes, come on over. The autopsy report is a bonus."

"Give me twenty minutes, maybe half an hour."

The cognac was where her father had left it, in the back of a cupboard which Carol hadn't opened since his death. Doc Crawford insisted it tasted every bit as good, if not better, than it had several years earlier. They chatted for several minutes as if the autopsy report were only an afterthought. It was Carol who finally insisted that she could no longer contain her curiosity.

"Love your company, Doc, but don't you want to tell me what killed Miss Lindstrom?"

"Why, of course. I just didn't want you to think I'm only interested in you when a murderer's on the loose. Anyway, the young woman's death isn't as much of a mystery as I figured it might be."

"No? What killed her?"

"Let me take it one step at a time. The body'd been frozen, and with our temperatures still pretty darn cold she hadn't had a chance to thaw. It took a couple of days to get the body temperature up enough so I could do a proper autopsy. What it shows is that she'd consumed a lot more alcohol than she should have. And I mean a helluva lot. It was off the charts. But the interesting thing is that she'd also ingested a lot of Rohypnol. Know what that is?"

"Why don't you tell me."

"It's the infamous date rape drug. I think they call it 'roofies' on the street. It acts like valium, only its many times more potent. The victim can be incapacitated in short order. She can't put up resistance to the rapist. She becomes a virtual rag doll. And the effect of the drug can be much worse if taken with alcohol."

"You're telling me Lindstrom was raped. How did she die?"

"No, I'm not saying she was raped. She was no virgin, but there was no sign of rape. Of course, we don't have all the fancy equipment the pathologists on those TV shows have. But what I'm pretty sure happened is that the mix of a lot of Rohypnol and a lot of alcohol killed her. It's not unheard of for someone who's taken a lot of that stuff to go into a coma or die. Your Miss Lindstrom was one of the ones who did."

"It's possible to know this after the victim's been dead for months?" Carol asked.

"It is. Remember, the body's been frozen, decomposition hadn't really started. You're lucky – in a manner of speaking, that is. Lucky she was left in that deep freeze cellar. Blood and urine tell the story."

"What about the head? She looked like she'd taken a beating."

"I'm sure it hurt. Assuming, that is, she was alert when she hit her head. But it wasn't fatal. It's impossible to be absolutely sure, but I'd put my money on a fall, probably when she lost consciousness from the effect of the drug. The skin was well preserved due to freezing, and there were nasty bruises. So somebody might have hit her around the face. But the skull was intact, no brain trauma."

Carol was digesting this information. Annika Lindstrom appeared to have been targeted for rape, a rape that may never have taken place because her would-be rapist realized that she was dead before he raped her. It looked as if she now had the answer to the question of how Annika had died. But Carol had the unpleasant thought that Doc Crawford's report had only increased the number of questions still to be answered. There was one more question, however, which he should be able to answer.

"When did Miss Lindstrom die?"

"Unfortunately, it's your investigation that will probably have to answer that question," he said. "If her body hadn't been frozen, I could give you a fairly precise answer. But then I wouldn't have been nearly as certain what caused her death, would I? All I can say is that it's likely she died in the winter. But I'm sure you've been assuming that, too. It's theoretically possible that she died from the Rohypnol a couple of weeks ago, got stuffed into a frozen food locker, and then was transferred to that lake cottage in time for the owner to find her there. But you wouldn't buy that, and neither do I. So, like I said, odds are she died sometime in the winter and froze almost immediately, probably in the cellar where she was found. If I were in your shoes, I'd be making the assumption that she died the night she disappeared. But I couldn't swear to it in a court of law."

Carol was mildly disappointed, but Doc Crawford's reasoning squared with hers. Then another question occurred to her.

"Could this have been a suicide?"

"Hypothetically," he said, "but she couldn't have been sure she'd die. Slip that stuff into the drinks of most women and they'd come around after awhile. They might not remember what had happened, but they'd survive. So I have trouble believing your Miss Lindstrom would have tried to kill herself that way."

"I'm sure you're right, but I had to ask," Carol said.

"Oh, and there's one more interesting thing. This young lady wasn't wearing any panties. This isn't a medical opinion, mind you, but I think it goes to prove that whoever gave her the Rohypnol had rape on his mind. Trouble was, she upped and died on him before he could do it."

Carol shuddered involuntarily. She could visualize the scene, and it wasn't a pretty picture.

Doc Crawford had nothing more to contribute, but he didn't seem anxious to leave.

"Please don't misunderstand me, Carol," he said after taking a sip of his cognac. "I'm not one to put my nose in other people's business. But we've been friends for a long time, going back to when I was close to your age and you were just a little girl. So I hope you won't take offense if I ask about that professor of yours. Word around here is that he's a real nice guy. Of course you wouldn't be interested in him if he weren't. But – oh, hell, why can't I just say it? I worry about what's going to happen."

Carol got to her feet and went over to Crawford, planting a kiss on his forehead.

"Doc, you're very sweet. But what are you worried about?"

"What I worry about is that you'll marry the guy or you won't."

"Want to explain that?"

"I'd love to see you happily married. Nothing could make me happier. But if you and the professor tied the knot, I fear you'd be moving down to the city, leaving us without our sheriff. And that would make me very unhappy. So do you see my problem?"

Carol shook her head and smiled.

"Your problem is my problem, Doc. And Kevin's – that's my professor's name. We'd both like to be married, at least I would and I'm pretty sure he would, too. But I can't imagine giving up a job I love and becoming just one of hundreds, maybe thousands, of police officers in the big city. And I don't think Kevin could imagine quitting Madison College and trying to find a position teaching opera up here. So we have what you might call a summer marriage – without benefit of clergy, of course. It's not ideal, but it beats the alternatives."

"I shouldn't have brought it up," Crawford said. "It really isn't any of my business. You've got enough on your plate without a semiretired old coot trying to play matchmaker."

"Don't be ridiculous, Doc. Tell you what, I won't resign as sheriff if you won't retire. Let's just not use the M word."

"I'll try to remember that. As for retiring, how can I as long as you keep sending me bodies to autopsy?"

"I'm afraid that's out of my control," Carol said as Crawford got ready to leave. Just as he reached the door, she stopped him.

"Wait just a minute. I want you to take what's left of the cognac. I'll never drink it, and I'm sure I speak for Kevin, too."

"You'd deprive me of an excuse to come over?" Doc Crawford said it with a laugh and when he left, the cognac left with him.

CHAPTER 19

Doc Crawford's report had clarified the cause of Annika Lindstrom's death, but had done nothing to help identify who was responsible. Moreover, it made it incumbent on Carol to place another call to Malmo, Sweden, something she dreaded doing. Although Annika's relationship with her parents had apparently not been close since the debilitating automobile accident when she was a child, they had not been estranged. An honest account of what had happened to the Lindstrom's daughter would still be deeply unsettling. But she had promised to let them know the result of the autopsy, and that meant that she would have to present the unpleasant truth in the least painful way possible. How could she tell Annika's parents that their daughter had been drinking heavily, had been drugged by a would-be rapist, and had died from the effects of this lethal cocktail? Ironically, it might be easier if she had to report that Annika had been shot to death by a stranger. The truth would only serve to tell the Lindstroms that Annika had probably been courting trouble by carelessly pursuing sex with relative strangers.

In any event, there was no one Carol could or should ask to place the call to Malmo in her stead. She steeled herself for the task with a second cup of coffee early on Tuesday morning. It would be midday in Sweden, and she was anxious to make the call before setting off for the office.

This time the person answering the phone was not Mrs. Lindstrom's nurse or caretaker. It was a man's voice, speaking, of course, in Swedish.

"Hello," Carol announced herself. "This is Sheriff Kelleher, calling from Cumberland, New York, in the United States. Is this Mr. Lindstrom?"

"Yes, Lars Lindstrom. Is this about our daughter?"

He had made the transition from Swedish to English without missing a beat, and, like his wife and late daughter, his English was excellent.

"That's why I'm calling. I promised Mrs. Lindstrom when I

called her about Annika last week that I would be in touch as soon as we knew more about what caused her death. I wish it weren't necessary to be making calls like this, but it can't be helped. I'm sure you want to know what happened to Annika. I'm now in a position to tell you. Are you all right? I mean, do you feel up to listening to me?"

"It's better that you're talking to me than to Helga. She's been having a particularly bad spell. Right now she's sleeping, and we let her sleep whenever she can. We knew that you'd be calling one of these days. I'm not sure I want to know how Annika met her death, but that wouldn't change things. She's dead, and I suppose we must know how it happened. I'm sitting at my desk, so you needn't worry that I may go into shock and fall down or anything like that."

"I think I can appreciate what you've been going through," Carol said, "although I have never lost a child myself. I do know that I'd rather be with you than talking long distance. It seems so impersonal. Anyway, I shall try to make it brief, but please ask any questions you have."

Carol paused, but Lars Lindstrom said nothing.

"As you know, back in January Annika attended a party with a number of her friends from the high school here in Southport. We called you when Annika didn't come home that night. During the course of that evening, she had quite a bit to drink. The doctor reports that her blood alcohol level was highly elevated. Sometime that evening – and we don't yet know when or exactly where, she ingested a powerful drug which is often used in situations of attempted rape. The drug typically has the effect of dulling the senses, making the person unaware of what is going on. In this case, the amount of the drug, together with the amount of alcohol in her system, caused her to lose consciousness. In effect, it killed her. I can assure you that whatever her assailant intended, he did not rape her."

For a long moment Lindstrom remained silent. When he spoke, what he had to say was not what Carol had expected.

"Much as Mrs. Lindstrom and I hate to admit it, our daughter had been having sex since she was thirteen. She was one of the most personable and charming young women you could ever hope to meet, but she was also one of the most irresponsible and promiscuous. That it should have come to this is heartbreaking, but it is not entirely surprising. She was living dangerously, courting trouble. Finally it caught up with her. There is no use in pretending that Helga and I are not at fault. We haven't had the energy – no, that's simply an excuse; we haven't had the will to make sure she lived more prudently. We even thought that it might help her to straighten out if she spent the year over there. It seemed as if a nice, small town family, good people with a daughter and son of their own, could provide a stable and nurturing home of the kind Helga and I had failed to provide for Annika. But we were naive. I do not blame the Kershaws. I'm sure they saw Annika's polite, personable side, not her wild streak. It's our fault. We abdicated responsibility for her years ago. She was mature beyond her years, so we figured she'd be fine. We were wrong."

Carol was waiting for questions, but they didn't come. There had been no expression of interest in knowing who had slipped Annika the date rape drug, nothing to indicate that Mr. Lindstrom was anxious to put this man or boy behind bars for manslaughter, if not murder. He, like his wife in the earlier conversation, had accepted what happened as the inevitable outcome of years of youthful irresponsibility and parental neglect.

"I am not ready to release Annika's body just yet," she said, turning to a more practical matter. "We'll be back in touch with you when that becomes possible."

"The more sensible thing, not to mention the less expensive, would be cremation. We would be most grateful if you could arrange to have that done over there. You can let us know the cost, and we shall make the funds available up front. Obviously, there is no hurry. I don't know much about such matters, but I can imagine that you may not be able to have Annika cremated until you have closed the case, whatever that entails."

"I wish I could tell you that we are close to an arrest. Unfortunately, we aren't. In fact, almost every day that goes by seems to increase the number of people who might have been involved in Annika's death. It isn't just a matter of who put the drugs in her drinks. We are also trying to determine who had means of access to the cottage where we found her."

As she said it, Carol realized that she had never told either Mrs. or Mr. Lindstrom where they had found the body. Now that she had carelessly shared that bit of information, she expected Mr.

Lindstrom to ask her about it. But he didn't. Apparently all the Lindstroms were interested in was burying their late daughter and moving on with what was left of their twice shattered lives.

CHAPTER 20

Deputy Sheriff Sam Bridges enjoyed working with his boss. When she was appointed, his initial reaction had been one of disappointment. Not because he felt that he should have had the job. Sam knew himself well enough to know that he would have been a poor administrator and, more importantly, that he didn't have the requisite people skills. But he had expected that Bill Kelleher's successor would be a man, probably Ernie Ackerman. But Ernie had been caught passing bad checks, a serious career mistake which not only cost him the job of sheriff but his position on the force.

When Carol Kelleher was tapped to succeed her father, Sam shrugged and wisely chose to reserve judgment. To his surprise, he came to like Carol, to appreciate her judgment and the tactful manner in which she handled difficult people. In the law enforcement business, one always encounters difficult people. The only problem Sam had ever had with Carol concerned Kevin Whitman. Not that he disliked Whitman. He barely knew him. But he thought that Carol tended to rely too much on her friend's advice, even to the point of sometimes letting him undertake investigative tasks which should have been reserved for her fellow officers. Fortunately, Carol herself seemed to have been aware of the problem, with the result that she had given Sam more responsibilities and made a conspicuous effort to discourage Whitman from trying to play detective.

On the Tuesday morning after the discovery of Annika Lindstrom's body in the Claymore's pump room, Sam was pleased to hear that his role in the Lindstrom case was about to grow exponentially.

"Sam, I'm going to need your help." Carol had pulled him aside after the morning squad room briefing and suggested that they have another cup of coffee.

But of course, Sam thought. That's why I'm your deputy sheriff. But the way in which she said it suggested that she was not about to give him some routine assignment.

"I can't remember a case when we've had so many people we need to question. Well, maybe the cast of that opera that was supposed to take place over at Brae Loch College, but I think this one is going to be even dicier. Trouble is, we need to move fast, and that means talking to a lot of interested parties right away. More than I can possibly handle. I'm going to have to ask you to do most of the talking."

"No problem," Sam said, unsure whether by interested parties she meant suspects in Lindstrom's death. Thus far, his involvement in the case had consisted of looking for evidence of a break-in at the Claymore cottage.

"Grab a pad and pencil," she said. "I'm going to have to give you a run down on who's who and what they may have to do with the Lindstrom affair."

And so Carol Kelleher and Sam Bridges sat down in a corner of the squad room and discussed everybody whose name had cropped up thus far in her investigation. It was, as she had said, a long list, and a majority of the names belonged to students at Southport High School.

They reluctantly agreed that there was no point in trying to catch the students off guard. Word would have spread that the sheriff was making the rounds, asking questions about relationships with Annika and who was where and with whom on the night in January when she disappeared. Indeed, there was no point in waiting to interview the students when they got home from school, assuming that home was their destination. Carol would alert the principal, and one by one the students she wanted Sam to interview would be called out of their classes, to be questioned in some quiet room. If any of them jumped to the conclusion that they were under suspicion, so be it.

As Sam waited in the back of an empty classroom for the first student on his list, a senior named Michael Stebbins, he was congratulating himself on his decision to begin with the boys. Or young men, as they surely thought of themselves. He had always found women, and before that girls, harder to figure out. He remembered with no great pleasure a couple of the girls he had pursued in high school. Just when he had believed he was making headway, they had suddenly dropped him and taken up with another guy. Stebbins would be easier, or so he hoped.

Stebbins entered the room and looked around, as if to assure himself that he wouldn't be answering questions in front of a third party. Such as the principal, or maybe his parents. He made no attempt to introduce himself, but stood awkwardly just inside the door until Sam invited him to have a seat.

"Mr. Stebbins," he said in what he hoped was a pleasant, disarming voice, "I'm Deputy Sheriff Bridges. Sorry to take you out of class like this."

"I don't mind. It's chemistry. No big deal."

"Well, it shouldn't take long. As you've heard, I'm sure, we're talking to a lot of Southport students about the late Annika Lindstrom. We understand that you knew her fairly well. Even dated her. I'd like you to tell me about her. What kind of person she was, what your relationship with her was, things like that. I'm going to set this recorder on the table here, just to make sure I don't forget what you've told me. Okay?"

Stebbins stood about six feet tall, but carried himself with slightly rounded shoulders like many teenage boys. Like Jeremy in the comic strip *Zits*, Sam thought. He wore his blond hair cut short, just a bit longer than what Sam would have called a brush cut. He had sharp features which managed to give his face an aquiline appearance. Not handsome, but not unattractive either. He looked uncomfortable.

"You want to know about Annika?"

"That's right. Everyone will have his own impressions of her, of course. What about yours?"

"Well, she was sort of–" Sort of what? He stopped without saying. Sam let him consider how best to describe her.

"What is it you want me to say?" he finally managed.

Sam shook his head.

"Come on," he said. "It's not a trick question. All I want is for you to tell me what it was about her that interested you. You did go out with her, didn't you?"

"I guess so. It wasn't a big thing. But, yeah, we did hang out together. Like some of the other guys did."

Hang out. It had not yet become a common expression when Sam was in high school. Did Stebbins mean that he and Annika did things with a group of their friends? Or did they go off someplace by themselves? And where did they go? It was unlikely to be a bar, inasmuch as Annika had been only 16 and he knew that the local joints regularly carded kids. Maybe it was the local ice cream parlor, or over to Yates Center for a movie. It might even have been an area motel.

"Okay, you hung out. What was your typical date like?"

Sam didn't know it, but this conversation was beginning to sound a lot like the one the sheriff had had with Eric Mackinson two days earlier. It was also likely that he would be asking much the same question of other Southport students in the days ahead.

"Just the usual stuff, nothing special. Sometimes just riding around in my car. One weekend we went over to Geneva, mostly to get away by ourselves."

Good, Sam said to himself. This was more like it. He wanted to ask if Stebbins had slept with Annika, but thought better of it. It probably didn't matter, and he wanted to avoid the appearance of prurient interest.

"Were you shocked when she disappeared?"

"Sure. Everybody was."

"Were you still going out with her when it happened?"

Stebbins thought about it before answering Sam's question.

"Yes and no. I mean we still saw each other, but it wasn't just me."

"So she was dating the field?"

"The field?"

"By the time Annika disappeared, she was dating several guys. Right? There she was, the most beautiful girl in the school, a great catch, and the guys all trying to get on the inside track. Is that the way it was?"

"I think you've got it wrong, sheriff. Annika wasn't playing us off against each other."

"When she disappeared," Sam asked, ignoring Stebbins's demurrer, "did it look like anybody in particular did have the inside track?"

"No, that's not the way it was. If Annika had a favorite, it wasn't anyone at the school. We were friends. I wouldn't know about Barry Claymore or Eric Mackinson."

Michael Stebbins had dropped these two names into the discussion so casually that Sam had no clue whether he was making a simple factual statement or deliberately trying to redirect the deputy sheriff's attention. Either way, Sam had no choice but to ask about Claymore and Mackinson.

"Are you suggesting that Annika may have been infatuated with these men?"

"Not really," Stebbins said, "but I know she'd hooked up with both of them. I don't know either Claymore or Mackinson very well, Claymore probably a little better. Annika didn't have a real close boy friend in the high school, that I'm sure of. But I honestly don't know how Annika felt about those other guys."

"How do you know she was dating Claymore and Mackinson?"

"With Mackinson, it was just common talk. He's a Southport grad, used to hang around the school. I think that's how it started. They must have met at a soccer game, and he probably looked more mature to her than guys like Rickie and me. I know she was with Barry, at least once, because we all went sailing on Rickie's boat back in the fall."

Sam quickly processed this information, searching his memory bank for evidence that it corresponded or conflicted with what the sheriff had told him. No problem with Mackinson. Claymore was another story. According to what Barry had told Carol, he'd never met Annika. Moreover, he had reported that his current visit to Crooked Lake was the first since the previous August. Yet Stebbins had gone sailing with Barry – and Annika – in the fall. Or so he said. Had he lied about it? Not very likely, inasmuch as Rickie Lalor could easily contradict such a lie.

"Are you sure that you went sailing with Barry Claymore and Annika in the fall? Claymore was in college in the fall, somewhere out in Ohio."

"I know, but he came back one weekend. It would have been late September. I remember he told us it was a party weekend at his school. He didn't have a date, so he decided to spend the weekend at the lake."

"I presume he stayed at his parents' cottage."

"Yes, he did."

"And that's when he met Annika?"

"Yeah," Stebbins said, apparently finding it easier to talk about Barry Claymore than about himself. "He met her at the yacht club when we were taking the boat out."

"I thought you said he was dating her when you went sailing."

Stebbins was anxious not to leave the deputy sheriff with

the impression that his stories were inconsistent.

"He wasn't when we met, but it changed pretty fast once we got out on the water. Annika wasn't there as anyone's date. It was just the four of us. But Barry, you could tell he was interested in her. Everybody was joking, having a good time, but he sort of put the moves on her. Before we called it a day, they were kissing and messing around. She'd come out to the yacht club with Rickie, but she left with Barry."

"As far as you know, did their relationship continue beyond that weekend?"

"I wouldn't know. It wouldn't have been easy, him being out in Ohio. Besides, she never seemed to have any one guy, if you know what I mean."

"So, like I said before, she was playing the field. How did you feel about that?"

"It didn't bother me," he replied.

Sam studied Michael Stebbins, but he was remembering how he himself had felt when girls he'd been dating shifted their attention to someone else.

"I understand that your girl friend is Jennifer Kershaw."

Stebbins started to ask where Bridges had heard that, but thought better of it.

"We've done some things together, but it's not serious. Actually, I first met Annika at Jennifer's house. I guess you know that she was staying with the Kershaws."

"What about the night Annika disappeared. That party back in January. Was Jennifer your date that night?"

"Not really. Nobody had a date like you're thinking."

"But Annika was there. And Jennifer. I've got a list of names here," he said, gesturing toward his jacket pocket. "What about Barry Claymore?"

"No. I haven't seen him since that time we went sailing back in the fall."

"Eric Mackinson?"

"No, there weren't any outsiders at the party, just a bunch of us from school."

"How can you be sure? I understand that your crowd spent most of the evening roving around. Wouldn't it have been possible for people to drift in and out, so you'd never be quite sure who was there? Who was with whom?"

"I suppose it's possible, but that's definitely not the way I remember it."

"When did you last see Annika that night?"

Once again Stebbins looked uncomfortable.

"You must think I'm stupid or something, but I don't remember. She was there for awhile, then she wasn't. I mean I saw her for awhile, then I didn't. Maybe she went home. Maybe she stayed at one of the places where the party had been going on after the rest of us cut out. Like Karen's or Sue's. I wasn't paying attention to her that night."

"Who were you paying attention to, Michael?"

"Probably Jennifer." He sounded as if he regretted having to admit it.

"I don't think you ever answered my first question. What was your opinion of Annika?"

Stebbins sighed audibly.

"Aside from being the prettiest girl in the school?" He smiled. "She was smart, fun to be with. The biggest knock on her, at least for the guys, was that she promised more than she delivered."

"Meaning?"

"You know, just when you thought you were going to score, she'd let you down."

When Michael Stebbins headed back to class, Sam was wondering whether he had ever 'scored' with Annika. Or if he had been among those whose advances she had first encouraged, then rejected.

CHAPTER 21

Sam was anxious to meet with Rickie Lalor. If he corroborated Stebbins story, they would be fairly certain that Barry Claymore had lied to them about knowing Annika Lindstrom and, perhaps more importantly, about when he had last used his parents' cottage. If Barry had violated his father's rule about the cottage in late September, might he also have done so again in mid-January? Stebbins hadn't seen him at the party, but it had apparently been the kind of party during which it would have been easy to miss somebody.

On second thought, though, Sam decided that wasn't likely. Surely *someone* would have been aware of Claymore's presence. More likely that Barry had come back from college but had skipped the party. That he had been in Southport, was looking for Annika or came upon her by accident, killed her and then left her in his parents' cottage.

This train of thought came to an abrupt end. Were she there, the sheriff would be shaking her head. Vigorously and negatively. You're getting ahead of yourself, she would say. Way ahead. And she would be right. All he'd done was interrogate one person, and that person was only a senior at Southport High School.

He stepped into the corridor to find a drinking fountain, and before he'd taken three steps he heard a deep voice.

"Sheriff?"

The owner of the voice looked like a fullback or a linebacker, which in fact he was. It was Rickie Lalor, who prided himself on being that rarity in modern day football, a two-way player. Of course the fact that he played both offense and defense had less to do with his talent than it did with the small size of Southport High and the limited number of boys who had gone out for the team. But Lalor had an athlete's build. He was also good looking, with curly dark hair and a handsome face which at the moment wore a big smile.

"I understand it's my turn to be grilled by the cops," he said. "Michael just told me you gave him a good going over."

124

Sam smiled back. Teen age bravado, he thought.

"I don't know about that," he said. "If you'll excuse me, I'd like a drink of water before we settle down for your grilling."

Unlike Stebbins, who had appeared uncomfortable throughout his session with the deputy sheriff, Lalor adopted what was – or what he thought was – an informal, cheery demeanor. When he took his seat across from Bridges, he draped an arm over the back of the next chair and stretched his long legs out under the table.

And waited.

"Let's talk about that night way back in January when Annika Lindstrom went missing," Sam said. "I'm sure you remember it. I suppose everyone here in Southport does. Anyway, we understand that you were among those present at a party that night, a party which Miss Lindstrom attended. What can you tell me about that night, especially about when you last remember seeing Miss Lindstrom?"

"You seem to know a lot about it already," Lalor said.

"We do, but I'm interested in hearing you tell us what you remember."

"There's not much to tell." Lalor leaned forward, putting his arms on the table. "I remember it was a helluva cold night. The guys all tried to go macho. You know, no jackets, no hoodies, just Ts. It was pretty stupid. The girls, they're not as crazy as we are."

"The girl I'm interested in is Annika Lindstrom. When was the last time you saw her that night?"

"No idea. If you'd asked me the next day, I probably could have told you. But now it's all one big blur."

"It's my understanding that she was your girl friend. I'd have thought you'd remember where she was. Are you telling me you didn't take her home?"

"Where did you get the idea she was my girlfriend?"

"People talk," Sam said, cryptically. "So you didn't take her home. Did someone else?"

"I honestly don't know. Could be, but I've no idea who it would have been."

"Who might it have been? Who else was she dating back then?"

"Who was she dating? You mean hooking up with?" Rickie laughed. "Depends what day you're talking about. Annika had fun leading guys on, making them think they were going to score, then letting them down. She was probably sleeping around, but that's not a nice thing to say about the dead. Anyway, it could have been someone from the party, even an older guy from town."

"An older guy from town?"

"There was talk she was seeing Eric Mackinson."

"Who's he?"

Lalor seemed surprised that the deputy sheriff didn't know about Mackinson.

"A guy who graduated Southport a few years ago. He seemed to be interested in Annika."

"How about Barry Claymore?"

"Claymore? At the party? He was going to college out in Ohio."

"I take it that's a 'no' – he wasn't at the party."

"Well, if he was I never saw him. Of course he could have been in the area. His parents have a cottage up on the West Lake Road. But it doesn't seem likely."

No, Sam thought, it doesn't. Not with college in session and the family home down in New Jersey. Unless, that is, Barry and Annika were in a relationship that compelled them to do unlikely things.

"Ever been in the Claymore cottage?" Sam asked. "It isn't insulated, no running water in the winter. It'd be way too cold to stay there in January."

Rickie Lalor had no comment to make about the Claymore cottage.

"Speaking of Claymore, did he ever sail with you? I've heard you have a boat."

"I sure do, a K," Lalor said, his smile broadening. "I'd go nuts over the summer if it weren't for *Snafu*. Barry, he went out with me a few times."

"Snafu? That's the name of the boat?"

"Right. You know, situation normal, all fucked up."

Yes, Sam said to himself, us ex-marines know all about snafu.

"How about Annika? She sail with you?"

"Same story – a few times. Once with Barry along."

"When was that?

"Back in September, not too long after she arrived in Southport. Just chance that Barry was back at the lake that weekend. It was Michael who saw him, invited him to join us."

"Did they seem to get along okay?"

Lalor laughed.

"Does Brad like Angelina? Hey, they couldn't keep their hands off each other."

"Did that bug you?"

"Now why would it do that? You couldn't count on Annika from one night to the next. It didn't take me long to get that message."

Sam chose to forego lunch in the cafeteria rather than be the subject of conversations and the object of stares from one corner of the room to another. He could have gone over to the town square for a sub or a panini, but he preferred to tackle another student on Carol's list. Sticking with the boys, he asked to have Bruce Bachman sent down to the faculty lounge. The room he had been using had been co-opted by a lit class.

Carol had given him little information on Bachman. As Sam reviewed his notes, it was apparent that Bachman was something of an oddity on her list. Jennifer Kershaw had mentioned that he was Annika's boyfriend and that Annika herself had referred to him as the sexiest man she had ever met. However, one of Jennifer's friends had apparently ridiculed that story. The only point on which people seemed to agree was that Bachman was not part of the group to which Annika's friends, male and female, belonged.

The young man who came into the faculty lounge at 1:25 made a positive impression on Sam the minute he crossed the threshold. Not only was he neatly dressed and physically attractive. He also introduced himself, said good morning to the deputy sheriff, and extended his hand in greeting. For all Sam knew, this could be a calculated ploy, designed to curry favor. But he appreciated it nonetheless.

"Bruce Bachman? Good to meet you," he said. "These little conversations are about Annika Lindstrom, as you may have heard. We need to learn as much about her as we can so we can determine why she was killed and who is responsible for her death."

"I'll be glad to answer any questions, but I'm afraid I don't really know much about Annika. Her disappearance was such a surprise, and then her death. I lost two of my grandparents within the last year, but that's different. It's the sort of thing you expect when people get to be their age. But Annika was just a kid, probably no more than 16 or 17."

"Yes, we can all agree it was a terrible thing. I need to ask you a few questions, mostly about your relationship with Annika. Let's start with the night she disappeared. It was in January, after a party here in Southport. Were you at the party?"

"No, I wasn't. Actually, I didn't know anything about it. Not before hand, I mean. Of course everyone knew about it within a day or two."

"Annika was there. We know that. So how does it happen that you weren't?"

"I don't understand. Parties like that involve friends. I know just about everyone in the school, but the kids who were partying that night – I guess you'd say they were acquaintances, but not really my friends."

"Maybe I've been misinformed, Mr. Bachman, but I was under the impression that you and Miss Lindstrom – Annika – were dating. That the two of you were really close."

Bruce Bachman could hardly have feigned the look of surprise on his face.

"Forgive me, sir, but who told you that?"

"I'm not sure it matters. What does matter is whether it's true."

The look of surprise on Bachman's face changed to one of amusement.

"I never had a date with her. I never even asked her for a date. We knew each other, of course, but we weren't close. Not even close to close. I'm sure anybody you talk to here at Southport would tell you the same thing. Has somebody said I had something to do with her being killed?"

Bachman had connected the dots.

"No, no. It's just that we heard that you two were – what's the right word here – intimate?"

"We were supposed to be intimate?" He practically shouted the question.

"That wasn't the way to put it. I'm sorry. The story was that Annika had a crush on you and that the two of you were going together."

"Do you know what I think, sheriff?" Bruce Bachman was no longer surprised or amused. He sounded angry. "I think that somebody made up a story he knows – or she knows – is simply not true. It's a malicious lie. And I'll bet that it's Annika, not me, who's the target of the lie. Someone's trying to smear her name."

"But how does linking her to you hurt her? Wouldn't it look like a compliment?"

"Thank you, sheriff, but the answer is 'no.' I'm not her type. No one would believe that she had a crush on me or that I had one on her."

"But what if someone told the lie to cast suspicion on you for Annika's death?" Sam had not given that idea any thought. It had just occurred to him.

Bachman wasn't buying it.

"Forgive me if I'm being rude, but that's ridiculous. Why on earth would anyone with a brain in his head suspect me of killing Annika Lindstrom? People don't go around killing people they barely know and hardly ever speak to."

Actually, sometimes they do, Sam thought. But those who do are usually mentally unstable. Bruce Bachman showed no sign of mental instability.

"Why don't we forget about you and Annika for a moment," Sam said. "I can assure you that the sheriff isn't going to consider anyone a suspect in this case without a great deal of hard evidence. Much more evidence than a casual comment that you and Miss Lindstrom were in a relationship. I do have a couple of other questions, though. Do you know Eric Mackinson?"

"I don't think so. Who is he? Is he a suspect in your case?"

"The answer to your first question is that he's a former student at Southport High who now works as a painter around the lake. The answer to the second question is that 'no,' he isn't a suspect. If you don't know him, let's talk about Barry Claymore. Do you know him?"

"I've heard of him, but I've never met him."

"Okay, next question. Have you ever done any sailing with Rickie Lalor?"

"No again. Of course I know Rickie. We're both in the senior class, and we played together on the school's football team for the last three years. Even in the same backfield – I was the quarterback and he was the fullback. He's a regular guy, but we aren't friends. Off the football field, that is."

"It's about time you got back to your classes. Final question: What do you think happened to Annika Lindstrom?"

Bachman had started to get out of his seat. He sat back down.

"I wish I could tell you that I have a great idea, that I've thought it out and come to the only logical conclusion. I like it when they do that in mystery stories. But the truth is, I don't have a clue. I'd like to think it was an accident. But that wouldn't explain her ending up in somebody's cellar, would it? A cellar in a locked house. Those are the best mysteries, the locked room mysteries. Have you ever read any?"

"No, Mr. Bachman, I'm afraid not. My job is solving crimes, not reading about them. But tell you what, if you have one of those locked room mysteries to suggest, I'll give it a try."

"Great. I'd suggest anything by John Dickson Carr."

When Sam left the school that afternoon, he briefly considered stopping at the public library. But only briefly.

CHAPTER 22

Joe and Ellie Cabot were not prepared to be taken to task for the second time in two days for having duplicated their key to the Claymore cottage. But Carol, temporarily freed from the interviews she had planned to have with Southport High School students, had made it her first order of business on Tuesday morning to pay the Cabots a visit. She had already accounted for five keys to The Summer House. One was still in the possession of the Claymores. She had relieved them, together with Bud Harbaugh, Eric Mackinson, and Barry Claymore, of four more keys, and she fully expected to make it a total of six that morning.

Carol felt no sense of urgency. When Sam left, she had placed a call to the high school and explained the need to release several students from class to speak with her deputy. There was never any doubt that the school would comply with her request, but she found it necessary to assure the principal that what she was doing did not imply that any of the students were under suspicion. Nor could she imagine that any of them might turn out to be suspects. After all, they weren't the ones with keys to the cottage. What is more, teenagers in quiet small towns weren't in the habit of killing their classmates. It might happen in drug and gun afflicted neighborhoods of large cities, but surely not around Crooked Lake.

Her conversation with the principal over, Carol sat for a moment, reflecting on her assumptions regarding Annika's former classmates. She knew she was right. Yet she was uneasy. Annika had died from ingesting large quantities of a drug – no, two drugs, Rohypnol and alcohol. Which undercut her conviction that drug deaths were a big city, inner city phenomenon. She knew that alcohol could be purchased in a variety of stores all over the area, and it wouldn't be difficult to obtain a six pack of beer (or two or three) even if one were underage. The date rape drug was another matter. She knew it was illegal in the United States. But Carol was not naive. She didn't know how it got to Southport or who brought it in and peddled it there, but she had to admit that it was probably no great challenge. So the problem wasn't how, but who. And once she thought of Annika's death in those terms, she would have to admit that she couldn't rule out people from the high school. Improbable, yes. Impossible, no. Especially with so many keys floating about.

Carol took the longer route to the lake. She did it deliberately, and with the windows rolled down. Whatever it was in the air that had brought on her bout with hay fever had gone away. The fresh air felt good. It was still nippy, but spring was clearly making a belated arrival. She passed Kevin's cottage, thought momentarily about making a stop, but decided to forego that particular pleasure. If the calendar in her mind was correct, he would be arriving back at the lake in less than a week.

The two Claymore cars were in place behind the cottage. She was pleased to see that Barry had his car back and wanted to ask him how long he had had to wait for it, but her mission was to talk to the Cabots. She drove the few extra yards and pulled in behind the hedge which separated the Cabot cottage from its neighbors to the south.

"We've been expecting you," Mrs. Cabot said as she greeted the sheriff at the back door. "Mr. Claymore mentioned that you are talking to his neighbors."

"That we are. I'm Sheriff Kelleher, and I'd like to speak with you or your husband for a few minutes."

"Of course. Come on in. Joe isn't here right now. I think it's his day to be at the high school. Anyway, I'll be happy to answer your questions."

They sat at the breakfast nook, spoke briefly about how terrible it must have been for the Claymores to find a dead woman in their basement on their return to the lake, and quickly turned to the issue of keys.

"I understand you have a key to the Claymore's cottage, that you use it to check up on the cottage during the winter."

"That's right. We've been doing it for them for several years now." The smile with which she announced their neighborliness vanished as soon as it had appeared. "I'm afraid we didn't so a very good job of it this winter. I feel kinda guilty about that woman being there."

"If you weren't negligent about locking up, there's no reason to feel guilty. You'll forgive me for being direct, but did you have occasion to go into their cottage over the winter?"

"Yes, we did. On two occasions."

"And are you sure you locked up when you left?"

"Oh, yes. I'm sure we did."

"Then you shouldn't feel guilty. It had to have been somebody else who was careless."

"I know, but I still feel badly. Bill was very upset when he talked with us about it."

"About the girl being in their cellar?"

"Well, yes, of course. But mostly about our missing key."

"You lost a key?" Carol's voice registered the shock she felt.

"Didn't Bill tell you?"

"No. I haven't talked to him since Sunday and he didn't mention it then. What happened?"

Ellie Cabot told the sheriff what she had told Bill Claymore, and gave her a detailed report on her exhaustive and unsuccessful search of the house for the missing key. Carol did not like what she was hearing. How was it possible that between Labor Day weekend and the following May two more keys to the Claymore cottage had materialized? And that one of them had mysteriously vanished?

Carol felt an impulse to join Mrs. Cabot in a second search of the house, but she knew it would be futile. She was sure that the Cabots, embarrassed by what had happened, would have gone through every room with the proverbial fine-tooth comb.

"Is there anyone else who had access to the house and, at least hypothetically, to the keys?" she asked.

"Just the family. Unless, that is, you count friends who were here from time to time. For dinner, things like that."

"Was either of the keys commonly in a place where it would be visible to these friends when they came into the house?"

"I guess so. It was on a hook in the mud room as you came in the back door. But why would anyone take it without telling us? There'd be no way they'd even know what it was a key to."

"I agree that it doesn't make much sense. But the fact remains that it's missing. You mentioned family. Do you have children?"

"Three. All boys. Ronnie and Boo are twins. They just recently turned nine. Benjamin is fifteen."

"Does Benjamin ever do work for the neighbors? Like mow the lawn, for example?"

Mrs. Cabot looked as if she were about to burst out laughing.

"In my dreams. He'll find any excuse to avoid work. It's all Joe and I can do to get him to mow our lawn. It's easier to do it ourselves."

"So he wouldn't have had occasion to need the Claymore's key to help them?"

"I sure can't think of one."

"Benjamin goes to school down in Southport, I assume. Is that where he is now?"

"I hope so. The bus picked him up at around 6:45."

"Unlikely as it is that they'll know anything about the Claymore key, I'd like to talk to your boys after school. When do they get home from school?"

"There's two different buses. Benjamin's usually home by 3:20, 3:30. The twins get here about fifteen minutes later."

"Either I'll be back or one of my men will. Thanks for your time. It may take awhile, but I'm sure we'll locate the missing key."

Maybe, maybe not, Carol thought to herself as she drove off for her next meeting.

For the third time in five days she pulled up in front of the Kershaw home in Southport. Amanda Kershaw had promised that she would search the house for the post card that Annika had allegedly sent from Ohio shortly after she disappeared in January. Her search had initially been fruitless, and she had concluded that she must have tossed it out. But Carol had urged her to keep looking, so she had persevered, going through files in which it might have been misplaced one day, leafing through books in which it might have served as a bookmark another. It was the previous evening that Amanda had left a message at the sheriff's office saying that the post card had finally been found. Carol was pleased with the news, but not confident that it would prove helpful.

"I was convinced I'd never find it," Mrs. Kershaw said after welcoming the sheriff. "You won't believe where I found it."

"What matters is that you did," Carol said. "I appreciate it that you kept looking."

"The thing is, it was right where I looked first. It had gotten caught in one of my desk drawers, so when I opened the drawer it didn't come out like it should."

Carol wasn't interested in the drawer; she wanted to see the post card. Mrs. Kershaw handed it over to her as if it were a precious stone.

"I'm sorry it's not in very good shape. It must have been bent back and forth every time I opened and closed that drawer."

The post card was indeed not in good shape. Any tell-take finger prints would have long since been made undetectable by the prints of postal service employees and various Kershaws. But the message on the card was still legible.

Don't worry, I'm all right. I'll tell you all about it someday. AL

The handwriting was an undistinguished cross between printing and cursive. Whether it resembled Annika's handwriting, Carol had no way of knowing without seeing something that she had written. She was willing to bet that it would not be a match. At best, it would be a crude effort to replicate Annika's handwriting. And, as Amanda had mentioned, there was no Annika, just the initials AL. Carol would have to ask around school if she had ever signed herself that way.

The postmark was badly smudged. It looked as if the date was January 19, but that would have been a guess. Nor was it clear where the card had been mailed. Ohio was recognizable, which accounted for the fact that everyone referred to it as the card from Ohio. The town was another matter. It began with a W, and it looked like a name of intermediate length. Carol held it up in front of her and squinted. Could it be Winesburg? Or was that because Barry Claymore's college was near Akron and so was Winesburg, Sherwood Anderson's famous fictional town? Two problems with that, Carol thought. She recalled from a college lit course that Anderson had based his stories on the town where he grew up, which was not Winesburg. More importantly, places near Akron came to mind only because she knew that Barry Claymore's college was near Akron. And she had no reason to suspect Barry, either of Annika's death or the probably phony post card.

"Mrs. Kershaw," she said after a couple of minutes of

staring at the card, "would there be a sample of Annika's handwriting anywhere in the house? I know that the diary was thrown out, but might there be anything else?"

"I'm sure there isn't. You have the suitcases, and they contain everything of hers that we didn't throw out. I'm sorry about the diary. There was no reason for us to get rid of it."

Carol wondered if she included herself in that 'us,' or if she was accusing her husband of the demise of the diary. She would have to pay another visit to the high school, talk to Annika's teachers, see if anyone had retained one of her papers or a test.

In retrospect, it had been a mistake not to involve herself more in Annika's disappearance months earlier. Why had she allowed the arrival of the post card to let her forget about the girl? In all likelihood they would not have saved Annika by pursuing the matter back in January, but they might be much closer to finding out who was responsible for her death.

CHAPTER 23

The digital clock had just turned over and now read 7:57. Kevin typed in the word FINI in capital letters at the bottom of page 33 of his paper, copied it to disc, and made himself a martini. It had taken him three long days in front of his computer to finish his venture into counterfactual history. Three days which he would rather have spent with Carol at the lake. But he knew he had done the right thing, knew that he had produced a paper which he would be proud to defend at the Copenhagen conference.

He hit print, and sat back to enjoy his drink while the printer produced a hardcopy of 'The Opera Verdi Never Wrote.' He was exhausted. This is what his students must feel like after putting in all-nighters to satisfy the requirements of his courses. Of course the students wouldn't have to put in all-nighters if they had planned better. And he wouldn't feel so frazzled if he had worked harder on the paper earlier in the semester. No matter. It was done. What is more, he would be back at the cottage in another week.

He would be giving the paper on Saturday, only four days away. He had rearranged his schedule earlier that day so that he would be arriving in Copenhagen on Thursday and leaving on Sunday. It meant that he would miss the final day of the conference, but it gave him two full days to enjoy the company of opera aficionados, most of them academics like himself.

Kevin surveyed the wreckage of his apartment. He had made no effort to pick things up and otherwise create some semblance of order. Uncharacteristically, he had not even made his bed or transferred dishes from the sink to the dishwasher. Carol would be horrified. But life presents us with situations in which we must make trade offs, he thought. Besides, I can straighten up in the morning. Now it's time to call Carol. There would be no need to tell her about the condition of the apartment.

She answered promptly, a product of a habit she had acquired after becoming sheriff.

"It's me, and you're the first to know that the paper is finished!" Kevin said it with feeling.

"That's marvelous. Congratulations. Now, wasn't I right to insist you get your priorities straight?"

"I'd already made the decision to put first things first, Carol. Let me take credit for being responsible."

"Be my guest. Anyway, that's good news. When are you off for Copenhagen?"

"Tomorrow night. And I'll be back Sunday, which means you'll be seeing me sometime late Monday. That schedule meet with your approval?"

"My only regret is that there's no transatlantic flight direct to Crooked Lake. Tell you what. I'll open the cottage, air things out, buy a couple of staples. Do you know what time you'll get here?"

"I can't see why I can't make it by mid-afternoon, four o'clock at the latest."

"Good. Then I'll make us a reservation at The Cedar Post."

"How's your investigation going? The one involving that Swedish woman?"

'Slowly. I'd be lying if I said I was just marking time until you get here, but it almost seems that way. The problem is that this is a crime that took place months ago. January to be precise."

"So, no progress?"

"Depends on what you mean by progress. We do know that the girl appears to have died from a walloping big dose of one of those date rape drugs. That and plenty of alcohol. So in a sense her death was probably accidental, meaning whoever slipped her the drug meant to rape her, not kill her. But whoever it was, he's still culpable. Unfortunately, there are a lot of people around Southport who might have done it."

"Sounds as if motive won't be a problem this time," Kevin said.

"Probably not, but I'm past the point of assuming anything."

"I must live a sheltered life up there, but I don't remember hearing that Crooked Lake had a lot of drug problems. What's been your experience?"

"I don't suppose there's anywhere in the country that's immune to it," Carol said. "We hear a lot about marijuana, of course, especially among the younger crowd. There's been a debate in the *Gazette* over a move to legalize it. Otherwise, this isn't a hotbed of drug trafficking. But I guess I live a sheltered life, too, because this is the first time I've heard about Rohypnol. Doc Crawford tells me it's cheap and not hard to get, but I don't recall a rape victim claiming she was drugged since I've been on the job."

"Rohypnol? Never heard of it."

"Well, that's what Crawford found in Miss Lindstrom's body. The street name is 'roofies.' By the way, do you happen to know a family named Claymore? They live on the West Lake Road, a few miles south of you. It's their place where the girl's body was found."

"No, I don't know any Claymores. I feel sorry for them, but I'm glad it was their cottage, not mine."

"I don't think there was any danger of her ending up in your cellar. Not, that is, unless you've given keys to the cottage to every Tom, Dick and Harry."

"I don't know about those guys, but you've got a key. Remember?"

"And, if my memory is good, so does your neighbor Snyder. Like you, Claymore had a neighbor keeping an eye on his place. Which makes him a person of interest, if not a suspect. So maybe you were just luckier than Claymore."

Kevin was dead tired, and finally admitted it.

"I want to keep you on the phone, but the truth is I'm practically out on my feet. Or in my chair. I've done nothing since our last conversation except work on that damn paper. Didn't set it aside until almost two this morning. If I don't get some sleep, I'll never make it to Copenhagen."

"Get some sleep. We can catch up next week. There's a lot to catch up on. But let me remind you, you're not to go looking for Lindstroms while you're over there. This is a professional trip, remember? Give your paper, talk opera, enjoy the sights, but stay away from Malmo."

"You can't really believe I'd do something like that, can you?"

"I can, and that's why I'm laying down the law. Verdi is your responsibility, Annika Lindstrom is mine."

"I know. I'll be on my best behavior in Copenhagen. I can't make any promises about Crooked Lake."

"Good night, Kevin. Have a good flight. I love you."

"Me, too."

CHAPTER 24

He may not have been particularly creative, but Deputy Sheriff Sam Bridges was thorough to a fault. It was a major reason why the sheriff trusted him with matters she didn't like to delegate to her other officers. Carol and Sam had missed each other at the end of the day on Tuesday, but he had left on her desk a neatly typed summary of his interrogation of the Southport High School students. She had spent most of the day learning what she could about the presence of the illegal drug Rohypnol in the Crooked Lake area, with the result that she had given little thought to Sam's assignment.

But with predictable efficiency, he had spent two days questioning the students who were reportedly closest to Annika Lindstrom. His report, all four single spaced pages of it, would be her evening's homework. She slipped it into her briefcase and set off for home.

She had finished supper and was ready to read Sam's report when Kevin called. For some reason, their conversation, brief as it had been, had the effect of spoiling her appetite for immersing herself in the musings of a bunch of high school students. She skimmed the report in search of a really critical piece of news, but finding none she decided she'd rather discuss it with Sam in the morning than spend the rest of the evening interpreting his analysis of what these 'friends of Annika' had to say.

It was not until Carol arrived at the office on Wednesday morning that she remembered that she was due to testify in court that day. It was not a particularly important case, and her testimony was unlikely to affect the outcome one way or another. As a result, she had given it little thought, so little that Ms. Franks' reminder that she was due in court in half an hour caught her by surprise.

"Damn it!" she exploded with a vehemence so unusual and so unexpected that her secretary winced.

"Sorry, JoAnne," she quickly apologized. "It's not your fault. See if you can get ahold of Sam for me."

Bridges was only next door in the squad room.

"Sam, we need to go over your report, but I've got to be down at the courthouse for heaven knows how long when I should be concentrating on the Lindstrom case. I've read the report, but I'm going to want you to give me more details on a few points. As soon as I'm free, I'll call you and we can find a place to get together."

"No problem. I doubt I can add much, though. It's amazing how little those kids can remember about who was where at that damned party. I'll bet some of them know more than they're letting on. Maybe you can get something out of the two Kershaw youngsters."

Kids? Youngsters? Adolescents, yes, but Carol knew that she would have to start thinking of them as adults.

It wasn't until the lunch hour that she was able to escape from the courtroom. Sam was in the vicinity, so they agreed to grab a quick sandwich at the Dockstreet Diner.

"I don't like to knock my fellow attorneys, Sam," she said as they took seats in a booth that still needed cleaning up after being vacated by the previous patrons. "I guess it's because I remember the times I screwed up in court. But you should have seen counsel for the defense this morning. No, let me take that back. You shouldn't have seen him. It was pure torture. Not to mention a waste of my time."

"Do you want to tell me about it? I promise not to quote you."

"No. I'm just letting off steam. I want to hear your reaction to what those Southport students had to tell you. Why don't –" She paused and waited while the waitress cleaned the table. They placed their orders, and Carol pulled out Sam's report and laid it on the table in front of them.

"It's a nice summary you gave me, but what I want is your unvarnished opinion. Whether you have a feeling that you're not getting the whole story. But first, let's just have a recap."

"Okay. Like I said, I'm reporting on what I heard from nine of the students. Make that eight. Bachman is just not part of the in-group. He could be lying, I suppose, but it's unlikely that all the rest of them got together and conspired to support him."

"Which means that Jennifer Kershaw is the one who's probably lying. Either that or Annika, for some reason of her own, fed her a line about being hot for Bachman. I'm hoping to corner Jennifer right after school today."

"The two things where there seems to be agreement are that Annika just vanished sometime during the party and that she and Barry Claymore had something going in September at a time when he was not supposed to be anywhere near the lake. Can we take the party first?"

"Go ahead."

"As you'd told me, it was kind of a casual affair. But I'm sure there was a method in its madness. Things started at the Leeds' house, but it didn't get interesting until the kids moved on to the Marinellis. By the time they got to the Selfridges, things had quieted down. The party seems to have settled into a kind of sleep over for a couple of the girls. The reason for the buzz about the Marinelli place – and some of them admitted as much – is that the parents weren't at home. Nobody said who was paired off with whom, but it's obvious that not everybody was watching TV or playing video games. They didn't bother denying that plenty of alcohol was being consumed either."

"When was the last time anybody saw Annika?"

"You mean when was the last time anybody said he saw Annika."

"Yes. He or she."

"Two of the girls said they saw her at the Marinellis. No one admitted seeing her later at the Selfridges."

"And no one admitted seeing Barry Claymore or Eric Mackinson during the party?"

"No, but I thought Lalor was going to say he'd seen Claymore. He didn't, but he went out of his way to say that for all he knew Barry might have been around."

"Interesting. Which raises a question. Forget for a moment what was said. Did you ever have a feeling that someone was concealing something? Or, more generally, acting or sounding at all strange? I know it's a hard thing to judge, especially when you don't know somebody. But why don't you just share your impressions with me."

Sam had thought a lot about it, and he had no trouble identifying things that hadn't sounded right.

"First, there was Stebbins. He acted nervous, all through our meeting. Of course it might be due to the fact that he was the first one I talked to. You know, he could have been uneasy because he didn't know what to expect. By the time I'd gotten to the others, word would have spread around. But no question about it, he was the most uncomfortable of them all. The contrast with Lalor would have been hard to miss. Lalor was real casual, even cocky. Maybe it's just his personality, but it was like he was overdoing the effort to be nonchalant."

"Let's skip Bachman and talk about the girls."

"They were pretty much all on the same page. Except maybe Marinelli. She didn't disagree with the others, but she didn't really have much to say. My guess is that it had to do with her being new at the school. Like Lindstrom. Her family didn't move here until after the semester started. I think her need to make friends more generally limited her relationship with Lindstrom. Aside from that, you'd have thought they'd all gotten together and decided what they'd tell me. You'd talked with the Leeds girls, so she'd have had a chance to talk to the others."

"I was afraid of that, but it can't be helped."

"What surprised me most was that they were all so open about the booze and the sex. It was like, oh, that's what we do. But like I said, no one ever put Annika in a bedroom with one of the guys."

"Maybe she stayed out of the bedrooms," Carol said. "Or maybe she didn't, and for some reason they all decided to lie. But why would they do that?"

"You think you should talk to some of them again?"

"What are you suggesting, the old 'bad cop, good cop' routine? Which were you?"

Sam smiled.

"Neither. I didn't think I should be aggressive."

"And you shouldn't have been. Not at this point," Carol said. "Do me a favor, will you, Sam? Eat your sandwich."

His egg salad with chips and a pickle had sat in front of him, untouched, for more than five minutes.

Carol let her colleague take a few bites while she studied his report.

"Now, while you're finishing lunch, let's talk about Annika and Barry. Your report says that both Stebbins and Lalor admitted sailing with the two of them one weekend in late September and that they were sure they had never met before that weekend."

"Right. And that before they got back to the yacht club Barry was kissing Annika. Not just a friendly peck on the cheek, either."

"Did you ask any of the girls about a relationship between Annika and Barry?"

"All of them. Well, at least all of them except maybe Sue Marinelli. They knew. I got the impression that anything Annika did was important, especially to the Selfridge girl. And to Leeds. They spoke well of her, but it was pretty obvious that she was competition."

"Did anyone say anything about Annika's relationship with Barry after that September weekend? Whether she talked about him, whether he had come back to see her, whether she had gone out to Ohio to see him?"

Sam had not pursued this line of inquiry, and he now had reason to regret it. It would have been a logical question to ask of the people he had been interrogating.

"I'm afraid I didn't ask," he said. "But wouldn't somebody have brought it up? I mean, these conversations were sort of like gossip sessions."

"You're probably right, but there may be reasons why gossips don't tell all. Especially when they're talking to the police. Not to worry, we'll be talking to some of these people again. Of that I'm sure."

Sandwiches finished, Sam and Carol went their separate ways. For Carol it was a drive down to Southport, where she expected to corner Jennifer Kershaw as she left school. In all likelihood, Jennifer would either be with friends or have made plans to spend some time with one or more of them. Today, those plans would have to be put on hold for at least an hour. Her one conversation with Jennifer had been all too brief, and it was imperative that she speak with her sooner rather than later. The urgency of such a meeting had been highlighted by Sam's report and Carol's conversation with him. How would Jennifer defend her allegation that Annika was enamored of Bruce Bachman? How would her remembrance of the January party compare with that of her high school acquaintances? How would it stand up to tough questioning? How would she respond to questions about Barry Claymore? About Barry Claymore and Annika Lindstrom? About Annika's diary?

Before setting off for the Southport High School, Carol sat in the car and leafed through Sam's report one more time. It mentioned nine names, which, together with Brian and Jennifer Kershaw but minus Bruce Bachman, added up to ten students who had been partying with Annika four months earlier. Except for her very brief contact with Brian and Jennifer, the only one of them she had spoken with was Karen Leeds. Much as she trusted Bridges, she was now aware that she, too, would need to talk with the others, or at least some of them. Particularly the nervous Stebbins and the cocky Lalor.

Then there were the Cabot children. And Helen Claymore's brother Roger. What is more, she would now have to pay a second visit to Barry Claymore. And Eric Mackinson. He had said that he wasn't at the now infamous party, and none of the students Sam interrogated had said that he was. But where had he been that night? Unlike the people Sam had interviewed, Mackinson had a key to the Claymore cottage. So did Barry. No one had claimed to have seen either of them in Southport the night of the party. But that didn't prove that they hadn't been there.

CHAPTER 25

There was a vacant space in the faculty parking lot, and Carol parked there rather than in the area set aside for visitors. It gave her a better view of the students who would be leaving school in approximately another ten minutes.

She was going over in her mind what she should ask Jennifer. More importantly, she was arguing with herself about how tough she should be. Being tough was not in her nature, if by tough one meant verbally aggressive. Perhaps it had something to do with her distaste for the general decline in civility which increasingly characterized public discourse. She hated the vitriolic blather which trumped rational debate on talk radio and the cable channels. And while she knew that police work was different from political commentary, she clung to the conviction that she was more likely to get the right results if she treated people with patience and courtesy.

Jennifer Kershaw was a difficult case. Carol didn't know her well enough to judge her. But there was something about the young woman that made her uneasy. There was the disrespect she had shown her father, the evasiveness with which she had characterized her relationship with Annika, her attempt to link Annika to Bruce Bachman. On the other hand, there was absolutely no reason to believe she had anything to do with the young woman's death. She was just a high school student with an attitude who had lived in the same house with her and had attended a party with her the night she disappeared. She didn't even have a key to the Claymore cottage, Carol thought. Why be tough?

When the doors opened to disgorge the crowd of Southport High School students, Jennifer Kershaw was among the first to leave the building. She was in the company of Karen Leeds and a girl Carol didn't recognize. They caught sight of the patrol car but kept on walking. Rather than get out, Carol gave a beep on the horn. If they ignore me and don't stop, I'll get tough, she said to herself. But they did stop, and after a moment's pause, all three of the girls walked slowly over to where Carol was parked. She leaned out of the open window.

"Hi, Jennifer. And Karen. I'm afraid I don't know you," she said to the other girl.

"Debbie Selfridge. And you're the sheriff."

"Nice to meet you. I hate to interfere with your plans," she said, "but I need to talk with Jennifer."

"Can it wait?" Jennifer said in a whiney voice. "We're going over to Debbie's."

"I'm afraid not. As you all know, we're investigating the death of your schoolmate, and it takes priority."

Carol knew that she'd be on tricky ground if she tried to compel Jennifer to get into the car. But she assumed that she was an authority figure the girls would reluctantly obey. She was right. Jennifer made no effort to hide her displeasure, but she told Karen and Debbie she'd be in touch and climbed into the car.

"Why do we have to do this now?" she asked as they drove carefully out of the parking lot.

"Because you're out of school and I happen to be in Southport. It shouldn't take long. We've never had a real discussion about Annika, just that brief meeting over on the square the other day."

"But I told you all I know, which is pretty much nothing."

"In my experience, Miss Kershaw, people usually know more than they think they do. It's a matter of listening, thinking, remembering. Or trying very hard to remember."

Carol was sticking with her decision not to get tough.

"Where are we going?" Jennifer asked.

"I thought it might be nice just to take a drive, maybe head up the hill where the wineries are, pull off the road on one of those lookouts. That sound okay?"

"Whatever."

And that is what they did. Seven minutes later they were parked on the side of a dirt road not far below the Gray Goose Winery. They had driven those seven minutes in silence.

"I'm anxious to hear your version of that party back in January," Carol said. "But there's something that's bothering me, and I'd like to clear it up first. It's about Bruce Bachman. While we were having ice cream the other day, you told me that Annika was dating Bachman and that she'd called him the sexiest guy she'd met since she came over from Sweden. What's bothering me is that Bachman denies ever going out with Annika. Are you sure you don't have him mixed up with someone else?"

It was hard to read Jennifer's face.

"No, it wasn't someone else. It was Bruce. Annika told me so herself."

"Why then do you suppose Bruce denies it?"

"I don't know. Maybe he's scared he'll be accused of doing something to Annika."

"Do you think he did something to Annika?"

The Q and A came to an abrupt halt. Either Jennifer hadn't expected the question or she was reluctant to share her thoughts with the sheriff.

"Let me tell you what I think," Carol went on. "I don't know why, but I think you made up this story about Annika and Bachman. I don't believe that they ever had any kind of relationship."

"That's crazy." Jennifer acted as if she was ready to get out of the car and start walking back to Southport. "I don't lie. Ask my friends. They'll tell you. I don't lie! Annika told me she was hot for Bruce."

"We asked several of your friends whether Annika was dating Bachman. Not only did they say she wasn't dating him. They all thought the very idea was ridiculous. What makes you think they'll back up your story when they've already told us that it's ridiculous?"

"Is this what you do? Mess around with people's heads?"

It was time to get tough.

"Jennifer, let me tell you something. Lying to any officer of the law is a bad idea. Lying to me is a particularly bad idea. If you can make up a story about Annika's love life, how can I take your word for anything you say about her? In fact, how can I believe anything you tell me?"

"Annika's dead," Jennifer argued, thinking she saw a way out of the spot she was in, "so you can't prove she didn't tell me she liked Bruce."

"I'd suggest that you cut it out. Now. You can forget about Annika, but what you're doing is malicious. Bruce is not amused. How would you like it if people made up stuff about you?"

Whatever Jennifer was thinking at the moment, it went

unsaid. Carol turned to the matter of the party.

"I want to talk about the party," she said. "My deputy and I have now talked to just about everybody who was there, so we have a pretty good picture of what went on that evening. Why don't you give me your version?"

"I thought you said you wouldn't believe anything I told you."

"Try me. I'll be the judge of whether it's the truth. Let's start with when you last saw Annika, and where."

"I can't remember. And you can't prove that I can."

"I wouldn't be too sure of that. Anyway, did you see her at all that evening?"

"Of course. She and I actually walked over to Karen's together from my house. It's after that I can't remember."

"Are you saying that after you got to Karen's you never saw her again?"

"I saw her a couple of times at Karen's, but I didn't see her leave there, and I know she didn't go over to Sue's with me."

"Sue's. That's the Marinelli place, right?"

"Yes."

"And then what?"

"Eventually the party moved on to Debbie Selfridge's before it broke up."

At least Jennifer had the sequence correct, and what little she had said was consistent with what the others had told Sam.

"Who were you with during the evening?"

Jennifer looked at Carol, a puzzled look on her face.

"I was with everybody," she finally said. "It was that kind of a party."

"At no time did you and one of the guys slip away to a room by yourselves?"

No puzzlement this time.

"Are you accusing me of hooking up with some guy?"

"I'm just asking a question. If you were off in some bedroom with someone, it would have been harder to keep track of where Annika was, wouldn't it?"

Jennifer thought about that for a moment and then turned her attention to a more worrisome matter.

"It's none of my parents' business, but if they thought I'd shacked up with someone they'd probably ground me."

For a fleeting moment, Carol tried to imagine how she would have reacted in a similar situation if she had a daughter. She didn't have any idea whether Jennifer was sexually active and, if she was, whether her parents were resigned to it or not, but she could appreciate that the girl would be mortified to have it known that at age seventeen she had been grounded.

"I have no intention of passing judgment on what you do when you go out to parties, and there is no reason why I would need to say anything about it to your parents. But the fact remains that your friends have already made it clear that this was a party in which drinking and sex were taking place. I'm investigating what happened to Annika Lindstrom. So I'd appreciate it if you'd dig into your memory and tell me anything you can about what Annika was doing that night and with whom. Did she ever say anything to you about whom she might have wanted to be with that evening? Did anyone else at the party mention to you whether she had paired off with anyone? In other words, whether you saw her or not after the party started, can you tell me what she might have been doing and with whom? You may not have liked Annika very much, but I can't believe that you want to obstruct our search for the truth about what happened to her."

"I know you won't believe me, but I've told you everything I know. I wasn't interested in Annika that night. I was so tired of her – Annika, Annika, Annika – you'd have to have known her to know what I mean."

Carol had to admit that what Jennifer had said was plausible. But it prompted one more question.

"You told me when we talked before that you were friends, just not close. That's not how you sound now. I'm curious. What was it between you and Annika?"

"Nothing important. It was just that she was such a big I-am. She was always the center of attention, and she loved it. She even got a kick out of telling people she was named after Annika Sorenstam. You know, the big golf star. Hell, most of the kids never heard of Sorenstam, but Annika liked to talk about her as if they'd been friends."

Carol started the car.

"I'm going back down to Southport. Do you want me to drop you at your house or at somebody else's?"

Jennifer had been expecting to spend another half hour or so with the sheriff. She looked both surprised and relieved.

"I'd appreciate it if you'd let me out at Karen's. I think you know where it is."

"I do, and I will," Carol said, interested that Jennifer had actually been polite for the first time since they had met.

They drove in silence until they reached the Leeds' house. As Jennifer opened the car door, Carol reached over and put a hand on her shoulder.

"I want you to think about what I said today. About lying. No more lies. They'll only catch up with you, and you'll regret it. I expect nothing less than your full cooperation with me. Do you understand?"

"Yes. Can I go now?"

"Of course. Call me if you remember something."

Whether Jennifer had more to tell and whether she would share it with her if she did, Carol did not know. There seemed to be three possibilities, she thought as she turned onto the West Lake Road. One: Jennifer may have decided to tell the truth. Two: she may have decided to lie because she is afraid of the possible consequences if she tells the truth. Or three: she may have decided to lie because she is protecting someone.

Carol thought about the possible reasons for lying as she drove. What might the consequences be if she told the truth? Would they be some form of punishment by her parents? Or would they be the end of a friendship or of an even more intimate relationship? And what if she were lying to protect someone? Who might that someone be, and what was he or she guilty of?

CHAPTER 26

Carol's trip north along the lake was slower than her trip down to Southport had been because she had to contend with school buses stopping every quarter of a mile or so to drop off students. One of those buses presumably was carrying one or more of the Cabot boys home. She had told Mrs. Cabot that she would be stopping by to question them about the missing key, but she had no reason to think that she would learn anything. She was simply tying up loose ends, even those with a probable relevance of near zero.

It turned out that a bus she had been tailing for several miles was indeed the one bringing the Cabot twins home from school. She waited until it had moved on, and then pulled off the road and parked beside the tall evergreen hedge. The boys stood on the porch, watching her. She recalled that one of them was Boo, but the other more conventional name eluded her.

"Hi," she said as she mounted the back steps. "Which of you is Boo?"

The shorter of the two boys, obviously not identical twins, raised his hand.

"I'm Ronnie," the other spoke up, making it unnecessary for Carol to confess her lapse of memory. "What are you doing here?"

It was a reasonable question, and it suggested that their mother had not mentioned that the sheriff might be paying them a visit.

"I have a couple of questions for both of you. And for your older brother."

"I'll bet it's about that mystery woman over at Mr. Claymore's," Boo said.

"Not exactly," Carol said. "Let's go inside and talk about it."

Benjamin, the oldest son, was making himself a sandwich in the kitchen and the sound of a vacuum cleaner somewhere in the house told her that Mrs. Cabot was also at home. Boo volunteered to get his mother, and a couple of minutes later they had all taken seats in the family room to hear what the sheriff had to say.

Carol hadn't planned to say much. She made her by now well rehearsed opening statement about the investigation, and then brought up the subject of the missing key.

"I am trying to account for every key to Mr. and Mrs. Claymore's cottage, and your mother has informed me that she and your dad had two of them. Unfortunately, one of them appears to be missing. I'm here today to ask a very simple question. Did any of you, for whatever reason, borrow that key? Or move it from its hook in the mud room?"

She watched for a reaction from the boys, for anything that might tell her more than what they chose to say. Benjamin looked at Boo; Boo looked at his mother. Ronnie looked up at the crown molding. Something's going on here, Carol thought. I wonder who will be the first to say something.

It was Boo who broke the silence with which they had greeted the sheriff's question.

"It wasn't me," he said, and his attempt to pass the buck precipitated a flurry of accusations and counteraccusations.

"You were the one who wanted to get in over there," Benjamin said. "You and Ronnie. It's your fault."

"I didn't take a key. I swear."

"But it was your idea."

Carol waited, interested to see how this disagreement would play out. It was Ellie Cabot who put a halt to it.

"What's this all about?" she asked of her sons. "Are you telling me that you went into the Claymore cottage? Why on earth did you do that?"

"It's because they wanted to take a peek at the Christmas presents," Benjamin said, glaring at his brothers.

"Yeah, but you're the one who took the key and let us in. I never touched the key, so it's not my fault."

"You know you aren't supposed to do that," Mrs. Cabot said, now angry with her offspring. "Why do you think we put the presents over there? It's so you won't snoop."

Carol decided it was time to take charge.

"Let me get this straight," she said. "You boys are apparently unable to wait to see what presents you'll be getting for Christmas. So your parents have taken to locking them up in the Claymore cottage until Christmas – or Christmas eve, whenever you open gifts. But this last winter, your curiosity got the better of you, so you broke into –"

"No, no," Benjamin interrupted. "We didn't break in. That's a crime."

This was not the time for a disquisition on the law of breaking and entering. In any event, Benjamin was technically correct. He had not gone into the Claymore cottage with theft on his mind, whatever his parents might have thought of what he was doing.

"Okay, you used a key. A key the Claymores had given your parents. What I'm interested in is what happened to the key after you'd checked out your presents."

"We just put it back where we got it, like we always do," Benjamin said.

"Meaning you've gone into the Claymore cottage more than once."

"I can't remember. Maybe twice."

Mrs. Cabot was not at all happy with what she was hearing, but she let the sheriff do the talking.

"You know for certain that you hung the key back up out in the mud room?"

"Of course. Where else would we put it?"

"That's what I'm asking you. If you put it there, why is it missing?"

"Maybe Dad used it later." Or Mom, but Benjamin didn't seem to think it desirable, with his mother right there in the room, to suggest that she had been the one to lose the key.

"Mrs. Cabot," Carol asked, "do you remember when it was that you borrowed the juicer? Or when either of you had to go into the cottage to check things out? Was it before or after Christmas?"

"It was before, I think. But, no, I'm sure Joe was over there sometime later in the winter. I guess I don't rightly remember the date."

"And when was it that you dropped a key in the snow and decided to have another one made?"

It slowly dawned on Ellie Cabot that the sheriff might not be accusing her sons of having lost one of their keys. If the extra key had been made after her boys had 'broken in' to the Claymore cottage for an advance peek at their Christmas loot, she and Joe were the ones who were more likely to have been careless.

"Oh, dear, I don't really know. Joe did it – insisted we

couldn't run the risk of not having a key if there was an emergency. It had to have been when there was a lot of snow on the ground. I think it was January."

All four of the Cabots in the living room were sure they had never lost or loaned a key to The Summer House. Joe Cabot had said the same thing, but he had said it over the phone from the high school, where he worked as a custodian. Carol realized that she would have to raise the issue with him in person.

She considered waiting for Joe to get home from work, but immediately thought better of it. He might not arrive for another hour or even two. Perhaps he was in the habit of working late. Perhaps he stopped off for a beer en route. In any event, she preferred not to have this discussion with him in the presence of his family. Maybe Thursday at the school.

After a brief stop at the office, Carol swung on by Cumberland's excuse for a deli and picked up something for supper. There was a brief e-mail message from Kevin waiting at home.

I'm on my way. By the time you're eating breakfast,
I'll be in Copenhagen, fighting off jet lag and trying
to enjoy the sights without you beside me. See you
Monday.

Love, Me

CHAPTER 27

It was one thing to talk with a Southport High School student while wearing her sheriff's department uniform. Asking if she might speak with the school's custodian while similarly dressed was another matter. There was no reason for her to start a rumor that Joe Cabot was in some kind of trouble. As a result, Carol traded her uniform for a pair of jeans, a casual blouse, and a windbreaker in the ladies' room at the office and set off for Southport. She parked as far from the entrance to the school as she could and made her way past the newly planted trees which were to be Annika Lindstrom's memorial to the main door on the northwest side of the building.

It was possible that someone would recognize her as the sheriff, but the fact that she was in mufti made it easier to dissemble and claim not to be on official business. In any event, the trouble she had gone to had not been necessary. Cabot was not on duty that day.

The woman on the desk where all visitors were expected to sign in not only told Carol that Thursday was Mr. Cabot's day off. She went on to explain why, something the principal surely would have preferred she not do. It seems that the economic slump which had affected Southport as it had much of the country had necessitated cuts in the school budget. The result was that some members of the staff had been 'furloughed' two days a month. Apparently custodians were not as essential as classroom teachers, and Joe was thus among the people furloughed. The woman cheerfully informed her visitor that Joe was doing just fine, having picked up part time work preparing the yacht club for the upcoming season.

As she walked back to her car, Carol was giving some thought to the fact that Joe Cabot was leading a life which intersected several of the strands of the Lindstrom case. He had two keys to the Claymore cottage, one of which was missing. He worked at the high school which many of Annika's friends attended, friends who were with her the night she disappeared.

And he was moonlighting at the yacht club where one of those friends, Rickie Lalor, had gone sailing the previous September with Annika and Barry Claymore. It was unlikely that any of this had any bearing on Lindstrom's death. But Carol knew that she would be unable to put it out of her mind.

She might have taken advantage of her presence at the high school to call Brian Kershaw out of class for his 'interview.' But she chose not to, instead driving into downtown Southport to pick up some medications at the pharmacy. It was while she was waiting at the counter there that she heard someone calling her.

"Sheriff," the voice said. "How lucky to have found you here."

Carol looked in the direction of the voice and saw Joyce Mackinson coming down the aisle toward her. She was surprised that the woman had recognized her out of uniform.

"Good morning, Mrs. Mackinson." And then, suddenly aware that the woman might think it strange that the county sheriff was not on duty on a weekday, she offered a brief explanation for her presence in the pharmacy.

"I know, there are days when I think a third of our income goes for meds," Eric's mother said. "I'm always taking some pill or other. But I'm glad I ran into you. Can you talk?"

The question sounded funny. Can I talk? Of course I can. But she knew what Mrs. Mackinson meant.

"I should be heading back to my office. What's on your mind?"

"It's Eric. I really need to talk to you."

Inasmuch as Eric Mackinson was what might be called a person of interest in her investigation of Annika Lindstrom's death, there was no reason to hurry back to Cumberland. Indeed, it would probably be a good idea to hear what Mrs. Mackinson had to say.

"Of course. Just let me finish up here and we'll go next door and have a cup of coffee, if that's okay with you."

"That would be very nice. I could use some coffee."

"Now," Carol said after they'd been served, "what's this about Eric?"

"Well, I know you've been trying to see him, and I began to wonder if it had something to do with that woman whose body was found here on the lake. What was her name? Something

157

Scandinavian, I think."

Carol had not told Eric's mother why she wanted to talk with him. It sounded as if Eric had not told his mother about his meeting with the sheriff up in the ravine. But apparently Mrs. Mackinson had figured out for herself what it was that the sheriff needed to discuss with her son. This should be interesting, Carol thought. Maybe even important.

"Yes, the person you're referring to is Annika Lindstrom. Her body was discovered just a week ago in a summer cottage on the West Lake Road. Does this have something to do with Eric?"

"Oh, no," Mrs. Mackinson said, "but I started to worry that you might think so."

"Why don't you explain why you've been worried."

"The problem is that Eric knew this girl, and I thought you might want to see him because you would be talking to people who knew her. I figured that somebody had told you about Eric knowing her."

"Actually, a great many people knew Miss Lindstrom. This is a small town, and the high school isn't very big either. Most of the students there knew her. So I'm not interested in everyone who knew her. I'm particularly interested in people who dated her. Did Eric date Miss Lindstrom?"

Mrs. Mackinson took a deep breath and proceeded to explain why she had wanted to talk with the sheriff about her son.

"In a way, I suppose he did. For a little while anyway. But it didn't last. We had a good talk about it, and he understood that he shouldn't have anything to do with her."

"Let's back up a bit," Carol said. "You say that Eric and Annika – that was her name – did date for awhile. How do you know this?"

"Because he brought her over to our house a few times. They usually sat around and watched TV. I could see why Eric might be interested. I mean, she was a good looking girl. Trouble is, that's what she was. A girl. I thought about it some after he told me she was in Southport High. And a junior at that. I figured she couldn't have been more than 16. Do you see my problem?"

"Not exactly."

"Eric is a man now. He's almost 25. Much as I don't like to think about it, I'm sure he's got a man's feelings. A man's needs. You know what I mean."

"You're telling me Eric might have wanted to have sex with Miss Lindstrom." Carol found it hard to believe that Eric Mackinson hadn't experienced those feelings, hadn't had those needs, long before he reached his mid-twenties.

"I worried about it, because if he did he could be charged with statutory rape. Eric would never force himself on anybody. But the girl could make it up, even if they hadn't had sex."

Such accusations weren't unknown, but Carol wondered why Mrs. Mackinson had conjured one up in her mind.

"Why do you think she might have done that?"

"Because she was angry at Eric."

"I'm afraid I don't follow you. You just said that Annika and Eric sat around in your living room and watched TV. Now you say she was angry with him. Why was that?"

"I didn't much like it that Eric was seeing this girl. She was too young for him. She was also from Europe and was going back there after just the one year at Southport. It just didn't seem like a good relationship. So I urged him to forget about her, to start looking for someone his own age, someone from this area."

"How did he react?" Carol asked. She could imagine that Eric would not be happy to have his mother trying to arrange his personal life. She remembered the cookies. Mrs. Mackinson was quite capable of intervening in her son's relationships with the opposite sex.

"Eric has a stubborn streak. At first, he didn't want to listen to me. But I told him he was just going to hurt himself, and he finally got the point. One night when that girl was over at the house, he got up the courage to tell her he wouldn't be seeing her again. She went wild. It was awful. She yelled at him, told him no one was going to treat her like that."

"How do you know she got so angry?"

The color rose in Mrs. Mackinson' face.

"I heard it all. You couldn't not hear her. Like I said, she started screaming at him the minute he said they would have to stop going together. I've never heard a lady talk like she did. When she left, I heard her say something about him not being the only stud in town."

If Mrs. Mackinson was to be believed – and why would she be making this up? – she might have reason to be worried. An angry girlfriend who had just been summarily dumped might well have been tempted to cry rape. Nor was it beyond imagining that she could have concocted such a story even if they had never been sexually intimate.

"When did this happen? I mean when did Eric tell Annika he wouldn't be seeing her again? When was it you heard Annika go ballistic?"

"It was after Thanksgiving. I don't remember exactly, but I know we hadn't put our Christmas tree up yet."

"Did you and Eric ever talk about what had happened?"

"He never said anything, and I didn't like to bring it up. But that was the last time I ever saw that girl in our house. Their relationship was over. So you see, my boy could not possibly have had anything to do with that girl's death."

Carol was very pleased that she had agreed to have a cup of coffee with Mrs. Mackinson. Eric's mother had wanted to talk with her because what she had to say would demonstrate that her son could not possibly have had anything to do with Annika Lindstrom's death. Ironically, what she had to say had had just the opposite effect. It suggested that her son might have had a motive for killing Annika.

According to Mrs. Mackinson, she had virtually driven her son to terminate his relationship with Annika. While her advice may have been sound, it might have had the perverse effect of prompting Annika to threaten Eric with a charge of rape. Or to simply report that he had sex with her, a sixteen year old minor. If she had, was it possible that he had chosen to avoid a trial and possible conviction for statutory rape by killing her? A follow-up conversation with Eric was now necessary. Had it happened as his mother had said? Had he ever had sexual intercourse with Annika? If he had, had he told anyone else about it? Had Annika ever threatened to claim that he had raped her?

As she drove back to Cumberland, Carol ran this scenario through her mind several times. Each time she reminded herself that she was always telling her colleagues to follow the evidence, not jump to conclusions prematurely. No matter what she had just heard from his mother, the case against Eric Mackinson was still weak. And then she thought of the keys to The Summer House. One of which had been in Eric Mackinson' possession all winter long.

CHAPTER 28

From where he was sitting on the hotel's stone patio, Kevin could see dozens of kayakers, all of them gliding effortlessly along the harbor in front of the Islands Brygge section of Copenhagen. For some reason he was reminded of the dragonflies that darted so swiftly just above the water's surface on a summer's day at Crooked Lake.

Kevin was enjoying the weather and the view so much that he had momentarily lost track of the conversation. One of his companions was trying to get his attention.

"Professor," he was saying, "has this girl been in the news over there?"

"I'm sorry," Kevin apologized. "I guess I wasn't paying attention. It's really your fault, though. Holding our conference in such a lovely city. Very distracting, don't you think?"

There were six of them, relaxing at the end of the first day of the conference, enjoying a drink and a chance to talk about something other than opera. Two of his colleagues were from the host country. Carl Rasmussen and Arne Thorvald. The others were from Italy, Canada, and Sweden. It was Rasmussen, one of the organizers of the conference, who had addressed Kevin.

"Hanson here was telling us about some blogger who's always attacking your country for one thing or another." Rasmussen nodded at Bengt Hanson, inviting him to take up the story.

The Swedish scholar smiled.

"We're pretty levelheaded people, you know," he said. "Not usual for one of us to be so – what should I say? – impolite? Even if it's true, we believe in rational discourse, not name calling. Anyway, there's this chap who started a blog back when Bush was your president. He took a disliking to his policies, which wasn't all that uncommon over here on this side of the Atlantic. But it wasn't long before he was going after almost everything American, not just the president."

Kevin was familiar with the fact that the United States was

not universally loved, but he hoped that he wasn't going to have to defend his country at a conference focussing on music, supposedly the universal language.

"I just happened to mention that this mad blogger has gotten a lot of attention over the last few days because a young Swedish student who was studying in your country was murdered. Raped and murdered. He really lashed out at you Americans. Wrote about out of control violence, the high percentage of the population in prison, a gun in every bedroom, mayhem in the streets."

Kevin was no longer paying attention to kayaks on the Inderhavn. A visiting Swedish student raped and murdered? Could a recent event in out-of-the-way upstate New York have acquired so much notoriety so quickly? Or had two Swedish students been killed on US soil in such a short span of time?

He passed on the opportunity to compare the blog under discussion with a 19th century Italian opera.

"Your blogger turned one death into an indictment of the whole American society and culture?"

"So you think he overdid it?" Franco Crespi, the Italian, said, more a statement than a question. "These generalizations, they are like a plague. It happens to us all the time. Poor Italy. A country run by the criminal class. Maybe by the Mafia."

"That's just what he did," Hanson said. "Of course it is worse when the victim is one of ours."

"Did the blog make any mention of the student's name? Or where this happened?"

"I don't have the time or the interest to track down everything that makes its way through cyberspace. But I know people who do, and this blogger has a pretty big following. What I heard was that it was a girl from Malmo and that she was killed somewhere in New York."

Kevin drew a deep breath. It was probably Carol's case. But how on earth would word of it have spread so far so fast? The girl's parents might have arranged for an obit in a local paper. That was probably how it started. But Carol had told him that the girl's death was the result of ingesting too much alcohol and a date rape drug, but that she had not been raped. Carol would surely not have told grieving parents that their daughter had been raped before she died. Had the parents misunderstood Carol's message? Perhaps their English was not as good as that of Bengt Hanson. Or had they been so upset with the failure of the Americans to provide for their daughter's safety that they had embellished the story, either by mentioning rape in the obit or talking about it when the blogger called?

Here he was, enjoying a drink with a group of fellow opera addicts on a beautiful late spring day in Copenhagen, and suddenly he was worrying about a case that Carol was struggling with several time zones and several thousand miles away.

"You're going to think I'm making this up, but it happens to be true. At least I think it is. I do know about the girl the blogger talks about, and I know about the place where she allegedly met her death. I think it's in a part of New York state a long way from the city, an area that not even a lot of Americans know about."

Rasmussen and the others had never met Kevin until that morning. For all they knew, he was as crazy as lots of opera fans were alleged to be. Perhaps he booed in a loud voice when the tenor missed a high note, or stormed out of the theatre when he didn't like a new production of a familiar opera. He may even have been the leader of a claque which demonstrated whenever his favorite diva's principal rival was on stage. They regarded him suspiciously, waiting for an explanation.

"You know this woman?" Hanson asked, his voice reflecting his skepticism.

"No. Only that her name is Lindstrom, and that she is from Malmo."

Hanson's eyes widened.

"I can see that Professor Hanson is no longer a doubting Thomas. Let me tell you what the blogger knows and what he doesn't know. And why he is spreading a malicious falsehood."

A nearby waiter saw Rasmussen's hand go up in the universal signal for another round of drinks.

"I have a summer cottage on a lake in upstate New York," Kevin continued. "It's several hundred miles from the city where I teach, a beautiful spot with lots of vineyards and wineries but not much of what you would call culture. What it does have is a sheriff who is also a lovely woman. I'm not sure what you'd call it over here, but the sheriff and I are in what I like to think of as a serious relationship."

Smiles broke out around the table. The Italian's was more of a smirk.

"My sheriff called me just before I flew off for Copenhagen to wish me a safe trip. And to tell me about the death of a young Swedish exchange student whose name is Annika Lindstrom."

Kevin started to tell his colleagues that Miss Lindstrom had gone missing back in January, four months before her body was discovered. But he thought better of it. It would only reinforce the blogger's opinion that not only was crime rampant in the States but that it flourished because the police were negligent.

"I don't know where your blogger got his information, but he's wrong about Miss Lindstrom being raped. The autopsy made it very clear that she had not been sexually violated. It isn't even clear that she was murdered. I suspect that the blog was designed to stir up animosity toward the US. The woman's death is, of course, a tragedy, but it isn't fair either to her memory or to her family to spread lies about it."

"Are you saying that it was an accidental death?"

Kevin had spoken with Carol about the case for little more than ten minutes in two phone calls. He had already said virtually all that he knew. He hadn't seen the blog, and he didn't want to further stimulate gossip by saying that Miss Lindstrom had died after drinking too much alcohol and doing it in the company of someone who had laced her drinks with an illegal drug.

"It's still under investigation. If the sheriff doesn't know, I surely don't. All I know is that the woman your blogger wants to turn into a cause celebre is not a very good argument for his anti-American crusade."

"Let me see if I understand what you're telling us, Professor Whitman," Rasmussen said.

"Kevin, please."

"Of course. Kevin it shall be. You have a summer cottage somewhere in the wilds of New York state. You are having a relationship with a sheriff who polices that part of your country. And your sheriff is investigating what happened to the woman from Malmo. Am I right?"

"You are."

"So I assume that sometime soon you will probably be going back to your cottage – and your sheriff."

"Right again. In fact, I expect to be seeing her next week. Perhaps as early as Monday, assuming I'm not detained in fair Copenhagen for defaming Giuseppe Verdi."

This drew a chuckle from his colleagues, especially Professor Crespi.

"Inasmuch as you appear to be better informed than our mad blogger, perhaps you will be so good as to let us know the true facts of the case at your early convenience. I am assuming, of course, that the sheriff will confide in you as her investigation goes forward."

Little did he know that in all likelihood Kevin would soon be involved in that investigation himself.

"I would like to second the suggestion of our good friend, Dr. Rasmussen," Hanson said. "Please keep us informed. You can communicate through me, if you like. I think you have my card. All of us here are intrigued, I dare say, by this story. But it is of much greater importance that misinformation being peddled through the blogosphere be challenged."

Kevin was not at all clear as to how Professor Hanson could effectively counter the version of Miss Lindstrom's death that now seemed to be spreading through Sweden and, for all he knew, much of Europe. But he agreed to stay in touch with Hanson, and expressed his appreciation that at least this sampling of the opera conferees was not reflexively anti-American.

The conversation drifted on to other subjects, and before long the six had left the case of Annika Lindstrom behind in favor of a spirited argument over several recent and highly controversial productions of old and familiar operas. On this subject, there was considerably more disagreement than there had been over the potential for mischief via blogging.

There were still plenty of kayaks on the Inderhavn when the small party settled their bar bill and headed across the Kalvebod Brygge for dinner in Tivoli. Kevin briefly considered placing a quick call to Carol for an update on the Lindstrom case, but remembered that back in upstate New York it was still early afternoon. No, he'd defer his call until later that night when he could reach Carol at home. Better that dinner conversation be about opera, something they all knew much more about than they did about the lives and deaths of Swedish exchange students in the United States.

CHAPTER 29

The ringing of the telephone early on Saturday morning startled Carol. She was in the process of pouring herself the first cup of coffee of the day, and a few drops of it landed on her hand rather than in the cup. Fortunately, no one was present in the kitchen to hear the expletive.

She had planned a leisurely morning, followed by a trip to the supermarket to stock Kevin's refrigerator, bread box, and cupboard for his Monday arrival back at the cottage. Now it looked as if trouble was brewing somewhere in Cumberland County and that her services were required. Kevin's call from Copenhagen the previous evening had put her in a good mood. It had lasted until exactly 7:30 the next morning.

"Good morning, Sheriff Kelleher," she said, trying to sound more cheerful than she felt. Why had she decided to be an accessible, neighborly sheriff by listing her home phone number in the white pages of the area's small phone book?

"I hope this isn't too early," the male voice said. "Would you like me to call back later?"

"Who's calling?" Carol asked, annoyed as she always was when a caller neglected to give a name.

"It's Brian Kershaw. Remember me?"

Annoyance was instantly replaced by interest. Intense interest. She had been intending to get in touch with Brian and arrange to see him. He had beaten her to the punch. Why? What had induced him to call her at home so early on a Saturday morning? He was about to graduate from high school; he was certainly old enough to know that one didn't phone strangers at an early hour on a weekend unless there was a good reason to do so. Of course she wasn't exactly a stranger. She had been in the Kershaw house several times within the past week. She was investigating the death of a young woman who had been staying with Brian's family until she disappeared just four months previously.

"Yes, of course. You surprised me. But I can talk now."

166

Carol corrected herself. "I would like to talk now. What is this about?"

"Can we meet somewhere? Not at my house. Probably not in Southport either. Whatever is convenient for you."

Very interesting.

"If you can give me time to get dressed, I'll meet you at the diner over in Yates Center. Can you be there by 8:15?"

"No problem."

Carol took a sip of the coffee and set it aside in favor of a quick shower. She would have her coffee and a bagel at the diner. There was no point in speculating on Brian's reason for the meeting. And for his insistence that it not take place at his home. Or even in Southport. That suggested that he didn't want members of his family to overhear what he had to say. Perhaps he didn't even want them to know that he had been in touch with the sheriff.

Kevin's impending arrival was all but forgotten as she drove the twenty-two miles down to the lake and over the hill to Yates Center. When she walked into the diner, Brian was already there, sitting in the booth furthest from the door. He spotted her before she spotted him, and was on his feet as she came down the aisle past the counter.

"I'm sorry to mess up your day off like this," he began, but she shook off his protest.

"You aren't messing up my day, Brian. I assume that we are here because there's something you want to tell me about Miss Lindstrom. Right now that's the most important thing on my agenda, so, please, no apologies."

Actually, Kevin was arguably the most important thing on her agenda, but he was still in Denmark and there would still be time to put the cottage in shape for his homecoming. At least there would still be time if what Brian had to tell her didn't require some immediate and time consuming action on her part.

"Have you had breakfast?" Carol asked. "I haven't, so I'm going to order coffee and a bagel. How about you?"

"Well, I did have something, but I'd be glad to join you. Could I have what you're having?"

Orders placed, they turned to the reason for their impromptu meeting.

"Do you remember that my family was all upset over a diary that Annika was keeping? The one that Dad found in Jen's room and said he'd trashed?"

"Yes, I do. I had the impression that your sister was irritated that your father had taken it. The two of them were having an argument about it when I was at your house to pick up Annika's belongings."

"I'm sure they were. You can't know my family very well, but we're an odd bunch. I don't know. Maybe that's too strong. I suppose lots of families quarrel. But we do a lot of quarreling. Dad and Mom do. And both of them argue with Jen all the time. We're none of us bad people, you know, but it can get kind of tense sometimes."

Brian had said nothing about whether he quarreled a lot with his parents or his sister.

"How about you? Do you join in these arguments or do you manage to stay out of it?"

"I try to stay out of the house as much as I can, but I guess I do my share of sounding off. It's hard to avoid it. Anyway, I'm not here to complain about my family. But I think you'll see why I had to meet you some place outside the house."

The coffee and bagels came, and Carol sat back and let Brian do the talking.

"It happened yesterday. I tried to reach you last night, but your line was busy. I thought it would keep until today."

Whatever it was had kept until the next day, but Brian obviously thought it important enough to try to reach the sheriff both on Friday night and again early on Saturday morning.

"My Mom has been busy getting ready for summer. She sort of does things like this every spring and fall. One of the things she does is go through the closets and send winter clothes to the dry cleaners. You know, the heavy stuff that we won't be wearing until it gets cold again in November or December. She'd sent out a lot of our stuff – mine, Jen's, Dad's, her own. She asked me to go down to the cleaners and pick it up after school yesterday. Which I did."

Carol was having trouble picturing where this account of Amanda Kershaw's routines was headed. But Brian would get to his point when he was ready.

"When I got there, they had several arm loads of clothing ready. Even helped me take it all to the car. But it seems they go through the pockets of everything before they dry clean it. Whatever they find, they put in a separate bag. Well, the bag contained all kinds of stuff – sales slips, coins, a couple of pens, small things like that. But the most important thing in the bag was a small pocket notebook. I'd heard enough arguing and name calling about Annika's diary that I was pretty sure that's what it was. I took a look at it, and it was in Swedish. At least it wasn't in English. I asked the man where he'd found it, and he showed me. It came from a deep inside pocket in one of Dad's winter jackets, one I hadn't seen him wearing in quite awhile."

"Do you have the diary with you?" Carol hoped that the rest of the story would not be about another round of argument when he reported the discovery of the diary to his family.

"Yes, I do. Here it is." Brian pulled the slim little notebook from his pants pocket and handed it to Carol.

"I take it you didn't tell your parents that you had the diary?"

"No way. I didn't tell Jen either. That would have caused a huge scene. Dad would have demanded I give it to him, so would my sister. Mom would have tried to mediate and she'd just have made a bad situation worse. Anyway, I knew you had been collecting all of Annika's things, and the diary was hers, so I figured you're the one who ought to have it."

God bless you, Brian Kershaw. Carol would be having a serious and potentially unpleasant conversation with the Kershaws about the diary, but she was hugely relieved to know that Brian had had the good sense not to mention it to his argumentative family.

"You did the right thing, Brian," she said. "It's quite possible that the diary doesn't tell us anything we don't already know. It certainly doesn't look much like a diary. But we'll get it translated and see what was on her mind when she wrote it."

Carol had no intention of studying the little booklet while she finished her bagel. A brief glance at it told her three things. First, it was very brief, no more than two and a half pages. Which meant that it was not really a diary at all. Second, it was in a foreign language, presumably Swedish. And third, it did mention names, six to be exact, one of which, Bob, was mentioned twice.

"You'll see your family before I will, and I'd appreciate it if you said nothing about finding this diary or whatever it is. I will call and make arrangements to meet with them right away, hopefully tomorrow if not today. And you should be present when

I talk with your parents and your sister. Now I know you have already explained why you wanted to meet with me. But we haven't had a real conversation since Annika's body was discovered, and I'd like to have a second cup of coffee and ask you a few questions. Okay?"

It would have been difficult for Brian to plead other business, and he didn't.

"What was your impression of Annika? I'm not looking for anything in particular. I'm just interested in how she struck you, what kind of person she was. In your eyes. After all, you lived in the same house with her for several months. You must have formed some opinion about her."

Carol had been prepared for an answer which was both respectful and nonspecific. But Brian surprised her.

"Funny, but I've thought a lot about that. About her. I think there were two Annikas. One was what everybody saw, you know, the self-impressed girl who figured she could do anything she wanted, have any guy she wanted. But my guess is that there was another Annika, just an insecure kid. Maybe I'm wrong. But there was something phony about her. I don't think any of us ever got to know the real Annika."

Carol was impressed. For all she knew, Brian was dead wrong, but his analysis was pretty sophisticated for a high school senior.

"Did you and she ever do things together?" She knew that Mrs. Kershaw had said that her son was interested, but that he had backed off because Annika had taken up with an older man, now identified as Eric Mackinson.

"I suppose half the seniors and juniors at Southport High thought about hooking up with her. So, sure, I thought about it. But you didn't ask Annika out, she asked you. I don't mean she actually asked guys to do things with her, but you know what I mean. She was in control. Know what I think? Maybe she didn't like me for a lot of reasons, but I think she figured it wasn't a smart idea to get involved with someone who lived in the same house she did – the son of the people who were her host family while she was living here. It would cramp her style, wouldn't it? Where would you go to make out?"

Brian hadn't mentioned Mackinson, so Carol brought up his name.

"As far as you know, did Annika date Eric Mackinson?"

"She did, and it became a big story around school. Nobody knew much about Mackinson until word got out that she was seeing him. All of a sudden everyone knew who he was. I'd never met him until he started hanging out during girls' soccer practice."

"Which brings up the matter of that party in January, the one when she disappeared. Did you see him that evening?"

"No, but Rickie said he did. Sort of hanging around on the edge of things. That's Rickie Lalor, one of my classmates."

"What do you remember about that night? My deputy and I have talked with just about everyone who was at that party except you. When was the last time you saw Annika?"

"It was a dull party. Just a bunch of kids roaming around, looking for booze, maybe a place to hook up. I left before eleven, so I can't tell you whether Annika was there later. I saw her last at Sue Marinelli's. She was with Rickie."

"What were they doing?"

"Just standing there on the back patio, talking. I remember thinking what a stupid picture they made. Rickie in his T-shirt, freezing his ass off, looking as if he was trying to crawl into Annika's coat."

"Did they go anywhere?"

"No idea. I was ready to go home, and I didn't really pay any attention to them."

In two minutes Carol had learned more about the party than she and Bridges had been able to coax out of the Southport students in several days. Assuming, that is, that Brian was a reliable source of information. He had sounded convincing. But why should she trust what he had told her? She knew no more about him than she did about anyone else.

"You were telling me about your impression of Annika," Carol continued. "How did she get along with the rest of your family?"

Brian had given no hint that he had to think carefully about his answers to the sheriff's questions. Now for the first time he seemed to hesitate.

"It was okay, most of the time," he said. "Mom worried a lot about how she was fitting in. But she's a worrier by nature. What bothered her most was Jen. My sister's not easy to get along with, and she'd decided that Annika was competition for the family's attention. Don't get me wrong, I like Jen, but she had a thing about Annika."

"And your Dad?"

Brian's hesitation lasted a bit longer this time.

"Dad and I have never been close. He's a good man, but he's – I don't know, sort of distant. I don't think I ever saw him talking with Annika. Except around the dinner table, of course. There was just once –" Brian stopped in mid-sentence, then left his unfinished thought there.

"Yes?" Carol asked. "There was just once. Once what?"

"It was nothing. Really nothing."

"Tell me about it anyway."

Brian Kershaw, who had been so willing to share his views about his family and their guest from Sweden, was having trouble when it came to his father.

"I mean it. It wasn't anything. But there was a day – actually it was one night – when I was on my way back to my room from brushing my teeth. Dad was in Annika's room. The door was open, and she was in her pjs. It looked like they'd been talking. He gave her a kiss on her forehead and then he left and headed down the hall to his room. He never saw me. I think she did, although she never mentioned it. But like I said, it was nothing. I shouldn't have mentioned it."

"What you mean is that your father was not displaying affection for Annika. He was just saying good night, like he would with you or Jennifer."

"That's what I meant."

"Brian, I know that this is an awkward subject. Please believe me when I say that I am not accusing your father of anything. But do you have any reason to believe that your father was interested in Annika in an inappropriate way?"

"Oh, no," he said in defense of his father. "He loves Mom. Besides, Annika was only 16. It never occurred to me that he had any bad thoughts about Annika."

Ah, Carol said to herself, I think you did wonder if he entertained such thoughts. You were probably wrong. But what is important is that you saw something which bothered you, something which didn't fit in your picture of your father as basically indifferent to your young house guest.

When the sheriff and Brian Kershaw went their separate

ways, Carol was feeling very grateful that her Saturday morning had been interrupted at an early hour by Brian's phone call. She would be paying the Kershaws another visit soon, if possible that very day. Right after she stopped by the Claymores to meet the unloved black sheep of the family, Roger Chase.

CHAPTER 30

She had seen many sisters who looked very much like each other. Likewise with brothers. But Carol did not think she had ever seen a sister and brother who resembled each other more than Helen Claymore and Roger Chase. The similarity of their features was remarkable.

As she and the Claymores had agreed, Carol had dropped by their cottage after lunch to meet Roger and be brought up to date on another of the keys to The Summer House. She expected it to be a very brief visit. Bud Harbaugh and Joe Cabot had unexpectedly copied their keys to the cottage, thereby complicating her search for the person who was responsible for Annika Lindstrom ending up in the Claymores' pump room. But Roger Chase would have had no reason to copy his key, and Carol viewed her trip to the Claymores as purely pro forma. Far more important would be her meeting with the Kershaws later that afternoon.

Nonetheless Carol accepted Helen's offer of a cup of tea and a piece of cake, which had apparently just emerged from the oven. She took a seat across from Roger and Barry, who occupied the living room couch, and immediately sensed that something was wrong. It wasn't what anybody said. Roger expressed his pleasure at meeting her, and the other hellos varied from cordial to better than perfunctory. But there was an unmistakable air of tension in the room, and neither Roger nor Barry was smiling.

Bill Claymore got straight to the point.

"I'm afraid that Roger forgot to bring his key to the cottage."

What he implied but didn't say was that he had made the importance of the key very clear and was more than a little upset that his brother-in-law had been so forgetful.

"Okay, Bill, I'm sorry. For the fourth time I'm sorry. You're going to change the locks anyway, so it hardly matters."

"That should prevent a repeat performance of what we've been through, but it doesn't explain how that girl got in here."

"But I've told you," Roger said, sounding exasperated, "I was nowhere near the cottage all winter. And I most emphatically did not kill anybody."

They had now gotten it out of their systems for the benefit of the sheriff. It didn't change the atmosphere in the room. While Bill and Roger continued to look grim, Barry looked as if he wished he were somewhere else. Anywhere else.

Helen reappeared with the tea and cake, and the gloom lifted momentarily, only to be replaced by silence all around as if it were impossible to enjoy the midday repast and talk at the same time.

Carol found the situation annoying, and finally said so.

"Excuse me, but I'm a little tired of this. Roger didn't bring his key with him. We all know that. What we don't know, or at least I don't know, is why everybody's so uptight. And I think it has to do with why Roger didn't bring his key."

She looked directly at Roger as she spoke.

"You haven't been in this cottage in several years. Isn't that right?" she asked. Roger nodded. "Now you've been invited and specifically told to bring your key because the Claymores are anxious about how that girl got into the place. You strike me as a perfectly intelligent man, so I'm sure you figured that the invitation to visit had something to do with the key. Yet you say you forgot. I don't believe you. I don't like to be rude, but I'm conducting a murder investigation and I don't like to be played for a fool. Why didn't you bring your key to the cottage?"

Roger gave Barry Claymore a surreptitious glance. Barry was staring at the floor.

"I think you can answer my question, Mr. Chase. And if you won't, I bet that Barry can." Carol knew from her days as a member of the bar that a lawyer should never ask a witness a question the answer to which she doesn't already know. She also knew that she didn't know the answer to the question she had just asked Roger. Nor did she know whether Barry knew the answer. But she thought she knew, and she hoped that the bluff would work. Perhaps she could add to the pressure by standing up, so that she could look down at the two men on the couch.

Carol stood up and took a step in their direction.

"I'm sorry, Barry," Roger said. "I guess a murder investigation trumps a promise of confidentiality."

Barry Claymore sank down into the cushions, but said nothing.

"You're right," Roger continued. "I didn't forget. I just didn't have a key to the cottage. I gave my key to Barry last fall."

"Now we may be getting somewhere," Carol said. "Why did you give Barry your key?"

"He couldn't find his, and he was worried about it. He knew his father would be upset if he asked for another key. It seems that Bill and Barry have had some trouble over the cottage, and a request for another key would have caused real trouble. So Barry asked me if he could have my key. He knew that I never came to the lake, so he thought it would be an easy way to avoid unpleasantness with his father. I mailed it to him a long time ago – last November, I think."

Bill Claymore said nothing. The expression on his face said volumes.

"Okay, Barry," Carol said, "it's your turn. Why couldn't you find your key, or maybe I should ask when did you realize that you'd lost it?"

"I can't remember just when it was. Sometime in the fall. Probably November, like Uncle Roger said. It just wasn't on my key ring."

"I don't understand. Do you think it just fell off the key ring?"

"That's what must have happened."

"Why don't you go get your key ring. I'd like to take another look at it."

Reluctantly, Barry went upstairs and half a minute later returned with the key ring, which he handed to the sheriff. She held it up so everyone could see it.

"This is what I'd call a very sturdy ring. I can't imagine a key falling off it. However, I can imagine someone taking a key off it. Did you have occasion to remove your cottage key from the key ring at some time last year?"

"I don't think so."

"That won't do, Barry. Think harder. Why might the key have been off the key ring?"

Unlike Bill and Helen Claymore, Carol knew that their son had visited the cottage when they were away. He had told her so the day his car had broken down. He had claimed that it had happened in the late summer. She had not believed him.

"Dad, I owe you an apology," Barry said reluctantly. "I'm very sorry I didn't tell you the whole truth at the time. I knew you didn't want me to use the cottage, and I didn't. Except the one time. It was just once. I promise I'll never do it again without your permission."

"What was so special about that one time?" Bill Claymore asked. Carol was surprised that his voice was so calm.

"It was after I'd started college. They were having their first party weekend, and I didn't have a date. I hadn't had a chance to get to know any girls yet. It was a nice weekend, so I drove back to the lake, and once I was here I stayed at the cottage. I knew I shouldn't, but – well, I hadn't thought it through, and I had to crash somewhere."

"I appreciate your candor, Barry," Carol said, relishing the irony. Without saying so, he had just admitted that he had lied to her about when he had used the cottage without permission. "But what does this have to do with losing your key?"

It was becoming increasingly clear that Barry Claymore's problem was larger than merely disregarding his father's instructions about use of the cottage.

"To tell you the truth, I'm not sure what happened to the key. I used it to let myself into the cottage when I got here on Friday evening, but after that I just don't know."

"I'm sure you understand that that isn't a satisfactory explanation," Carol said. "Let's think a little harder about it. What did you do that weekend?"

"I went sailing on Saturday, and there was a party that night. That's about it."

"Whom did you go sailing with?"

"A guy I knew from the summer, Rickie Lalor. And a friend of his named Stebbins."

"And the party? Who gave this party?"

"Some girl in Southport, a friend of Lalor's. I think it was Brenda Miles. No, it was Karen Leeds."

"And then what?"

"That's what I don't remember."

"You're saying that you went to this party and then – what? You blacked out? You fell asleep at the party and spent the night there? You drove back to the cottage?"

"I think I had too much to drink. I must have passed out, and one of the guys drove me home. To the cottage. I just don't recall anything until Sunday, when I got up and drove back to Ohio."

"You must have used your keys the day you left. Were they all there?"

"I don't know. I mean I didn't look to see. Why would I?"

"You'd have had to lock up the cottage," Carol said, trying not to sound impatient. "Was the cottage key on your key ring?"

Barry thought about it for a moment, then shook his head and once again said he didn't know.

"I wouldn't have needed the key. All you have to do is set it to lock, then pull the door shut behind you."

It was at that moment that for the first time since Carol's arrival Barry Claymore looked animated.

"Wait a minute," he said, the implication being that he'd just thought of something. "What if the guy who drove me home took it with him? That could explain why I lost it and why I needed to ask Uncle Roger for his key."

Very clever, Carol said to herself. This young man who's been lying to his parents and to me has just managed to shift attention to an unnamed somebody who had driven him to the cottage back in September. To somebody who acquired a key to the cottage that night. To somebody who might have used that key to get into the cottage in January and leave Annika Lindstrom's body there. Assuming, that is, that his story about getting drunk and needing a ride to the cottage was true, a big assumption.

"Who was it that drove you back to the cottage that night?"

"I have no idea. Like I said, I'd passed out." Barry was no longer saying he might have passed out and needed a ride. It had now become a fact.

"Would it be safe to say it was one of the people at the party?"

"I guess so."

"Okay, who was at the party? Who might have given you a lift?"

"A bunch of people. I didn't know most of them. It could have been Lalor. None of them was really a friend, but Rickie knew me best."

"Where was your car on Sunday morning?" Carol asked.

The question seemed to puzzle Barry.

"Where was it? Why, right behind the cottage, where I'd –"

The problem occurred to Barry some time after it had occurred to Carol.

"In other words," she said, "either you drove home by yourself on Saturday night or at least two people helped to bring you here after the party. One to drive your car, the other in a second car to take your good samaritan friend back to Southport."

"You're probably right," he said. "I mean about there being two cars. But I swear I didn't drive back by myself."

Carol decided not to torture Barry further. She knew that he'd catch it from his father after she left. Roger, in spite of his role in what had just transpired in the Claymore living room, was temporarily off the hook. What was important was that Barry had accomplished two things during that tense and unpleasant hour. He had done his best to cast suspicion on Rickie Lalor as Annika's killer, without, of course, ever even mentioning her death. But he had also done a pretty fair job of placing himself in a bad light. There had been the lies about his use of the cottage, and then the admission that he had been there in late September rather than during the summer. He had first told her that he had eventually found his key in an old pair of jeans. Now the story was that the key had been lifted from his key ring when he was too drunk to notice. Barry and the truth were strangers to each other.

Carol was even beginning to wonder if the business of too many keys to The Summer House would turn out to be a red herring.

CHAPTER 31

Instead of discussing Annika's 'diary' with the Kershaws on Saturday afternoon, Carol reverted to her original plan, which was to stock the larder at Kevin's cottage and otherwise ready the place for his return to the lake on Monday. She would have liked to confront the Kershaw family with the small notebook which the dry cleaner had discovered in Mr. Kershaw's jacket. But that could wait one more day, provided that Brian kept his promise not to mention it unless the sheriff was present.

By the time she had a chance to call the Kershaw residence, the family had scattered. Jennifer had gone to a neighboring town where the softball team was involved in a regional playoff game. Bob was at the country club playing golf with what Amanda called the rest of his usual foursome. Amanda herself was about to drive over to Geneva to meet an old friend and do some shopping. Brian, who would presumably be at the center of the brouhaha when Carol produced the notebook, was not in the house and he hadn't told his mother where he was going. A meeting was arranged for the following afternoon at two, and Mrs. Kershaw set off for Geneva still wondering what was on the sheriff's mind.

The delay gave Carol an opportunity not only to prepare for Kevin's homecoming, but to puzzle over the notebook more carefully than she had been able to do when Brian had handed it to her that morning. She sat down to do just that in Kevin's study after putting the groceries away.

The sky had clouded over, so that the afternoon sun had no opportunity to brighten the room. She found it necessary to turn on a light. She had already flipped the circuit breakers to start the refrigerator humming, and had finally figured out how to open the pipes and start the pump which brought water into the cottage from the lake. She was reminded, of course, of the fact that Mr. Claymore had had to perform the exact same task just a little more than a week ago, and that in the process of doing so he had made the macabre discovery in his own pump room. Kevin's cottage was of somewhat more recent vintage, which had made the task of opening the cottage less challenging. Nevertheless, and in spite of the fact that she looked forward to sharing the cottage with Kevin for the rest of the summer, she was glad that she didn't have to go through this seasonal ritual in her own home. Inevitably, these ruminations got her to thinking about the cottage as their home, if and when they got married. What would they have to do to make the cottage livable for all twelve months of the year? Then came the reality check. How could they live at the cottage for the entire year when he had to be down in the city meeting his classes and attending faculty meetings? What was it that she was saying to herself about marriage?

Carol turned her attention back to the diary. It had been less than a year ago that she had tried to make sense of another diary. Father Rafferty's notebook, like the one now before her, had not really been a diary. Certainly not in any conventional sense of the word. But it came much closer than the much smaller and much briefer document on Kevin's desk. This one was no larger than a middle sized envelope, and weighed barely more than one. It had a pale olive green cover and contained less than twenty pages. It more resembled something that one might use to make a list for grocery shopping. Unlike the Rafferty notebook, it looked like nothing she had seen in any store. Perhaps Annika had picked it up in Sweden.

Only two pages had been written on, two pages and two lines on a third page. It didn't look like a list – more like a single long paragraph. The handwriting offered no clue to the writer. It was reasonably neat, but hardly a good example of exemplary penmanship. What is more, it didn't look at all like the post card from Ohio. She assumed that it was Annika's, and in this case that was a fairly safe assumption. Carol didn't know Swedish, and would have been unable in any case to be absolutely sure that what she was looking at was Swedish. For all she knew, it could be Danish or Dutch or Czech. But it wasn't. It was Annika's, and it was written in Swedish.

Had it been in French or Spanish, Carol might have spotted enough words to make an intelligent guess as to what Annika had been writing about. But other than the six names, none of it made any sense. And she knew no one who could translate it, although somewhere in the county there would probably be someone who would be able to help.

The names posed no problem. Brian and Jen obviously referred to the two Kershaw children. And Amanda and Bob had to be Mr. and Mrs. Kershaw. Bob was mentioned twice. Then there was Ricki. Annika had known and had probably dated Rickie Lalor. Carol was willing to ignore the spelling, and unless there was another Rickie in her life, she was probably referring to Lalor. Following that logic, Michael was in all likelihood Michael Stebbins.

What did the names have in common? Four were members of the family she was staying with. The others were boys she had dated, and they seemed to be good buddies. The list, if it was a list in some sense of the word, seemed incomplete. Three boys, but only three. How about Barry? How about Eric? How about others she had almost certainly dated? And no girls, other than Jennifer Kershaw. What kind of a list would include the Kershaws and two other boys? The answer would probably be simple, but it didn't occur to Carol at the moment.

The sun came out from behind a cloud. Carol got up and went to the window. She stared, almost hypnotically, at the lake, her mind wandering from the notebook to the summer that lay ahead, a summer of swimming with Kevin, a summer of sleeping with Kevin. Even of solving the Lindstrom case with Kevin.

At no time since they had met had Carol ever slept over at the cottage when Kevin was not there. She had never given much thought to why, but it had become such an ingrained habit that only on rare occasions had she even considered doing otherwise. But on this afternoon in May, as the clouds vanished and the lake waters turned blue under a sunny sky, Carol made an impulsive decision. She'd sleep at the cottage that night. There was plenty of food on hand; she'd taken care of that herself. She went into the bedroom and quickly found what her memory told her was there – a nightie, a robe, and a change of underwear for the morning. The shelf in the bathroom cabinet which she had reserved for herself in summers past was similarly well stocked.

A smile on her face, Carol danced into the kitchen and took a bottle of Chardonnay from the fridge. Just two more nights, she said to herself as she pulled the cork.

CHAPTER 32

May 16th. Eleven days after the discovery of Annika Lindstrom's body. The day Kevin was due back at the lake. She had expected the hours to drag by at a snail's pace until he arrived. But it hadn't worked out that way.

Sunday's agenda had been modest, consisting of but one important task, the confrontation with the Kershaws. But to her surprise, there had been no fireworks when she produced Annika's 'diary.' Instead, she had spent less than an hour at the Kershaw house on Mountain View Road. Reflecting on it later, she realized that she shouldn't have been surprised.

The notebook had been found, not by a member of the family, but by someone at the dry cleaning establishment. Brian could hardly be criticized for turning it over to the sheriff. Mr. Kershaw had the most explaining to do, inasmuch as he had claimed to have tossed the notebook out with the trash. Much as he might have wished to have it back, he knew that that was impossible. So he did what Carol expected him to do. He said that he had intended to throw it out and thought he had done so. The person least likely to buy that argument was Jennifer, but all she could do at this point was to repeat her criticism of her father's invasion of her privacy.

There had, of course, been a lot of talk about what Annika might have written, but it was now Carol, not Jennifer or her father, who would be finding someone to translate those two pages. If either Jennifer or Mr. Kershaw was worried that the translation would prove embarrassing for them, there was nothing they could do about it.

The meeting with the Kershaws had been interesting less for what had been said than for the the body language with which the several members of the family had reacted to the news. Brian, of course, knew what was coming, and he obviously enjoyed watching those reactions. Mrs. Kershaw had been opaque throughout the meeting. Either she was better than the others at masking her emotions, or she was simply not as interested in the notebook. Mr. Kershaw had tried hard to put on a face which said 'I am indifferent.' Actually, he had tried too hard. When Carol produced the notebook, his face had registered shock. It lasted only for a fleeting moment before it disappeared, but it had been there. Jennifer, initially unhappy that her father had taken the notebook from her room, was now clearly worried that it was in the sheriff's hands. She had alternately nibbled on her finger nails and bitten at her lower lip. She was clearly worried about what Annika might have written.

Carol had promised that in due course she would let them know what their house guest had had to say in the notebook. In the meanwhile, the father and the daughter could keep right on worrying. Having taken care of that bit of investigative business, she went back to the cottage and made what for her was a strange decision as to how to spend the rest of the afternoon. She would listen to one of Kevin's operas. He had tried, albeit gently, to interest her in his academic subject and his other love. He had even tried to stage an opera at Brae Loch College, and had done so in part because he thought it might lead to a visiting appointment at the college, thereby giving the two of them an entire year together at the cottage. Another of the murders which had afflicted Crooked Lake recently brought an end to that plan, but not to Kevin's efforts to turn her into a fellow lover of opera.

Carol still preferred blue grass. But she wanted to share Kevin's interests, so she spent awhile looking at his collection and reading the liner notes which told the stories and commented on the music. She finally settled on *Rigoletto*. It was an opera she had heard of, and she knew that Kevin was fond of Verdi. Fond enough to go to Copenhagen to deliver a paper on an opera that Verdi had wanted to compose but never got around to writing.

To her surprise, she liked it. The overture promised excitement, and the opening scene was full of music with a pulse which grabbed her attention and led her to pick up the libretto, the better to follow the plot. As the opera unfolded, she realized that she had actually heard some of the tunes. Kevin would have called them arias, but whatever the proper name, they were tuneful. Carol was hooked, at least on this particular opera. By the time it had come to its tragic conclusion, with Monterone's curse on the eponymous hero fulfilled, the sun was setting. Carol had not once looked at her watch. When she finally did, it told her that Kevin had arrived back in the city from Copenhagen. And that there were fewer than 24 hours before he would be joining her at the cottage.

He should probably take another day to overcome jet lag and pack properly before setting off for the lake. But she knew that he wouldn't dream of it. And she didn't want him to.

Monday went by as rapidly as Sunday had. Carol had paid too little attention to the source of the date rape drug, having turned the matter over to Bridges. After morning roll call, Sam gave her a detailed report on the state of his efforts to identify someone who had been peddling Rohypnol in Cumberland County. The report may have been detailed, but it was inconclusive. Sam had talked with several people who had been known to sell drugs; a couple of them had actually done a little time. They weren't helpful. He had spent time with school officials who monitored such things, and while he learned quite a bit about the inroads which pot and even coke had made among the youth of Southport, he learned nothing about Rohypnol. It wasn't easy, but he had actually picked up the names of several high school students who were known to be into drugs. With the exception of one cocky kid named Schuster, they all acted innocent and declined to be drawn into a discussion of the matter. Schuster was willing to admit what he'd been taking, rattling off a list of drugs, some of which Sam had never heard of. But he had nothing to say about where he had acquired them. Before they were through with it, Sam concluded, Schuster might have to be subpoenaed. Schuster and who knew how many others.

Carol would have liked to believe that a drug dealer would help them identify the person responsible for Annika's death. But she doubted that that's what would happen. It was more likely that they would find Annika's killer by other means, and that the guilty party would then tell them from whom he had obtained the Rohypnol.

A particularly full in-basket of matters unrelated to the Lindstrom case occupied the better part of three hours, and she spent another hour trying to talk Officer Byrnes out of quitting the force. She would miss each of her officers should they move away or decide to take another job. But Byrnes was special in ways she had not fully appreciated until they sat down in the squad room to discuss an offer he had received from a company that designed web sites. When their meeting ended, nothing had been decided.

But he had agreed to give it more thought.

Carol checked her watch. It was 2:55. She hadn't even had lunch. It was while she was debating whether to duck out for a bite that it occurred to her that Kevin would now be only about an hour and a half or less from the lake. No need to spoil dinner by having a late lunch. In fact, no need to spend more time at the office. She rarely called it a day so early, but this was a special occasion. What is more, she rationalized, she had put in a lot of extra hours recently. She cleared her desk, gave Sam a heads up, and told Ms. Franks where she could be reached.

Forty-five minutes later she was back at the cottage. She had traded her uniform for jeans and a favorite wool sweater, and put up a crude, hand written sign that said 'Welcome Home' on the back door.

Kevin announced himself with a beep on the car horn as he pulled in behind the cottage. She met him at the door with a warm hug which reminded him that in addition to all of her other attributes, Carol was physically strong.

They exchanged kisses for the better part of a minute until Kevin disengaged himself and suggested that they might want to resume snuggling inside, away from the prying eyes of his neighbors.

Carol brushed aside his protests and brought his luggage in from the car. He was checking out the contents of the fridge and the cupboards when she came in with the last of his things, a lap top and a small shopping bag.

"Why all the stuff?"

"I didn't want to take the time to pack smart. That's the nice thing about driving. You can throw everything into the car and not worry about whether it'll fit into the overhead bin."

He picked up the shopping bag, and emptied it on the kitchen table.

"I needed a couple of good knives, and Denmark makes good knives. Here's a little something that caught my eye the other day."

He picked up a small box and handed it to Carol.

"You need to wear things like this," he said. "probably not when you're in uniform, but they'll look great with that burgundy jacket of yours."

She was looking at a pair of unusual gold earrings. No

words were necessary. She gave Kevin another hug and went down the hall to the bathroom to put them on.

"What do you think?" she said, obviously delighted.

"I think I made a good choice. Found them in a museum shop. They were designed with you in mind."

"I was going to ask how you found time to do any shopping, but I can hardly complain, can I?"

"I've got a lot to tell you about Copenhagen. And I'm sure you've got a lot to tell me about this Lindstrom woman. When's our dinner reservation?"

"5:45. I never did get around to lunch, so I thought it'd be a good idea to have an early dinner."

"Neither did I. Hate those thruway stops. So let's not talk Copenhagen or murder until we get to The Cedar Post and they bring us our wine. Let me freshen up and we'll be off. I'll bet they'll take us even if we're a bit early."

The Cedar Post hadn't changed. It looked just as it had when they'd had their last dinner there the previous fall. As a matter of fact, it looked just as it had ten, even fifteen years earlier. The decor – or lack thereof – was familiar. Kevin was prepared to swear that some of the bottles behind the bar had been there when he first met Carol. Orders for those liqueurs were rare. For all he knew, such orders were nonexistent. He wondered whether the liqueurs improved with age the way bourbon and cognac did. Even some of the faces in The Post, particularly those sitting at the bar, looked familiar. He had the wild thought that some of these locals might have endowed bar stools.

Carol had been frequenting the place for so long that the hostess knew exactly which table she preferred. So it was that at close to half past five they took their accustomed seats in a corner of the restaurant, ordered two glasses of Chardonnay, and began to play catch up.

"Let's talk about Copenhagen," Carol said. "You've been there for three days. I've been wrestling with the death of Annika Lindstrom for a week and a half, and it will take me more than a single evening to brief you on the dramatis personnae involved in the case."

"No problem, as long as you aren't trying to keep me at arm's length from your latest murder. And by the way, you probably won't believe this, but while I was at the conference I actually spent the better part of an hour talking about Miss Lindstrom and what happened to her."

"You did?" Carol was genuinely surprised. "I thought we'd agreed that you were going to concentrate on Verdi."

"So did I. But one evening a few of us were sitting on the patio of my hotel, enjoying a drink, when a Swedish chap mentioned that some blogger had been writing about the death of a Swedish girl over here in the States."

"He brought it up himself? You didn't raise the subject?"

"I most certainly did not. Seems this blogger has acquired quite a reputation as a critic of the US of A. Somehow he'd heard about a Swedish girl who was living over here and had been raped and murdered. We started talking about this guy's anti-American blog, and I realized that the case sounded like yours. It didn't take but a few minutes to realize that that's just what the blog was about."

"But I told you about the Lindstrom girl. She wasn't raped, and we're not even sure she was murdered."

"I know, and when I realized that I knew about the case we were discussing, that's what I told them. My Swedish colleague had no idea where the blogger got his information, or misinformation. But he's been using the case to trump up anti-American sentiment, claiming that we're a lawless country that treats our foreign guests badly."

"That's terrible. Why didn't you tell me this?"

"I thought about it, but figured it would just get you all worked up. There wasn't anything you could have done about it, so I decided it could keep until I got back."

"I can't imagine where this blogger got his information. It doesn't sound like anything Annika Lindstrom's parents would have given out to the press. They might well have arranged for an obit in the local paper. But somehow I can't imagine them saying that Annika had been murdered. And raped. I can understand that they might have assumed she'd been murdered, but I told Mrs. Lindstrom specifically that she wasn't raped."

"But you've never met the woman. Do you really know anything about her? How stable she is? How she felt about her daughter coming over here in the first place?"

"All I know is that she's bedridden, and has been since a bad car accident some years ago. And that she admits that she and her husband hadn't been all that close to their daughter. But nothing in my brief conversations with her suggests that she would make up a story like the one on this blog."

"I think I'm beginning to regret that I didn't go over to Malmo and try to meet with Mrs. Lindstrom," Kevin said.

Carol shook her head.

"I don't think that would have been a good idea. You didn't know enough about the case, and odds are she had nothing to do with the misinformation on the blog. It would just have upset her. Maybe she doesn't know about it. Let's hope so."

"Anyway, what bothered me most when I heard about it was the hostility to the United States in this guy's blog. It was as if Lindstrom's death is just one more piece of evidence, if any more were needed, about what a dreadful society we have over here."

"Let's hope most Swedes think he's a crank and ignore him. On the other hand, we do have our share of not very savory characters, even on Crooked Lake. Do you realize that this is the sixth murder – if it is a murder – we've had in my jurisdiction in less than four years? And you know as well as I do that compared with most other civilized countries we have a terribly high rate of incarceration. Not to mention a fixation with guns that mystifies our friends overseas."

The conversation gradually turned to other things, such as how his paper on Verdi's non-opera had been received, the sights and sounds of Copenhagen, and how much better the food was at The Cedar Post than it had been on the flights to and from Europe. By the time coffee was served, they both knew it was time to talk about the Lindstrom case. Except that Kevin had run out of steam.

"While I was driving up to the lake I imagined us doing three things tonight," he said. "I'd report on the conference, you'd tell me all about this Swedish exchange student, and we'd be sharing a bed again. I'm going to have to take a pass on your case, much as I want to hear about it. I always thought jet lag wasn't so bad when you're flying east to west, but I'm bushed. Let's do it tomorrow when I'm not just pretending to be awake."

"Of course. I couldn't do justice to all that's happened, even if you weren't tired. And don't worry about sharing the bed. It's all made up, just waiting for us. But tonight I'll let you sleep. Just tonight, though. Okay?"

"Thanks. Now, will you drive me home?"

CHAPTER 33

"Come on, get up!" Carol ordered as she shook Kevin awake.

"What?" He pulled himself up onto an elbow and stared in Carol's direction, his eyes not yet in focus.

"You heard me. I have to get to work, and I'm not about to walk out without a good-bye kiss on our first morning of the summer."

"You have to go now?"

"If you get a move on, I'll join you for breakfast. It's ready, keeping warm in the oven. I'll give you three minutes to visit the bathroom and run a comb through your hair. Three minutes max."

Kevin crawled out of bed, located his bathrobe, and disappeared down the hall. He got back to the breakfast table in just under three minutes, still looking half asleep.

"You're welcome to go back to bed after I go, but I wasn't going to leave with just a note for you. You went to sleep so fast last night that we never got around to talking about what we'd be doing today."

Kevin stared at his pancakes.

"Have some coffee," she said. "And don't let those things get cold. I went to a lot of trouble to make you a nice breakfast."

"Sorry about last night."

"That was then, now is now. Eat your breakfast."

Kevin made a conscious effort to shake off the cobwebs and tackled the pancakes.

"I think I may finally have your attention," Carol said. "So let me tell you what's up. I'm off to the office, and I expect to be busy big time until five, five-thirty. There's a copy of the *Gazette* on your desk. It'll give you a very rough idea of what happened to Miss Lindstrom, but it's already dated and doesn't say anything about my major worry, all those keys to the Claymore cottage. You won't get any idea from it who might have been responsible for the girl's death. They don't have the staff do any investigative reporting, so what they print is mostly what my office tells them.

190

And we're not saying much. Not yet. If you'll make supper, I'll bring you up to date on what we've learned and what we still don't know. That is if you don't fall asleep on me again."

"I'll be fine," Kevin said as he poured some more maple syrup on his pancakes. "There's a lot to do around here. I'll probably have to wait until Mike Snyder's available before putting the dock in, but I want to get started on making the place look like summer's here. I need an oil change and have to get the tires rotated, which means a trip to Yates Center. How about my hair? Do I need a cut?"

Carol had gotten up to put her dishes in the sink. She came up behind him and ran her fingers through his hair.

"It's your call. It looks good to me, but get a trim if you like. Just don't do something stupid like a Mohawk."

"Are you kidding? Me, a self-respecting academic with a Mohawk?"

"I just wanted to be sure you knew my limits. Anyway, I've got to be off."

She leaned over and gave Kevin a kiss. And then she was gone.

Kevin resisted the temptation to go back to bed, and after cleaning up the kitchen and unpacking set off on his round of errands. As he had anticipated, it took him the better part of the day to do all that he needed to do. The decision about what they'd have for supper had been made for him by what he found in the fridge and the cupboard. He was just putting the finishing touches on a Greek salad when Carol drove up at 5:40.

"How's it feel to be back?" she asked as she shed her gun holster.

"Better now that you're here," he said. "Of course, I'm not sure I'm ready for spaghetti and meatballs after living on a diet of smorrebrodsmad for several days."

"Are you trying to impress me with your knowledge of Danish cuisine, or is it your command of the language?"

"Okay, I'm showing off. But it's really good – roast beef and horseradish sauce on rye bread."

"We can get that at the deli in Southport, and we call it a roast beef sandwich."

"Very clever, Carol. Anyway, the Danes do it better. By the way, I'm not knocking spaghetti. You did a great job of shopping

– looks like we have enough food on hand for at least a week."

"It was in my interest, too, inasmuch as I'm taking my meals at the cottage."

Time for another in a series of welcome home kisses.

"I want to hear about the Lindstrom case," Kevin said as he put the last of the supper dishes in the dishwasher. "Only the details, of course. Are you close to wrapping it up?"

"I have the feeling I've barely gotten started. Every day seems to bring some new wrinkle I hadn't anticipated. The key to the case still seems to be keys – of which there are too many."

"I like that. Keys are the key. Tell me about it."

"Like I told you, the problem is that the body got into the Claymore cottage because somebody had a key. And as it turns out, several somebodies had a key. There are just too many keys."

"But all those keys don't explain how she ended up dead, which seems to have been a precondition for sticking her in the cottage."

"I know. But whoever was responsible for her death had to have had a key to the cottage. By my calculation – subject to tomorrow's new wrinkle – there are at least eight keys. Are you up to hearing the names of people you don't know, people who had those keys?"

"Sure. I've got a pretty good short term memory. I think I can keep track of eight people, even if I've never heard of them before."

"Here goes then. There are the Claymores, Bill and Helen. He teaches at a university in New Jersey, and they spend their summers at the lake."

"What does he teach?" Kevin interrupted.

"I don't know, but I very much doubt that it's opera. Their son, Barry, also has a key, and here it gets interesting. He's just finished his freshman year at a college in Ohio. But his parents don't want him using the cottage in their absence. Seems he and some friends trashed it once, and his Dad laid down the law to him. Barry ignored Dad's instructions last fall, however, and spent a weekend at the cottage. Trouble is, the key he used to get into the cottage disappeared. Let me get back to that in a minute. To cover his tracks, he got Helen Claymore's ne'er-do-well brother Roger to give him his key. Got that? So now Barry once again has a key, or did until I took it off his hands."

"This guy Barry sounds like a slippery character. He's one of your suspects?"

"I don't have suspects yet. Nor do I know whether slippery is the appropriate adjective. He has definitely lied to both me and his father. Anyway, that's four of the keys. Two others belong to neighbors of the Claymores named Cabot. They keep an eye on the Claymore cottage over the winter, and have a key just in case. But sometime this last winter they made a copy of their key for what sounds like an innocent reason. Which makes two keys for the Cabots. But like Barry, they seem to have misplaced one of their keys. I've got to have a sit-down with Joe Cabot about that key."

"You've accounted for six keys so far, and two of them can't be accounted for. That sounds confusing, but you know what I mean."

"I do. I'll get back to the missing keys in a minute, but first those other two. Seems the Claymores had a contractor named Harbaugh doing some work on their upstairs bathroom last fall. He had a key, and wouldn't you know, he had an extra made so a subcontractor could paint the bathroom. The sub's name is Eric Mackinson, and he admits he had a key. 'Had' because I relieved him of his key just as I did Barry Claymore."

"Sounds like keys multiply up here during the off-season. The Cabots make a duplicate. The contractor makes a duplicate. Barry Claymore doesn't make a duplicate, but he does the equivalent – he gets a relative to give him a key to replace one he lost. I'll bet the Claymores aren't very happy about this."

"You're right, and I don't blame them. It makes my job that much tougher, too."

"You were going to tell me about the Claymore's son losing a key."

"It's one of those important wrinkles, not least because that missing key may also have somehow turned into two keys, or who knows how many. Barry had a hard time getting his story straight, and I'm still not sure what the final version is. But he thinks he may have gotten drunk at a party the night he was here back in September and had to be driven home. Which leads to the possibility that whoever drove him home took the key to the Claymore cottage with him."

"Do you believe this?"

"My next order of business is going to be talking with a couple of guys Barry knows in Southport, guys that could have driven him home. But you see why my problem is too many keys."

"Too many keys and another problem, if I understand what you've told me. If I recall correctly, your forensics guy thinks the Lindstrom girl was set up for a rape – you know, the drug and the alcohol. In other words, somebody wanted sex which he didn't think she'd consent to, but he got much more than he'd bargained for. No sex and a dead woman on his hands. You've met all these people with keys. As far as you know, did any of them have a relationship with Lindstrom?"

"I know that two of them had dated her. Mackinson, the painter who had worked on the Claymore cottage, saw her back in the fall. That relationship ended, according to his mother, leaving Annika angry with Mackinson. Barry Claymore denies a relationship with Annika, but two Southport High School guys have told us that he dated her back in September. They make a good case, and I'm sure Barry will eventually admit it.

"Mackinson is in his twenties, and Barry's just started college. The other men are older. I'm pretty sure Harbaugh's not going to become a suspect. I keep missing Cabot, so I'll reserve judgment until I've talked to him. But what if an acquaintance of Barry's did take his key? And what if he had dated Annika? That's about it, except for Bob Kershaw, and I have a hard time imagining him in any kind of relationship with Annika. Not to mention that he doesn't have a key to the Claymore cottage."

"Who's Kershaw?" Kevin asked.

"Lindstrom was staying with the Kershaws. I wouldn't even have mentioned his name, except for the fact that he's been more than casually interested in a a small diary Annika was keeping. I don't have any idea what it's about, but he's mentioned in it a couple of times."

"Why the mystery?" Kevin asked.

Carol chuckled.

"It's in Swedish. Nobody reads Swedish, so everyone's worried about what all those strange words might be saying about them. Ironic, but we're also interested in something else that Annika wrote. Or didn't write. After she disappeared last January, the Kershaws got a post card from Ohio telling them not to worry,

194

that she was okay. But I'm certain she didn't write that card. Or that she was ever in Ohio."

"Wait a minute," Kevin said. "Didn't you mention that Barry Claymore was in college in Ohio? Doesn't that suggest that he was the one who wrote the post card, pretending to be Lindstrom?"

Carol was about to challenge him when Kevin interrupted.

"No, that doesn't make sense. More likely that someone else wrote the card and sent it from Ohio to cast suspicion on Barry."

"You're playing detective again, aren't you?" Carol said. "Your logic is okay, but don't you have trouble visualizing someone going all the way to Ohio just to mail a post card?"

"Not if it would shift suspicion for Lindstrom's death to someone else, in this case Barry Claymore."

"You're incorrigible, do you know that? You've been back for little more than 24 hours and you're already involving yourself in my investigation."

"All I'm doing is turning your story of the Lindstrom case into a two-way conversation, Carol. You wouldn't want me just to sit here passively, would you?"

"I don't think it would matter what I wanted. But no, I don't want you to be passive. In any event, I'm not sure you could be. I've seen too much evidence to the contrary. I think you know what I mean."

Kevin knew exactly what she meant. The rest of the story of Annika Lindstrom's untimely death might have to be postponed until tomorrow.

CHAPTER 34

Carol's story about Annika Lindstrom's diary – or whatever it was – came to mind during the night when Kevin awoke with a cramp in his leg. The cramp disappeared quickly, but the diary remained on his mind until he fell asleep ten minutes later. Kevin had always had trouble remembering dreams. He could remember having them, but was rarely able to recall what they were about. He had no trouble recalling the story of the diary or the thoughts it had inspired in the middle of the night. As a consequence, he brought up the subject over breakfast.

"There's something I'd like you to do today," he told Carol as he spread jam on his toast.

"Always glad to be of help, provided it doesn't interfere with my official duties."

"Not only won't it interfere. It will make your duties easier. I'd like you to make a copy of Miss Lindstrom's mini-diary. Just what she wrote. What was it, a little over two pages? I can come out to your office and pick it up. It could wait until tomorrow if necessary, but I'd like to do something with it, and the sooner the better."

Carol set her coffee cup down and put on what she thought of as her stern face.

"So this is how it's to be," she said. "You aren't going to be satisfied to get me into the sack. You want to be in on the action while I track down whoever's responsible for Miss Lindstrom's death."

"But of course. Did you ever imagine that I was going to keep house all summer while you rounded up criminals?"

"Why don't you tell me about this great idea of yours."

"It's not a great idea. Really. All I'm proposing is a short cut. You told me you need to get the Lindstrom girl's diary translated so you'll know why the Kershaw family's so worried about it. I doubt you have a lot of Swedish speakers on the force. But I have a good friend on the Madison College faculty who is Swedish, and I know she'll be happy to provide a quick translation, free of charge. What do you say?"

"I could say that I'll tap into my vast circle of Scandinavian friends and get the diary translated without your help. But you wouldn't believe me. Okay, you can call on your friend. Who is she, by the way?"

It momentarily crossed Kevin's mind that Carol might be wondering if this woman was more than a faculty colleague.

"Her name's Ingrid Cohen. She teaches lit."

"Cohen? That doesn't sound very Swedish to me."

"It's her married name. I have no idea what her maiden name was, but I can assure you that she hails from Sweden. She's always talking about visits with family back in Norrkoping."

"Okay. I think Ms. Franks could run off a copy of the diary in ten seconds."

"Why don't I drive out to your office and pick it up. That way I could start the ball rolling today."

"It'll be ready no later than 9:30. I'm assuming you'll be dressed by that time."

"Bet I'll be ready before you are," Kevin said, pushing away from the breakfast table. Two minutes later the shower was running.

It was shortly after ten when Kevin punched in Ingrid Cohen's phone number. He studied the copy of the diary while the phone rang in his ear. As Carol had said, it didn't look like a diary. But it would pose no challenge for Ingrid. Provided that she was at home, not off to Norrkoping or some more exotic spot across the Atlantic.

Five rings into the call, a woman's voice said good morning and announced that she was Professor Cohen.

"Ingrid, hi. This is Kevin Whitman. So glad to have caught you. I was afraid you might have abandoned the city, just like I have."

"Oh, hello, Kevin. No, I have no immediate travel plans, just some lazy days to make up for all those end of term papers. To what do I owe the pleasure?"

"I have a small favor to ask. I need something translated. It's very short, shouldn't take long at all. But I don't read Swedish. If you'd be willing to do it, I could fax it to you today. Do you have a fax machine?"

"Of course I'll do it, and I do have a fax machine. But I must say I'm surprised. Off hand I don't know any Swedish operas. Somehow that's an art form that never really made it across the Baltic."

"I could suggest a few Russian composers, but that isn't the point. This doesn't have anything to do with opera. We've got a problem up here in the Finger Lakes where I spend my summers. Seems a Swedish exchange student died in strange circumstances. She left what could called be a mini-diary, only about two pages long, that might help explain what happened to her. I was hoping you could give us a hand."

"Now I'm surprised all over again. What accounts for your involvement with a Swedish exchange student?"

"I never met the girl, but the local sheriff is a friend of mine. We got to talking about it, and it occurred to me that you might be able to help out."

"I'd be delighted to translate for you. I wish it didn't have to do with the death of a student. An exchange student at that. How sad."

"What makes it worse is that some blogger in Sweden has used her death to indict American culture."

Kevin explained his recent trip to Copenhagen and what he had heard about the blog from a Swedish colleague.

"I can be as critical of this country as anyone, but that strikes me as more than a bit unfair. Sweden's hands aren't clean either, if you think about it. Whose are? Anyway, I'll get back to you right away. Got a pen handy to take down my fax number?"

He did, and Ingrid gave it to him.

"Why don't you e-mail me your translation," Kevin said. They exchanged e-mail addresses and the conversation drifted off to other matters for a few minutes. It was Ingrid who finally had to plead other business.

"Sorry to cut you off, but I'm meeting someone. You be sure to let me know whether the diary offers any clues to what happened to this student."

"Thanks, Ingrid. I'll stay in touch."

As promised, Kevin promptly sent the copy of the diary off to the city. There were many things which might have commanded his attention during the rest of this Wednesday in mid-May. But he chose to concentrate on what he had learned from Carol the previous evening about the Lindstrom case. Somewhere in all those names and all those references to keys there would be something which had his name written on it, something which he could be doing to help move Carol's investigation along. As was his wont, both at the college and at the cottage, he settled down at his desk, pulled out a yellow pad and a pen, and began to brainstorm.

CHAPTER 35

Instead of going directly to the office on Wednesday, Carol drove to Southport. She wanted to talk with the pharmacist about the pills which Annika had been taking. She was familiar with a couple of them, but had no idea what the others were for. It was a conversation she should have had earlier, but it had become more urgent since Doc Crawford had found evidence of Rohypnol in Annika's system. It was highly unlikely that what was in the one unlabeled bottle was the date rape drug. Why would Annika have it in her possession? But Carol had to be sure.

The pharmacist was temporarily out, so she left the bottles with a hastily scribbled note, told the clerk that they were important to a criminal case she was working on, and set out for Cumberland. As she circled the town square, she spotted a young man who looked familiar coming out of the coffee shop. It took a moment to place him. He had been identified for her by Betty Engelman at the memorial service for Annika Lindstrom. His name was Rickie Lalor.

Carol pulled over to the curb, rolled down the window, and called out to him.

"Mr. Lalor?"

His turned in his tracks, a puzzled look on his face.

"Over here," she said. "I'd like to talk with you."

He paused, then slowly retraced his steps until he came along side the official car.

"You're from the sheriff's department?"

It was a pretty good guess inasmuch as it said so on the door panel.

"I am the sheriff," Carol said. "Come on, hop in."

Lalor looked around, trying to make sure that no one he knew could see him as he climbed into the sheriff's car.

"What's this about?" he asked.

"I think I should be asking you the first question," she said. "This is a school day, and it looks like you aren't in school. How come?"

"Oh, that," he said, visibly relaxing. "I'm graduating in about three weeks, and nothing much happens at the end of your senior year. I've already been admitted to Syracuse, so I can afford to coast. How come you're rounding up truants today?"

"I'm not rounding up truants. You should be in school, but that's between you, your parents, and the principal. I thought I'd take advantage of the fact that you're skipping school to ask you a few questions."

"How did you know who I am?"

A reasonable question, Carol thought.

"Two reasons. My colleague questioned you several days ago, and he gave me a pretty good description. Better yet, you were pointed out to me at the memorial service for Annika Lindstrom. So I know quite a bit about you even if we haven't met. By the way, congratulations on your admission to Syracuse. Are you going out for the football team this fall?"

"I doubt it. They'd tell me I'm too small or too slow. I don't kid myself. Southport High isn't where they recruit guys for Division 1A schools."

Preliminaries out of the way, Carol got down to business.

"I know that Officer Bridges talked with you about Annika Lindstrom. I'd like to ask you about Barry Claymore. It's my understanding that both you and Barry went out with Miss Lindstrom. Let's go back to last fall. Claymore was in college out in Ohio, but he came back to Crooked Lake one weekend in September. While he was here, he went sailing with you and Annika and – well, to put it bluntly, he hit it off with Annika. Where did you stay while he was here that weekend?"

"At his parents' cottage, I assume."

"You assume. You're not sure?"

"It's the logical place, isn't it? I mean, he didn't stay at my house, and I'm sure the family Annika was staying with wouldn't have let him stay there. Why, does it matter?"

"It matters because Barry thinks he may have gotten drunk at a party and needed to be taken home, meaning the cottage. Did you drive him back to his parents' cottage?"

Rickie moistened his lip as he thought about the sheriff's question.

"Yeah, I may have. That was a long time ago. It's hard to remember just what everyone did."

"So, I'm right that there was a party that weekend. A party at which people could have gotten sloshed."

"Probably."

"Probably what?" Carol asked, trying to keep her frustration under control. "That there was a party or that people got sloshed?"

"Both. There was a party, I'm sure of that. And I think Barry was drunk."

"And you drove him to the cottage."

"It must have been me or Michael."

"Who's that?" Carol was sure he was referring to Michael Stebbins. But she was interested in how Rickie would characterize the relationship.

"Michael Stebbins. He's a friend of mine. He knew Barry, too. Maybe he drove Barry home."

"Or you did."

Rickie looked out the car window, away from the sheriff.

"Now that I think about it, both of us must have gone with him. I think Michael drove Barry's car, and I drove my own car. That's because we had to get back to Southport. I guess it's a good thing we didn't run into you people. You know, the police. We must have been – what did you call it, sloshed? I don't need a DUI on my record."

"No, it's not a good idea. What's worse, you could end up in a hospital, maybe the morgue."

Whether his memory had clicked in or he'd decided to tell the truth, Rickie Lalor was now being more forthcoming. She doubted that he'd be as candid regarding the key.

"I've had a long talk with Barry," Carol said, "and he tells me that he lost the key to his parents' cottage. He thinks it happened that weekend we've been talking about, the party weekend back in September. Did he say anything to you about losing the key?"

"Not that I remember. But I don't see how he could have lost his key. He couldn't have used the cottage if he didn't have it."

"He was drunk, so I assume you or Michael had to open the cottage and let him in. Did you put him to bed?"

"Something like that. It's kinda coming back to me. He was out of it, so we carried him upstairs and dumped him in one of the bedrooms."

"You understand that it's important that I get this straight," Carol said. "You unlocked the cottage, got Barry into his bed, and then came back to Southport. What did you do with the key to the cottage?"

Rickie frowned.

"The key? We left it there, of course. I think Michael put Barry's key ring on the kitchen table where he couldn't miss it in the morning."

"There's no chance the cottage key came off the key ring while you guys were taking care of Barry?"

"I can't imagine why," he said. "Anyway, it must have been there. Barry would have needed it in the morning when he left."

"Not necessarily. You can lock most doors from the inside and then just pull them shut."

"Why is the key such a problem?" Rickie asked.

Surely this young man, already admitted to Syracuse University, would know the answer to his question if he had been paying any attention to the news about the discovery of Annika's body.

"Would you like to hazard a guess?"

"It seems to me that it wouldn't be hard to get a replacement. His parents obviously have a key and could easily make a copy for him."

"Yes," Carol said, "that's very true. But what if in the meanwhile the lost key found its way into the hands of whoever put Annika's body in the Claymores' cellar?"

"Oh, I see," Rickie said. He looked pensive. "Do you suppose Barry never lost his key, just said he did?"

"Why would he do that?"

"Don't get me wrong. Barry's a friend, sort of, and I'm not accusing him of anything. But think about it. What if he killed Annika? Claiming he didn't have a key to the cottage would pretty much let him off the hook, wouldn't it?"

"Is that what you think happened?" Carol asked.

"No, of course not. But it makes sense in a crazy sort of way."

"But only if Barry lied about losing the key. I have to assume that he may be telling the truth. In which case, I have to keep looking for someone else who had a key to the Claymore cottage. And that is why I must ask you if you kept Barry's key after you put him to bed that night."

Rickie Lalor was no longer looking out the car window. He was looking directly at the sheriff.

"That is absolutely ridiculous. Why on earth would I want the key to Barry's cottage? So I could put Annika in the cellar? Good God, what kind of a monster do you think I am? I don't have a key to the Claymore cottage, and I didn't kill Annika. She was a good friend."

"There's no need to get excited, Mr. Lalor. I didn't say you killed Annika Lindstrom. Or that you kept Barry's key. The one thing – at the moment the only thing – I know for sure is that whoever is responsible for what happened to Annika had a key to get into the Claymore cottage back in January. There are quite a few keys to that cottage, which makes it necessary for me to ask questions of people who must be innocent of any wrongdoing."

"I'm sorry, sheriff," Rickie said. "I didn't mean to sound off like that. You've got a tough job. Actually, I've given some thought to majoring in criminal justice myself. It's a big field these days, as best as I can make out from reading college catalogues. One of these days I might even find myself doing what you're doing, like they do on NCIS and some of those cop shows. Of course I'd have to be careful about drinking and driving."

He added that last with a smile. I wonder if he has ever really considered the criminal justice field, Carol asked herself. Or whether he thinks that saying so might impress me.

She used her cell phone to call Southport High School and soon found herself talking to the woman who had told her that Joe Cabot had been furloughed two days a month. And that he had weathered this personal economic crisis by finding part-time work at the yacht club.

"Hello, this is Sheriff Kelleher. I believe you're the person who told me about your custodian's schedule. That would be Mr. Cabot. I was calling to see if he's at the school today."

Carol remembered that Thursday was his day off, and she knew she could wait until the next day to seek him out at the yacht club. There would be fewer people around, and it would be easier to have the conversation about the key there than at the high school. But she was already in Southport and she was getting tired of these daily trips up and down the lake.

"Why, yes, Joe's in today. Would you like me to buzz him for you?"

"Yes, please, I'd appreciate that."

Joe Cabot must have been in his basement office, because he answered almost immediately.

"Joe, there's somebody here who wants to speak with you. It's the county sheriff."

Carol was annoyed that the secretary had identified her as Cabot's caller. Somebody should give the woman lessons in discretion.

"Mr. Cabot, this is Sheriff Kelleher. I've missed you at your home, but I happen to be in Southport and wondered if we could find a moment to have a brief chat. It's close to lunch time. Would you be able to get away and join me for a sandwich over on the square?"

"Good timing, sheriff. I usually bring a bag lunch, but today I have to meet with my accountant in town and planned on lunching there. Glad to have company."

"I don't want to embarrass you by meeting you at the school. Why don't we meet at Merrill's in, say, ten minutes."

"Good. I'll be there."

Joe Cabot hadn't sounded like someone who was reluctant to be seen with the sheriff. Or someone who might have abused his role as keeper of one of the Claymores' keys. Make that two of the Claymores' keys.

The sheriff had the advantage of being just across the street from Merrill's, so she was already in a booth when a burly, dark haired, ruddy faced man came through the front door. Carol assumed that this was Mr. Cabot. He was sure she was the sheriff.

"Sheriff? I knew we'd be meeting up one of these days soon. The wife told me you were looking for me. It's about that missing key, isn't it?"

"Hello, Mr. Cabot. Yes, I have keys on my mind. Indeed, I guess you could say I have a key fixation. Just like Bill Claymore. And for the same reason. I haven't ordered yet. I thought I'd wait for you."

They made small talk for two or three minutes, placed their orders, and then got around to the reason for their meeting.

"You have two keys to the Claymore cottage, and it seems that one of them is missing. Do you have any idea where it might be?"

"I'm sure it's in the house. I know Bill is worried, and I can see his point. I probably shouldn't have had that extra key made. But I know the key didn't get into the wrong hands. It'll come to light one of these days. Ellie will find it when she cleans, or it will have fallen into some of the stuff in that messy mud room."

This isn't what Carol had wanted to hear. But it was more likely than that Annika Lindstrom's would-be rapist had the key. In any event, there was no point in berating Cabot.

"Do you recall just when it was you went into the Claymore cottage last winter?"

He had obviously anticipated the question, and provided her with dates and reasons why his presence in their house was required. He claimed that on no occasion had he had need to go down to the pump room.

His affiliation with the school might have given him the opportunity to get to know Annika. Carol asked him whether he had known her.

"I knew who she was. I expect everyone at Southport High knew who she was. Pretty girl. Tall, too. But I don't talk much with the students, not unless they're interfering with my job. Like some kids were doing just yesterday, down in the furnace room where they don't belong."

Carol could imagine students sneaking off to the furnace room for a quick smoke.

"Favorite place for a cigarette, is it?"

"Sometimes, especially in the winter. But they weren't smoking yesterday. Just having a big argument. I thought it was going to get out of hand, and I wasn't hired to be a policeman. It's a shame. That Lalor boy's a darn good athlete. Too bad he has such a temper."

"Rickie Lalor? I didn't know he had a bad temper."

"You know him?" Cabot sounded surprised that the sheriff would be familiar with any of the teenage crowd at Southport High School.

"Barely. I've been talking with everyone who ever dated Annika Lindstrom."

"I don't know about that. He's a big shot, but he was really angry with a buddy of his, name's Stebbins. Him and that Jennifer Kershaw. You see how it is. I don't really know any of the students, but it's not a big school and over the course of a few years you get to know who pretty much everybody is."

Carol was suddenly more interested in Joe Cabot's off the cuff remark about an argument in the furnace room than she had expected to be.

"I've met the kids you mentioned. The Lindstrom girl was living with the Kershaws. Do you have any idea what they were arguing about?"

"Not really," he replied. "I just wanted them out of the room with nobody hurt. I think it had something to do with somebody keeping his word. Or her word. I wasn't paying attention to what they were saying. Look, I'm sorry to have to break this off, but Miss Kershaw's father will be waiting for me. He's my accountant."

Carol wasn't sure what to make of it. Probably nothing. Why should she assume that an argument among three young people who had known Annika Lindstrom was about Annika Lindstrom? Better to concentrate on the keys to the Claymore cottage.

CHAPTER 36

It must be the most beautiful house on Crooked Lake, Carol thought. The rich brown and cream colored house blended so well with the plantings on the property that it looked as if it had been carefully set down among them by some benevolent genie. Long rather than tall, the house appeared both reclusive and welcoming. If any of the hundreds of cottages which occupy the shores of the lake had a better outlook, she had yet to see them.

Her appointment with Eric Mackinson had been set for ten o'clock. She had anticipated that they would meet at the home he shared with his parents in Southport, but he suggested that she meet him at the lake house where he was repainting the interior. No one will be at home there, he said, the implication being that they could talk without the hovering presence of his mother.

It was not quite ten, and Carol didn't know whether Mackinson would have heard her drive up. She parked next to his white paneled truck and walked around the house to the beach. The owners had not yet moved summer furniture out onto the deck which faced the lake, but she could readily imagine what a lovely setting it would be for cocktails before dinner. It was while she was admiring the view that he appeared at the door onto the deck behind her.

"Good morning, sheriff."

Mackinson was wearing a paint-stained shirt and jeans and looking even younger than she had remembered. If she hadn't known better, she might have assumed that he was one of those college kids who advertises for pickup summer jobs.

"This must be a nice place to work," she said.

"It's great. They're nice people. They picked the colors and then left me alone. I hate the ones that hang around and keep making suggestions or wonder if the walls shouldn't be a little lighter. Or darker."

Eric Mackinson was in his element discussing house painting. She fully expected that he'd be less at ease when she began to question him about the things that were on her mind.

"Can we sit out here?" he asked. "I'm not dressed to be sitting on their chairs, except maybe in the breakfast nook."

In the absence of deck furniture, they'd have to sit on the steps. But it was a nice morning and the temperature had reached 60 degrees, so Carol agreed to stay outside even if she would have liked to see how this elegant house was furnished.

There were two things on her mind. One of them was the breakup between Eric and Annika, presumably engineered by his mother. The other was what he had been doing on the night of the January party. He had told her the day they had met in the ravine that he had not attended the party, not having been invited. But she now felt a need to probe further into just where he had been that night.

"You must be wanting to talk about that Lindstrom girl," Mackinson said. "I don't know that I can help you. I told you all I know about her when we met the other day."

"In my experience, people always know more than they think they know about things." Carol wasn't even sure this was true. But it had become part of her investigative routine, a cliche she used because it might stimulate further reflection. "So let's talk a bit more about your relationship with Annika. You told me that by the time of that party when she disappeared you hadn't dated her in a month, or something like that. Why did you stop dating her?"

"Nothing in particular. I guess we sort of realized it wasn't as much fun as we thought it would be. No hard feelings, just no magic."

"Did your parents not approve of Annika?"

It was a question which Eric had not expected. He looked as if he wasn't quite sure how to answer it.

"They didn't pay much attention to who I dated," he finally said.

"Your mother tells me she likes to bake cookies for your girlfriends. Did she bake cookies for Annika?"

"She may have." This was a conversation that he clearly didn't wish to pursue.

"Who took the initiative when you and she stopped seeing each other? Was it her or you?"

"I guess it was mutual."

"You say there were no hard feelings when you and Annika

broke up. I got the impression from one of her friends that Annika was angry that you had ditched her."

"Who told you that?"

It had, of course, been his mother, not one of Annika's friends.

"I think it was just a rumor, but I thought I'd mention it," Carol said, finessing the question. Eric was now conspicuously uncomfortable, and probably assuming that it was Annika herself who had told her friends at school that she was angry with him.

"Well, it's not true. We still saw each other occasionally."

"I thought you said you hadn't seen her in a month when she disappeared."

"I meant I hadn't gone out with her." Eric was now both uncomfortable and flustered. "But I saw her, you know, around town. She seemed okay."

"Did you see her the night of that party in January when she disappeared?"

"No, I didn't."

"Where were you that night, Mr. Mackinson?"

"I was at home, all evening long. Why are you asking me all these questions?"

"How does it happen that you remember where you were on that particular night four months ago?"

He could not have misunderstood the reason for the sheriff's question.

"If you think I'm trying to create an alibi for that night, you're wrong. I don't need an alibi, because, like I've told you, I didn't have anything to do with what happened to Annika. But when she went missing, everyone heard about it. All of Southport was talking about her. You couldn't help but remember what you'd been doing."

"So you were doing what? Watching TV with your parents, something like that?"

Another question that had caught Mackinson off guard. He looked at the sheriff, then turned his attention to his paint covered hands.

"Were you home alone that evening?" Carol asked.

"Yes, I was," he admitted reluctantly. "Mom and Dad play bridge most Saturday nights. With the Wainwrights. I'm sure that's where they were."

Eric could have claimed that his parents could vouch for the fact that he was home on the night Annika disappeared. But he knew that the sheriff would be asking them for confirmation. Better to admit being home alone without an alibi than to fabricate an alibi which would quickly be exposed as a lie.

Carol had already told a lie of her own when she said that a friend of Annika's had told her that Eric's former girlfriend was angry with him for dumping her. She considered telling another lie to the effect that Eric had been seen somewhere near the now infamous party that night in January. The temptation to do so was strong. But she decided against it. It was a card she could play another day. The fact that none of the party goers had reported seeing Eric that night didn't mean that he had not been hanging around. Had he really seen Annika for the last time the night she'd been so angry with him? For some reason that she would have been hard pressed to explain, Carol didn't think so.

When she left Eric Mackinson to get back to the task of painting the interior of the beautiful house with the beautiful view of Crooked Lake, she placed a call to Kevin at the cottage. Not surprisingly, he had not heard back from his Swedish colleague about the mini-diary.

"Too soon," he said. "I'm sure she's busy. But I know she'll get back to me in a day or two."

They agreed on plans for dinner, and she called her office.

"Have there been any calls for me?" she asked Ms. Franks. The answer was that there was nothing that could not be handled by Sam or one of the other men.

"Oh, wait a minute," Diane said. "I think Officer Parsons has something he wants to tell you. He's out on the lake, of course."

"Okay. I'll give him a call."

Lake traffic was still light, and Parsons was involved in a routine patrol. He picked up promptly.

"Bill, Carol here. Ms. Franks tells me you have something for me."

"Don't get your hopes up. It's nothing, just something that Barrett said yesterday. Remember when Sam and I were going through the Claymore cottage the day after the body was discovered there? We found that one of the window sills looked like it had been gouged by something. I think we talked about it that day. We were thinking about forced entry. Because it was on the inside, though, we put it out of our minds. Then Barrett said something yesterday about a squirrel that had gotten into his place. He said it had chewed around two of the window frames, trying to get out. I should have thought of it sooner. That explains those gouges on the sill at the Claymores. Just a squirrel, not someone trying to stash Miss Lindstrom in the cellar. I'm sure they can tell you when it happened. Lucky they were able to chase the little devil out of the cottage before it did more damage."

"Funny thing," Carol said. "I'd forgotten all about that. I guess I'd already figured that whoever had gotten into the cottage had done it with a key. But thanks anyway."

"You been following the weather report?" Parsons asked.

"No, why?"

"We're in for some rough weather over the weekend. Not sure we'll be getting a lot of rain, but talk is that the wind will be up. Enough to maybe do some damage to some of the beaches. I've been talking to a few people who don't seem to have things buttoned up. It may be a tempest in a teapot, but Saturday could be a doozy. I'd suggest we put the other boat out, if you think we could take guys off the roads. There'll be people who'll need help"

"Let me think about it. High winds could create problems on the roads, too. But I appreciate the heads up.'

Carol wasn't eager to use the second patrol boat. It needed work, which was a major reason why it wasn't on the water already. But the budget was tight, and the work hadn't been done. Frequently the weather forecast for the area was overly pessimistic. She hoped that would be the case this time. She'd wait until Friday night to make her decision.

11:24. Carol's day was just beginning.

CHAPTER 37

For Carol, the rest of the week went by in a blur. Three of her officers called in sick. She had never known any of the three to be guilty of malingering. They had obviously caught whatever bug was going around. Ms. Franks left on Friday morning to attend a grandfather's funeral in Buffalo. The Lindstrom case got little attention, and Carol acknowledged that she was poor company for Kevin.

She had managed to see the pharmacist in Southport and get his report on Annika's medications. As it turned out, however, she learned nothing of importance. He assured her that none of the pills she had inquired about were Rohypnol or any other type of date rape drug. She had been sure that they wouldn't be, but it helped to have a professional opinion.

Unlike Carol, who had become increasingly tired and irritable over the course of the week, Kevin bounced back from jet lag only to find himself frustrated by the absence of anything constructive to do. He was willing, even eager, to involve himself in the investigation of the murder case de jour. He had sent a Swedish colleague at the college the mini-diary, but so far the anticipated translation into English had not come back. As a result, he had been reduced to puttering around the cottage. Mike Snyder was too busy to help put the dock in, but Kevin had handled the canoe by himself and had kept boredom at bay by taking it out for a few trips up and down the lake.

It was while he was paddling north in the direction of West Branch that it occurred to him that there might be one other thing he could do which might help Carol in her investigation. He didn't need her approval for it, and it was doubtful that he'd learn anything of great consequence. But he had been intrigued by what Carol had called the Ohio connection. That was where Barry Claymore was attending college. It was also the state from which a postcard had been sent back in January announcing that Annika Lindstrom was okay, that there was no need to worry about her. Of course there had been every reason to worry about her, and the postcard had almost surely not been written by her.

A college teacher himself, he had begun to think about the McLean College calendar. Was the college in session when Annika Lindstrom had disappeared? If so, had Barry Claymore cut classes to return to Crooked Lake? If not, might Barry have taken advantage of a long weekend to return to the lake to renew his relationship with Annika? The first of these questions could be answered by a call to the college. The second question might elicit an answer if he knew Barry's schedule and if his teachers took attendance. Kevin was well aware of how closely colleges and universities guarded the privacy of their students. Or tried to. But he could at least learn something about McLean's schedule, and with luck he might learn something about what Barry had been up to.

He hoped that when he got back to the cottage he would find an e-mail with the translation of Annika's mini-diary. Unfortunately, getting back to the cottage would prove more difficult than he had anticipated. It had been a normal May day when he set out in the canoe, but as he paddled briskly north a wind had come up from the south. At first it was just a moderately stiff breeze, but within a matter of minutes the wind was gusting at what he estimated to be thirty or even forty miles per hour. The prudent thing to do was to turn around and head home. Kevin had not been prudent. By the time he finally reversed course, the wind was whipping the waves into white-capped fury and he found himself making headway very slowly and then not at all. He guided the canoe in toward shore, the better to take advantage of the somewhat quieter waters in the coves. Even so, it was a painfully slow and tiring trip.

Such a wind was not that common on the lake, but it was not unprecedented. It will spend itself in an hour or so, he thought as he beached the canoe. As was his practice, he turned the boat over so that it lay at an angle which would keep it from filling with water should rain start to fall. As he walked up the lawn to the cottage, a cluster of small tree branches from a neighbor's fire pit flew past him, driven by the wind. Walking into that wind was proving to be a challenge.

Kevin stopped on the deck and looked out over the lake. Several gulls were struggling without success to fly against the wind. A lone power boat was making its way laboriously toward shore, its bow rising and then falling hard against the waves. The sound of those waves as they crashed on the beach was as loud as any Kevin could remember. He was tired and much relieved to be safely home.

Just as he was about to go in, the wind picked up sharply. He felt it through his windbreaker. At that very moment he witnessed something the like of which he had never seen before. His canoe took off from the beach and sailed like a large errant kite, low over the ground, until it crashed against a tree two cottages away. A gust of wind had caught it where its hollow shell was exposed. The light frame was not sturdy enough to anchor it to the beach, and it had become airborne as if it were no more substantial than an abandoned newspaper.

The sight of the flying canoe was so shockingly unexpected that Kevin stood mesmerized for a moment before the realization set in that this source of so much summer joy had just been badly damaged, perhaps beyond repair. There was no point in going up the beach to check on the canoe, much less trying to bring it back. Crumpled against the tree, it would not be going any further. When the wind subsided, he'd check on the canoe's condition. He wasn't optimistic.

Cursing himself for his failure to lash the canoe to the iron post he had installed on the beach, Kevin went on into the cottage to change out of the clothes which had been soaked by the spray as he struggled back to the cottage against the wind. Now warmer and dryer, he turned on his laptop. Professor Ingrid Cohen's e-mail was waiting for him. It didn't compensate for the loss of the canoe, but it did improve his mood a bit.

Ingrid's message made the predictable disclaimer that she didn't know how useful her translation would be. She went on to offer the opinion that the diary – actually little more than a brief note – was a Christmas shopping list. It wasn't constructed in the way lists usually are, but rather as an extended paragraph which read more like her thoughts about what would and would not make appropriate gifts.

Kevin skimmed quickly over Ingrid's prefatory remarks and got to the translation from Swedish to English. It was so short that Ingrid wondered why he'd referred to it as a diary.

What am I going to give people? I suppose I don't have to give Ricki and Michael anything. Why should I? Just because they're still my friends even if I haven't let them fuck me? What kind of a reason is that? My American family's another matter. What will they expect? Or should I be asking what they deserve? Brian's okay, even if he's not that mature for 17. I don't know where to begin. I might go for a bottle of aquavit, but the family would disapprove. Perhaps a cologne. There must be something for all of them, even if I don't much care for Jennifer. What's the cure for jealousy? I think she pigs the bathroom on purpose to spite me. I'll think of something. Amanda doesn't pose much of a problem. She's always complaining about the cold, so I may pick a woolen scarf I've seen in a shop down in the square. It'll cost too much, but she tries hard to be nice, so I think that's what I'll do. She worries about everything. It must be hard for her. Now for Bob. The gift he'd most like is to get into my pants if he could figure out how to do it without screwing up his marriage. He's really pathetic. What I'd like to do is give him a framed nude photo of me. Wish I had one. That would cause a scene when Bob opens it on Christmas morning. But I'll be a nice little girl and give him something like a box of toffee. What a family.

What a family indeed, Ingrid had remarked at the end of the translation. Then she added that she would really appreciate a more detailed explanation of what this was all about. Kevin sent a quick note of thanks to her, together with a promise that he would let her know if and how her translation helped to solve the mystery of Annika Lindstrom's death.

The canoe momentarily forgotten, Kevin moved from the desk to the big chair in the corner of his study. He read and reread the mini-diary in its English version, confident that Ingrid had correctly captured what Annika had intended. It was too brief to offer a nuanced picture of the four members of the Kershaw family, but it managed to provide a fairly effective thumbnail sketch of each of them.

It was immediately apparent, however, why Mr. Kershaw

had been interested in the thin little notebook. Annika had not said just what it was that he'd said or done, but it was clear – at least to Annika – that his interest in her was more than that of a conscientious host. Mr. Kershaw would be aware of what he had said and done, and he might well have worried that Annika would have commented on it in the 'diary.' Not wanting his family to know that he had behaved inappropriately toward the exchange student, he had taken steps to make sure that any comments she might have made about his behavior did not posthumously fall into the hands of his wife and children.

Kevin speculated on what Mr. Kershaw might have said or done. Had he been circumspect, leaving it to her to infer that he was interested? Or had he told her of his feelings? Had he been so bold as to kiss her? To touch her in ways that made his intentions clear? Kevin had never met the man, much less observed him interacting with the girl or, for that matter, with members of his own family. But he was sure that Carol would want to pursue the possibilities suggested by Ingrid Cohen's translation of Annika's musings about Christmas gifts. For all he knew, she already suspected Mr. Kershaw of an unhealthy interest in the girl.

His interest in the case stimulated by Ingrid's e-mail, Kevin decided to place the call to McLean College that he had been considering. The college's information service was both efficient and polite. Good public relations, he thought. They confirmed that the January weekend in question had indeed been a long one due to Martin Luther King's birthday. If he wanted information as to Barry Claymore's class schedule, he would have to speak with the registrar. That office, as he expected, was mindful of the privacy issue, and Kevin had no persuasive reason for needing to know what classes Claymore was taking during the recently completed semester. Carol, calling in her official capacity, might fare better. Kevin thanked them for their help, such as it was, and went back to the living room where he could watch the wind-battered lake through the big picture window.

CHAPTER 38

Carol put on a happy face when she walked through the door, but it didn't fool Kevin.

"Are you okay?" he asked, sounding worried.

"I'll survive," was her not very comforting reply. "It's that blasted wind. I haven't seen it blow like this in years."

She indeed looked wind blown, but Kevin knew that it had been a difficult week and that her problems were not all attributable to the fact that the wind was now gusting close to sixty miles an hour.

"Go on and change. I'll uncap the beer. Or will it be wine tonight?"

"Truth is, I don't care. You decide."

Kevin hoped that his news about Annika's thoughts on Christmas presents would cheer her up. He took a peek at the casserole simmering on the stove top and took two beers out of the fridge while Carol disappeared into the bedroom to shed her uniform.

He was surprised to see her emerge five minutes later in a nightgown and bathrobe.

"Sorry about my outfit, but I didn't think I was up to two changes of clothes tonight. I've been looking forward to getting ready for bed ever since lunch."

"You look great," Kevin said. And she did, except for the fact that she was obviously tired.

"It's not true, but thanks anyway. God, what a week. What a day! This storm's the last straw."

"At least it hasn't started to rain. Can you imagine what that would be like?"

"We've been short handed, and with the weather like it is we could have used everyone. You were lucky not having to go anywhere."

Should he tell her about the canoe, or would that simply further dampen her day? She'll find out soon enough, he thought. Better give her the full story.

"I didn't have to go anywhere, but unfortunately I did."

Carol shook her head.

"Why am I not surprised?" she said.

"All I did was take the canoe out. It was fine when I set off, but it didn't last. No point dragging this out. I had to come back against the wind. As you see, I made it, but it was a workout. The canoe didn't fare so well."

"Meaning what?"

Kevin told her about the big gust of wind that lifted the canoe and drove it into a tree up the point. He tried to make light of it, but Carol loved the canoe almost as much as he did, and she didn't take the news well.

"I'm sure I can get it fixed. I've never used Barton's Boat Shop, but I know a couple of people who swear by it. Soon as the wind goes down, I'll get Mike Snyder to give me a hand. We can run it up there on his pickup, probably have it back in a week or two."

He was too optimistic, as it turned out. Kevin and Carol would not be using the canoe for more than a month.

"Any more depressing stories you'd care to share with me?" Carol asked.

"No, but I've learned something which should make you happy." Kevin considered what he had just said. "Well, maybe happy isn't the right word, but I think it will help your investigation."

"You're going to tell me that you're playing detective again, right?"

"I already told you that I was sending a colleague at the college a copy of Annika's diary. Her translation came back this afternoon."

Carol's face brightened.

"That's great," she said. "At least I hope it is."

"I printed it out. I'll go get it for you."

Kevin disappeared into the study and was promptly back with Ingrid Cohen's translation of Annika's note.

It took Carol less than a minute to read it.

"I'll be damned," she said. "A Christmas list for the Kershaws. Maybe not exactly a list, but it amounts to the same thing."

"I'm sure her choice of presents isn't what's most interesting," Kevin remarked, stating the obvious.

"I had no idea what to expect. But this is more than just interesting. It's a good thing the son was the one who picked up the dry cleaning. If it'd been Mr. Kershaw, we'd still think it went out with the trash. Amanda – well, I don't even like to think about it. And heaven knows what Jennifer would have done with it."

"What do you make of Annika's impressions of the Kershaws?" Kevin asked. "You know them and I don't. Do you think Annika had them pegged? Especially Mr. Kershaw? I guess what I'm asking is whether you believe her, or do you think she was imagining his interest in her."

"I wish I knew. I never met her, so what I know about her is what Amanda and half a dozen of Annika's school mates have told me. That includes Brian and Jennifer Kershaw. Oh, and there's a teacher at Southport I know fairly well who offered her opinion. I've heard that Annika was in the habit of leading guys on. You know what I mean – making them think she'd be an easy lay, then backing off. She's been described as awesome, but it seems pretty clear that Jennifer was jealous of her. So what Annika says about Jennifer suggests that she had her figured out. And I find her comments about Amanda pretty much on the money, too. I'm not sure Brian is immature for his age, but I can imagine that Annika thought so. The book on her is that she was mature beyond her years, so she may well have viewed most of her peers as immature by comparison. That leaves Mr. Kershaw, and I guess I'm inclined to believe Annika. But that's only because I think she's right about the other Kershaws."

"You said she'd been called a tease. Who said that?"

"Bridges questioned the guys at the high school," Carol said, "and the two who seemed to know her best said pretty much the same thing – that she gave guys the come on, then let them down. Both of them dated her, although we're not really sure how close to her they were. They denied that their relationship with her was serious, but it's hard to know whether they were being honest with us. Annika's little Christmas list certainly suggests that they were serious enough to try to have sex with her. And that she disappointed them."

"I'm not so sure I'd agree with what Annika said about Mr. Kershaw," Kevin said. "Think about it. If the guys who dated her are right about her being a tease, isn't it possible that she egged Kershaw on, leading him to believe that she was interested? That wouldn't excuse him if he began to get ideas about a teenage girl, but it would tell us that she wasn't the innocent young thing she sounds like in the little notebook."

"I doubt very much that she was an innocent," Carol said. "She'd lost her virginity long before she came to Southport. Even her parents acknowledge that. But that doesn't mean she was wrong about Mr. Kershaw. The problem is that it won't be easy to find out what if anything happened between them. He'll deny it, and who's going to prove that he's lying?"

"I'll tell you what I'd do. I'd raise the issue in front of the whole family. The way you describe it, the Kershaws aren't exactly the Cleavers – you know, one big happy family. Daddy would deny everything Annika wrote, somebody would say something like 'what about that time when,' and before you know it there wouldn't be any family secrets left."

Carol looked at Kevin in shocked amazement.

"Are you serious? That would be a terribly cruel thing to do. We're not trying to ruin the Kershaws' marriage."

"No, but you are trying to solve the Lindstrom case. If Mr. Kershaw was as besotted with Annika as she implies in her note, he might well have been angry when she rejected his advances. Angry enough to want to have his way with her, by rape if necessary."

"You're telling me you think he's the would-be rapist, the guy who stuffed her in the Claymore's cellar?"

"No, of course not," Kevin said. "What I'm saying is that you should be treating him as a suspect if you believe what Annika wrote about him."

"It doesn't make sense, Kevin. Mr. Kershaw didn't have a key to the Claymore cottage. He couldn't have gotten in to put her in the pump room. So it's hard to believe he's guilty of attempted rape."

"You're probably right. But how do you know he didn't have a key to the Claymore cottage? You haven't accounted for the missing Cabot key. You don't know what his relationship is with the other people who had keys to the cottage. The contractor, Mackinson, Barry Claymore. Or maybe he's guilty of trying to rape Annika, she drops dead, and he gets someone else to help him dispose of her body. Somebody who does have a key to the cottage."

"If I remember correctly," Carol said, "you're the one

who's always telling me that the simplest, most obvious explanation for things is usually the right one. You can't believe that the simplest explanation for what happened to Annika Lindstrom is that Bob Kershaw tried to rape her and then somehow hatched a plan to get her body into the locked cottage of people he almost certainly didn't know."

Kevin gave her a big smile and got up to get two more beers.

"I'm just settling into my role as your off-the-wall detective partner," he said as he went into the kitchen. "But I wouldn't rule Kershaw out as a suspect. You yourself said that you found the translation more than just interesting, and I doubt you were referring to Annika's choice of Christmas presents."

"All right, I'll remember to keep Bob Kershaw in mind. And I know I have to confront him with what Annika said about him. But I don't intend to read her note to the assembled members of the family. I need to speak with him alone, see how he reacts. I suspect he was worried that the diary made some derogatory remarks about him, that that's why he took it from Jennifer's room and kept it. Now we know that he was right to be worried."

"Promise me one thing, though," Kevin said. "If necessary, I hope you'll take steps to see what kind of a tempest Annika's note stirs up in the Kershaw household. That may be a lot more interesting – and more important – than how Mr. Kershaw reacts to Annika's opinion of him."

CHAPTER 39

It was not until nearly nine o'clock on Saturday morning that Carol finally rubbed the sleep from eyes and climbed out of bed. She glanced at her watch. Almost twelve hours of sleep! She remembered breaking off the discussion about Bob Kershaw and Annika Lindstrom at an early hour and retreating to the bedroom without giving a thought to the evening's romantic possibilities. Kevin had not tried to change her mind, but had cleaned up the kitchen and retired to the study with a book.

The coffee smelled good. Kevin had obviously already eaten breakfast and gone back to his book.

"Were you going to let me sleep all day?" Carol asked as she poured herself a cup of coffee.

"You needed it. I don't know when I've seen you so dog-tired. Do you even remember what we were talking about?"

"It was Annika's list and Mr. Kershaw's interest in her finer qualities. Yes, of course I remember. But my body told me when I'd reached my limit. Sorry to walk out on you like that."

"There will be other nights. Like tonight. How about some breakfast?"

"Just let me nurse this coffee for a few minutes," she said. "What are you reading?"

"*The Hollow Man*. It's one of John Dickson Carr's best locked room mysteries. Have you ever read him?"

"You own a copy of it?" Carol sounded surprised.

"Sure. It's one my favorites. I hadn't read it in years, but it kept me occupied for a couple of hours after you hit the sack."

"Funny thing," she said. "I'd never heard of Carr until Bridges mentioned locked room mysteries one day. He'd never heard of Carr either, but one of the students he'd interviewed suggested he make his acquaintance. Somehow the discovery of Lindstrom's body in a locked cottage brought it to mind."

"Smart kid. Who is he?"

"His name's Bachman. Nobody who was involved with Annika," Carol said. "Bridges talked to him because Jennifer

Kershaw had said that Annika was crazy about him. He denied it, said he hadn't been interested in her and couldn't imagine that she'd have been interested in him."

Hmm," was Kevin's laconic reaction. "Do you suppose he was lying?"

"No. No one but Jennifer ever suggested they were in a relationship, and I'm sure she's the one who's lying."

"Anyway, I'd recommend *The Hollow Man*. Or any of a dozen other Carr novels. By the way, have you noticed the weather? It was just getting warmed up yesterday. Take a look at the lake."

They went into the living room to survey Crooked Lake through the big glass window. It looked angry.

"I checked the weather report. They say this will keep up until sometime late in the day. We could be getting rain squalls before the wind subsides."

"Where's the canoe?" Carol asked.

"You really were paying attention last night, weren't you? Come over here."

Kevin pointed to the remains of his canoe, wedged against a tree some thirty yards up the point.

"Do you really think it's salvageable?"

"I hope so. If it'll cost more than a new one, I'll give it a decent burial and we'll go shopping for a replacement."

"So, what are we going to do today?"

"It looks like a good day to stay inside by the fire, don't you think?" Kevin said. "We might even make up for last night. But first, why don't you have some breakfast? I've still got a lot of batter left for pancakes."

"Hey, Michael. Time to get your ass out of bed."

"Who's this?" Michael Stebbins sounded groggy, which he was, having just been awakened from a sound sleep.

"It's Rickie. Who'd you think would be calling you on a Saturday morning? Come on, get up. I want to take advantage of this weather and get in some sailing."

"Sailing?"

"Yes, sailing. The wind's great. You don't get many chances like this to test the K-boat."

"Why do we have to do it now?" Michael, still sounding

sleepy, wanted to know.

"Because it won't last, dummy. We do it when we can. And this morning we can. No school, no games, no one else on the lake. It's perfect. So get yourself out of bed. I'll meet you at the yacht club at 9:30. That's just over half an hour. Okay?"

"Give me forty-five minutes. I've gotta get dressed and have breakfast. And drive to the club."

"Okay, but get a move on."

Joe Cabot turned off the West Lake Road and into the parking lot of the Crooked Lake Yacht Club. It was not Thursday, when he normally spent the days he was furloughed from the high school at the club. But there were things he knew needed doing, things he hadn't finished two days earlier, and he figured this would be a good day to do them. A good day because the weather would keep weekend sailors off the lake and hence out of the yacht club. Sailing required wind, of course, and the common complaint among the members was that there often wasn't enough of it when races were scheduled. But really high winds made sailing treacherous for the small boats which race on Crooked Lake. And the wind which swept across the lake on this morning in May was unusually high. Only the foolhardy would challenge such a wind.

Before unlocking the clubhouse and going inside, Joe walked down to the main dock past a long line of K-boats and other craft belonging to club members. He was still a good twenty feet from the water's edge when he first began to feel the spray from the waves that pounded the beach. Joe was not a sailor. The boats were expensive, and he had chosen to invest such money as he had for recreation in a power boat which he could use for family excursions, water skiing, and fishing. But he enjoyed watching the races at the yacht club, and he had developed friendships with several people who kept their boats there. So in spite of the fact that he did not own a sailboat, he was at home around those who did and he enjoyed the days he spent at the club.

Joe steadied himself against a pole at the end of the dock and watched the waves as they came rolling in. He was enjoying the clean fresh air, in no hurry to start the work he had come to do, when he heard a car behind him. The sound of the wind and the waves was so loud that at first the car's engine didn't register. But this car came to a stop on a lane of blacktop which ran right down to the water's edge only a dozen feet off to his left.

It was Rickie Lalor who got out of the car and came over to where Joe Cabot was standing at the end of the dock.

"Hi, Mr. Cabot. What are you doing here?"

Joe recognized Lalor, as he did most of the students at Southport High School. His memory had been refreshed very recently when he had chased Lalor and two of his friends from the school's furnace room where they had been engaged in a heated argument.

"Mr. Lalor, I believe. As for me, I do some work for the yacht club occasionally, and that's why I'm here."

"Well, that's great. Sorry, by the way, for that little rumpus the other day. You were right to kick us out."

"Yes, I was. The furnace room is my kingdom, you know. Out of bounds for those of you who're supposed to be getting an education."

Lalor wasn't sure exactly how to respond to this witticism. He didn't.

"You haven't seen my friend Stebbins, have you?"

"No. No one's been here this morning except me. Everyone else is smart enough to stay home on a day like this."

"That's why I'm here. Me and Michael. We'll have the lake to ourselves."

"What are you talking about?"

"We're going to take my boat out. Got to test it against this wind."

"Are you crazy? There's too much wind."

"Not for me," Lalor said. "That's why we're doing it. No challenge to go out most weekends."

"Have you ever tried to sail when the lake's like this?" Joe asked, both worried for these young men and angry with them for risking life and limb so foolishly.

"I've been sailing since I was eight. And I'm good. Ask Michael. Where in hell is he?"

The question had no sooner been asked than Stebbins drove up, stopping just behind Lalor's car.

"I was beginning to worry that you'd changed your mind," Rickie said.

"Hello, Mr. Cabot." To Joe's surprise, Michael Stebbins reached out to shake hands.

Joe tried his common sense speech on Stebbins, but it had no more effect than it had on Lalor.

"Don't worry about us. We'll be fine. Rickie's a born sailor, and I've learned a lot from him. We do this all the time."

"Not in weather like this," Joe said.

"Like I told you," Lalor said, "that's why we're here. It's a challenge, not like those pussy cat days we get most of the time. Come on, Michael, let's get *Snafu*."

The two young men left Mr. Cabot at the the dock, shaking his head at their foolishness. He determined that he wouldn't bother to watch them wrestle with the boat, and headed back for the clubhouse.

Bill Parsons had known it would come to this. The sheriff had hoped that the storm would abate, that the wind would calm down to a manageable twenty miles an hour. It hadn't. She would have liked to put their other patrol boat in the water, but had reluctantly decided that it was not in good enough shape to challenge the strong wind and waves. The result was that on Saturday morning Bill and his partner, Officer Jim Damoth, were in the department's only serviceable patrol boat, making their way around the lake, eyes open for boaters in trouble. It wasn't easy going, even with the wind at their back.

It was approximately 10:50 when their patrol boat came around the end of the bluff from the east arm of the lake. They were heading directly into the wind and approaching the widest part of the lake where the two arms of the Y converged. Bill had intended to hug the shore line and follow the west arm of the lake north in the direction of West Branch.

His plan changed when he spotted a sailboat close-hauled and far out in the middle of the lake about a quarter of a mile below the bluff. Even at that distance he could see that the boat was heeling way over, its deck nearly under water on the port side. It was moving at a rapid clip. There appeared to be two men on board, one at the tiller, the other riding high above the water as ballast.

"What are those darn fools doing out there?" Bill asked his

younger partner. It was a rhetorical question.

The patrol boat shifted course and headed down lake toward the K. It had gone no more than a dozen choppy yards into the wind when Parsons and Damoth saw the sailboat come about. Almost immediately, the man providing ballast disappeared and in a matter of seconds the boat went over onto its side, its sails in the water.

Parsons tried to increase his speed, but the headwind was too strong. The waves battered the patrol boat, making its approach to the floundering sailboat painfully slow. In spite of its water logged sails, the K was drifting steadily north, bobbing like a cork on the angry surface of the lake.

By the time Parsons and Damoth were close enough to get a good look at the sailboat, it was clear that only one man was clinging to its side. His efforts to right it had been fruitless. Parsons shouted toward the man in the water, but it was impossible to make himself heard over the wind. Eventually, they were able to maneuver into position to haul a very tired and very scared young man aboard the patrol boat.

The capsized sailboat remained a problem, but their first priority was the missing member of its small crew.

"Where's the other man that was with you?" Parsons asked.

The man who lay in the well of the patrol boat choked, coughed, and finally spoke.

"He's gone. He didn't duck when we came about. It must have been the wind. He didn't hear me."

The hell with the sailboat, Parsons thought. He steered the patrol boat clear, and began to circle back toward where he believed the K had capsized, looking for the other man. For another ten minutes he and Damoth searched the area. It had become clear that the man was indeed gone. If he had been knocked unconscious or even badly injured by the boom, he would have had little chance in these cold, rough waters.

Reluctantly, Parsons turned the boat back toward the north. They caught up with the sailboat and, after a great deal of trouble, were able to fasten a line to it and headed for the shore near a marina. Pushed by a powerful tailwind, they were able to make good time.

"Who are you?" Parsons asked the young man in the well of the parole boat.

"Rickie Lalor," was the weak answer. "I can't believe this happened. He was my best friend."

"Who is he?" Parsons used the present tense.

"Michael Stebbins. We thought it would be fun to do it in this wind. I can't believe he's gone."

There would still be a search, a more thorough one than had been possible this morning. Without a doubt it would be unavailing. But it would have to be undertaken as soon as the wind subsided. This was not the first drowning he had encountered during his years on the force, but Bill Parsons was involuntarily shaking. These deaths were always tragic, but invariably unnecessary, the result of carelessness or reckless behavior. Now someone named Michael Stebbins would join the list of those unnecessary deaths.

Bringing the K-boat safely into shore was not easy, but Officer Damoth managed it while Parsons tended to Lalor. He was cold and shivering, and he kept repeating that Michael had been his best friend and that he couldn't believe that he was gone.

"I'm going to drive this young man over to the hospital, Jim. You call the sheriff and report what happened. You'll reach her at the cottage of a Kevin Whitman. I don't have the number on me, but it'll be listed."

"Is he going to be okay?"

"I think so, but we're not going to take any chances."

They helped Lalor out of the boat and walked him up the beach to the marina office.

"Hi, Howard," he said as they encountered the manager. "I need you or one of your men to give me and this fellow a ride up to where my car is parked. It's just this side of West Branch at our launch site. He's going to the hospital, and we've got to get there right away."

"That his boat on the beach?"

"It is, and I'll see that it's taken care of after we make sure he's in good hands. He's been in a bad accident. We think a buddy of his drowned. I'll tell you more later, but I really need to get him to the hospital."

"That's awful. But sure, there's no business here today, not with this weather. I'll do it."

Forty minutes later, Rickie Lalor was under observation at the Yates Center Hospital. Parsons had tried unsuccessfully to reach his parents, but decided to leave it to the sheriff to notify the Stebbins family.

Carol was now used to being called at Kevin's cottage. Her officers had long since become aware that their boss was in a relationship with the professor. There was the occasional in-house joke about the sheriff and her 'opera man,' but she was respected, and if she liked him, he, too, merited respect.

But Officer Damoth's news about the drowning of Michael Stebbins was something she could not have imagined. She was initially shocked, then angry. Why did kids do such foolish things? Did they think they were immortal? Now a second student at Southport High School had died in the short span of four months. A second memorial service would have to be held. Another student, Rickie Lalor, would have to live with the knowledge that he shared responsibility for his friend's death. In all probability, some girl at the high school would be crying when word got out that her boyfriend was suddenly, shockingly, dead. Hadn't she heard that that girl might be Jennifer Kershaw?

Carol hadn't really known Stebbins. In fact, she didn't really know any of the kids who had been Annika Lindstrom's friends. They were of interest to her only because they had been part of Annika's short life in Southport, because they had attended a party with her the night she disappeared back in January.

She hated to have to make the phone call to the Stebbins, people she had never met, people whose names she didn't even know. That difficult mission accomplished, she would then have to be in touch with the equally unfamiliar Lalor family, although she assumed that Rickie would already have contacted his parents from the hospital. And then there would be Jennifer Kershaw. Which meant another trip to the home where Annika had lived before her untimely death. First the father who had allegedly fantasized about a relationship with Annika. Now the daughter who had not only been jealous of Annika but who had presumably been dating Michael Stebbins. How would the deaths of these two people alter the life of this troubled young girl?

CHAPTER 40

Carol had tried to reach the Stebbins' home without success. This was not the time to leave a message. You don't tell parents via voice mail that their son is dead, nor do you tell them to get in touch with the sheriff right away. She would keep trying. It was while she was repeating Officer Damoth's news to Kevin that Joe Cabot called. In view of what had happened, she figured that the call was more likely to be for her than for Kevin, so she picked up the phone.

"Is this the sheriff? It's Joe Cabot."

"Hello, Mr. Cabot. How did you know where to find me?"

"Let me apologize for bothering you there, but I'm worried. I called your office, and the person who answered gave me two numbers. This was one of them."

There goes the last vestige of my privacy, she said to herself.

"No apology necessary. What is the problem?"

"I've been working at the yacht club today, and a couple of the boys who have privileges here took a boat out this morning. They should have been back by now, but they aren't. They shouldn't have gone out in this weather. I tried to talk them out of it, but you know how kids are. Anyway, I thought you should know about it."

"Did they give you their names?"

"I know them from school. The one whose family owns the boat is Rickie Lalor. His friend is Michael Stebbins. I wasn't sure what I should do. I was about to go home, but I didn't want to leave the club with them still out in this wind storm."

Carol would have to share the bad news with him.

"I already know about this," she said. "Unfortunately, there was an accident, and it looks very much as if Mr. Stebbins may have drowned. A couple of my officers were patrolling the lake and saw the boat go over. They saved Lalor, but couldn't find Stebbins. That was a couple of hours ago."

There was a quick intake of breath on the other end of the

231

line, then a moment of silence.

"How terrible," he finally managed to say. "I should have kept them from going out there."

"You couldn't have done that, not if they were determined to go. It isn't your fault. I'm going up to the hospital right away and see how Mr. Lalor is doing. He must be absolutely devastated. We just have to hope that he'll be okay. I'm sure you didn't expect to hear what I've had to tell you, Mr. Cabot, and I don't envy you the task of sharing this sad news with your family. But thank you for calling."

Carol bundled up against the wind and gave Kevin a peck on the cheek before going out to her car.

"I'm afraid this takes precedence over the Lindstrom case," she said. "I can't be sure how long I'll be. If I'm running late, say after five, I'll give you a call. Don't worry about dinner. We can finish up what you made last night."

"Drive carefully," Kevin urged.

"Always do," she said as she closed the door behind her.

When Carol got to the hospital, Parsons had left to resume his patrol of Crooked Lake. She spoke briefly with the duty nurse on the floor, and was informed that Lalor was doing fine but, on doctor's orders, was being kept under observation at least until evening.

"Have his parents been here?"

"No. The officer said that no one answered at his home."

So neither the Stebbins nor the Lalors knew of the bad news. Wherever they were, they were probably enjoying the day, unaware of the tragedy which had struck their families.

Carol stuck her head in the door of Rickie's room. There were several magazines beside the bed, but he wasn't reading. He was staring at the ceiling.

"Rickie," she said softly, deliberately avoiding the more formal 'Mr. Lalor.'

He looked in her direction, then turned his attention back to the ceiling. He said nothing.

"Rickie," she said again, "I'm here to tell you how terribly sorry I am about the accident. About Michael. I'm also glad that you are going to be all right. I can't begin to know how you feel, but I'm sure you will feel better if you can talk about what happened. It may not be easy, but it's worse to keep it all inside.

May I sit down?"

Carol took his silence as an invitation and, moving a couple of magazines aside, sat in the chair across from his bed.

"Officer Damoth explained it to me. It was lucky for you that he and Officer Parsons were close by when your boat capsized. We can only regret that they were not closer."

She didn't want to sound as if she were critical of him for being out on the lake in such a high wind. Better to concentrate on what happened when they tacked that one last and fatal time.

"Why don't you try to tell me what you think happened?"

Lalor took his eyes off the ceiling and stared at the sheriff.

"I don't know. It happened too quickly."

Carol was surprised that he had chosen to talk. Surprised but pleased.

"Presumably you had been tacking for some time, and it had been okay. Was there something different about the time the boat capsized?"

Was it her imagination or had Rickie Lalor's eyes, so lifeless before, suddenly focussed more sharply on her?

"What do you mean, something different?"

"That tack didn't go well. Do you have any idea why?"

Rickie looked at the ceiling again.

"My officers saw it all," she continued, "but they were too far away to see anything clearly. They just suddenly lost sight of one of you and then a second or two later the boat was over on its side. Maybe the wind was too loud for you to hear each other."

"Yes, that must have been what happened," Rickie said. It was the first time he had spoken above a hoarse whisper. "It had to be. I think that's what I told the officers."

"Were you at the tiller?"

"Yes. Michael was crew."

Carol was not a sailor. Certainly not one with the experience Rickie Lalor was alleged to have. But she had a fairly good mental image of tacking, and she knew that whoever was at the tiller would control the mainsail. And hence the boom.

"So you think Michael didn't hear your command and the boom swung around and knocked him off the boat?"

"It must have been like that. Like I said, it happened so fast I didn't know anything was wrong until we capsized. I didn't even see that Michael wasn't in the boat."

As he spoke, Carol was trying to visualize those few moments when the boat changed course. Perhaps a sudden, even more violent, gust of wind hit them. There had certainly been a failure of communication, probably due to the wind. Or was Rickie's reputation as a sailor exaggerated? Was he over his head out there in the broadest and deepest part of Crooked Lake, trying to cope with dangerously high winds and high waves?

"Had you and Michael sailed together very often?"

It was a straight forward question. Rickie considered it.

"I don't know what you mean by often."

"Did you sail together three or four times? A dozen times? Frequently over several summers?"

All Carol knew for a fact was that they had sailed together once with Annika and Barry Claymore. But she had formed the impression that sailing was something the two friends did often. And well.

"We did it when we could. When Dad and his friends weren't using the boat."

It was a surprisingly vague answer. In fact, Carol was beginning to believe that Rickie had been vague ever since she had joined him in his hospital room. But that was unfair, she thought. This young man had just lost a close friend. He was undoubtedly blaming himself for putting the boat through a maneuver which had cost Michael his life. And for having gone sailing with him in such foul weather in the first place.

"Rickie," she said, "as I'm sure you know, there will be an inquest into the accident. You will have to testify. I know that it all seems a blur to you now, but you will have to answer questions about what happened to the best of your ability. The inquest will bring back bad memories. It won't be pleasant. But I know you will do just fine.

"I appreciate it that you're willing to talk with me. I understand that you won't be here much longer. I'd suggest that we try your parents again. I have to talk with them, but they'll want to hear your voice. They'll be relieved that you're okay, and they'll want to come and get you. If they haven't gotten home by the time the doctor releases you, I'll arrange to take you home, or get one of my men to do it. Do you know your Mom or Dad's cell phone number?"

"I've got it in my wallet. But I'll try the house first. And don't worry about me getting home. If for some reason I can't reach them, I can get a ride to the yacht club with a friend. My car's there."

"That's not a good idea, Rickie. Your parents should be the ones who take you home. The car can be collected later. Go ahead and make that call."

Reluctantly, Rickie dialed home. No luck. The wallet had, of course, been in the lake, and the note on which he had written a bunch of numbers, including his parents' cells, was now unreadable.

"Please keep trying the home number," Carol said. "I'll do the same."

She was preparing to leave when Rickie had a question.

"You've probably had experience with things like this. Do you suppose I'll ever get over it? Right now I feel sick. Not like I could throw up or anything like that, but what I've heard people call sick at heart. I've never lost a friend before. He was just 18. He won't be sitting next to me in math class on Monday."

Carol had not particularly cared for Rickie Lalor, but at the moment she felt almost painfully sorry for him. No wonder that he was sick. He was going to be all right physically, but it would be some time before he recovered emotionally from the morning's tragedy.

Before she left the hospital, Carol got in touch with Bridges.

"I've heard," Sam said. "Bill called me, said you might be needing my help."

"I'm afraid I do. We've got one dead boy and another one hospitalized, and neither of their parents can be reached. I'm on my way down to Southport where I hope to see both families. It may take awhile. My first priority has to be Michael Stebbins' parents. I'm going to call them as soon as we hang up, and if they don't answer I'm going on to their house, see if anyone in the neighborhood knows where they are. I'd like you to start calling the Lalors. Rickie didn't say anything about them being out of town or gone for what he thought would be a long time. So just keep calling. And if you get them, let them know he's in the hospital at Yates Center but that he's in good shape and will be released today. You'll have to tell them what happened, but don't say too much, just that the boat capsized and our rescue team saved Rickie but couldn't find Michael. Say that I'll be in touch just as soon as I've seen the Stebbins. Okay?"

"No problem. I'm glad you'll be the one to speak to that kid's family. I'm not sure I could tell a parent a son had been killed."

"Yes you could, Sam, but it wouldn't be easy. I'll do my best."

Carol hated to be the bearer of bad news just as much as Sam did. In fact, she had experienced a moment of relief when her call to the Stebbins' residence produced only a brief recorded message. But all that had done was postpone the inevitable.

She had checked the address, and realized when she turned onto Edgeware Lane that the Stebbins lived on the same short street as the Mackinsons. Southport is indeed a small town, she thought. The garage door was open and there was no car in it or in the driveway. She parked and rang the bell anyway, but no one came to the door. She had no idea how long she would have to wait.

While she was considering her options, Carol noticed that the official car had attracted a small contingent of curious kids. The oldest looked to be under ten. She opened the door, stepped out, and called him over.

"Do you live on this street?" she asked, adopting what she thought was a child-friendly tone.

"Sure. Over there."

The boy pointed to a house across the street on the corner. It was next door to the Mackinson place.

"So you must know the Stebbins family," she said.

He acknowledged that he did, but immediately announced that they weren't at home.

"Would you happen to know where they are or when they might be back?"

"No," he said, but did not elaborate.

It was while they were having this terse and unproductive conversation that Carol noticed that Eric Mackinson had come out onto his porch.

She excused herself and walked across the street.

"Mr. Mackinson," she said, "good to see you again."

Eric didn't look as if he was glad to see the sheriff, but his curiosity, which had brought him onto the porch, also led him to ask why she was there.

"Those of us in my business are always busy, even on weekends," she said, ignoring his question. On the spur of the moment she decided to take advantage of the fact that the Stebbins weren't home to ask Eric the question she hadn't asked when they had met on his paint job.

"Funny how I seem to keep coming back to that evening in January when there was a party going on down here in Southport. The one you didn't go to because you weren't invited."

Carol remembered several of the young people saying that these parties weren't by invitation. Friends just knew, by corridor chat or tweets or whatever, that a party was in the works.

"You're here to talk to me?" Eric sounded surprised. "You're parked in front of the Stebbins' house."

"I guess I am. Maybe I'll talk to them, too. But I've been wondering about that party again. I'm sure that one of the high school students said you were hanging around that night. You know, outside one of the houses where they were partying."

"Somebody told you that?"

"As you know, I've been talking to a lot of Annika's friends. One of them – I don't remember who it was – said that he'd seen you that night." Carol wasn't sure why she'd said 'he' instead of 'she.'

"But I was home that night," Eric protested.

"No reason why you couldn't have left the house. Maybe you went to Jack's Tavern for a beer, or to the coffee shop. Or took a walk. I just wondered if you remember leaving the house here."

"Does it matter?

"I really don't know. We're only trying to get a fix on where people were that night. It's the way an investigation like this works."

"I don't think I left home, but that was way back in January. All I know is I was watching TV. I know I didn't have anything to do with the party or those high school kids."

"How about your neighbor, Michael Stebbins? Do you remember seeing him that evening?"

"I think he was at the party. It was his friends mostly."

"Speaking of Michael, you wouldn't happen to know where the Stebbins are today, would you?"

"You need to talk with them?"

Yes, I do, Carol said to herself, but not about you.

"That's why I parked across the street."

"Mr. and Mrs. Stebbins left around noon. I haven't seen Michael. The twins are visiting their grandparents."

Thank God, Carol thought. They have other children.

"I may be around for awhile," she said. "I need to see them, today if possible."

When she went back to her car, Eric stayed on the porch for a long minute, presumably wondering what it was that the sheriff needed to talk about with the Stebbins.

CHAPTER 41

It had been an emotionally exhausting afternoon. But the wait for Mr. and Mrs. Stebbins was not as long as she had feared it might be. She had killed some time by driving around town a couple of times. It was on her second circle of Southport that she spotted people getting out of a car in the Stebbins' driveway. Four of them.

As it turned out, the Stebbins and the Lalors had been making a circuit of area antique barns and stores together. The upside of this fortuitous happenstance was that Carol had to tell her sad story only once. The downside was that the one couple had been elated to hear that their son had survived while the other was devastated by the news that they had just lost theirs. The Lalors, of course, could not have been more sympathetic. And the Stebbins made it clear how glad they were that Rickie would be all right. But it was a very bad half hour. Carol thought it was the worst she had experienced since she had become sheriff of Cumberland County.

Mary Jane Stebbins broke into tears as soon as Carol told her what had happened and her crying quickly turned into hysteria. Neither her husband nor the Lalors were able to calm her, and Carol wisely gave up trying to provide details of the tragic accident. She realized that she would have to discuss the inquest later when Mrs. Stebbins had recovered, although she wasn't sure what would constitute recovery in a situation like this.

When she later reflected on those terrible thirty minutes, one thing other than Mrs. Stebbins' hysteria stuck in her mind. It was something Mr. Stebbins said and the brief exchange that followed.

"Michael was a follower," he had said in one of the few moments when everyone was not comforting Mrs. Stebbins. "He was always doing what Rickie wanted to do."

The Lalors knew that this was not a time to challenge this implied criticism of their son.

"I know. Rickie has always been a risk taker." It was Dave

239

Lalor, Rickie's father. "This was one risk too many."

Carol remembered wincing, wondering how the Stebbins would take this tactless understatement.

But Mr. Stebbins hadn't seem offended.

"Michael wanted to go to Syracuse, just like Rickie will be doing, but his grades apparently weren't good enough. He was still filing college applications right up until –"

He had paused, choking back tears of his own, and then went on.

"I drove with him to look at a couple of colleges. Some small place in Ohio and another one near Pittsburgh. Now he won't even get to graduate from high school."

It had been but a brief interlude of more or less normal conversation in what was otherwise a period of shared grief. But Carol would remember it for two things, the picture of Michael as a follower of Rickie Lalor and as someone who had visited a small college in Ohio. Was it McLean, Barry Claymore's school? It hadn't seemed appropriate to ask what would have appeared to be an irrelevant question while Mary Jane Stebbins was sobbing over the loss of her son. But Carol would have to find the right moment to ascertain whether Michael had contemplated applying to McLean.

The Lalors had been anxious to leave for the Yates Center Hospital, but reluctant to say so. Eventually Harold Stebbins had told his friends that they should go and see their son, that he would take care of Mary Jane. There had been hugging all around. By four o'clock the grieving parents were finally alone, the sad but relieved parents were on their way up the lake, and Carol was heading for Kevin's cottage.

As a rule, Kevin and Carol didn't pour themselves a drink as early as 4:30, but this had not been just any old day. Carol was tired. The previous evening she had been physically tired, and she had recovered by going to bed early and sleeping late. Tonight she was emotionally tired; the strain of her meetings with Rickie, his parents, and, most of all, Michael Stebbins' mother and father clearly showed.

"Do I look as bad as I feel?" she asked Kevin as she emerged from the bathroom and a face to face confrontation with herself in the mirror.

Kevin knew better than to say 'yes' to this question, but he had to agree that Carol looked as if she had had a harrowing day.

"I'm about to pour you a glass of an excellent Pinot. I have every expectation that you'll feel fine in a matter of minutes."

"And I have every reason to believe that I'll like the wine but still feel miserable. This isn't the kind of day you can exorcize with a stiff drink."

"Wine isn't classified as a stiff drink, Carol, but I take your point. It has been a bummer, hasn't it? I'll bet the meeting with the boy's parents was excruciating."

"It was. You and I, we've never had kids, so we can only imagine how hard this would be for the Stebbins. She simply went to pieces. He's a stiff upper lip type, but he wasn't fooling anybody. I hate to say it, but it was a huge relief to get out of that house. Trouble is, their grief is just kicking in. I hope that they have good support from their extended families and friends. They're going to need it."

"Excuse me while I get the wine," Kevin said. "Then I want to hear about the day."

"I'll try."

They talked for over an hour, or rather Carol talked and Kevin listened, tossing out a question every so often. It was close to six when Kevin called for a time out and put the pot on the stove to reheat what was left of the previous night's meal.

"I'd completely forgotten that I didn't have lunch," Carol said as she tackled a second helping. "This is even better than it was last night."

"Thanks for the compliment. I guess. I don't think restaurants get many points for serving yesterday's specials today."

"Anyway, here I am, right in the middle of the Lindstrom case, and Crooked Lake claims another victim. I don't mean to sound indifferent to Michael's death, which you know I'm not, but this is going to take me away from the investigation. I dread an inquest like this."

"How do you know that Michael's death isn't related to the Lindstrom case?"

Carol put down her fork.

"Would you mind repeating that?"

"I just asked how you could be sure that what happened to Stebbins isn't related –"

"I heard what you said," Carol interrupted. "What I don't understand is why you said it."

"It's just a fugitive thought that popped into my mind. What if they are related?"

"Why would an accidental drowning be related to the death of a young girl who's been fed a date rape drug?"

"Well, why not look at it this way? If the victim of drowning is a fry cook in West Branch or a bank manager in Yates Center, neither of whom had ever heard of Annika Lindstrom, I don't think I'd ever think the two events are related. But we've got a rather different situation here. The guy who drowns is a young man from Southport who not only knew Annika, he went out with her. He attended the party from which she disappeared. You and your men have been questioning him for over a week about Annika, and I don't believe you're doing it because you're working your way through the Southport phone book."

"But that's a pretty big leap in logic."

"Maybe. Maybe not. I know you don't believe in coincidences. But it would strike me as a rather big coincidence if two people who knew each other well – who'd been friends and had a dating relationship – both died in unusual circumstances within a span of just a few months. Suppose it isn't a coincidence. Suppose that the two events are in some way related?"

Carol pursed her lips, looking pensive.

"I see what you mean," she said, "but it just doesn't make sense to me. Annika's death resulted from an attempted rape that went bad. We're dealing with a crime. Michael's death was the result of poorly thought out youthful bravado. It was an accident."

"You're probably right. But what if Michael's death wasn't an accident?"

"Are you suggesting that Rickie Lalor intentionally killed his friend Stebbins?"

"No. All I'm doing is reminding you of your aversion to coincidences."

"How about another glass of that Pinot. Nice wine."

Kevin brought out the bottle and refilled their glasses.

"You're thinking, right?" he asked. "You think I may have a point."

"I pride myself on maintaining an open mind, Kevin. I'll entertain any theory, no matter how far fetched. There's one thing

I do know, however, and that's that there's no way the upcoming inquest into Michael's death can find Rickie Lalor guilty of deliberately killing his friend. Bill Parsons is a smart, sensible guy. He says that there was no other boat anywhere in sight when he spotted Rickie's K-boat. And he was too far from it when it capsized to see what happened. The inquest will be a formality. Unpleasant for the family, of course, but there will be a finding of accidental death by drowning."

"And that's probably the truth of the matter. If, on the other hand, Rickie was responsible for Michael's death, you'll have to find it out in some other way. Sorry about that."

"I know. As they say, I'll have to connect the dots."

"Yes," Kevin added, "and if it turns out that Rickie killed Michael, it might well mean that Rickie also killed Annika."

Not for the first time, Carol found herself wondering about the circuitry in Kevin's brain.

CHAPTER 42

Carol was concerned about both the Stebbins and the Lalors, but she was also very much interested in the Kershaws. She
had spent a restless night, worrying about how she should organize
what promised to be an unusually busy Sunday. She would need to
visit with the Stebbins again, more as an act of simple human
kindness than because she needed to ask questions. The same was
true of the Lalors. It would give her a chance to see how Rickie
was doing and to see how the family was coping with the fact that
their son might be morally responsible for the death of Michael
Stebbins.

But what she was most anxious to do was spend some time
with the dysfunctional Kershaw family, the family which Annika
Lindstrom had so devastatingly dissected in her reflections on
Christmas gifts.

"I wish I could invite you to come along with me today,"
she said to Kevin over breakfast. "It might help to be able to
compare impressions of the Kershaws when we discuss Annika's
Christmas list. But it's not proper police procedure, as I'm sure
you know. So you'll have to busy yourself at something else while
I make the rounds of these troubled Southport families."

"The life of a undercover cop," Kevin sighed. "Always out
of sight."

"You'll manage. Why don't you give some thought to how
many other suspects in Annika's death you can come up with? Just
don't do something rash."

"Like what? I don't do rash things."

"Last night you as much as said Rickie Lalor killed Annika
Lindstrom."

"I did not," Kevin protested. "It's known as brainstorming.
Besides, I think your killer is going to turn out to be Roger
Chase."

"You can't be serious."

"No, I'm not. It's just my way of saying that what you've
been telling me since I got back from Europe is that it could be

anyone, as long as he or she has a key to the Claymore cottage. Which means that I have no idea what happened to Annika, and inasmuch as I get my cues from you, it means that you have no idea either."

"I'm afraid you're right. Look, I'm going to have to call and make sure all of the Kershaws are at home when I arrive. I can just drop by unannounced at the the Stebbins and the Lalors, but I want the whole Kershaw family present when we discuss Annika's so-called diary."

Carol called, Amanda Kershaw answered, and it was agreed that the sheriff would meet with the family at eleven o'clock, by which time everyone would be up and about and presentable. No point in bothering the other families at an earlier hour, so she decided to stop to see them on her way back to the cottage.

After Carol had departed for her meeting with the Ker-shaws, Kevin got dressed and went out to survey the damage to his canoe. The wind that had tormented the lake on Saturday was now but a quiet breeze. It was hard to believe that the storm could have been so deadly. The canoe was in one piece, but it had taken a beating which Kevin guessed would cost a lot to repair. He couldn't remember the fine print in his insurance policy, but he would talk to the company. Maybe he should write it off as a complete loss and shop for a new one. A few of his neighbors were also out, sizing up the damage to the beach or collecting debris which had been blown ashore. They commiserated with him over the canoe and passed along remembrances of other storms, all of which seemed to have been much more devastating than this one. When he returned to the cottage, he had the feeling he'd been told he was lucky to lose nothing more than a canoe.

Carol had little time to enjoy the return of decent spring weather. She went over in her mind several times what she would be saying and not saying to the Kershaws about Annika's opinions of them. It might prove to be a fairly delicate exercise. She hoped it would also be revealing.

According to the bell in the steeple of the town's Baptist Church, it was exactly eleven o'clock when she pulled up in front of the house on Mountain View Road. Right on time. They were waiting for her. Amanda met her at the door, and she was greeted by the sight of Bob, Brian and Jennifer sitting in a neat row, as if ready for the teacher to commence the first class of the day. There were perfunctory nods and subdued 'good mornings,' but nobody got up to welcome her.

Okay, she thought. We'll just dispense with the preliminaries.

"Have you all heard about the accident on the lake yesterday?"

Three heads bobbed in unison. It was Jennifer who did not acknowledge that she had heard about Michael, but Carol had no doubt that she had.

"We got the news yesterday afternoon," Amanda said. "It was Mrs. Levinson who told us. She lives down the street."

"And what was it that you heard?"

"Mildred said that Michael and the Lalor boy had gone sailing, and that a high wind came up and capsized the boat and that Michael drowned. She didn't have any details."

"Actually, we don't have many details either," Carol said. "But it looks as if that's what happened. One of my department's patrol boats happened to spot the boat when it went over. Otherwise Rickie Lalor could have been lost as well. Officially, we don't know that Michael has drowned. His body has not been found. But I'm afraid that his chances would have been practically nil."

Jennifer, who had been linked with Michael in student gossip, had still said nothing. In fact, Carol thought, she doesn't seem well. In spite of the fact that her eyes were on Carol, there was something about the way she sat, the way she looked, that said she was barely aware of what was going on around her.

"Jennifer," Carol began, "this is a terrible thing for everyone, especially the Stebbins' family. But I know that you were close to Michael. I'm so very sorry."

"I loved him," Jennifer said, but nothing in the way she said it or in her body language added emphasis to those three familiar words.

The other members of her family turned to look at her, obviously surprised.

"You never told us, my dear," Amanda said. "You didn't say anything when we heard about it. This must be terrible for you."

"Nobody cares what I think," Jennifer said. Her voice was flat, lifeless, her words lacking the angry edge the sheriff had come to expect. Carol didn't think Jennifer had moved a muscle since they had begun talking about Michael's death.

"This really isn't the time to do this," Carol said. "I'm sure we can't imagine your feelings, Jennifer. Why don't we leave what happened to Michael aside for the moment and talk about what I came here to discuss with you all. That would be Annika's diary. Okay?"

They all knew that this was the morning's agenda. But did they all really want to discuss it?

"Mom says you had it translated," Brian said. "Are you going to read it for us?"

"I don't think so, Brian. It would be better if I just gave you the gist of what she wrote. Because, you see, it really isn't a diary, or even a fragment of a diary."

"But we want to hear it," Brian persisted.

"Let's let the sheriff do what she thinks best, Brian," Mr. Kershaw said. "No need for us to insist on knowing everything that was on the poor girl's mind."

This was the time for Jennifer to remind everyone that her father had been very much interested in what was on the poor girl's mind. But she didn't. Sphinx like, she remained rigid and silent in her chair.

Brian was not happy to hear that his role in putting the non-diary in the sheriff's hands would not be rewarded with a verbatim report of what Annika had written.

"I said it isn't a diary," Carol said. "It's a Christmas gift list, or something very much like one. What Annika did in the little notebook was set down some thoughts about what she might give people she knew for Christmas. She was obviously contemplating buying presents for the four of you and for two other people she regarded as friends, Rickie Lalor and Michael Stebbins."

Jennifer recoiled from what she had just heard as if she had received an electric shock. But she quickly recovered her poise and said nothing.

"Let me ask a question," Carol said. "Did Annika actually give each of you a Christmas present?"

"Of course, she did." It was Amanda. "She knew she was a guest in our home, and she did the proper thing, just as her parents would have taught her to do."

"Then let me ask another question. I'd be interested to hear what Annika gave to each of you."

No one had a hard time remembering. It had been a scarf for Amanda, a bottle of cologne for Brian, a box of toffee for Jennifer, and a recording by the Swedish group, Abba, for Bob. Pretty much what she had planned, Carol thought, except that the toffee went to Jennifer rather than Mr. Kershaw. Was the gift of sweets to the girl who had been anything but sweet to her a subtle criticism? More likely, Annika had already bought the toffee when it occurred to her that she could, with equal subtlety, remind Bob that he, like Abba, was yesterday's news. No one would ever know what Annika had been thinking, and it didn't really matter.

"Is that it?" Brian asked.

"I don't think it is necessary to say anything further except that Annika was quite frank in what she had to say about all of you. She may have been well brought up, as you have suggested, Mrs. Kershaw, but she also had a sharp tongue – or should I say a sharp pen. And unfortunately what she had to say about the four of you was not, on the whole, complimentary. The Christmas list was not just a series of names matched with presents. It was more of an excuse to express some personal thoughts about her host family. So you see why it is that I won't be reading Annika's 'diary.' It would be embarrassing for everyone."

"But I'd like to hear the truth," Brian spoke up with feeling. "What could she have said that we don't already know if we only had the guts to admit it."

"That will be enough, Brian," his father said sternly. "The sheriff is right. What Annika was writing has nothing to do with her death. So it's of no further interest to any of us. This chapter in our lives is closed. Let's leave it that way."

Carol was sure that Mr. Kershaw had a pretty good idea of what Annika had said about him. She was equally sure that he was relieved that the sheriff would not be reading or commenting on what she had said. What she didn't know was how concerned he was about what the sheriff now knew about his relationship with Annika. Bob had just told Brian that what Annika was writing had nothing to do with her death. What Bob didn't know was whether the sheriff agreed with him.

When Carol left the Kershaws to worry about Annika's Christmas list, she was less concerned with their worries than she was about the fact that Jennifer had been a veritable zombie throughout the meeting. It was entirely possible that she had indeed been in love with Michael Stebbins and had been crushed by news of his untimely death. But her intuition told her that there was something else bothering Jennifer. That nagging thought bothered her as she paid her respects to the Stebbins. It continued to bother her as she tried to talk with Rickie Lalor in his room, where he had closeted himself ever since coming home from the hospital. And it was very much still on her mind when she arrived back at the cottage.

"There's something we've got to talk about," she told Kevin. "I want you to pretend to be Jennifer Kershaw."

CHAPTER 43

The risers on the stairs to the second and third floors of the Lake Bank Building were unusually steep, probably due to the age of the brick structure on Lake Street. Whatever else he did to stay in shape, Bob Kershaw would be giving his calf muscles a good stretching every day he came to work. By the time she reached the third floor, Carol was slightly winded, which surprised her. She would have to find time in a busy schedule to get in more exercise.

The frosted glass announced that the office was that of Robert K. Kershaw, Certified Public Accountant. The light shining through the glass told her that the CPA was in. She rapped on the door and opened it to face a middle aged woman with an unattractive hair do and a pair of old fashioned glasses pushed up on her forehead. The small sign on the desk said that this was Mary Louise Kimball.

"Good morning," Carol said, taking the conversational initiative. "I'm Sheriff Kelleher, and I don't have an appointment. But I'm sure that Mr. Kershaw will be happy to see me."

"He might be busy. Let me check." Ms. Kimball did not use the phone, but disappeared into the inner sanctum, closing the door behind her. She doesn't want me to hear her conversation with the boss, Carol thought. Whatever they were saying to each other took almost two minutes, but when the door opened it was Bob himself who came out to greet her.

"Sheriff Kelleher, so nice to see you again.," he said, extending his hand to her. "Come on in. Mary Louise, why don't you get the sheriff some coffee. How do you like it?"

"I think I'll take it black this morning. And thank you."

They were soon seated in old, comfortable leather chairs in an office that smelled of furniture polish and the barest hint of a pipe tobacco that reminded her of something her father had smoked. The walls were decorated with diplomas and plaques attesting to Bob Kershaw's civic virtue. Coffee appeared so quickly that Carol assumed that it had already been prepared.

"Now, to what do I owe the pleasure of seeing you twice on

250

a weekend in May?"

So, Carol said to herself, no idle chit chat, no verbal skirmishing before we get down to business.

"I've come to talk with you about Annika Lindstrom's Christmas gift list. Yesterday you graciously concurred with my decision not to discuss it in front of your family. But I feel that I must share with you what Annika wrote, and that I must hear what you have to say about her comments."

"I rather thought that that was what you had in mind," he said. "I wouldn't put any stock in what the late Miss Lindstrom had to say about anyone, if I were you. She was pleasant enough when she chose to be, but she was quite capable of being nasty. Always in a calculating way. In any event, please go ahead and let me hear what she had to say about me. And about the rest of my family if you wish."

Carol regarded this as a preemptive disclaimer. She wondered how he would react to the specific words Annika had used to characterize him.

"As you will see, it would have served no good purpose for me to read the so-called diary yesterday," she said, choosing not to comment on Bob's characterization of Annika. "But now I think it is appropriate to read what she wrote."

Carol removed her copy of the English translation from her jacket pocket, smoothed it out on her thigh, and read the passage which applied to Mr. Kershaw.

Now for Bob. The gift he'd most like is to get into my pants if he could figure out how to do it without screwing up his marriage. He's really pathetic. What I'd like to do is give him a framed nude photo of me. Wish I had one. That would cause a scene when Bob opens it on Christmas morning. But I'll be a nice little girl and give him something like a box of toffee.

She had read it so often that she had it virtually memorized, enabling her to watch for Bob's reaction. His face did not change expression, but the color rose in his cheeks. When she finished, however, a smile spread across his face and he leaned back in his chair.

"What a piece of work she was," he said. "A little tart with

251

a vivid imagination. I'm sure she spoke of the rest of my family in similarly gross language. I didn't much care to be characterized as pathetic, but beyond that it's all a pack of lies. What I think is that little Miss Lindstrom would have liked for me to lust after her, and when I didn't pay her the time of day she was angry. It's obvious that she vented her anger by transferring her fantasies to me. I'm afraid that it's Annika who was pathetic."

This was just about what Carol had expected Mr. Kershaw to say. What else could he say? That it was true? That he had indeed lusted after Annika, but that he had been discrete and never coarse?

"What you are saying, Mr. Kershaw, is that you never gave Miss Lindstrom any reason to believe that you were interested in her physically?"

"That's exactly what I am saying. She was just someone who was living in our house because my wife wanted to promote good international relations by hosting an exchange student."

"If your wife and children were to read what Annika said, do you believe that they would agree with you that she just made it all up?"

The question took Bob by surprise. For a brief moment he struggled to respond coherently, but quickly regained his composure.

"You wouldn't read this pack of lies to my family, would you? What purpose would it possibly serve? You made it very clear that you didn't wish to embarrass us."

"That's right. I do not wish to embarrass your family. But my question was whether they would interpret what Annika wrote as you have."

It was not a particularly warm day, and the heat in his office had not been turned up that morning. But Bob Kershaw was sweating.

"What are you suggesting? That you might like to ask my wife if she thinks I was interested in Annika in a way that was improper? Or my son, or my daughter?"

"I'm not suggesting anything, Mr. Kershaw. I'm only asking what you think they would say about your interest in Annika."

"I believe that they would support me. But you have been in our house a few times. You know that we are hardly what you would call a close-knit family. Sometimes we rub each other the wrong way. Heaven knows what Jennifer would say. She resents almost everything I do, when all I'm trying to do is be a good father."

"And your wife?"

"Look, sheriff, ours isn't a perfect marriage. Amanda and I aren't still honeymooning. We have our own lives to lead. We live and let live. No big problems."

"Perhaps Annika was a little problem."

Mr. Kershaw got up and walked over to the window, from which he could see the comings and goings of people in the town square.

"I thought that you were investigating Miss Lindstrom's death," he finally said, "not my alleged interest in her."

"I am investigating her death. One of the things I have been trying to do is learn everything I can about the people who were an important part of her life while she was here in Southport. And about her relationships with those people. I do not believe that her death was caused by someone who was a stranger to her. So I'm interested in your alleged interest in her in much the way I'm interested in everyone else's interest in her. I can't simply take a person's word for it as to how they felt about her. If I did, I'd be a pretty poor cop, and chances are I'd never figure out who was responsible for her death."

"You're proceeding on the assumption that I'm a suspect in Annika's death?" Bob asked. It had occurred to him that this was about more than whether he was another middle aged man who'd taken a fancy to a young girl.

He came back from the window and sat down again.

"It is probably about this time when suspects are advised to get themselves a lawyer," he said. "If I thought there was any reason, however bizarre, why you'd suspect me of killing Annika, I would indeed be calling Ken Sturdivant. But I don't believe that is necessary. Let me be candid. Annika was a beautiful young woman. It would have been hard to live in the same house with her and not be aware that she was sexually attractive. For all I know, I did occasionally look at her in ways that could have been misunderstood. Let's call it the male reflex. I probably told her that I was glad to have her in the house, that she brightened up the place. I may have complimented her on her clothes, maybe her hair, maybe that perfect Scandinavian skin of hers. God, I might even have told her she was beautiful. What's wrong with that? She was beautiful. If she misinterpreted my intentions, that's not my fault."

Carol had heard what was probably as close to a confession that Bob Kershaw had been smitten by Annika Lindstrom as she was likely to get. There was no point in pushing the issue further. There were, however, two more questions she had to ask.

"You will remember that I removed everything of Annika's from your house awhile ago. I inventoried things quite carefully, and they were about what you'd expect. But I didn't find a cell phone. I didn't find an iPod. I didn't find a laptop. In fact, I didn't find any of the electronics most people her age would regard as absolutely necessary. Did you take any electronic items from Annika's room after she disappeared?"

"Why would I do that?" he asked.

"Mr. Kershaw, please let's not go down that path again. You went to considerable trouble to find Annika's diary, and I think we know why. Why not her laptop? Or any device which could have entries which mentioned you?"

"Okay," he said with resignation. "I did look for things like that. I never found a cell, an iPod – none of the little gadgets. Figured she probably had them with her when she vanished. That they were on her when you found her body. Were they?"

"No, they weren't. What about a laptop?"

"I did find that, back when we cleaned out her room. I took it."

"And where is it now?"

Mr. Kershaw got up slowly and went to a closet across the room from the window. He rummaged around for a minute and produced a small laptop.

"Nothing on it," he said. "I mean nothing that has any bearing on your case or on me and my family."

"Is that because you deleted things?"

"No. I might have if I'd found anything which could have been misconstrued. But the stuff which could have been revealing about her personal life just wasn't there. It was almost entirely school related. Not even Facebook."

"Then you won't mind if I take it."

"I think you can assume that the fact I haven't junked it

proves it contains nothing of interest."

"Thank you for calling that to my attention," Carol said. For whatever reason, Bob Kershaw had pulled himself together, decided that he had nothing to fear from being more candid, and was even beginning to enjoy this little contest of wills with the sheriff.

"I had a second question. Do you remember ever being inside Bill Claymore's cottage?"

"Claymore? No reason to be. I don't know him. I wouldn't even know where it is if I hadn't been doing a small job for a neighbor of his, Joe Cabot. We met at Cabot's place once back in the winter when he was working on his taxes."

"I had no idea accountants made house calls," Carol said.

"We aim to please," Kershaw said with a smile.

When she walked out of the old brick building and into the bright sunlight, Carol was no more certain than she had been when she arrived that Bob Kershaw was a suspect in the Lindstrom case. But at least she now knew that he had a relationship, however tentative, with the Cabots, the family which had made an extra copy of a key to the Claymore cottage and then lost it.

CHAPTER 44

"Hi, sheriff. It's Karen Leeds. Remember me?"

The voice was one Carol thought of as perky. Or chipper. She would have known who it was even if Ms. Franks had not told her. Short, cute. The girl who had referred to Annika as awesome.

"Hello, Karen. Nice to hear from you. What's on your mind?"

"A lot of things, I guess. Everybody's in a funk over Michael. That was so terrible. I don't think anyone paid attention to their classes today."

"Michael was really well liked, I take it?"

"Oh, yes, But, funny, you don't know how much someone means to you until something like this happens. Rickie's table, we were all crying at lunch. Well, maybe not really crying, but you know what I mean."

Carol assured Karen that she did, then waited. She doubted that the call had been prompted by a need to share the sorrow of Southport students over Michael Stebbins' death.

"There weren't many of us there today. At Rickie's table, I mean. Michael was gone, of course, and Rickie, too. They say he's going to be out for a few days. It was mostly just the girls. Anyway, we got to talking about what an awful downer it was, and how we missed Rickie. I mean, he was the leader. Always saying something or doing something that made lunchtime fun.

"But he wasn't there, and we just sat around and picked at our food and said stupid things. It got me thinking about something Rickie had said one day over lunch just after they found Annika. It was about who'd done it, and know what he said? Eric Mackinson."

"Rickie told you that Mackinson had killed Annika?" Carol asked, making no effort to conceal her surprise.

"Well, not exactly. But everybody was talking about who might have killed her, and we were throwing names around. That's when he said something like 'how about Mackinson.' I don't think most of us even knew who Mackinson was."

"But you did?"

"I wouldn't have if it hadn't been for what I saw the night of that party when Annika disappeared. I should have said something to you, but I'd forgotten all about it. Annika and other kids were coming over to my house first. I remember that I was on the front porch when I saw some guy stop Annika as she came up the street. She sort of ignored him and came on up to the house. I asked her who that was, and she said it was a creep named Eric Mackinson. They'd been together before and he wanted to hook up with her again, but she told him to get lost. When you asked about what happened that night, I was just thinking about the kids at the party. Then today I remembered what Rickie had said, and it reminded me of Annika and this guy she called a creep."

Why hadn't she heard about this before? She had told Eric that someone had seen him on the street the night of the party, but it had only been a ploy to get him to admit that he had left his house that evening. Now she had an eye witness to the fact that he had indeed been on the street – and with Annika Lindstrom. But Rickie hadn't mentioned his belief that Eric Mackinson might have killed Annika. Neither had anyone else, including Michael Stebbins, who lived practically across the street from Eric.

"Are you sure of these things, Karen? That Rickie suggested Mackinson might have been responsible for what happened to Annika? That Annika met up with Mackinson the night of the party, and that she told you he wanted to hook up with her again?"

"Oh, yes, I'm sure of it. I'm sorry. I should have told you this back when we talked about Annika. Like I said, I wasn't thinking about anything but who was at the party and when I last saw Annika. Do you think it's important?"

"I don't know," Carol said. "We're still investigating what happened to Annika. And to Michael, of course. Two friends of yours, both gone now. I'm so sorry for you and for everyone at the school. But, no, I don't know whether what you've told me is important. What I can tell you is that I very much appreciate this information. It may turn out to be important; it's just too soon to know."

"I hope it helps. And I really am sorry I didn't say something before. But it's just awful about Michael. I hear Rickie is real sick about it, blames himself for trying to sail in that weather. And Jennifer Kershaw is upset, too. She was with us today, but she didn't say anything, just sat there, staring at her food. She and Michael were trying to get it together. I'm worried about her, and about Rickie."

"It will take time for both of them, Karen. They're going to need friends like you to help them get through this. I know you'll be there for them."

"I've got to go, but I wanted you to know about this guy Mackinson. Please don't let any more bad things happen to us."

Carol shared Karen's hope that the kids at Southport High School had experienced their last tragedy. She knew that there would be others in the course of many of their lives, but she fervently wished that the current year would end without the loss of another school mate.

Karen's phone call changed Carol's priorities for the day. She would have to go back to Southport, at least that's what she would do if she could locate Eric Mackinson and arrange to meet him. She tried his cell and was pleased that he answered after only a few rings.

"Mr. Mackinson, this is Sheriff Kelleher. I need to talk with you again, and I'd like to do it today if at all possible. I assume you are on a job. Where can I meet you?"

"Is something wrong?" Eric answered, his voice betraying his anxiety.

"Not that I know of, but something occurred to me that suggests we should have another chat. What's your schedule?"

"I'm working at a place on the outskirts of Yates Center. It's up Piney Branch Road. But I can be back in Southport by five, give or take a few minutes."

"Let's meet in Southport. I'll be on one of those benches in the town square park at five o'clock. Let me give you my cell number in case you're delayed."

Carol gave him the number and brushed aside his proposal of an alternative meeting place.

"I'll see you in the square," she said and put her cell back in her pocket.

It was ten after the hour when Eric Mackinson approached across the square. She hadn't noticed the arrival of the panel truck. Perhaps he had driven home and then walked back into town.

"Here, have a seat," Carol said. "This shouldn't take long."

"Has something happened?"

"Like what?" Carol asked.

Eric looked as if he didn't understand the question.

"I don't know. I thought I'd answered all your questions."

"Well, I have some more questions," Carol said. "I'm afraid I always seem to be going back to the night of that party in January. The one you missed. You were home alone that night, you told me. Let's talk about that."

Eric was obviously uncomfortable. Carol had the impression that of all the people she had talked with about the Lindstrom case, Eric Mackinson had been the one who was most ill at ease each time they met.

"When we first met," Carol continued, "you claimed that you hardly knew Annika. But it has since become clear that you knew her quite well, that you and she went out together. Then after awhile, you tell me, your relationship with her wasn't going so well and you stopped seeing her."

"Like I told you," Eric interrupted, "we may have seen each other in town, but we never got together again."

"Okay, but the relationship had ended, sometime before Christmas and well before the infamous January party. I must tell you that I am having trouble believing that that is the whole story. There are two things that bother me. In the first place, I believe that there was much more to your relationship with Annika than you have let on. Frankly, I believe that you and she were physically intimate, that you had intercourse with her back in the fall. Moreover –"

Eric was no longer merely uncomfortable. He was agitated, and he tried to interrupt again.

"No, let me finish. When you broke off the relationship I believe she got very angry with you. And you began to worry. What if she were to bring a charge of rape against you? She was only sixteen, and even if she had given her consent, it would be statutory rape. Your life would be in ruins. So I think you tried to make up to her. You met with her and suggested that you should give it another try. In fact you were actually seen with her on the night of the party. The night she disappeared. And the way I hear it, she rebuffed you."

"It wasn't like that at all," Eric blurted out. "We split with no hard feelings. Everything was fine, really it was."

He was insisting that the breakup was amicable. Not that

they hadn't slept together. Not that a charge of statutory rape hadn't entered his mind. Just that they had parted as friends.

"Perhaps. But what if I'm right. What if you realized that Annika was no longer your friend, but rather a vindictive girl who could cause you a lot of trouble? I don't know what happened next. Why don't you tell me? Did you shrug your shoulders and go back to the house to watch TV? Or did you become obsessed with changing her mind, doing whatever you had to do to make her see things your way? What did you do about Annika that night after she walked away from you? After she told you to get lost?"

It was too late in the game for Eric to claim that he'd forgotten. He had already lied or shaded the truth about his relationship with Annika one time too many. He didn't know how the sheriff had come to know so much about him and Annika. He tried to avoid her question by asking one of his own.

"You think I killed her, don't you?"

"I don't know what to think, Eric. That's why we're talking. That's why I'm talking to a number of people. Sooner or later I'll learn who was responsible for her death. In the meanwhile, I'm asking questions. It's as simple as that. My question for you is, did you kill Annika Lindstrom?"

"No, I didn't kill her. I loved her."

When Eric Mackinson left the park bench to go home for dinner, he was worried – worried that the sheriff believed he had killed Annika. The sheriff didn't know whether she believed that or not. But she did know that she needed to talk with Rickie Lalor, who had apparently identified Eric as a suspect in her death. What did he know about Eric? Why had he told his school friends that Eric might have been guilty of killing Annika? She resolved to pay a visit to Rickie. Rickie Lalor, currently grieving the death of his friend Michael Stebbins. Rickie Lalor, the leader of the clique of Southport students which had included Annika. Rickie Lalor, the strong willed risk taker who had presumably been a problematic role model for Michael.

CHAPTER 45

The drive back up the West Lake Road took Carol right by the Claymores' cottage. She was surprised to see both Barry's car and Barry himself. He was raking the back yard, which was covered with branches and odds and ends of detritus which had accumulated there during the wind storm. On the spur of the moment she slowed down and pulled over onto the shoulder a few yards from the hedge which shielded the Cabot residence from its neighbors.

"Barry, I didn't know you were still here," she said as she walked over to where he was standing, leaning on the rake.

"Hi, sheriff. Yeah, I guess it was easier to procrastinate about getting that summer job than I thought it would be. Maybe a good thing. This way I get to help clean the place up, get back into Dad's good graces."

"It was quite a storm, wasn't it? Did you people lose your power?"

"No, we did okay. Actually, I had planned to be on my way, but Mom and Dad didn't think it was a good idea to be on the roads with the weather like that. I'm leaving tomorrow."

"And going where?"

"Back to Ohio. I've got some new friends there. One of them called to ask if I'd be interested in a lifeguarding job at a neighborhood pool near the college. I didn't say yes, but it's worth a look."

Carol leaned against the car that Barry had so recently failed to service in a timely way, leading to their impromptu lunch in Yates Center.

"I take it you like it at your college."

"Sure. It's harder than I expected, but it's fun. You know, more freedom than you get at home. I've been lucky with my roommate. We're going to do it again next year."

"You've heard, I presume, about the boating accident on Saturday. I remember that you knew Michael Stebbins."

"That was so unbelievable," Barry said. "Like I told you,

I'd been sailing with him. Him and Rickie. He wasn't a friend, but I knew him pretty well. It's just awful. And he was thinking about going to my school next fall."

"Michael was going to McLean?" She remembered her conversation with Mr. and Mrs. Stebbins and the mention of a trip Michael had taken with his father to look over a college in Ohio.

"I don't know, but he talked about it. He came out to visit the school, talk to the admissions people. He even suggested that maybe me and him could room together."

"He knew you that well?"

"Not really, but I think he was nervous about rooming with someone he didn't know. I think he wanted to go to Syracuse, live with Rickie, but that didn't work out. Anyway, it wouldn't have worked at McLean with me either. Clay and I really hit it off. It started out as a joke, but we got along good and decided we'd room together next year, too."

"What started out as a joke?" Carol asked.

"The Claymores. His name was Clay Moore, actually Clayton Moore, but everyone calls him Clay. So we became the Claymores. We thought it was funny. I wondered if somebody assigning roommates had a sense of humor, but truth is I think it was just chance."

Carol found the idea of two Claymores mildly amusing, but she was more interested in the young man who wouldn't be going to McLean.

"Let's talk about Michael's visit to your college. When did he do that?"

"It was last January, the end of the month."

"You're sure?"

"Yes. I remember because it was on the weekend when I came down with the flu. He hoped I could join him and his father for dinner, but I was feeling lousy. It hit the campus real bad for about two weeks. I missed three days. Even had a couple of my classes canceled because the profs were sick."

Carol had been assuming that Michael's visit to McLean had probably taken place in the spring. Not so. Someone who knew Annika was missing had been in Ohio not two weeks after her disappearance, and that someone was Michael Stebbins. No, she corrected herself, there could have been two people. It was possible that Barry Claymore had also heard about Annika. She wasn't sure who was responsible for it, but presumably one of them had mailed a postcard to the Kershaws, a postcard signed AL, a postcard that assured them that Annika was all right. And that would mean that one of the two had, at a minimum, been involved in creating the illusion that Annika was alive when in fact she was almost certainly already a frozen corpse in the Claymore cottage's pump room.

"Tell me, Barry, where were you on the three day weekend when Martin Luther Kings' birthday was celebrated last January?"

Barry wrinkled his brow. It suggested that he was thinking hard about the sheriff's question.

"That was before I got the flu, wasn't it? Yeah, it had to be. It was just after college started spring term. I guess I was right there in my dorm. Maybe I took in a movie or something. It's hard to remember."

"Maybe we could ask the other Clay Moore," Carol said. "I'll bet he'd remember."

Barry pulled a rake full of small broken tree limbs over to the pile he had been assembling in the corner of the yard.

"I'm not sure that's necessary. It's coming back to me. That was the weekend Annika disappeared, wasn't it?"

"It was, and I was wondering if you were taking advantage of the long weekend to drive back to the lake to see her."

"You want to know if I was here when it happened, don't you?"

"That's what I said."

"Well, if you must know, I thought about it. About coming back to see Annika, I mean. I'd spent the Christmas holiday with the family back in Jersey, and they had a lot of things planned so I couldn't get away then. It had been quite a while since I'd seen her, and we'd hit it off pretty good."

Carol sighed silently. When she had first spoken to Barry he had denied even knowing Annika.

"You weren't into the spring term yet, and you thought it would be a neat idea to spend a day or two with Annika again. But did you actually come back to Crooked Lake?"

"Well, no, I didn't."

"Why not? Too long a drive? Too much snow and ice on the roads?"

"She had other plans. I called her, and she said it wasn't a good time."

"But I thought you and she had hit it off pretty good. Couldn't she have juggled her plans, knowing she'd have a chance to see you again?"

"I tried to get her to change her mind. I even told her I'd reserved a motel room."

Nice move, Carol thought. And sensible, what with the cottage closed up for the winter and freezing cold.

"What motel was that?"

"I don't remember. I'd never stayed in a motel up here before, didn't figure I'd be doing it again soon."

Carol knew there weren't that many motels close by. He knows I'll be checking all of them, she thought.

"Did you cancel your reservation?" she asked, hoping that he hadn't, thereby improving the chances that some desk clerk would remember.

"I must have, otherwise I'd have been stuck with the bill." Barry resumed raking, but kept talking. "You suspect me of being up here that night Annika went missing, don't you?"

"I'm only trying to clarify just where everyone was on that January night. If I sound as if I don't trust your answers to my questions, don't take it personally. By this time there are quite a few people around here who probably feel just like you do. In the law enforcement business, I'm afraid you develop the not very nice habit of treating what people tell you with a certain amount of skepticism. Even the truth can acquire a subjective cast."

"Well, I wasn't here when something happened to Annika. I wanted to be, and I did make a reservation. But I wasn't here, and I did cancel the reservation. I'm sure you will ask around, and I hope people will confirm what I've told you."

Later, as Carol drove back to Kevin's, she was reviewing her conversation with Barry Claymore. She was not prepared to accept his statement that he had not visited the lake that weekend. There was no way to prove that Annika had told him that she had other plans. It might be possible to verify that he had made and then canceled a motel reservation, although she wasn't sure how good the records of local motels would be more than four months after the fact. She'd put Bridges on it tomorrow. The easiest way to confirm or refute Barry's story would probably be to call Clayton Moore. She had chosen for the present not to make Barry even more anxious by asking him for Clayton's phone number. But she did not know where Clayton was from, and if the college declined to give out his phone number or at least his family's address, contacting him might be a problem. Perhaps Kevin would have an angle.

That evening, Kevin promised that he would try, but he had already discovered that McLean's privacy rules might not be easy to overcome.

Carol gave Kevin a thorough report on what she had learned – and what she had intuited – over the course of the day, and they both agreed that the list of suspects in the Lindstrom case was coming into focus. But it was after dinner and before bed that Kevin confronted Carol with the question that had been on his mind all day long.

"Yesterday you gave me an assignment, but we got side-tracked by other things and I never did ask what on earth you were talking about. Do you remember, you told me that you wanted me to pretend to be Jennifer Kershaw? Now I think of myself as being a reasonably intelligent guy, but really, Carol. Pretend to be a junior in high school, and a girl at that? What are you talking about? I'm sure you don't expect me to play like an undercover cop, dressed up in something a 16 year old girl would wear. I know they do that on TV, cops pretending to be hookers to trap a john. But I don't have the cleavage for it. So what were you talking about?"

"Don't be ridiculous. I wouldn't dream of asking you to make an ass of yourself. What I want you to do is try hard to think like Jennifer might be thinking. Try to put yourself in her position, knowing what we know about her. She's a troubled kid. And it's more than just typical teenage hormones or hostility to the limits parents try to enforce. I've talked with her several times, and gotten a feel for her personality. She's not an easy person. Chip on her shoulder, obviously and not surprisingly much more at home with her peers than with adults. But when I met with the Kershaws after Michael Stebbins' death, she was a different person. You'd expect her to be sad. Word has it that she and Michael were interested in each other. How close they were, I don't know. But I'm sure there's more going on than grieving for Michael. Jennifer was more than numb and unusually quiet. There's something on her mind, something that scares her. She looked blank, but not in the way people can look when they're simply shutting everyone else out. I'm not sure how good a judge of these things I am, but what I think I saw was fear."

"So Jennifer may be a girl who is frightened, and whatever she's frightened of seems to be related to Michael's death. Is that it?"

"I guess that's what I'm saying, although I'm not really sure. That's why I want your help. Let's talk over everything we know about Jennifer. About her personality, her friends, everything. Even if it's just hearsay. Then I'd like you to go into your brainstorming mode and see what ideas you can come up with that might account for what I've seen."

"Is there any chance that I could meet Jennifer? Maybe you and I could see her together. It's hard to form an opinion about someone you've never even seen. I know that it helps me get a fix on my students when I actually see them for the first time, when I can picture what they look like. No promises where Jennifer is concerned, but I'd like to meet her."

Carol thought about it.

"I don't suppose it'll make a difference one way or another if she sees me with you, so I don't see why not. I'll give her a call and see if I can set something up for tomorrow or Wednesday. Unless, that is, you've got some urgent business to take care of."

"I'll cancel it," Kevin said with a smile. "I know my priorities."

By the time they climbed into bed for the night, it had been arranged, albeit reluctantly. Carol had suggested that she and Jennifer meet the next day in the town square right after school. Jennifer had insisted that this was not a good idea. After some discussion, it was decided that they would meet inside St. Patrick's at 4:30. Carol did not mention that Kevin would be there, too.

CHAPTER 46

St. Patrick's Church was three blocks south of the public square in Southport, which made parking easier than it would have been in the commercial center of town. Why Jennifer had chosen it as their meeting place, Carol did not know. What she did know was that Jennifer wasn't willing to meet in the town square.

They parked in front of the church just a few minutes ahead of 4:30 and made their way into the church. It was quite dark inside, and there was no sign of Jennifer. Or anyone else for that matter. Carol assumed that they were early, and suggested to Kevin that they take seats in the back of the church, from which they could better keep an eye on the door.

To her surprise, a soft voice from somewhere ahead of them and off to the left called out.

"Is that you, sheriff?"

Carol stood up and looked around. A young woman emerged out of a dark side chapel ahead of them and walked slowly their way. It was Jennifer Kershaw.

"Jennifer," Carol said. "I thought we had arrived before you got here."

"Who is that man with you?" Jennifer had stopped about ten feet away from them.

"Everything is all right. This is Kevin Whitman, a good friend of mine, who needed a lift into town this morning. I promise you that it's okay to say anything in front of him that you'd say in front of me."

"Hello, Jennifer," Kevin said in what he hoped was his best avuncular voice.

Jennifer looked uncertain as to what her next move should be, but after a moment's hesitation she slid into the pew in front of them and sat down. In spite of the fact that the church was poorly lit, they could see that she was nervous.

"Jennifer, I don't want to take any more of your time than I have to. But I wanted to talk with you for a few minutes about Michael Stebbins."

The young woman in the pew in front of them stiffened perceptibly.

"You want to talk about Michael? I thought you would want to ask me about Annika's diary."

"I'd be delighted to talk about that, too, if you'd like to. I probably didn't answer everybody's questions at your house the other day. But my reason for being here is Michael."

"I don't understand. What is there to say? He's dead, he's not coming back. I think they're going to have a memorial service for him at the high school. But I'm coping."

"I'm glad to hear that. It has to be terrible to lose a good friend like this. I've been worried about you."

"Why are you worried?" Was it Carol's imagination, or Kevin's, that this question was not Jennifer's way of saying 'don't worry, I'm fine?' It sounded more like a question prompted by a need to know if there was some reason why the sheriff thought she should be worried. It was dark in the church, but not so dark that it disguised the reappearance of what Carol would have described as fear.

"Let me be frank with you, Jennifer. I'm worried about you because you seem to me to be worried. I don't know why you are worried. I can understand why you are depressed, why you are sad. You've just lost your friend Michael. But why are you worried?"

"I'm not worried," she said defensively.

"But you asked that we not meet today in the town square, which is out in the open, where anybody could see you talking with me. Instead, you wanted to meet here, away from downtown, a place where nobody would see us. That suggests worry. Do you see my point?"

Jennifer bit her lip.

"I just don't want my friends to see me with you. They'll think I did something wrong."

"Have you done anything wrong that you're worried about?"

Jennifer looked around. It was an involuntary action. She was facing the door, and it was obvious that no one had come into the church.

"No. Why are you asking if I've done something wrong?"

"Like I said, you seem worried. And nervous. Just like you

did when I last met with your family. It isn't like you. Naturally, it makes me concerned about you."

Jennifer looked at Kevin for the first time since she had sat down.

"Is this man really just a friend of yours? He's not an undercover policeman, is he?"

Kevin an undercover policeman? Both Kevin and Carol would laugh about this later. But not now. Jennifer clearly knew nothing about undercover cops, other than misinformation she had picked up from television. Nonetheless, the question spoke to an anxiety, the cause of which they did not know.

"I really am concerned about you, Jennifer. Kevin just happened to be with me today. If you'll be more comfortable, I can ask him to wait for me outside."

This was not what they had agreed on, but Carol had a feeling that Jennifer might be willing to speak more candidly if Kevin were not present, and that, after all, was more important than giving him a chance to further form an impression of the young woman. For whatever reason, Jennifer decided she was willing to tolerate Kevin's presence.

"Never mind. Anyway, you're wrong. I'm not worried. And I don't know why you think I'm nervous. I'm never nervous, except maybe before exams. So I don't know what we're talking about."

"I guess I was wondering if there's something that's bothering you. Is it something about Michael, not just that he's dead, but that his death has got you thinking about something? Something that worries you? I know you said you aren't worried, so maybe that's not the word I should use. Let's say that you're puzzled. There's something you don't understand, and Michael's death has brought it to mind."

"If you like, I can say this over and over again. But I'm okay. There really isn't anything more to say. I ought to go now."

Reluctantly, Carol agreed. She could think of no other way to get Jennifer to open up.

"Can you wait until after I go before you leave?" Jennifer asked. "You know, give me ten minutes start before you leave the church?"

"Of course," Carol said. And they watched while Jennifer went to the church door, cautiously peered out into the street, and then hurried on her way.

"What better demonstration that she's afraid," Kevin said. "And it's not just that her friends will realize that the sheriff is questioning her and wonder why. It's someone specific. She doesn't want him or her to know that she's talking to you."

"I think you're right. Otherwise, why this business of making her meet me in this church, blocks away from more obvious meeting places. I don't think she's even Catholic. Why not the Baptist Church – it's right on the town square."

"The church has nothing to do with it," Kevin said. "It's location. And it's indoors where you can't be seen. Pretending to be Jennifer is going to be tough, and I'm making no promises. But I agree with you, she's in some kind of trouble and she's not willing to talk about it. Not yet."

"So what do you think of Miss Kershaw?" Carol asked.

They had talked a bit about it en route back to the cottage, but it was now the cocktail hour and time to get serious.

"No question, you're right. She's nervous, and it's pretty obvious that she's afraid of someone. This isn't your typical high school student being coy about something. When she says she isn't worried, she's lying. She wants you to think she's okay, but at the same time she's sending signals that she's not. Frankly, I think she almost wants you to know she's scared. I know that doesn't make sense, but my guess is that Jennifer is confused. She's got a problem and she doesn't know what to do. She probably hopes it will go away, but she doubts that it will."

"I'm glad you see it like I do," Carol said. "Of course, we may both be wrong, but I don't think we are. Like I said before you met her, she's not the same girl she was the first couple of times I talked to her. She was testy, argumentative, hard around the edges. Now she actually seems less grown up, or at least not so grown up as she liked to think she was. She needs help."

Kevin refilled their wine glasses and then went over to the window where he could see the late afternoon sun lighting up the bluff across the lake.

"You wanted me to put myself in Jennifer's shoes. To try to get inside her head. Sorry if I'm mixing metaphors or something like that. It's a challenge. We know too little."

"Why don't you give it a try?"

"If you cut me some slack, I will," Kevin said. "Now I've at least got a mental picture of what she looks like and sounds like. She looks like a fairly typical teenager. And sounds like one. Except that she's worried, nervous, scared, all those things we've said about her. Then I have your description of her family, her closest friends, what they say about her, what she says about them. My theory is that whoever she's afraid of is likely to be a member of her family or one of those friends."

"Do you think it could be a family member?"

"Initially it seemed like a good possibility. But I don't really think so. You've made it clear that there's a fair amount of tension in the family, but that's the old Jennifer. What could her parents be doing that she'd find threatening, that would scare her? Threaten to ground her? Hardly. That would bring out the old Jennifer. I can think of things parents might do that would upset a child. Plan to move across country, taking her away from her friends. Send her to some private school to get her to knuckle down, clean up her act. But that would make her angry, not scared. Tell her they're getting a divorce? I suppose that could do it for some kids, but I don't see it as turning Jennifer into the girl we saw this afternoon.

"And then there's her brother. You've indicated that their relationship is a bit prickly, but not that unusual. I'd assume that she'd take any serious trouble between the two of them to her parents, no matter how much they may annoy her. I can't conjure up a scenario in which Brian would scare her, make her afraid to be seen with you."

Kevin resumed his seat on the couch and turned his attention to other people in Jennifer's life. But not before Carol interrupted his train of thought and brought him back to the family.

"How about the fact that Bob Kershaw, her dad, seems to have had what I'd call an unhealthy interest in Annika?"

"I've thought about that," Kevin said. "I'll bet she's been observant enough to know that daddy had an eye for Annika. Maybe she even saw them in some kind of compromising situation. But Annika's been gone from their lives for months. Why would something that happened back then – or something she thought happened back then – become a problem now? I suppose it could have come up one day when she and her dad were having one of their spats, but what could he do that would scare her? That would make her afraid to be seen with you? He knows that you're already familiar with Annika's little Christmas list. No, I don't think Jennifer's problem has to do with a family member."

"Which leaves you where?"

"With someone she knows here in Southport, I guess. Of course it's possible that her anxiety is related to plagiarism on a school paper, or a theft from a local store. Who knows? But you're not investigating things like that, and I don't think you're worried about what kind of trouble Jennifer's gotten herself into unless it's somehow related to Annika's death. Or maybe the family, and I like to think I've ruled that out. So let's talk about non-family members that have surfaced in your investigation. And let's try eliminating some of them."

"I'm listening," Carol said.

"Okay, let's begin with Barry Claymore. You have no evidence that Jennifer really knows him. Oh, they may have met, but he wasn't a part of her group and he's been out in Ohio. If Barry killed Annika last January, he surely wouldn't have told Jennifer about it. And I can't imagine he would have told someone else, who then told Jennifer. Moreover, we know that Barry had nothing to do with Michael's death. So why would Barry have any reason for threatening Jennifer, and why would she have any reason to be afraid of him?"

"Eric Mackinson?"

"Well, from what you've said, there's a better chance that he was responsible for Annika's death than Barry was. But why would Jennifer be afraid of him? Once again, like I said about Barry, it's doubtful that they really knew each other. If he did kill Annika, how would Jennifer know? And if by some chance she did, why wouldn't she just tell you instead of hiding from Mackinson? Anything is possible, I suppose, but I'm sure Jennifer isn't worried about Eric Mackinson."

"So far we seem to be in agreement," Carol said.

"Are we going to drink ourselves into a happy haze, or shall we give some thought to dinner?"

"My limit is two glasses, and yours should be. I love listening to you pretending to be Jennifer, so let's not worry about cooking up a storm. We can make do with what's in the fridge. Why don't we move out to the kitchen, you keep talking, and I'll put something together."

While Carol tackled the challenge of supper, Kevin focussed on Jennifer's circle of friends.

"You didn't mention any pecking order among the girls, just that Karen Leeds, Debbie Selfridge, and Sue Marinelli were her closest friends. It's probably sexist to say so, but I have trouble picturing teenage girls as being as threatening as teenage guys. I know, girls run with gangs, commit crimes, just like guys do. But why would Jennifer be afraid of them? Because Karen or one of the others threatened her if she went to the police? Went to the police about what? To report that her friend had killed Annika? Please. Annika was the victim of an attempted rape. Doesn't that sort of rule out the girls? And what else might any of the girls do which would make Jennifer afraid? Sorry, but no matter how hard I rack my brain, I can't think of anything."

"Actually," Carol said, "it hadn't occurred to me that any of the girls could be the cause of Jennifer's change in mood. So whom does that leave?"

"Theoretically, quite a few, but the only ones you've mentioned to me are the contractor – Harbaugh, isn't it? – and the Claymores' neighbor, Cabot, plus a guy named Bachman and Rickie Lalor. Oh, I almost forgot Helen Claymore's brother Roger. But Harbaugh, Cabot, and Roger aren't friends or acquaintances of Jennifer's, and nothing you've told me suggests any reason why she would be afraid of any of them. I didn't think very hard about Bachman, mostly because you didn't seem to think he was an important player in the mystery of Annika's death. And then there's Lalor. And after eliminating all of the other people on your roster, he's my candidate for the person Jennifer's worried about, afraid of, threatened by, whatever."

"But he's feeling guilty about Michael." Carol protested. "He's pretty much locked himself in his room. Didn't go to school today, doesn't seem to talk to anyone. Sounds like he's suffering a load of remorse. How can he be threatening to Jennifer?"

"I know it doesn't feel right," Kevin said. "But if I'm right about the others, who else is there? Some anonymous guy you haven't even thought of, much less given a name to?"

"I think you're suggesting that my investigation hasn't been very thorough. You may be right."

"Come on, Carol. I know how thorough you are. And I'm not saying that just because I love you. I've watched you handle these cases now for several years. Can you believe it? It seems like yesterday you actually thought I might have killed John Britingham. Remember? All I'm suggesting is that you need to take another, good hard look at Rickie Lalor. Partly because I can't see anyone else that Jennifer might be scared of. And partly because I have a hunch – just a hunch, mind you – that he could be the one who caused Annika Lindstrom's death and put her in the Claymore pump room."

"Rickie." Carol spoke the name as if she were savoring the sound of it.

"Yes, Rickie. Let me tell you why."

CHAPTER 47

By the time Carol and Kevin had retired for the night, they had discussed everything they knew about Rickie Lalor, everything they thought they knew about him, and quite a few things that they didn't begin to know about him. It had been a discussion that began as an effort to find a reason why Jennifer Kershaw might feel afraid of Rickie, and ended as a discussion of why Rickie was the most likely suspect in Annika Lindstrom's death.

Kevin, in his brainstorming exercise, had soon come to the conclusion that Jennifer's trouble was related to Annika's death. He had initially suspected a family problem, but it hadn't taken long to disabuse himself of that notion. He was briefly reluctant to abandon the possibility that Mr. Kershaw was somehow the source of Jennifer's problem. But that would be true, he decided, only if Jennifer knew that her father had become sexually involved with Annika. That in turn got him to thinking about Annika, and in no time he found himself assuming that whomever Jennifer feared must have had something to do with Annika's death and her presence in the Claymore cellar. And how could that be her father?

"Somewhere along the way," he had told Carol, "I became convinced that Jennifer knew how Annika had met her death, and that the person who was responsible for her death knew that she knew. The more I thought about it, the more likely it seemed to me that that person was Rickie Lalor. So let me give you my picture of Rickie. It's based, of course, on what you've told me, but I've added a few flourishes. I'm sure you'll tell me if I've gotten something wrong."

His thumbnail sketch went something like this. Rickie was good looking. He was strong, a presumption based on his letters in football. He was reasonably intelligent, otherwise he would not be college bound. He was an accomplished sailor; the accident that had cost Michael Stebbins his life was being attributed to poor judgment rather than a lack of good seamanship. His fellow students seemed to look up to him and accord him a special status.

Witness the fact that the group of students who shared the school lunch hour with him referred to the table where they habitually sat as Rickie's Table. At least one of those students seemed to walk in his shadow, treating him as his role model. That would have been Michael. Moreover, Rickie had a reputation as a risk taker, someone who was always ready to push the envelope, to take chances. He seemed to have a way with the girls, but, if Annika was to be believed, he had failed in his quest to have sex with her.

Carol had nodded her agreement as Kevin ticked off these personality attributes.

"That sounds like the Rickie I know," she said. "Or the one I've heard described. But you're going to have to tell me why you think it makes him our man."

"I think his profile offers some clues. But let me focus not just on who he is but on what we know he's said and done."

Carol listened as Kevin cited things which might have a bearing on the case.

"First, he told you he was at the party that night in January. Which means he was very much around when Annika disappeared, almost certainly in the same homes she was during the course of the evening. But you don't know where he was or with whom at any particular time. Nobody seems to have said, oh, I saw him having a snack in somebody's kitchen at 10:30, or he'd snuck off with so and so to a back bedroom at around 11:15. In effect, we don't know anything about what he was doing that evening.

"Second, you know that he dropped the hint to his friends in the cafeteria that they might want to bring up Eric Mackinson's name when they talked with you about Annika. But why did he do this? He didn't say. Did he really believe that Eric had something to do with Annika's disappearance? Or, for reasons of his own, did he want his friends to think so."

"My turn," Carol interrupted. "Let's talk about last September. In spite of the fact that Rickie has been deliberately vague, we know that either he or Michael drove a very drunk Barry back to his cottage that weekend he visited the lake. In either case, Rickie had to have been at the cottage because they had to have a second car to get back to Southport. Rickie would have had Barry's keys in his possession that night, both to drive his car and to open the cottage. He claims that he left the keys behind. That has to be true of the car key, but what about the key to the cottage? Barry wouldn't have needed it to lock up. Rickie could easily have lifted it from the key ring and taken it with him. We know that Barry claims he later missed that key and got his Uncle Roger to give him a replacement.

"At first I was just trying to account for all of the Claymores' keys. Then I asked myself why Rickie would have wanted to steal Barry's cottage key. Rickie certainly would not have lifted a key in September so that he'd be able to hide Annika in January. But what if it occurred to him that an empty cottage could be a great place to make out with a girl. It was still warm in September, and I doubt he'd thought ahead to cold weather."

"I suppose that's possible," Kevin said. "But you don't know that he took the cottage key."

"No, and he'll deny it. But I'm pretty sure that's what happened, and I'm assuming that he did. Let's go on to something else. Remember that the school custodian, Cabot, found Rickie along with Michael and Jennifer in the furnace room. They weren't there to sneak a cigarette. They were arguing vehemently and Rickie was really laying into them about something. Cabot didn't know what they were arguing about, but suppose it had to do with Annika and the fact that I'd been asking them some tough questions about their relationships with her."

"Which brings us to what occurred just this past weekend," Kevin said, taking up the narrative. "I'm talking about Rickie going sailing with Michael on that terribly windy day. He was at the tiller of the boat when it capsized and Michael was swept overboard. It would have been Rickie who suggested they go sailing, not Michael. It's his boat, he's the risk taker, Michael's the follower. Now ask yourself why Rickie had to go sailing that day and take Michael with him, and keep your mind open to the possibility that he planned to have an accident. Why? Ready for my theory about what happened to Annika?"

Carol had no quarrel with any of Kevin's 'facts,' but he was putting them together in ways which necessitated a lot of guess work. But she had asked him to put himself in Jennifer's shoes, and if he thought Jennifer's fears had something to do with who had done what to Annika, she was willing to bear with him.

"Go ahead. Just don't be surprised if I don't jump on your bandwagon right away."

"I think you will," he said. "But first, let's weed out some of the other suspects in Annika's death. There may be more, but first let's consider Eric Mackinson, Barry Claymore, and Bob Kershaw. I have trouble buying into any of them. Where would Jennifer's dad have had an opportunity to establish a relationship with Annika that could have led to her death? Not at the Kershaw house, that's for sure. At his office? I'll concede that it's possible, but highly unlikely. You've learned that she was set up for a rape, suggesting that she wouldn't have had sex willingly with her partner that night. In view of her 'diary,' it's a good bet that she wouldn't have consented to sex with Kershaw in any event. That, I suppose, is an argument in favor of daddy as the would-be rapist. But it's awfully hard to believe that Kershaw infiltrated the party and persuaded Annika to accompany him back to his office. Anyway, I'd rule him out because he didn't have a key, hence no access to the Claymore cellar."

Carol stopped him.

"Don't forget that he had been in the Cabot house back in the winter to help them with their taxes – and that the Cabots had conveniently lost a key to the Claymore cottage. What if Bob Kershaw swiped that key?"

"Why would he do that?" Kevin asked.

"So he could hide Annika's body," Carol said.

"But that assumes he was planning to kill Annika. You don't believe that, do you?"

"All I'm doing is reminding you that in my book he's still a suspect."

"How about Barry? Do you really believe he makes a good suspect?" Kevin asked. "He certainly knew Annika less well than the others. He saw her briefly back in September and was admittedly enamored of her. As far as you know, he never saw her again. He admits to considering coming to the lake in January, and that he had made a tentative reservation at an area motel. But he says he canceled it and didn't make the trip."

Carol reminded him that Barry may not have canceled the reservation, or that perhaps he did cancel it, came anyway, and stayed elsewhere. She had put one of her men on it, and hoped to have more information soon.

"Okay, so we can't rule Barry out," Kevin continued. "For the sake of argument, I'm willing to assume that he was at the lake. But if he was, no one's reported seeing him that night. In any event, I can't see him coming to the lake determined to have sex with Annika even if he has to rape her. Do you really think he carries those roofies around in his jacket pocket, just in case? Surely if he tried to talk her into the sack and she refused, he'd be unlikely to find any Rohypnol in Southport on the spur of the moment that night. But all of that's beside the point. The case against Barry falls apart when you consider where Annika was found. He had a key, no problem, but I just can't imagine him doing something so stupid as stashing her in his own parents' cottage. Wouldn't you agree?"

"I agree," Carol said, "that it's counterintuitive. But there's no accounting for what people will do when they're confronted with a situation they hadn't counted on. If he'd tried to rape her, he'd have been in a panic when he realized that he had a dead girl on his hands."

"All right," Kevin said. "I'll concede that he could have acted irrationally in the circumstances. If, that is, he was anywhere near Southport that night. But I'm almost certain that he wasn't."

Carol turned to Eric Mackinson.

"If what his mother told me is true, he might have had a motive for killing her. He had had sex with Annika, had made her angry by terminating their relationship, and might have feared that she could charge him with statutory rape. That's plausible."

"But what isn't plausible," Kevin said, "is that he would compound his problem by trying to rape her. Your source says he did approach Annika that night, apparently hoping to rekindle the relationship. But she rejected him. So what are you suggesting? That he refused to take no for an answer, followed her, lured her into his house, fed her more alcohol and the Rohypnol, and tried to have sex with her? I know you don't think Eric's the brightest bulb in town, but I can't imagine him courting real trouble like that."

"But the word on date rape drugs is that the girl doesn't remember what happened. I'll bet Eric would have known that."

"I don't know what he knows about drugs," Kevin said, "but why would he run any risk with a girl whom he'd been afraid would cry rape? No, I very much doubt that Eric and Annika got together that night, or if they did that he tried to rape her. He did have a key to the Claymore cottage, but in the circumstances that seems irrelevant."

"So you're inclined to dismiss Kershaw, Claymore, and Mackinson as probable suspects in Annika's death. Which means, I assume, that you're going to try to make the case for Rickie Lalor as the killer. Sorry, I mean as the one who slipped Annika the roofies and accidentally caused her death."

"I am. But you're right that none of these people, including Rickie, tried to kill her. He wanted to have sex with her, things went wrong, he had a dead girl on his hands, and he had to find a way to get rid of the body. Get rid of her quickly and in difficult circumstances."

"We're pretty sure Annika's death wasn't premeditated," Carol agreed. "But when I talk with people, I always tell them that Annika was killed, not that she died from the drugs she consumed. I've been half hoping that somebody might slip and say something that tells us that he knew how Annika had died."

Kevin and Carol had agreed earlier that they would limit themselves to two glasses of wine, but they had been at it for quite awhile and Kevin finally suggested that, just this once, they have a third. Pleading a busy work day tomorrow, Carol demurred, but Kevin refilled his glass.

"I'm still thinking clearly," he told her, "so don't expect me to start rambling. Now here's my case against Rickie.

"The party was planned for a night when the parents weren't home, at least at the Marinellis. We both know that this meant that alcohol would be consumed and that there would be opportunities for people to hook up. Don't you love that phrase? I used to call it 'make out.' I have no idea how many of the kids intended to hook up, have sex, whatever you want to call it. Maybe they didn't either. Things sometimes happen spontaneously.

"But it's my theory that Rickie had a plan. He had characterized Annika as a tease. He'd been going with her, after a fashion, but she wouldn't have sex with him. He may have known that she was putting out for Eric Mackinson and it bugged him. It doesn't really matter. But he saw an opportunity to make out with her, and because he knew from experience that she wasn't likely to go all the way, he got himself some Rohypnol. Somewhere along the way, probably at the Marinellis from what you've said about the way the party progressed, he coaxed her into one of the bedrooms. No problem. Annika had almost certainly been drinking a lot and she was typically willing to fool around. Up to a point. Just to make sure this would be his night, Rickie put some of those tablets in her drink. She started to lose her will to resist him and he started to take her clothes off. Then the drugs kicked in, she blacked out and fell, hitting her head. Now Rickie had a problem he hadn't counted on. A problem which becomes much worse when he discovers that Annika is dead.

"This is where my theory gets a bit fuzzy, but I think I'm on the right track. Jennifer and Michael are in the house, and Rickie needs help. Somehow he manages to get the attention of one or maybe both of them. Everybody is pretty well smashed, inhibitions are relaxed, nobody is going to be shocked by the fact that sex might be taking place. So we now have Rickie, Michael and Jennifer in a room with Annika, trying to figure out how to get her out of there. Without it being obvious that she's dead, of course. It would be much easier with the three of them than if Rickie tried to do it alone. What to do with the girl's body in the middle of a cold night in January? Then he remembers that he has a key to the Claymore cottage. He probably had to go home to get it, but he has two helpers now. Chances are they waited until they were quite sure the rest of the group had decamped for the next house. They were probably sure no one saw them leaving with Annika – I can just picture them trying to walk her to where they could get her into one of the cars. I have no idea how long it took them, or just how they did it, but in due course Annika is in the Claymore's pump room and they are back in Southport, hugely relieved that they have solved a very large problem. At least temporarily."

Carol had been listening in silence.

"You should be writing whodunits," Carol said, her face breaking into a broad smile. "If I hadn't been conducting this investigation, you might have lost me some time ago. But it makes sense. Let me see if I can finish your scenario."

"If you promise to wrap it up before midnight."

"No problem," Carol said, now confident that they were on the same page. "It looks like Rickie has solved his immediate problem, but he's now facing another one. Two other people know what's happened, and where Annika will be spending the winter. They are good friends of his, which is why he enlisted their help. Michael is his best friend, and someone whose relationship with

Rickie is almost worshipful. Jennifer is dating Michael, and Rickie knows she's not fond of Annika. Both of them can probably imagine themselves in Rickie's shoes, and whatever they thought about what had happened, they have become his accomplices. Rickie, I'm sure, swore them to secrecy. Can't you just see the three of them, sometime that night, promising each other that they'll say nothing to anybody? Ever? They've gotten away with something, and I'll bet they actually had an adrenaline rush after it was over.

"But inevitably," she continued, "Annika is discovered. They knew there would be an investigation, but back in January it seemed a long way away. They could see no reason why the investigation would focus on any of them.

"That was then. Now is now. I've been spending a lot of time with the Southport crowd, asking a lot of questions. And I've been at the Kershaws so much that I could be paying rent. Michael and Jennifer begin to worry, and they'll inevitably talk with Rickie about it. Should we make up some story to explain what happened? Should we tell the truth and hope they'll understand that we were scared and acted impulsively? I have no idea what was said, but I can imagine that Rickie wasn't having any of it. But what if he started to worry about Michael and Jennifer? What if they backed out of their promise not to talk to the police? What if they fingered him as the one who was responsible for Annika's death? He insists that they've got to stick together. That's probably what they were arguing about when Cabot caught them in the furnace room."

"Right, and Rickie can't be sure they'll keep their mouths shut," Kevin added. "He's a risk taker, and the stakes are high. It becomes time for him to look out for number one, maybe even get rid of Michael and Jennifer if he has to."

Carol shook her head 'no.'

"I refuse to believe Rickie deliberately killed his friend. Anyway, we'll never be able to prove that Michael's death wasn't an accident."

"It doesn't really matter," Kevin insisted. "Maybe Rickie set out to kill Michael. Maybe he intended to scare him into keeping his mouth shut. Maybe it was just an accident, as you say. One way or another, Michael's dead. Rickie doesn't have to worry any longer about him telling the truth. But not only don't you know whether Rickie killed Michael deliberately. Neither does Jennifer. If you were in her shoes, you'd be scared. Like Michael, you'd been talking to Rickie about changing his story and now Michael is dead. If you think it's possible that Rickie killed Michael to make sure he doesn't talk, you could believe he'd kill you, too."

"Why am I having such a hard time believing that a high school senior would go to such lengths to avoid admitting he had something to do with an accidental death?"

"I know," Kevin said. "But remember that Rickie's a self-confident guy. Life's dealt him a good hand, he's about to set off for a good college. Why mess it all up? Especially when your instinct is to take risks. Anyway, if I'm right, we've got our explanation for what's wrong with Jennifer. Maybe she's got no reason to feel threatened, but I don't blame her if she does."

By the time they decided to pack it in, they had agreed on most things. The case against Rickie Lalor seemed to be compelling. It was a circumstantial one, to be sure, but it looked better than the alternatives, even if they could not be dismissed out of hand. Now Carol faced two decisions. How to guarantee Jennifer's safety, if she was indeed in jeopardy. And how to persuade Rickie Lalor to show his hand, if indeed he had been the would-be rapist and the person whose key had gained entrance to the Claymore cottage that night in January. As fate would have it, she would have very little time to make those decisions. Less than two days, to be exact.

CHAPTER 48

Jennifer heard the ring, but barely. Roused out of a deep sleep, she reached across to the bedside table, groping for her alarm clock. Her hand couldn't find it. And then it did. The ring continued. She wasn't sure how many times she heard it before she realized it was her cell phone. But when she finally picked it up, it went dead. There was no one there. She tried to focus her eyes on the clock. It seemed to say 3:50, but she wasn't sure.

She turned over, mumbled something unintelligible, and soon fell asleep. When the ringing started again, a faint memory of what had happened the last time kicked in, with the result that it was her cell phone rather than the alarm clock that she reached for. Unfortunately, her hand was not steady, and she knocked it onto the floor. By the time she had located it and brought it to her ear, she was almost wide awake. Once again there was no one there. It was now 4:45, and she was both puzzled and strangely uneasy.

It was way too early to get up and she was very tired. But the urge to sleep was giving way to a half conscious effort to make sense of the fact that her cell had rung twice in the wee hours of the morning. Unusual, to say the least. That no one had been there was even harder to comprehend. A wrong number? Probably. But she was unable to make herself comfortable and settle down for another hour's sleep before she would have to get up and face the day. She had turned over in bed for perhaps the sixth or seventh time since the second call when her cell rang again.

Annoyed, she grabbed the cell and in a sharp voice asked who was calling. This time the phone did not go dead. She thought she heard breathing, and then she did hear a single word. 'Michael.' It hit her like a punch to the gut. For the briefest of seconds a wild thought crossed her mind: Michael has somehow miraculously survived! But of course that could not be so, and a terrible truth took hold of her. Her caller was warning her, warning her that the fate that had befallen Michael could also be hers. The fear she had experienced over the last two days swept over her. She started to cry.

In spite of the fact that she and Kevin had talked late into the night, Carol left early for the office on Tuesday. She had not slept well. Too much to think about. But it promised to be an unusually busy day, with Jennifer Kershaw and Rickie Lalor at the top of her agenda. It was these two young students at Southport High School that she had been thinking about when she would rather have been sleeping.

To her surprise, Ms. Franks was already at her desk and on the phone. She signaled to Carol as she walked in, indicating that she wanted her to wait.

"Yes, I understand. The sheriff just came in, so if you'll wait just a minute, she'll be with you."

Franks put her hand over the phone and spoke to the sheriff.

"It's that Jennifer Kershaw. There was already a call from her before I got here. It came in at six, if you can believe that. She sounds terribly upset. I guess she must have been to call so early."

"Did she say what she wants?"

"No, just that she's got to talk to you right away. She's really all worked up. I'm not good at voices, but she's been all breathy, if you know what I mean."

Carol hurried into her office and picked up the phone.

"Jennifer?"

"Thank God you're there. I have to see you. It can't wait. I told you yesterday I wasn't scared, but I am."

"Okay, just slow down and we'll see what we can do. Where are you?"

"In bed. I told Mom I'm feeling sick and can't go to school. But I'm not really sick, so I can meet you. Can we do it now? I mean just as soon as I can get dressed."

"Of course. Do you want to tell me what's the matter?"

"My cell's been ringing all night. He woke me up three times."

"Who's calling you?"

"Please, can I see you? Right away? I'd rather not talk on the phone."

"I'll be there. I'm on my way to Southport right now."

"No, no, not here." Jennifer almost shouted it, then lowered her voice. "I don't want you to come to the house. And I don't think I should come to your office either. Is there some place where nobody would know where we are?"

This is, indeed, one scared young woman, Carol thought. She was going to suggest the church again, but had a better idea.

"I'm thinking of a place, but how are you going to get there? You said you're supposed to be in bed."

"I know, but I already talked to my brother before he left for school. He said he'd drive me if it was an emergency."

Carol had gotten the distinct impression that Jennifer had a contentious relationship with Brian, much like the one with her parents. If she had turned to him for help, she must really be in serious trouble. Or thinks she is.

"Then let's meet at the cottage of the man who was with me at the church yesterday. It's on Blue Water Point, which is about eight miles north of Southport."

She gave Jennifer the address of Kevin's cottage and told her she'd be there within half an hour. It would probably take Jennifer a bit longer to tell her mother she was feeling better, get dressed, walk to school, and prevail upon her brother to leave class to drive her up the lake.

Carol called the cottage. Kevin was up and about, but not fully awake. She instructed him to put some clothes on, make sure that there was enough coffee for guests, and prepare himself for a visit from Jennifer Kershaw.

She set off for Blue Water Point without touching anything on her cluttered desk or stopping for a second cup of coffee in the squad room.

"Tell them I'm on my way to see a terrified young woman," she said to Franks, and hurried out to her car.

It was already apparent that this was going to be a beautiful day, perhaps the warmest Crooked Lake had had all spring. It was a drive Carol normally enjoyed, but today all she could focus on was Jennifer, who like herself, had had a bad night.

As she had expected, Carol reached the cottage before Jennifer and her brother did. Kevin had dutifully followed Carol's 'orders.' He was more presentable than when she had last seen him at around 7:30, and the smell of fresh brewed coffee permeated the cottage. She quickly briefed him on the gist of her conversation with Jennifer and told him to expect a very anxious young woman. And her brother.

Carol had given no thought to whether Brian would wish to go directly back to school or wait for his sister. Kevin could drive

Jennifer home, of course, but it was possible that Brian would want to sit in as they talked about Jennifer's problem. She decided that that would be up to Jennifer.

Not more than ten minutes later a ten year old Ford with a banged up front fender pulled in beside Kevin's Camry and the official sheriff's department car.

They watched as the two Kershaws jumped out and hurried across the grass to the back door. Jennifer was conspicuously nervous, even here, looking around at neighboring cottages and back at the road as if expecting to see someone she knew.

"Come on in. Hello, Brian. Let me introduce you to Kevin Whitman. Jennifer has met him."

"I'm not sure what this is all about. Jen's treating it like a secret, but she's convinced me that she had to be here. What am I supposed to do?"

"You're welcome to head on back to school. It's really up to you and your sister. Jennifer?"

"Can we sit down some place. I smell coffee. Could I have some?" She then remembered to say please, and asked if she might have cream and sugar.

Kevin obliged, and Jennifer addressed the sheriff's question.

"Maybe it's a good idea for Brian to hear what I want to tell you. He'll know soon enough anyway. We'll all know. I mean Mother and Dad."

Having frantically called the sheriff twice that morning and driven all this way to unburden herself of what sounded like a terrible problem, Jennifer suddenly seemed reticent. She sipped at her coffee, smiled nervously, and looked as if she were having trouble getting comfortable on the couch. They waited. It was Carol who became the prompter.

"I think, Jennifer, that you need very much to share something important with us, but that it's not easy to talk about it. Why don't you begin by telling me about those calls on your cell phone in the night."

Jennifer talked about what had happened and about her growing sense that something other than hers being a wrong number was the problem. Then she lapsed into nervous silence once more.

"You've come here to do more than share your anxiety,

Jennifer. I believe you want to tell us what's bothering you. Or should I say who's bothering you. Would it be easier if I guessed? If I'm wrong, you can tell me and I'll apologize for making a stupid guess."

"Do you think you know?"

"That's the way I would put it. I don't know, but I think I do. I think you are afraid of Rickie Lalor. And I strongly suspect that he's the one who placed those calls to you during the night."

Jennifer at first looked relieved, but almost immediately became unhappy once again.

"I'm sure I must be wrong," she said, her eyes brimming with tears. "He's been a friend. There's no way he would want to hurt me. I don't know whether I'm scared of him or just scared of being scared."

"We have lots of time this morning," Carol said. "You must have a lot of things you need to talk about. Just take your time and tell us what's been on your mind."

Kevin spoke up for the first time since greeting Jennifer and Brian when they arrived.

"I don't know whether you've had breakfast. But I can easily rewarm some left over Danish. Let me do that, and refill your coffee."

Without waiting for her answer, he disappeared into the kitchen.

"I guess I've been worried ever since Michael drowned," Jennifer began. "I know it was an accident. I mean, it had to be, with that awful wind and everything. Rickie just lost control and Michael went overboard. That's what everyone's been saying, and they must be right. But I can't get it out of my mind that maybe Rickie wanted Michael to drown. That he did it on purpose. Maybe he took Michael out sailing that day so it would happen that way. Is that possible?"

"We don't know, Jennifer," Carol said. "It was probably an accident. What matters is why you think it might not have been an accident. That's why you called me, isn't it?"

"Yes, it is." Jennifer made a conscious effort to straighten up in her seat. "Michael and I had been talking with Rickie about things, and he didn't agree with us. In fact, he got awfully mad, told us we were wrong. So when Michael drowned, I wondered if Rickie was still mad – you know, so mad he'd do something bad like losing Michael out there on the lake."

It was obvious that the real story about Jennifer's fear of Rickie Lalor would have to be pulled out of her slowly, one thing at a time.

"Okay. You and Michael had an argument with Rickie. It would take quite a serious argument to cause Rickie to kill Michael and threaten you. I want to know just what that argument was about."

"Well, it goes back to the time that Annika disappeared." She said it reluctantly, but the ice had been broken.

"Good. That's more specific. Something happened that night in January that you and Michael and Rickie all knew about. The problem is that you haven't agreed on whether you should tell people about it. My guess is that you want to talk about it – and so did Michael – but Rickie doesn't. Am I right?"

"I guess so."

"No, Jennifer, you know so, and you believe that Rickie feels so strongly about it that he could kill Michael, and possibly you, to keep you from talking about it. That's why you're frightened, and that's why you're going to tell me what happened to Annika in January."

"Brian, I'm so sorry. This is going to be a terrible thing for you and Mom and Dad. I should never have done it. But I'm so scared of Rickie. You've got to try to forgive me and help."

Brian looked confused, but he offered the assurances of love and affection that his sister so obviously needed at that moment.

"It was at Sue Marinelli's house," Jennifer began. "Like those parties usually go, we'd been dancing and stuff, but it wasn't long before everyone was looking for somewhere to hook up. You know how it is."

She glanced hopefully at Carol and Kevin for a sign that they would understand.

"Michael and I were kinda looking for a place. Not to have sex, just to have some fun. We were on the second floor and suddenly, just ahead of us, a door opened a little bit and there was Rickie. He was seeing if anybody was out in the hall, and as soon as he saw us he whispered to us to, quick, come on into the room. I wish he'd never seen us. We could have been at Debbie's or someplace else, but we were right there. Well, Rickie's a friend, and he sounded as if something was the matter, so we went in. It was so weird. There was Annika, lying on the floor. She didn't have anything on from the waist down except some leg warmers. I remember thinking she was so beautiful. We knew Rickie must have been having sex with her, but she was on the floor and he sounded all confused, trying to tell us that Annika was sick or something."

"Was Annika breathing?" Carol asked.

"I figured she'd passed out from too much to drink and fallen down. It looked like she'd hurt her head. At first, that is. But Rickie kept saying it was more serious. I think it was Michael who figured out she might be dead. We all tried to see if she was breathing and if her heart was beating. It was awful. There she was, dead, on the floor with no clothes on, in the Marinelli house. Rickie was going crazy."

Once started, Jennifer seemed to be reliving that evening. Any inhibitions about telling the sheriff and her friend and her own brother disappeared.

"I remember that Rickie said we had to get her out of there. So he made up a plan. We got her dressed in a hurry. Didn't even bother with her panties. I was to stand guard to make sure no one else saw them, and Rickie and Michael were going to get on either side of her and sort of walk her down the back stairs and outside. It was lucky that everybody else had apparently gone on to Debbie's. Anyway, we didn't run into anyone, and the last time I saw them that night was in the backyard. Rickie said they were going to get a car."

"You didn't see either of them again that night? Or know what they did with Annika?"

"No. Rickie just said not to say anything to anybody and they left. It wasn't until the next day that I heard from Rickie. I met with him and Michael down by the waterfront, and they told me they'd left her in a summer cottage somewhere. I didn't even know it was Barry Claymore's parents' cottage. We agreed that none of us would say anything to anyone, just that as far as we knew Annika had disappeared without saying good-bye. Rickie made it sound like an oath. Michael and I had gotten mixed up in it, so we had to swear to keep it a secret. And that's pretty much all that happened until you found Annika in that cottage a couple of weeks ago. All except for the postcard from Ohio. I know that Michael sent that when he went out there to visit a college."

It was all very much as Kevin had said it was the night before. Carol could readily imagine that Rickie would be worried that Michael and Jennifer might renege on their promise not to tell anyone what had happened to Annika. Worried enough to threaten them, to kill Michael? Whether Jennifer was in any real danger, Carol could believe that she thought she was. The phone calls in the night would have ratcheted up her fear. Had Rickie known that Jennifer had met with her the previous day in the Catholic Church? How could he have known that? But if he thought he might be facing serious criminal charges if what he had done became known, he might well have gone to extreme lengths to monitor everything Jennifer was doing. And with whom she was meeting.

"Did Rickie ever say anything to you about what happened to Annika that night at the Marinellis?"

"No, just that they were going to have sex–and then she passed out."

Carol would have liked to ask Michael the same question, but that was no longer possible. Rickie might have told him about slipping the roofies into Annika's drink, but it was highly unlikely that he had told Jennifer about it. Chances were that she believed Annika had died from the fall. Better leave it at that for the time being.

"Do you remember anything else about that evening that you think I should know?" she asked.

"Only that Rickie was really upset until we got Annika out of the house, but by the next day he was his old self. He said he was sorry Annika was dead, but he didn't talk a lot about it. I didn't much care for her, but for her to die like that, just when she was getting it on with him – I mean, that was so terrible. What mattered most to Rickie was that no one should find out what happened."

Kevin would probably tell Carol he'd told her so.

"So he wasn't as broken up about it as he was about Michael's death?"

Jennifer thought about the question.

"That's one of the things that worried me. He's been acting like he feels real bad about Michael. Not going to school, staying in his room, telling whoever calls he feels awful. What if it's a big act? What if that's just what he wants us to think? I think he knows I met with you in the church. How would he know that if he was home in bed, crying about Michael?"

"You don't know he knows we met yesterday, and I doubt it. His call last night suggests that he still hopes to scare you into keeping your word not to talk. Let's assume that that's what he's thinking. I'd like you to go back home, get back into bed, and stay out of sight in the house until I've done a few things. I don't believe you're in any danger, but I'll have one of my men keep an eye on the house."

It was Brian who asked the question that must have been on Jennifer's mind.

"What will happen to my sister? Will she be charged with some crime?"

"Let's take this one step at a time. Jennifer, you came forward and told me what happened. That's what in the legal profession is called a mitigating factor. It makes you look a lot better. Besides, if what you tell me is true, you had nothing to do with Annika's death. You did try to cover up what happened, and that's not a good thing to have done. But your situation shouldn't be anywhere near as serious as Rickie's. So, please, try to relax."

At that moment, Jennifer Kershaw was the least relaxed person in Kevin's cottage.

CHAPTER 49

"Would you be willing to talk with Rickie again?" she asked Jennifer. "Maybe do a bit of acting?"

Of course no one knew what Carol was talking about, but Brian spoke right up.

"She's a good actor, all right," he said. "Look how she kept her family in the dark about Annika. But she really is good. She played Titania in our school play. I couldn't believe it was my sister."

"Titania?" Carol asked.

"*Midsummer Night's Dream,* Carol," Kevin said. "Shakespeare at his most fanciful."

"Oh, yes, that Titania." She smiled, then immediately became serious.

"What I'd like you to do, Jennifer, is have a frank talk with Rickie. I'd like you to tell him you really think it's time to confess what happened with Annika. I'm sure you've said this to him before, but it's important that you give it one more try. The difference is that this time I'd like you to be wearing a recording device so that we could have a record of what Rickie says. What I have in mind is –"

Jennifer stared at the sheriff in disbelief.

"You want me to tape Rickie like they do on those TV shows? In secret?" Her voice betrayed what she was thinking about the idea. "No way. People get killed doing that. Besides, I couldn't do it to Rickie."

"I would never put you in danger, Jennifer. We'd do this in a public place, and I'd have my officers nearby. They'd be out of uniform, so Rickie wouldn't be suspicious. I know you want to put an end to this mess you're in. You want Rickie to own up to what happened so you won't have to be afraid any more. It'll all come out eventually anyway, and the sooner the better. For Rickie's sake, as well as yours. He's in trouble, and it will only get worse. Trust me, you'll be helping him."

"He'd never forgive me."

293

"If he's the man you want him to be, he'll understand. What happened was terribly unfortunate. You all panicked, made some bad choices. But I don't believe that Rickie is a truly bad person. And I know that you aren't. We need your help."

Jennifer continued to look unhappy, but she didn't say anything.

"We won't do this unless your mother is willing to go along. I'll talk to her, explain it all to her, assure her that you'll be fine."

"What about my father?"

Carol wasn't eager to involve Bob Kershaw, although she knew it might be impossible to keep him out of the loop. Technically, he wasn't off the hook as a suspect himself.

"Let me talk to your mother first," she said, non-committally. "I don't want you to have the wrong impression about what you'll be doing. You aren't going to sound as if you've made up your mind to tell me what you know. You'll be trying to convince him that it's a good idea and that you want his support. What I'm hoping for, of course, is that he'll say things about what really happened back in January at the party. We can't be sure how he'll respond, but it's likely that if I talk to him about what you told us today he'd just deny it. He'd say you're a mixed-up girl, making it all up. It would be 'she said,' 'he said,' and that wouldn't be much help."

"That sounds complicated," Jennifer said. "It's not like you have a script to memorize. He'd see right through me."

"No he wouldn't. It would be just like the other conversations you and Michael had with him. He'll be the one who'll be doing most of the talking. You'd just keep asking him why. Why does he still insist that you keep the secret? Or why not. Why wouldn't he want you to to tell me the truth? Then all you'd have to do is say you'd think about it."

Jennifer sat there on the edge of her seat, unconsciously rubbing her hands up and down the legs of her jeans.

"When are you going to talk with Mom?"

"I'm going to call her this afternoon. But I don't want to discuss this on the phone. I'll need to sit down with her. You can be there. You realize, of course, that this means your mother will know what happened in January. Brian already knows. And we're not trying to keep it from your father, either. The whole Kershaw family is going to work together to make this come out right. Do you understand?"

Carol fervently hoped that she was right about that. She was reasonably confident that Amanda would come around. It would be painful, but she was a sensible woman who loved her daughter, no matter how difficult she may have found her.

When Jennifer left to go back to Southport, she was obviously making an effort to come to terms with what she had told the sheriff and what she had consented to do. It wasn't easy, but Carol believed that she'd see it through.

"It looks like you had it about right," Carol said to Kevin when they had the cottage to themselves. "Do you think she's convincing?"

"I do, and I can tell you think so, too. Trouble is, there's no Michael to back up her story. It won't be easy to nail Rickie for anything unless he says something incriminating to Jennifer."

"And just what are we trying to nail him for?" Carol asked, rhetorically. "There's no premeditated murder in Annika's case, like you think there might be with Michael. According to Doc Crawford, it can't even be statutory rape because they didn't actually have sex. But he did give her an illegal drug, and that contributed to her death. That's serious, and I'm sure there's at least a manslaughter charge in there somewhere. I'm not quite sure what we could get him on for hiding her body. Breaking and entry, of course, but there's got to be something worse than that. But that's down the road. The first thing is to get Amanda Kershaw to agree to my plan and then to set up the meeting between Jennifer and Rickie."

Carol started to chuckle.

"Excuse me if I laugh. I've been sheriff now for, what, four years? Or is it going on five? We've never wired anybody before. And here I am, proposing to do it, not with Bridges or Barrett or one of the guys, but with a sixteen year old girl."

"There's no chance Rickie will catch on, is there?"

"It's extremely unlikely. Remember, she's not going to present him with an ultimatum. She's trying to find common ground with a friend, that's all."

"I wish I were as confident as you are. Maybe I should be somewhere close so I could help if things get out of hand."

"Then again maybe you shouldn't. You'd hear him raise his

voice and you'd go running over to save her. That would screw everything up."

"That's how they blow it on TV, isn't it?"

"We're not going to blow it. Anyhow, right now I've got to have a talk with Amanda Kershaw. I'll let you know the minute Jennifer has set up the meeting with Rickie Lalor. I hope we can do it tomorrow, but stay off the phone so I can reach you."

Carol got ready to leave.

"Hey, how about a kiss," she said. "And try to enjoy the rest of your day. I'll see you when I see you, hopefully at a decent hour – like no later than six. Have a cold one waiting."

CHAPTER 50

Carol pushed the button and listened. A brief silence, and then the familiar voice.

"How're you doing?"

"Not good."

"It's because of Michael, isn't it?"

A pause.

"I'll never forgive myself."

"I miss him. I'd give anything if he was here right now."

"Me, too."

"He could say this better than I can."

"Say what?"

"That it's time to tell them about Annika."

"I already told you we can't do that. Why don't you leave it alone?"

"I'm so messed up. It's driving me crazy. Why can't we just start over? We made a mistake, but we didn't kill her."

"They'll never believe that. If I admit putting her in the cottage, they'll be sure to think I did it because I killed her."

A pause.

"Wouldn't it look better if you admitted what we did? What if the sheriff finds out, then it'll really look like you've been hiding something."

"She'll never find out. I got rid of the key long ago. No-body'll find it at the bottom of the lake."

"What about me? I get nightmares about it."

"Nightmares are a helluva lot better than jail time. So forget it. You made a promise, and you've got to keep it. Michael would have."

"But he wanted you to confess."

"He changed his mind."

"He did? When?"

A pause.

"While we were sailing. He said he couldn't let me down.

He's the best friend a guy could – I mean he was. What am I –"

Carol terminated the conversation. It had actually gone on for another couple of minutes, but it no longer pertained to Annika. Instead, Jennifer Kershaw and Rickie Lalor had shared their grief over Michael Stebbins' death.

"How do you think it went?"

"She did well, I thought," Kevin said.

"I should hope so. We certainly practiced it enough."

Indeed they had. Mrs. Kershaw had, not surprisingly, been shocked to hear that her daughter had had a role in Annika Lindstrom's January disappearance. But once she had come to terms with the implications of what had happened, she agreed to Carol's plan to wire Jennifer and record her conversation with Rickie. As long as there were a lot of the sheriff's men in the immediate area. They had rehearsed for the better part of an hour until Jennifer herself had finally admitted that it wouldn't be that difficult.

The only difficulty had occurred when Mr. Kershaw had quite unexpectedly walked in the front door when everyone assumed that he would be at the office. However, he had been so relieved that the sheriff's mission had nothing to do with him and his relationship with Annika that he went along with her plan with very little protest.

It had been agreed that the town square and the high school grounds were not good places for the meeting because the critical conversation could so easily be interrupted by well meaning friends. After much discussion, it was decided that Jennifer and Rickie should meet on a bench outside the elementary school, which was conveniently located several blocks away from the main part of town. And so they did, at a little after one o'clock the following day.

One of Carol's officers sat in an unmarked car across the street, apparently taking a midday nap. A second, dressed in work clothes, appeared to be part of a cleanup patrol, picking up papers, cigarette butts, and the occasional discarded soft drink bottle that had collected in the street gutters. Another was engaged in examining a house with a foreclosure sign tacked to its front door. Kevin had prudently stayed at the cottage.

Now he was sitting across from Carol in the cottage study, thinking about what they had learned from the taped conversation between Rickie and Jennifer.

"It happened the way Jennifer said it did, that's pretty clear," Carol said. "Nothing about trying to rape Annika, but I never expected that. Guys may brag to their buddies about such things, but I can't imagine Rickie telling Jennifer."

"So now what?"

"Now I talk to Rickie. I won't mention Jennifer as a source, just say I figured it out all by myself."

"Good luck with that," Kevin said, sounding doubtful.

Carol caught up with Rickie the following day as he was leaving his home.

"Going somewhere?" she said, leaning out her car's window.

'Nowhere in particular. I just need some fresh air. Maybe I'll go back to school tomorrow."

"Come on, sit with me for a minute or two. Michael still on your mind?"

"Yeah, all the time."

Having admitted he didn't have an agenda at the moment, Rickie reluctantly climbed in beside the sheriff. They talked about Michael, about how his family was coping, about whether he'd ever get over the loss of his friend.

"By the way," Carol said, suddenly changing the subject, "you were responsible for Annika ending up in the Claymore cellar, weren't you?"

The question caught Rickie off guard.

"What?"

"You heard me. After Annika died, you hid her body in the Claymores' cottage."

"Did Jennifer Kershaw tell you that?"

"Jennifer? No, I've just been thinking about it. For days, maybe even a week now."

It wasn't exactly a lie. Rickie himself had told her, thanks to the wire which had caught his conversation with Jennifer.

"Well, you're wrong. I had nothing to do with Annika's death. Or with her being in that cottage."

"I think you put her in the cottage, Rickie, and I think you had something to do with her death."

"That's ridiculous." He was angry, but Carol was sure he

was also afraid. Was it something in the way he said it, or was it simply because she knew he couldn't help being afraid?

"No, it's not ridiculous." It was time to get tough. Carol was sure she now held the upper hand. "I'm sure you didn't mean to kill her, but it happened. I think you drugged her and she went into a fatal coma."

"You can't prove –" Rickie stopped in mid-sentence, aware that he may just have made a serious mistake.

"You were about to say that I can't prove you drugged Annika because the drug becomes undetectable in a very short time. Unfortunately for you, that's not the case when the body is frozen shortly after ingesting the drug. And Annika froze quickly in the Claymores' cellar. Her body contained a lot of alcohol and, more importantly, a lot of a drug called Rohypnol. To have sex with Miss Lindstrom, you were going to rape her if necessary, weren't you?"

"None of this is true," he said, "none of it!"

"In your panic, you grabbed for any lifeline. It took the form of a key to the Claymore cottage, a key you'd taken from Barry Claymore back in September when he was too drunk to drive. With Annika hidden away where no one would think of looking for her, you could go on with your life, confident that your secret was safe. But the truth –"

Rickie suddenly bolted from the car, ran across the street to his own car, which was parked in the Lalor driveway. Almost before Carol realized what he was doing, he backed out of the drive and sped off down the road in the direction of the high school.

Officer Grieves was the first to respond to her call. In a matter of minutes he and another of her men were on the road to look for Rickie Lalor. Unfortunately, they were up county, many miles from Southport. Carol swung by the high school, but found no sign of Rickie's car in the parking lot.

Carol decided that her best strategy was to go back to the Lalor home and see if anyone there could help her. Marie Lalor, Rickie's mother, was at home, and the sheriff got right to the point.

"I was talking with your son just now, and he suddenly became very upset. He got into his car and drove away without telling me where he was going. I need to find him, and it may be urgent. Did he by any chance call you?"

"No, he didn't." Now it was Mrs. Lalor who was upset. "Is something the matter?"

"What's the matter is that Rickie was telling me something and then – I'm not sure, but I think he had a panic attack. I checked the high school, but he's not there. Would you please call him on his cell?"

Mrs. Lalor started to ask more questions, but Carol urged her to make the call first. She did, but Rickie didn't answer. Carol had not expected him to.

"You know your own son far better than I do," Carol said, trying to avoid sounding as worried as she felt. "Where might he have gone? Is there any place you know of where he likes to get away and be by himself?"

"I really don't know. He's been so depressed ever since Michael drowned. He hardly eats, hasn't been to school. Do you want to take a look at his room to see if you can find something that might help?"

The fact that she'd been given a green light to check out Rickie's room told her volumes about how anxious Mrs. Lalor must now be.

"Yes, of course. Let's do it. What makes you think we'd find something in his room?" Carol asked as they climbed the stairs.

"It may not mean a thing, but Rickie has a black box up there that he keeps stuff in. He taped a big note on it that says 'Do Not Open.' I try to give him his privacy, but I couldn't help but be curious. Anyway, it's mostly just photographs of him, most of them with friends. Like Michael, and quite a few of him with Annika Lindstrom."

Carol couldn't imagine why the black box, or anything else for that matter, was likely to provide a clue as to where he had disappeared to when he tore out of the Lalor driveway.

The room was neater than she had expected, except for the fact that the bed had not been made. A quick glance at the desk and dresser told her nothing. The box sat on the floor under the room's lone window. It was nothing more than an old file box. Ignoring the hand lettered 'Do Not Open' sign, Carol opened it.

As Mrs. Lalor had said, most of what she saw were photos. There was a Swedish-English phrase booklet which didn't look as if it had been opened. A small tube of colorful lipstick gloss rolled across the bottom of the box when she moved the pictures aside But if the box contained any clue to where Rickie had gone, it would have to be found in the photos. Most of them were of Annika. Annika in her soccer uniform. Annika in a bathing suit. Annika in a group picture with several girls, most of whom looked familiar to Carol. There were also a couple of pictures of Michael. But most of the pictures were of Annika and Rickie, and the majority of them had been taken at a place which Carol recognized instantly. It was a lookout on the end of the bluff, high above the place where Crooked Lake's two arms come together to give it its shape of a letter Y.

What were the odds that Rickie had gone up onto the bluff to what must have been a special place for him? She didn't know, but that's where she would go.

Carol was in a hurry, and she didn't spend any time explaining to Mrs. Lalor what may have prompted her son to drive off so impulsively. She did tell her that there was nothing to be worried about, although Carol herself was very worried. After all, she had been in the process of telling Rickie that he was responsible for Annika's death when he bolted. What would the young man do? Try to run away? Worse yet, commit suicide?

CHAPTER 51

"Kevin, glad I caught you. Look, I'm going to be late, and I have no idea how late. It's about Rickie Lalor. I was letting him know that he may be in a serious pickle – the date rape drug, the Claymore's pump room, the whole thing. And he ran, jumped into his car, and took off like a bat out of hell. I should have been quicker, but I lost him."

"What do you think he's up to?" he asked, using his thumb to increase the volume on his cell phone.

"I don't have a clue. The point is I'm on my way to a place where he might have gone. It's a long shot, but it beats driving up and down the highways and byways of upstate New York. Unfortunately, my men are all in the wrong places. Can you believe it, nobody anywhere near where I hope he is and where I'm heading. Even if I find him, I'll be tied up for heaven knows how long. So don't wait supper."

"Sorry to hear this," Kevin said, knowing that Carol would be blaming herself for what had happened. "But there'll be a piece of rhubarb pie waiting for you when you get back to the cottage. A neighbor told me that the Log Cabin farmer's market out on county road 36 has the first pies of the season, and I'm on my way there now."

"You're on 36? Where?"

"Oh, about four miles beyond the turn off to the upper bluff road."

"Turn around." Carol made it sound like an order. "I want you to take the bluff road out to the end, to where there's that small lookout parking area. I have no idea where he went, but there's a chance that he headed for the end of the bluff. He's got a whole slew of pictures that were taken out there, most of them with Annika or Michael."

"What am I supposed to do?"

"You're closer to the bluff road than any of my men. Probably at least twenty miles closer. Just get down there to the end and see if he's there. Have you turned around yet?"

"I'm doing it as we speak," Kevin said. "But what if he is there? I've never met the guy and I don't know what kind of car he's driving."

Carol was beginning to sound impatient.

"He's in a dark green Pontiac. I'd say it's five, could be seven, years old. He's young, you know that. Husky kid, around six foot tall, dark wavy hair. If he's there, talk to him until I arrive. Or if not me, one of my men. Maybe I worry too much, but it has occurred to me that he may be suicidal."

"Why, does he have a gun? Unless he does, how can he commit suicide out there?"

Kevin and Carol both knew the bluff well. The slope at its south end was gradual, the lake far below and not easily accessible from the lookout. There was no place for jumping which would produce more than a few bruises or at most a broken bone or two.

"Suicide's just a guess on my part. I'm pretty sure he doesn't have a gun with him. Maybe he could switch off onto that narrow dirt road that winds down toward the lake. There's a place where he could run his car off into that little quarry. Hell, I don't know. Just get there."

"What do I talk about if I find him?"

"Be creative. It's your favorite place in all the world, you go there to commune with nature, you're thinking of buying a plot of land out there. Just keep him talking. And keep him away from the quarry."

"I'll do my best."

"Are you on the bluff road yet?"

"Almost. But I have no intention of having an accident just because you think there's a chance Annika's killer may be out there."

"I know," Carol said, trying to remain calm. "Be careful. And thanks."

She floored the gas pedal. Thank goodness traffic was light. Had she been able to get to the end of the bluff as the crow flies, she could be there in a just a few minutes. Unfortunately, she had to drive all the way up to Yates Center, then go west to the bluff road and drive all the way back south to a point not more than a mile and a half across the water from where she was at that moment. Much as she loved Crooked Lake, she would have to acknowledge that parts of it were hard to get to.

She tried Grieves again, then Byrnes and Barrett. Nothing to report. No need to have them head for the upper bluff road. Kevin would beat them to it. So would she unless she encountered an accident or a paving crew. Better to leave her officers scouring the area roads for an aging green Pontiac. Why had she been so sure that Rickie would have headed for the bluff lookout? It may be a pleasant spot, with one of the best views of the lake, but it was also a virtual dead end, a cul de sac from which escape would have to be via a narrow, winding, dirt road where speeds in excess of 15 miles per hour would be dangerous. Perhaps Rickie had not thought of that. On the other hand, perhaps he had no intention of trying to escape.

Kevin had always enjoyed the bluff, both from his cottage, especially at sundown, and from the road along its crest. But today Carol had sounded anxious, and he had no idea what lay ahead of him at the south end of this hill which divided the lake for roughly half its twenty-two mile length.

He passed only three cars on the drive, testimony to the fact that there were very few farms or homes up there. Unlike the hills which rose up from the eastern and western shores of the lake, the bluff was devoid of vineyards. It was, he thought, a lonely place. Lonely but attractive in its own strange way.

As Kevin approached the lookout, he was alarmed to see no car parked there. But just as quickly he relaxed. After all, Carol had not been certain that this was where Rickie was headed when last she saw him. He pulled his car to a stop at the end of the parking area closest to the winding dirt road which ran from it down the hill in the direction of the cottages that clung to the shoreline of the bluff far below. He started to walk down the dirt road without giving much thought to just why he was doing so. But as he walked, he began to worry that Rickie might already have been there and then chosen to leave via the narrower and more difficult dirt road. Kevin knew that Rickie's car had not passed him on his way to the lookout.

He had gone no more than a hundred yards, however, when he saw the green Pontiac. It was parked on what passed for a shoulder of the dirt road, around a corner and out of sight from the lookout. Not far ahead of the car a single figure was seated on an old tree stump. It had to be Rickie. His posture made it impossible to gauge his height, but he had the dark wavy hair Carol had mentioned and he had the body of an athlete who works to keep himself in good physical condition.

Kevin made it a point to scuff his shoes over the dirt road, dislodging small stones and making his presence known to Rickie while he was still at some distance from him.

"Hi," he called out when the young man turned his head to see who was approaching. "Lovely place, isn't it?"

Rickie didn't reply. The expression on his face was one Kevin had seen many times in his classrooms. It spoke to the gulf which so often exists between adolescents and those a generation older than themselves.

Kevin did not wish to walk on by as if he were preoccupied with his own agenda. Nor did he want to appear overly friendly. He considered sitting down a few feet away, but thought better of it. He paused near Rickie and used a sleeve to wipe away nonexistent sweat from his brow.

"Beautiful spot. I love the view of the lake from here. Must be you do, too."

"Not really."

"Oh, sorry. I didn't mean to intrude. It's seemed like such a great day, I figured you'd feel like I do."

He hoped that Rickie would say something, anything which would invite a conversation. He wasn't sure what he would do if he didn't.

"That's okay. I wasn't trying to be rude. It's just been a bad day."

"I guess we all have them from time to time," Kevin said. "I hope being up here will help. It always helps me."

Rickie didn't change his position on the stump, but he shrugged his shoulders as if to say that the view from the bluff was unlikely to help.

"Excuse me," Kevin said, taking a seat on a long dead, moss covered log. "I've got some gravel in my shoe. Don't pay any attention to me."

He removed his shoe and busied himself removing the gravel.

"You come here often?" Rickie asked.

Kevin was surprised at this cautious overture to a conversation.

"As much as I can. Sometimes just because it's a beautiful day and I want to get out of the house, enjoy the fresh air. Other times it's like you. A bad day, and I figure I'll feel better if I come up here. The thing I like about it is that it's so quiet. Nobody to bother me."

He laughed.

"Nobody to bother me, and here I am bothering you. I'm sorry."

"No need to be sorry. You didn't know I had a problem."

"Well, that's true, but I shouldn't be making assumptions."

Rickie looked at this stranger, a puzzled look on his face.

"Funny," Kevin said, "but I was reminded of something that happened a few years ago. I'm a teacher, you see. A college teacher. This student came to me, all upset, wanted me to give him an extension on a paper that was due. He said that he had too much on his mind, that he couldn't possibly do it. And I remember lecturing him – you know, he had an obligation, his grade would suffer, he just had to suck it up, that sort of thing. Then he told me what his problem was. He had been driving with a friend that weekend, lost control of his car, and crashed into a tree. His friend had been killed. I felt like a fool."

"That's awful. What did you do?"

"I told him how sorry I was and gave him the extension. He stopped by my office a couple of years later to say hello. He still hadn't gotten over the loss of his friend, and he probably never will. But he was trying to get his life together. I guess talking to me helped, though I'm not sure why."

Rickie didn't say anything. Nor did his face change expression. And then he lowered his head into his hands. Kevin could no longer see his face. Was he crying?

"I'm sure you don't want to hear about other people's problems," Kevin said. He couldn't imagine why the story he'd just shared with Rickie had come to mind. It was an old story, not a recent one. It had happened during his very first year at Madison College, at a time when he was very conscious of his newfound authority and perhaps unconsciously distancing himself from his own very recent student days. He knew that what Rickie had done was not really comparable to what that former student had done. But he also knew that Rickie was probably every bit as miserable.

For the first time since he had begun to think about Rickie, he found himself actually feeling sorry for him. And angry with himself for believing that Michael's death had been no accident. Then again, perhaps it hadn't been an accident. As Carol had insisted, they would almost certainly never know. But at that moment he thought he could understand Rickie's pain, no matter what his responsibility was for what had happened to Annika and Michael.

He put his shoe back on and looked at his watch. It told him what time it was, but not when Carol would make it to the lookout. If Rickie Lalor was suicidal, he shouldn't leave him. On the other hand, if he didn't move on fairly soon Rickie might begin to wonder about this stranger who had chosen to sit down on a log and make small talk.

Fortunately, it was only several minutes later that he heard a car pull into the parking lot above them, and shortly thereafter he heard Carol's voice.

"Rickie?" she called out as she came around the bend.

Both Kevin and Rickie looked in her direction. Kevin stood up, but Carol ignored him as she came down the road.

"I thought I'd find you here," she said to Rickie. "I see you have company. Somebody else enjoying the view, I presume."

Kevin got the message. He mumbled something that sounded like 'hello,' told Rickie he'd enjoyed their conversation, and set off in the direction of the parking lot.

"How did you know where to find me?" Rickie asked the sheriff.

"I saw your pictures, the ones of you and Annika and Michael that were taken here. I thought maybe you'd decided to drive up here and do some thinking."

He nodded.

"What's going to happen to me?" he asked.

"I honestly don't know. But I'd urge you to call home now. Your mother should be there, and she needs to know that you're all right. Tell her you're with me and that we're taking care of things."

Taking care of things entailed returning to Southport. Rickie locked his car and joined Carol in her car for the second time that day. When his mother answered his call, he did not try to explain his problem in any detail, but he did tell her that he was with the sheriff, that he was in trouble, and that they'd be home in half an hour or so. By the time they got there, Rickie's father had come home and had already called and spoken to Milton Avery, an old family friend. Avery was not only a friend, he was also a highly regarded defense lawyer, a former state legislator, and one of the most influential people in Cumberland County.

CHAPTER 52

It was more than half an hour before Avery joined them, during which time Rickie looked depressed and remained silent while Carol told the Lalors about their son having been responsible for spiriting Annika Lindstrom's body away from the January party in Southport and hiding it in the cellar of a cottage on the West Lake Road. She did not mention either the attempted rape or the participation of Michael Stebbins and Jennifer Kershaw. These things would become public knowledge in due course, but it seemed unnecessary to mention them at the moment. It was bad enough that she had to let the Lalors know that their son had been involved in covering up what might be a serious crime. They had reacted in quite different ways. Mrs. Lalor had found the news devastating. All she could talk about was how, with a son in jail, she wouldn't be able to face her friends. Mr. Lalor ignored his wife's fears and tears.

"He's not going to jail, Marie," he said in a stern voice. "Do you hear me? Not one day in jail. Milton will take care of that. So stop blubbering."

Carol had no idea whether Rickie Lalor faced time in jail. She doubted that he would simply walk away from this mess and begin his freshman year at Syracuse as if nothing had happened. But she knew it would be hard to prove that Rickie had put the Rohypnol in Annika's beer, however likely it was that he had done so. Nor was she sure what charges Ed Stokes, the county attorney, would wish to bring for concealing Annika's death. She would have to pay him a visit after she left the Lalor house. One thing she did know, however. As capable as he was, Stokes would be up against a master in Milton Avery.

When Avery walked into the Lalor living room, he immediately took charge. It was obvious that it was a role with which he was thoroughly familiar.

"Hello, Jim. Marie. You must be Rickie," he said as he shook hands with the young man. He then turned to Carol. "By a process of elimination, you would be the sheriff. Of course the uniform's a dead giveaway. I have no idea what's been said here, but let's get one thing straight. Rickie, you aren't to say a word to anyone unless I say it's okay. You're not guilty of anything, and you're not going to be found guilty of anything. So let's –"

"Rickie!" The voice came from the foyer, and then Jennifer Kershaw herself burst into the room. "She made me do it. Honest. I'm so sorry."

The five people who witnessed this unannounced intrusion were all surprised, but they reacted in different ways.

Dave Lalor was annoyed, and started to say so.

Marie Lalor looked shocked by this breach of good manners.

Milton Avery rose to his feet to intercept the girl as she rushed toward Rickie.

Sheriff Kelleher braced herself; she knew that a storm was brewing.

Whatever he was thinking, Rickie Lalor's face registered no emotion.

It was Mr. Lalor who spoke first.

"What are you doing here?"

Jennifer completed her rush across the room to where Rickie was sitting on the couch. She ignored Mr. Lalor's question.

Avery, who had failed in his effort to stop Jennifer, asked the more important question, one that should have been on everyone's mind if they had been listening to what she had said as she entered the room.

"Who made you do what, young lady?"

"Never mind, it's all right." It was Rickie, speaking for the first time in many long minutes. Instead of pushing Jennifer away, he freed one of his arms and wrapped it around her. "It's going to be okay, and it isn't your fault."

Carol was watching, fascinated. Why wasn't it Jennifer's fault? Because Carol had told him that she herself had figured out what had happened? Or was it because he knew or had guessed that Jennifer had shared his secret with the sheriff and had forgiven her for doing so?

Avery was demanding an explanation for what he had just witnessed. And heard.

"I don't know who you are," he said to Jennifer, "but I am here to represent Rickie Lalor's interests, and I insist on knowing what you're talking about. Who made you do what?"

Jennifer half turned away from Rickie to look at Avery.

"I was just on my way home from school when I saw her car out front." Jennifer pointed at Carol. "You came to arrest him, didn't you? You told me I had to do it, and then I did and then you arrested him. Oh, Rickie, I'm so sorry. I was wrong."

Jennifer slumped into a seat on the couch next to Rickie.

"What are you talking about?" Avery practically shouted the question.

Carol could see where this was going. It was only a matter of time before Rickie's attorney would be taking action to suppress the tape of Rickie's conversation with Jennifer. It was time to leave the Lalors to their discussion of strategy with Milton Avery. She was confident that Avery would be counseling Rickie not to leave the country. Or Southport.

"Jennifer, the family needs to talk privately with Mr. Avery. I'm leaving. I'm quite sure Rickie is willing for you to come with me. Like he said, he'll be all right. So let's go. I'll drive you home."

Rickie urged a very reluctant Jennifer Kershaw to go with the sheriff. After saying again how terribly sorry she was, she followed Carol out to her car.

It was well after nine o'clock that evening that Carol and Kevin finally had some of the rhubarb pie which he had picked up at the Log Cabin on his way home from the bluff.

As she had predicted, it had been a very long day.

"God, I'm emotionally exhausted," Carol said.

"Small wonder."

"And I feel guilty even saying that. Can you imagine how this has hit Southport? The whole lake for that matter. First a young visitor from overseas dies. Then a local boy is drowned. Now a popular high school student is arrested, and may be facing jail. If that's not enough, Jennifer Kershaw tells me she wishes she were dead, claims she should never have agreed to making that tape."

"That's not all," Kevin said. "How about those parents who never bothered to supervise the kids? Just left them alone to get drunk and have sex. None of this would have happened if they'd been home when that party took place."

"Your Swedish blogger may have been right after all. About our culture, I mean."

"It isn't us, Carol. I'm sure things like this are happening all over. Except maybe in those places where girls wear burkas and can't go out of the house without a brother or an uncle or someone like that. I wouldn't trade our problems for theirs, would you?"

"Of course not. But all the drugs, the booze, the casual sex. It's damn discouraging. I don't know what I believe any more. I used to think it was wrong to send young guys off to war but not let them have a beer. Now I'm not so sure. It's a crazy world."

"We're talking about kids being kids, Carol. You and I have been there, done that. Things just got out of hand here. And don't forget the key. If Barry had stayed sober way back last September, he'd have driven to the cottage by himself and Rickie would never have had a key. No key, no Annika in the pump room."

"Yes, but she'd still have been dead, and heaven knows where she'd have been found."

"So what's next?" Kevin asked.

"I laid out the facts for our county attorney. It's complicated, as he was quick to point out. If, on reflection, he thinks he can make a case that Rickie really did put the drug in Annika's drink, the charge could be manslaughter. Probably not second degree murder, but that's possible. After all, Rickie would have intentionally given Annika an illegal substance which has the potential to cause death. But frankly, I think the defense won't have much trouble demonstrating reasonable doubt. After all, lots of people could have dropped something into Annika's glass during the evening, and no one saw Rickie do it. And we know that Rickie says nothing about the matter on the tape, even if it survives Avery's effort to suppress it."

"And how about the body in the pump room?"

"What Rickie did was not only wrong, but illegal. We don't countenance concealing a death or unlawfully removing a dead body. But I've got a hunch that there will be a sympathetic understanding of panic in a case like this. Not enough to let him off scot-free, of course. The prosecution is going to have to give a lot of thought to this one."

"What would you like to see happen?"

"I wish I knew. If I was absolutely sure Rickie popped the pills into Annika's drink so he could rape her, I'd be willing to throw the book at him. I wish we'd been able to get our hands on whoever sold the Rohypnol. If he did drug Annika, Rickie has nothing to gain and everything to lose by giving up the name of the pusher. So count me among those who believe in guilt only if it's established beyond a reasonable doubt. It's the American way, Kevin."

"I'm with you, and I'm sure you're not surprised. To be perfectly honest, though, I can't help feeling sorry for Rickie."

"That's what makes this so damnably hard. I want very much for him to be guilty of nothing more than poor judgment and theft of a key to the Claymore cottage. But I will never feel sorry for a rapist."

"How about Jennifer?"

"She's one confused girl. First she's part of the cover up. Then she wants to tell the truth. Now she's sorry she wore the wire. We know she went along with Rickie; she told us all about it, and I've even got it on the tape. If it's admitted as evidence. My guess is that she'll get off with probation because she confessed to what happened and the part she played in it. She may regret blowing Rickie's cover, but it's too late to deny it."

"Interesting, isn't it," Kevin said. "There's been a lot of collateral damage in this case, with Jennifer the prime example."

"I know what you mean, but I hope that it's been a wake-up call for the Kershaws. They actually seemed to be functioning like a real family at the end. At least they were trying to. Heaven knows, Jennifer needs their support."

Carol sighed.

"You know what?" she said. "I hated this case!"

"You really need a break. You've got to get away from Crooked Lake and its problems for awhile."

Carol shook her head.

"You know I can't do that."

Kevin moved closer on the couch and took her hand.

"I think you can. And I know how."

"You're very sweet, but the best I can do is a long weekend once in a blue moon."

"No, there's a way. It's called a wedding, which is customarily followed by a wedding trip. I believe they still call it a honeymoon."

Carol looked at Kevin as if he'd just announced that he was

moving to Uzbekistan.

"A wedding?"

"Yes, it's what people have when they get married. I want to get married. To you. This summer."

Carol's face broke into a smile, but it was a tentative smile, as if she wasn't quite sure whether he was serious.

"But we've been over this before, and you know –"

"We have indeed been over it, but I've decided we've been looking at it through the wrong end of the telescope. No, I can't move to the lake, and no, you can't move to the city. But why have we let that rule out marriage? I've got a colleague who lives in the city while her husband has a job up in New Hampshire. It may not be ideal, but they love each other and they seem to cope pretty well. Why not us? And if we get married, I'm sure the good citizens of Cumberland County wouldn't have any objections to our taking a wedding trip somewhere. Where'd you like to go?"

"Is this a proposal?"

"I'll let you sleep on it, but, yes, it's a proposal. We'll still have our summers together, plus those long weekends you mentioned, and any people who have moral qualms about you spending nights at the cottage can relax."

"I'd have to stay Carol Kelleher, you know. They're used to a Sheriff Kelleher up here."

She's going to do it! Kevin suddenly felt giddy. He threw an arm around her and gave her a big hug.

"You can call yourself anything you want to. Kelleher, Whitman, Miss Crooked Lake."

"You don't have a date in mind, do you?"

"No, that's going to be a joint decision, and I promise to give you time to catch your breath and sort things out with the powers that be in the county."

"I think I feel better already. Speaking of promises, will you promise to carry me across the threshold and into the bedroom on our wedding night?"

"I can do better than that," Kevin said. "I'm going to carry you across the threshold right now."

Made in the USA
San Bernardino, CA
02 December 2019

60728360R00182